# LES MISÉRABLES

# LES MISÉRABLES

A Novel by Leonore Fleischer
Based on the Screenplay by Rafael Yglesias
From the Novel by Victor Hugo

CORONET BOOKS
Hodder and Stoughton

First published in Great Britain in 1998
by Hodder and Stoughton
A division of Hodder Headline PLC

A Coronet paperback

The right of Leonore Fleischer to be identified as
the Author of the Work has been asserted by her in
accordance with the Copyright, Designs and Patents Act 1988.

10 9 8 7 6 5 4 3 2 1

A CIP catalogue record for this title
is available from the British Library

ISBN 0 340 71758 0

Typeset by Hewer Text Ltd, Edinburgh
Printed and bound in Great Britain

Hodder and Stoughton
A division of Hodder Headline PLC
338 Euston Road
London NW1 3BH

CONTENTS

# Chapter One

### A STRANGER

The night winds of autumn and winter sweep blistering-raw over the mountains surrounding the northern French town of Digne. They swirl down filled with the promise of snow and ice. During the longer days of spring and summer, the sun's rays warm the mountain-tops enough partially to melt the snowcaps on their summits. Rills and streams and rushing rivers pour down from the heights, moving stones and granite boulders out of their paths. Then the fields become fresh with moisture; spring flowers turn the meadows into medieval tapestries of colour. Sheep and goats grow fat on their uphill pasturing.

But even in summer the sun must go down. Then, as soon as its rays disappear behind the mountain summits, the temperature drops sharply and the winds begin to blow from above, bearing icy blasts in their long, invisible fingers. Then all of Digne shivers; people close their shutters and lock their doors. Fires are lit in stoves and on hearths; stools are drawn up to the warmth; cats scratch on the kitchen door, begging hoarsely to be allowed into the house.

Summer in the north is brief, and autumn arrives soon. By October, the shorter days bring early darkness and, with the dark, comes the severe threat of the harsh winter ahead. Tall stacks of firewood crowd the sheds behind the farmhouses. In Digne, the more prosperous residents lay in supplies of coal for their stoves; the less prosperous burn the harder, rougher-burning greyish coke.

Rich and poor alike have already stored away jars and bottles of preserves, barrels of grain, pickled meat and fish in kitchen and cellar. The jars of the well-to-do contain cherries, pears, plums, berries and other summer treats, frequently floating in delicious flavoured brandies. Their barrels are filled to overflowing with the finest wheat for baking white bread, fatty salted beef and pork, veal tongues and other savoury delicacies.

As for the poor, their jars hold pickled turnips and beets, cabbage leaves, hearts of nettle and anything edible that can be gleaned from the autumnal fields. Their barrels hold only millet and barley, slabs of salted cod, leeks, onions and potatoes, and whatever parts of pig and calf the rich despise – hearts, lips, ears, livers, trotters, teats – any offal that can be cooked into brawn or head cheese for winter sustenance. Digne is a prosperous town, and even the poor do not go hungry, although farmer dines on far humbler fare than mayor or merchant.

So, by the time that summer is over, Digne has shut itself away from the cold, its doors double-barred against the winds, and the chinks in its walls stuffed with straw. Fires blaze indoors, and hot food steams on its tables – all in defiance of the icy blasts from the mountains that turn the nights into a freezing hell.

It was this town that a stranger entered one late afternoon, just before nightfall in October of the year 1815. The sun was nowhere to be seen, thanks to the heavy rain-clouds over the mountains. Rain had been falling for several hours, and the air was frigid. On the traveller's back was an old ragged knapsack, and in his hand he carried a large knotted stick to help him on his journey. He was an unusually tall man, long of leg and wide of shoulder. Next to him, your average-sized man appeared nothing larger than a child. His hands were huge, sinewy and rough, very strong, and his legs and thighs were full-muscled under his loose-fitting pants, which were frayed over his knees. He wore a ragged grey jacket with a hood, which kept out very little of the cold. On his feet were a pair of ancient hobnailed shoes, cracked and broken.

The stranger's hair was close-cropped, but his face was masked by a battered old hat pulled low on his brow; also by a short, rough beard which grew thickly, obscuring his cheeks and chin. Under his hood the man's eyes were narrowed against the wind. It was impossible to discern their size and colour, but they were large and blue. Those eyes had seen far too much of the miseries and injustices of the world, and they wore an expression compounded of suspicion, anger and bitterness. Those eyes mistrusted the entire human race and regarded other men with hostility and aversion.

The fellow was actually between thirty-five and forty years of age, but his face was so beaten and burned by wind and weather that he might be mistaken for someone decades older. He walked slowly, legs trembling with fatigue. He had come a very long distance on foot, walking for four days over bad roads and roads that were no roads at all, merely rutted cart-tracks filled with rocks to trip up the unwary traveller. He was exhausted, hungry and thirsty. Most of all, because of the rain, he was stiff with cold. His patched and tattered clothing was all very old, and so threadbare that it offered almost no resistance to the cruelty of the weather. Like the piteous cat, he too wanted to howl at the kitchen door that was locked against him: Let me in! Let me sit by the fire and get warm!

As he entered Digne, the man realized that he had gone as far as human flesh would allow. He desperately needed to rest, to eat, to drink, to get warm and dry, and to sleep. Tomorrow he would be on his way again, but tonight he couldn't take another step. There was some money in his pocket; not a great deal, but more than enough to pay for a hot supper and a bed of straw in some humble inn or even a warm barn. He'd been on the road for four days, and so far had spent scarcely a sou on himself. He had slept in the open, and eaten what tiny morsels he could glean out of empty fields which had already been harvested and gleaned before him.

Once or twice he'd attempted to catch a rabbit, or a squirrel or pigeon. Once, he'd even gone after some fieldmice. But small creatures like these were too fast for him, and always got away. Ah well, he told himself with bitterness, they would only meagrely repay the effort to catch them. There was virtually no meat on them.

In the last three days he had eaten almost nothing. Now that he had come this far north, with mountains all around him, their stern heads looming like angry magistrates, there were few fields to search through for the odd parsnip or carrot or bit of winter cabbage. Worse, it was too cold to sleep out in the open; a man had to have shelter at this altitude. So a couple of his precious francs, scraped together with such pain and effort, would have to be squandered on what could not be obtained for nothing.

He tried to keep from thinking about food and warmth, but his stubborn mind was fixed on wheaten bread and rich sheep cheese, and a pewter pot of country ale. He could almost taste them, almost feel the heat of the firelight on his weary limbs. Leaning on his stick, moving very slowly in a curious kind of shuffle, a shuffle he had developed over many years of having his legs and ankles shackled by heavy chains, the man descended from the path above, into the town, looking for an inn.

But first, as he realized with a sinking heart, he had to do what the law required of him. He had to go to the local prefect of police and present his papers, just as any traveller was obliged to do. He knew what the outcome of that would be, but he hoped that he could get some food and drink and shelter before the inevitable consequences made that impossible.

As he made his way to the centre of town, looking for the town hall, the stranger was followed by the curious glances of the local men and women, who were going about their customary business in the streets. His ragged, unkempt appearance, his impressive size and the odd way he shuffled along made him the natural object of their curiosity. They nodded their heads at one another, and pursed their lips knowingly. *This was one to keep an eye on*, they said without words. *He must be very thirsty*, they noted. *Look at him gulping from the public fountain.*

The stranger drank and drank, as though he could never drink his fill, and still he was thirsty. He looked up from the water to see five little street urchins staring curiously at him.

'Where's the town hall?' he growled at them.

'I'll show you,' offered the most forward of the boys. With the others trailing after them, the urchin led the tall man to a large building on the square, and pointed. 'There.'

A gendarme was dozing on a stone bench outside, near another public fountain. The stranger stopped to drink again, then approached the policeman, waking him up. Out of his jacket pocket he took a folded document – bright yellow, the warning colour to all police and magistrates that the bearer was to be treated as a criminal – and handed it to the gendarme.

'I'm supposed to report.'

Without bothering to stand, the gendarme took the yellow

passport and read it. 'Just here for one night,' the stranger offered. 'I'm going to Pontarlier.'

The policeman returned the yellow paper and jerked his head at the door. 'Inside.'

'What?'

'Inside. You report to the captain.'

'Not to you?'

The gendarme shook his head gruffly. 'No. It's not my job.'

The stranger scowled angrily. 'Why'd you read it, then?'

'You gave it to me.' The policeman stood up and gave his trousers a hitch. 'Got a complaint?'

The stranger balled up his fists, but said nothing more. Long years of enduring unfair treatment parcelled out by authority had taught him to keep silent. He moved past the gendarme and headed into the town hall.

'Who is he?' demanded one of the urchins.

'A convict from the galleys. Stay away from him. Go on!' He shooed the curious boys away. 'Go home, puppies.'

Having presented his documents to the authorities, the stranger hurried as fast as he could through the town, looking for an inn and a meal. The first house he encountered was a large building of stone, La Croix de Colbas, owned and operated by the man Labarre. La Croix de Colbas was generally agreed to be the finest in Digne, its patronage largely made up of wagoners, who always know the best places to eat.

As soon as the man entered the inn by the kitchen door, his senses were assailed by savoury odours so overpoweringly delicious that he staggered back and nearly fell. Large cast-iron pots were simmering on the stove, and a long spit was turning over the fireplace; it held a couple of plump game birds, three rabbits and a sizzling roast of marmot. Fat from the spit dripped on to the coals, and the aromatic smoke that arose made the stranger's mouth water uncontrollably. His hunger, which had been a gnawing ache in his belly, suddenly became a ferocious pain, an agonizing need above all others.

'Good evening. What can I do for Monsieur?' the landlord asked with an ingratiating smile. Although the traveller's appearance promised little, one could never tell what he might be carrying in that knapsack. It cost nothing to be polite. Even so, it was the better part of wisdom to be cautious, and find out what one could.

'Food,' the tall man answered shortly. 'Food, ale and a bed to sleep in.'

'Nothing easier,' smiled Labarre, adding, 'If you can pay for it.'

'I can pay,' replied the other, taking a leather purse from his jacket and shaking it to make the coins jingle.

Labarre's smile broadened and he rubbed his hands together. 'Ah well, then, *bien, bien*. Right this way.' The landlord led the tall man into the large dining room, where a group of wagon drivers were drinking ale and cider and waiting hungrily for their dinner to be brought from the kitchen. The stranger drew a low stool up to the fire and sat down to warm himself while the landlord headed back in the direction of the kitchen and his stewpots.

Meanwhile, the traveller was almost warm and almost dry. He was beginning to feel drowsy, and only his painful hunger kept him from falling asleep. He didn't see the gendarme outside the inn window, beckoning the landlord outside, or notice the two men talking together. The first thing he did know was the landlord shaking him roughly by the shoulder.

'Monsieur, you will have to leave. I cannot serve you or give you a room.'

'But I have money—' the tall man protested. 'Put me in

the stable. I'll pay for the stable. Give me bread and a bowl of soup. I'll eat here in the kitchen. I won't bother your . . . fine guests. I'll sleep in a corner of the hayloft and I'll clear out before sunrise.'

'Nevertheless . . .' Labarre shrugged. 'I have no food and no room. Nothing is available.'

'You have plenty of food!'

'All reserved for them.' The landlord pointed to the hungry wagoners, who were waiting impatiently for the delicious contents of stewpots and spit. 'You must go. Now.'

'No.' The stranger shook his head stubbornly. 'This is an inn, and I am a legitimate patron, the same as these others. I will stay. I've walked for four days. No one will give me room. I need to eat—'

'Look.' The landlord pointed through the window, and the tall man could see the gendarme waiting outside. 'You don't want to start something.'

Labarre leaned closer to the other man, so close that his piggy little eyes looked directly into the stranger's, and the tall man could see the flecks of spittle in the corners of his mouth.

'Do you seriously think I don't know who and what you are?' Labarre hissed. 'I'm no fool. I sent to the police to find out. Now go away before I have you thrown out bodily.'

The stranger's heart sank. He had no answer to make. Resigned, he stood up, put his knapsack on his shoulder and took up his stick. Slowly he shuffled away from the welcoming fire and back out into the rain.

'Where am I supposed to go?' he asked the gendarme plaintively. 'Tell me. Want to put me in jail for the night? That's okay. I'll go. I'll *pay* to sleep in jail.'

The gendarme shook his head. 'The jail is for criminals. Have you committed a crime?'

'Just tell me where to go,' the stranger pleaded. 'Tell me where I can eat and where I can sleep.'

The policeman shrugged his shoulders carelessly. 'It's none of my business. Stay where you please. You're a free man.'

A free man. The stranger's lips twisted in bitter irony. What kind of freedom was this? Very soon his identity would be the talk of the entire town. His only hope was to find someone within the next hour who was willing to take him in for the night, because they were either greedy or sympathetic. He had little faith in the sympathy of the human animal, so he expected to pay.

But it was already too late. The gendarme's report, combined with the speed of town gossip, had already turned Digne against the stranger. Every inn, even the meanest and humblest, slammed its door in his face. Slipping on the wet cobbles, which were slick from the rain, he went from cottage to cottage, knocking on windows, offering francs in exchange for food and shelter. But there were no takers. Nobody was willing to take a chance on accommodating the stranger. They were too cowardly, too afraid of what the police had said about him.

At last, wet through and through, stumbling with exhaustion, he found a small shed lined with straw, crept into it and curled up to sleep. Only a moment later, the man was shocked into wakefulness by the savage snarling of a large dog. The beast was fierce and huge, capable of tearing him to pieces. It was close enough for the man to smell its fetid breath; close enough for him to realize that its bared teeth were about to sink into his flesh. Moving swiftly out of fear, the stranger scrambled to his feet and dashed out into the rainy night. He barely had time to retrieve his knapsack and stick.

It was only because the dog was chained that he managed to escape at all.

His heart burned with rage. Every human face was set against him; every human hand was raised to strike him or drive him away. Now even the animals had joined them. Here was the ultimate degradation! To be ejected from a doghouse! By its rightful owner! He was no better than a dog himself to be treated this way. Less than a dog, who was entitled to sleep warm and dry while he himself was not!

'I am a dog,' he roared into the uncaring night. 'I am only a dog.'

Weariness finally overcame the stranger as he staggered into the town square, and he sank on to one of the public benches near the cathedral and laid himself down, his knapsack under his head for a pillow. The bench was of rough stone, and it was wet with rain, but to the traveller comfort had ceased to matter. He closed his eyes and drifted off into uneasy sleep.

Barely an hour later, a hand shook him awake. The man started up, his eyes widening in fear, but he saw a kindly face, an elderly woman dressed entirely in the black of widowhood, a prayer book in her hand.

'Why are you sleeping here?' she asked him gently.

'Why do you think?' was the bitter reply.

'You don't have money.'

The tall man shook his head impatiently. 'Leave me alone.'

'I have only five sous,' said the widow gently, 'but you are welcome to them.'

The stranger snatched the coin from her hand. 'It's better than nothing,' he muttered grudgingly.

The woman was persistent. 'Did you knock on doors and ask people to help you?'

'I asked. I asked everywhere.' His head down, the stranger answered through teeth gritted in anger.

'You didn't ask there,' the woman said softly.

He turned his head to follow her pointing finger. Across the square, near the cathedral, he saw a small house, modest and neat, attached to a large palatial mansion that was the Digne hospital. There was a small garden in front of the house, and a rusting gate on to the street.

'There? No, I didn't ask there. Why?'

'Knock on that door,' said the old woman, smiling.

Stiffly, groggy with exhaustion, the stranger got to his feet and took up his knapsack. He shuffled across the street, shivering with the cold and the damp, and pushed the garden gate open. The rusting metal hinges squealed in protest, a strange, plaintive sound. He went up to the old, plain wooden door. Hesitating, he raised his hand and knocked, once, twice. Then he knocked again.

'Come in,' called a man's voice, a gentle voice, a welcoming voice. 'Come in. The door is never locked.'

## Chapter Two

### THE BISHOP

The stranger hesitated, but when he heard the invitation repeated, he pushed the street door open and stood in the doorway, taking in the scene within. He saw a middle-sized room, with a fire blazing cheerfully in the hearth. In the centre of the room was a dining table with six chairs around it, but right now it was being used as a writing desk. A cheerful-faced man with white hair, perhaps sixty-five years of age or older, was sitting there, making notes in a journal. He was working by the light of waxen tapers burning in two tall candlesticks that appeared to be of solid silver.

The candlesticks, heavy, ornate, costly, stood in strange contrast to the rest of the room, which was simplicity itself. The furniture was solid and practical, but very plain, with no carving or gilding; it was close to peasant furniture. The man himself was dressed in a simple cassock. Also in the room was a plump woman of roughly the same age as the man. Wearing all black except for her white cap and snowy apron, she was setting the table for dinner, laying two places. The knives, spoons and forks, which she was taking out of the basket she wore over her arm, seemed also to be made of the same heavy silver as the candlesticks.

The tall man might have been ignorant and uneducated, but he was far from stupid. At once, he comprehended the scene. The man was a priest, and to judge by the simplicity of his dress and the plainness of his surroundings, he could be of no rank higher than a parish priest attached to the cathedral. The rich silverware must belong to the Church itself and not to these people. As for the woman, she was no doubt his housekeeper, one of that legion of pious dragons who live only to guard their priestly employers, keep their houses spotless and put nourishing food in their bellies.

But the stranger's understanding was limited in this case. True, the man was a priest and the woman was indeed his housekeeper, but that was by no means all the truth. In actual fact, Bishop Myriel, the wearer of the cassock, was the bishop of the cathedral and the Digne diocese, a man of great piety, spirituality and godliness, but also of great power. He represented the Church itself to the town of Digne. The plainness of his dress and his home were by his own choice.

Charles François Bienvenu Myriel had come to Digne nine years earlier as its bishop. His designated home was a magnificent palace, with large rooms, fine, ornately decorated furniture, marble-and-gilt mantels, tall windows and high, painted and stuccoed ceilings, adorned with cherubs and saints. Next door to it was the public hospital for the poor, a small structure, humble, its handful of rooms crowded with too many beds, and suffering from a lack of fresh air owing to the few and small windows. Over the years many patients had died there who might have lived if conditions in the hospital had only been better and more healthful.

To the bishop there seemed to be only one obvious answer: the bishop's palace should become the hospital, and the shabby little hospital would be the domicile of the bishop. This was soon effected, and the man settled down to a life of simplicity, service, charitable works and prayer. Of his generous salary of fifteen thousand francs a year, fourteen thousand were given immediately to the poor – to widows, to orphans, to the hospital and anyone else who needed help. He would have given more, except that his housekeeper absolutely forbade it, swearing that a thousand francs a year was barely enough to put food on the table, plain as that food was. Of all the rich gifts heaped on the bishop by the wealthy, none was kept. All were sold at once, and the proceeds distributed to the poor.

Is it any wonder that the poor people of Digne thought of their bishop as blessed, a true saint, absolutely guaranteed of beatification on his death? But they didn't dare mention this in the bishop's hearing. He had forbidden them to speak of his goodness. He preferred to keep as anonymous as possible his pious deeds and acts of charity. The bishop sought no fame, reward or even thanks. To him, giving came as easily as breathing.

As to the rich silverware, that had escaped being sold only because it was all the bishop had left of his former life. The pieces were a family heirloom, and therefore of great sentimental value to the man. It was his only treasure, because it had belonged to his mother and to her mother before that. The housekeeper always kept the basket of tableware under lock and key, and she would have hidden away the candlesticks as well, if the bishop had allowed it. The house was always unlocked; the bishop insisted on it. He feared no man. What could anyone take from him that he would not willingly give? Besides, everything that happened was the will of God.

'Come in,' the bishop called, looking up from his work and seeing the tall man filling the doorway with his unusual height and the width of his shoulders.

'Excuse me . . . I'm sorry . . .' the stranger stammered anxiously, without leaving the doorway. 'Do you have food you can spare for me? I'll pay for it. I've come all the way from Toulon. I've been walking for four days. I've had nothing to eat. I have money . . . Please?'

'Why didn't you go to an inn if you have money?' demanded the housekeeper before the bishop could hush her.

The stranger shook his head. 'They won't take me. I'm a convict. My name is Jean Valjean. I served nineteen years' hard labour. They let me out four days ago. I'm on parole. I have to report to Pontarlier by Monday or I go back to the galleys. So I've been walking. All the way from Toulon. Here – this is my passport.'

From his ragged jacket he withdrew his grimy papers. Opening the document, Valjean thrust it towards the bishop.

'I can't read, but I know what it says. "He is very dangerous." They're right,' he added with a bitter laugh. 'I'm very dangerous, but I can pay. I got a hundred and nine francs and fifteen sous. That's for nineteen years' hard labour. I need a meal and a bed. I don't care how much you want. I'll pay. I'll pay the whole nineteen years for a bowl of soup and a night's sleep.'

With a sweet smile, the bishop shook his head. 'Monsieur, you are welcome to eat with us. This is Madame Magloire.' He turned to his housekeeper. 'Supper is ready, am I right, madame? You'll have to set another place. And, after our guest has eaten, you'll make up the bed in the alcove. Please come in, monsieur.'

Valjean stood amazed, rooted to the spot. What sort of man was this? Could such kindness be genuine? Was there some trap here? But over his suspicions he could smell the cooking food, and he began to feel faint again. He shut his eyes to keep the dizziness away.

'It's chilly,' said the bishop. 'Come in and close the door, monsieur.'

Jean Valjean opened his eyes, but he couldn't yet take the few steps that would bring him into the room. He still felt the need to explain himself.

'You mean it? I've been honest. I'm a convict. See my passport?'

'I know who you are,' the bishop said gently. The gendarmerie had already brought him news of Valjean.

'And you're going to let me into your house?'

The bishop shook his head. 'This isn't my house, monsieur. It belongs to Christ.' He rose from the table and took Valjean by the arm, leading him across the threshold and shutting the door behind him.

And so Jean Valjean, a convict with a yellow passport, was soon amazed to find himself in a warm room, sitting at a table in front of a bright fire, chewing on dense-textured rye bread and eating a steaming bowl of hot, savoury soup, rich in vegetables because the bishop did not allow the luxury of meat at his solitary meals. He was even drinking wine, because the bishop had commanded a reluctant Madame Magloire to bring in a bottle of the best from the little they had.

Even more curious, they were eating by the light of wax candles in tall, heavy silver candlesticks, and even the spoon that brought the tasty soup to his lips was made of genuine silver. Valjean rubbed his thumb along the handle and looked closely at the spoon.

His interest did not escape the sharp eye of Madame Magloire, who sat glumly, regarding the stranger with fear and suspicion. 'What crime did you commit?' she asked him bluntly, ignoring the disapproving look she knew she was getting from the bishop.

'Maybe I killed somebody.' Valjean shot her an evil smile, enjoying her jump of terror. He could see that the priest was not afraid of him, so he turned to him next.

'How do you know I'm not going to murder you?' he asked, his grin widening.

'How do you know I'm not going to murder *you*?' replied the bishop calmly.

Valjean was taken aback by the priest's words, and soup dripped from his spoon on to the table. 'What's that? A joke?'

'I suppose we'll have to trust each other,' the bishop said simply.

The directness and kindness in the bishop's words disarmed Valjean. 'All right, I didn't kill anybody,' he admitted grudgingly. 'I'm a thief. I stole food. I was hungry. I stole, but I paid for it. I wore chains for nineteen years. They chain you even when you're sick. But I didn't get sick.'

His voice dropped into deep bitterness. 'I worked hard. Got to. Slack off and they give you the lash. Bitch about the lash and they give you solitary.'

'You've suffered a great deal,' the bishop said compassionately, with tears in his eyes.

Jean Valjean nodded. He had suffered. 'So they let me go. And they gave me a yellow passport.' The man's lips twisted angrily, and his tone became more vehement. 'What can I do with a yellow passport? No one will give me work. I have to go to Pontarlier, report to my parole officer. And then what? Starve to death?'

He laughed, a harsh, grating sound with no mirth in it. 'Nineteen years and now the real punishment begins.'

The bishop shook his head with a deep sigh. 'Men can be unjust,' he allowed sadly.

'Men?' Valjean exploded angrily. 'Not God?' He saw the priest's head jerk back as though he'd been struck, and he softened his tone somewhat. 'All right. Well, whoever you are, I thank you. A meal and a bed. A real bed to sleep in. In the morning, I'll be a new man.'

\*　　　\*　　　\*

But sleep didn't come easily to Jean Valjean. Ironically, the bed itself was at fault; it was too comfortable, too soft, too warm. Valjean was well used to sleeping on thin straw pallets on a cell's stone floor, or on the bare planking of the convict ship galleys. He wasn't accustomed to a real mattress. He could use a stone for a pillow, but not this luxurious collection of feathers and down under his head. For hours his body tossed restlessly from side to side, while scraps of painful memory fevered his brain. And he had nineteen years of painful memories ready at hand to torture him. At last, not many hours before dawn, he fell into a fitful sleep. At once he began to dream again of the unspeakable tortures he'd experienced.

He woke a couple of hours later, his mouth dry, his head raging in pain, still wrapped in the horror of the dreams that had attacked his short sleep, dreams in which he was back at the oars in the galleys, his shoulders straining, his arms nearly out of their sockets as he rowed. He dreamed that, because of his exhaustion, he'd dozed off and the guards had caught him dozing. With whip, fists and feet, they set on him, beating him bloody, ignoring his moans of pain and pleas for them to stop. Tonight it was a dream, but on numerous occasions in Jean Valjean's miserable life it had been a bitter reality.

He kicked off the covers and sat up, aware of his terror and his headache. His breathing was harsh and loud, his heart pounded in his broad chest; the room was not cold, but gooseflesh stood out on his arms, making him shiver almost uncontrollably. It was near dawn; soon it would be another morning.

Sitting on the edge of his bed, the tall man felt something else, something even stronger than the pain and the fear. Anger. He was racked by fury at the injustices he'd suffered for close to two decades, and even before that the injustice which had forced a humble man, who was willing to work, into such circumstances of poverty that he had stolen a loaf of bread to keep alive.

A loaf of bread. Worth, at most, perhaps five sous. That had been Jean Valjean's offence. For that theft he had been sentenced to five years at hard labour. Those five years had swelled to nineteen because of his repeated attempts to escape. Had he been subdued at the beginning, had his spirit been broken by the repeated cruelty of his guards, he would have served his five years and been put back in the world some fourteen years earlier.

But Jean Valjean could not be so easily subdued. There was a fierce spirit in him, an independence, a desire for justice that could not be quenched. He knew what the consequences would be for an attempted escape and recapture. He understood well that it was more prudent to bear his injustices in silence and get out of prison years sooner. Yet he couldn't help himself. Again and again he tried to escape; again and again he was recaptured and the term of his sentence extended by even more years. And so Valjean endured many more years of beatings, starvation, degradation and unbearably hard labour under the most wretched circumstances.

Having been transformed by an indifferent but authoritarian society from a simple man into a raging animal, having been infected with a burning hatred of humankind and a deep resentment of God, Jean Valjean was turned loose in the world with a bitter legacy, a handful of francs in payment for his decades of hard labour, and a yellow passport proclaiming him a convict, a criminal, a dangerous person.

Now that they'd robbed him of any way of earning a living, that indifferent, authoritarian society restored Jean Valjean to life. What a bitter joke!

He got off the bed. He was fully dressed apart from his broken boots, which he now put on. Stealthily, he explored the room around him, his eyes accustomed to the dark. He found nothing to reward his search.

But in the other room there was a basket of silver. Valjean had watched Madame Magloire restore the freshly washed tableware to its basket, and the basket into a cupboard under lock and key. That silver must be worth something!

A slanting ray of pale moonlight, the last ray of the night, came through the window and dimly lit up the corner of the dining room where the cabinet stood. It was almost as bright as day. Silently, Valjean tiptoed into the room and made his way to the cupboard. He had confidence in his strength. Nineteen unrelenting years of hard labour had given him muscles like the twisted limbs of ancient oak trees, iron-hard, gnarled masses in his shoulders, arms, thighs, legs and chest. He was confident that he could force the silver cabinet open with little trouble.

But when he reached the cupboard he started in surprise. It was, indeed, locked, but the key was still in the lock. Valjean supposed it was simple carelessness on the house-keeper's part, but nothing could be further from the truth. Madame Magloire would have guarded that silverware with her life if necessary, even slept with it every night under her pillow, had she been allowed. No, it was the fault of the bishop, whose orders to leave the key in the cabinet lock as a sign of trust in all his visitors she did not dare to disobey.

Jean Valjean knelt down and turned the key. He reached inside the cabinet and pulled out the basket. It was filled with silver tableware; by the last dim rays of moonlight he could make out the gleaming surfaces of the carefully polished knives, forks and spoons. Hastily he thrust it – leaving the basket behind – into his knapsack. The silverware made a loud metallic sound and Valjean froze. Then he sat up, the hairs on his nape prickling in alarm. Footsteps. Slow, almost shuffling, but definitely footsteps coming his way.

Valjean grabbed his knapsack and moved as silently as a nocturnal predator until he was standing behind the open door, out of sight. His jaw was set and his fingers tightened on his walking stick.

A shadow appeared in the doorway; it was the bishop, dressed in his nightshirt. A very light sleeper, he'd been roused by the muffled sounds in the other room and the metallic chinking of the silverware. He peered into the dining room, unable to make out anything much, until his eye fell on the open cabinet lit up by the moonlight.

'Is anybody there?' he asked.

There was a sudden movement behind the door, and before the bishop could turn or raise an arm to defend himself, Jean Valjean's heavy stick came crashing down on his head, and the old man crumpled to the floor with a soft moan.

Valjean knew he had to hurry if he wanted to get away. The old man wasn't dead, and would soon be calling for help. Dragging his bulging, heavy knapsack, he loped towards the street window and threw it open. He tossed his bag and stick outside, and threw his leg over the sill. Then, quietly, he dropped to the ground, picked up his bag and disappeared into the misty dawn.

## Chapter Three

### A GIFT TO GOD

**G**ive thanks to the Almighty, Bishop Myriel was not dead, nor even seriously hurt. This was indeed a miracle, because Jean Valjean was a man of great strength and his stick was a thick and heavy one. But his awkward position behind the door restricted his movements and made the blow a glancing one, hard enough perhaps to cause a mild concussion, not hard enough to break the skull. Know this: had Valjean been forced to kill the bishop for his silver, he would have done so without hesitation. But he was satisfied to see that the old man was merely unconscious. No, the true victim was poor Madame Magloire, who was even now sitting at the dining-room table weeping over the empty silverware basket as though over the coffin of a beloved. She had not shed quite so many tears at the funeral of her husband.

In fact, the bishop, his wounded head dressed in a gauze bandage, soon felt well enough to put his gardening smock on over his cassock and go out to dig in his garden bed of root vegetables. Even outside in his precious garden he could hear the noisy sobs of his bereaved housekeeper.

'Don't cry,' he called into the house. 'We'll use wooden spoons.'

How could he know that those words would not be a

consolation, but would in fact make Madame Magloire wail even louder?

'I don't want to hear any more about it,' cried the bishop; it was the closest thing to a cross word he had ever spoken to his housekeeper. Sighing, he turned back to his weeding.

There came the sound of heavy footsteps. The bishop sat back on his heels and waited. Around the garden wall came three uniformed gendarmes, a plump senior officer in the lead and two following behind. Between the latter two policemen, dwarfing them by his superior height, was Jean Valjean, a prisoner, his hands bound by a rope behind his back. His eyes were cast down, his face grim with despair.

'Monseigneur, I'm sorry to disturb you—' the plump gendarme began. 'We found this man—'

'You caught him!' interrupted a joyful cry from within the house, and a smiling Madame Magloire came running out with a light step, her eyes searching for her precious kidnapped silverware. 'Oh, thank God!'

The bishop raised a cautionary hand and placed it firmly on Madame Magloire's arm. At once, the woman understood and fell quiet.

'I'm very angry with you, Jean Valjean,' said the bishop mildly.

'What happened to your head, Monseigneur?' asked the gendarme.

Monseigneur! Valjean raised his head and his eyes widened in surprise. This pompous fool of a policeman kept calling the priest Monseigneur! This old man could be no simple priest; he must be the Bishop of Digne himself! That would explain the costly silverware. His heart sank, and he cast his eyes down again. Things were about to go very badly for him indeed. The very least he could expect was an immediate revocation of his parole and a new sentence of hard labour for the rest of his life, but who knows what kind of special, unique tortures lie in store for the wretched idiot who robs a monseigneur!

But the bishop was not interested in satisfying the gendarme's curiosity. 'Didn't he tell you he was our guest last night?' he demanded.

'Yes,' the policeman nodded. 'We had our eye on him, you know. He carries a yellow passport. He's a dangerous man; it says so right there in his papers. After we searched his knapsack and found all this silver, he told us he slept here last night.' Then he shook his head and laughed sarcastically. 'He claims you gave it to him.'

'Yes.' The bishop nodded calmly. 'Of course I gave him the silverware.' Behind him, Madame Magloire uttered a strangled gasp of horror, like a high-pitched mouse's squeak.

'But Monsieur Valjean,' the bishop continued, his tone gently chiding, 'why didn't you take the candlesticks? That was very foolish. Madame Magloire, fetch the silver candlesticks. They're worth at least two hundred francs. Why did you leave them?'

Jean Valjean stood stunned, unable to believe his ears. He stared at the bishop; they all stared at the bishop. What was this nonsense? Had the blow on his head cost the old man his sanity?

'Hurry up,' the bishop urged his housekeeper. 'Monsieur Valjean has to get going. He's lost a lot of time.' With a low moan of anguish, Madame Magloire turned to go into the house. To have loved and lost, not once, but twice! It was more than a virtuous woman should be required to endure, yet she didn't dare disobey Bishop Myriel. She went to fetch the tall silver candlesticks. But she walked very slowly, hoping against hope to be summoned back.

'Did you forget to take them?' the bishop asked Valjean,

who still stood stupefied, unable to respond. He wasn't sure what was happening here. Were they making a mockery of him? Were they all in it together – the gendarmes, the bishop, even Madame Magloire? Torture him thus, give him hope, then lock him up and throw the key away? It was beyond Jean Valjean's comprehension, and he didn't know what to say; he could only stand there mute.

The senior gendarme was still suspicious. Something fishy was going on here. This man was nothing but a common convict; he even carried the yellow passport to prove it. What had he to do with a bishop's silverware? *Non*, it didn't add up. 'Pardon, Monseigneur, but are you saying he told us the truth?'

The bishop nodded. 'Of course. Thank you for bringing him back. I'm very relieved.'

What could a policeman say or do in the face of the bishop's calm certainty? With a jerk of his head, the senior gendarme nodded to the two men holding Valjean. One of them cut the rope around his wrists, freeing his hands.

'You're really letting me go?' muttered the tall man in disbelief. He was still in shock.

'Didn't you understand the bishop?' huffed the plump gendarme. He glared at Valjean, as angry as a predatory house cat who's just had its mouse prey snatched out of its jaws.

The housekeeper was also glaring angrily at Valjean when she returned from inside the house, carrying both large candlesticks. The bishop took them from her reluctant fingers. He had to pull to release them.

'Madame Magloire, offer these men some wine,' he instructed. 'They must be thirsty.'

Immediately, the scowl disappeared from the plump gendarme's features. 'Thank you, Monseigneur.' He smiled, and all three officers followed the fuming housekeeper into the dining room. First the silver goes, now the wine! *Mon bon Dieu*, where would it end?

The Bishop of Digne placed the candlesticks carefully into the knapsack and shoved the bag into Valjean's arms, while looking seriously up into the tall man's face. 'Don't forget, don't ever forget,' he told him solemnly, in an undertone that the others couldn't hear. 'You've promised to become a new man.'

At last Jean Valjean found his voice. 'I ... I don't understand,' he stammered. 'Why are you doing this?'

The old man straightened, and from his face shone a beatific radiance that made Valjean long to look away; it was too bright; it hurt the eyes. But Jean Valjean couldn't tear his glance from the bishop. Some greater power kept his eyes locked on that painful gaze.

'Jean Valjean, my brother, you no longer belong to evil,' the bishop said slowly, but with great conviction. 'With this silver, I've bought your soul. I've ransomed you from fear and hatred. And now—' The man's voice rose in power, swelling like organ music. 'I give you back to God.'

The bishop's words and, even more, the power and saintliness behind them threw a chill upon Jean Valjean's soul. He shivered and shook, but he could not speak. Everything inside him screamed in protest. No! No! How could he part with his fear and hatred? They were what kept him going, made him strong! He *needed* his hate; he *craved* his fear. The bishop's phrases resonated in his soul like the tolling of the cathedral bell, causing him agony. He couldn't bear it. He had to get away. With a strangled cry, Valjean turned and fled, clutching the precious knapsack to his breast.

Valjean trudged for several miles, the knapsack growing heavier and heavier, until he was forced to stop. By the side of the road was a clearing, and he decided to rest a while there, where he could keep a lookout for all comers. He sat down on a rock, and placed his bag between his legs. Unable to resist a peek, he loosened the top and looked inside.

The gleam of silver should have reassured him, but somehow it didn't. His thoughts were still confused, and still haunted by the words of the bishop. He, Jean Valjean, had been given back to God, body and soul? It was not a blessing, it was a curse! He looked at the silver again. It was, according to the bishop, the price of his soul. But hadn't Judas Iscariot also valued his soul at the going price of silver? Redeemed or damned. Which? With a low groan, Valjean sank his head into his hands.

For nineteen years the soul of this man had been living in darkness, while his body and spirit were continually brutalized by those in authority over him. Once he had been a creature of the light, like other men, with a hope of heaven to come as a reward for the miseries of this world. He had long ago been robbed of that hope; indeed, he had been robbed of all belief in heaven. Only hell seemed a reality to Jean Valjean.

The man had lost two decades of his life. He was only dimly aware of what had been going on in the world while he was shut away from it; he'd missed most of the Napoleonic era, the wars with Austria, England, Russia fought by Bonaparte in the name of France, the triumphs at Austerlitz and Borodino, the defeats at Moscow and Waterloo. He'd missed the progress of Napoleon himself – from soldier to commander-in-chief, to First Citizen, to consul, to First Consul for Life, to dictator absolute, to king, to emperor, to outcast exile.

By the time Jean Valjean first entered prison, he had lived through the French Revolution with its stirring ideals of *Liberté, Egalité, Fraternité*. He'd lived through the terror that saw Louis XVI's head roll into the dust, to be followed by his queen's, and hundreds – no, thousands – of his nobility. He'd known about the squabbles among the revolution's leaders that had resulted in the deaths of most of them.

Yet in his simplicity of mind and spirit Valjean had believed that, without a corrupt king and court, the aims of the French Revolution would be fulfilled. The poor people, honoured by the titles 'Citizen' and 'Citizeness', would benefit; there would be work in plenty for all; bread would be cheap, and hunger would be abolished, never again to force a man to steal food. There would be no more degradation of the lower classes that sent women out into the streets to earn a few sous with their bodies, that made infants and children die of malnutrition and the other diseases caused by poverty.

But what did Valjean find now that he was back out among free men? Where was the promised brave new world? Where were the wonderful conditions that were meant to change society? Nothing appeared to be changed. Another king, Louis XVIII, now sat on the throne of France. The 'citizen' poor were still hungry, still degraded. A brand-new class of oppressive nobility had sprung up. The bourgeoisie still ran things for their upper-class masters; the Church was still powerful and still in collusion with the rulers, all of them allied against the common people. Over the decades a great deal of blood had been shed, and it appeared to Valjean it was all for nothing. So much for the revolution with its grand ideals of 'Liberty, Equality, Brotherhood'. All that still seemed to matter to men was money and power, as it always had.

With such bitter thoughts Jean Valjean contemplated his new-found wealth. A man could do a great deal with the hundreds of francs the silverware would bring, particularly the candlesticks. Vague plans began to form in his mind. He could change his name and appearance – cut his hair, shave his beard, start life over again in a town where nobody knew him. Maybe he'd buy himself a tavern, or even an inn. He would live comfortably, sell strong drink and rob any drunken patron unwary enough to take his eyes off his purse. Soon he would be rich, and with wealth would come power. There was no telling how far he could go. Never again would he be a fool or a victim. Valjean made up his mind to be shrewd, cunning, afraid of no man, and willing to do anything to gain his ends.

The sound of whistling disturbed his thoughts and made him look up in alarm. Swiftly, his pulled his knapsack closed, and shoved it under his feet.

A young chimney-sweep, no more than eight or nine years old, black all over with chimney soot, appeared out of the trees lining the road, and came towards Valjean, whistling happily. He wore a filthy hat cocked jauntily on the side of his head. His day's work was done, and he had a few sous in his pocket, earned by dropping down a filthy chimney, breathing soot and ash and cinders, brushing and scrubbing until his hands were raw. But now he was free for the rest of the afternoon, and he was happy, because he was only a child, with a child's desire for some playtime. Jean Valjean watched him intently, his eyes narrowing.

'Good morning, monsieur,' the boy greeted him cheerfully.

As quickly as a striking snake, Valjean reached out and grabbed the child. 'I'm no monsieur, I'm a thief,' he growled. 'Got any money?'

Roughly, he searched the chimney-sweep's pockets, finding a coin. Forty sous. He clutched it in his huge hand, laughing cruelly.

The little boy's dirty face crumpled. 'I just got paid!' he protested. 'Please give it back.'

But Valjean merely held on to the coin more tightly. His grin widened; he was enjoying the child's misery.

Now a feeble indignation took hold of the little chimney-sweep. He pounded on Valjean with one small fist, while trying to pry open the man's hand with the other. 'Give it to me! It's mine!' he demanded.

With a curse of annoyance, Jean Valjean roughly pushed the child off him, throwing him to the ground. The boy landed hard, momentarily stunned. Now the chimney-sweep was really frightened; this large man was capable of doing him real harm. He scrambled to his feet, tears rolling down his cheeks, making streaks in the soot, and ran pell-mell down the road.

Jean Valjean stood still, watching him go. The mean pleasure he'd taken in tormenting the child vanished like mist, leaving him holding . . . forty sous. What had he done? He owned a fortune in silver, and he'd just stolen a miserable forty sous from a little boy. What kind of man was he? He knew what kind of man he was, a dangerous one, a thief, capable of anything. Forty sous was forty sous, he told himself. He was even richer now, even if only by forty sous. So why was he having these second thoughts?

He looked down at the coin in his hand, and he suddenly heard the bishop's words resounding in his head. 'Jean Valjean, my brother, you no longer belong to evil. With this silver, I've bought your soul. I've ransomed you from fear and hatred. And now I give you back to God.'

And he had stolen from a child! How much more evil could he be? Who really had custody of his soul, God or Satan?

'Boy!' he shouted suddenly. 'Come back! I was teasing!'

The boy didn't turn or slow down. His skinny little legs

kept pumping until he had rounded the bend of the road and disappeared from sight.

'I don't want your money! Come back!' Valjean picked up the heavy knapsack and began to run after the chimney-sweep. His legs were long and strong, but the bag was very heavy and awkward to carry. It slowed him down, so by the time he came to the bend in the road, the agile little sweep was long out of sight.

A great pang of mingled frustration, guilt and unhappiness swept like a strong wind over Valjean, shaking him to his very centre. The boy's coin burned like fire in the palm of his hand. He wanted to throw it from him, but he was unable to let it go; the pain of burning was part of his punishment.

'I don't want it! Take it back!' he yelled to the empty road. But there was no answer, and no glimpse of the sooty little child who had whistled so cheerfully only a few moments before. All around him was silence.

What was happening? What kind of painful struggle was going on inside him? Jean Valjean looked up to heaven, his face a mask of uncertainty. He was terrified by his own feelings, by what they might portend for the life he was planning. 'Don't do this to me,' he whispered, half pleading, half demanding.

All around him was silence.

Valjean shook his head, tears filling his eyes, and this time his whisper was only pleading. 'Let me go,' he begged. 'I can't be good. I can't . . .'

All around him was silence still.

His mind in a turmoil, his heart in conflict, Jean Valjean took the yellow convict's passport out of his pocket and slowly tore it to bits, scattering the pieces in the road. All at once, a strong wind blew across the clearing, picking up the pieces of the passport and scattering them in all directions.

In a moment they had disappeared. And, with them, his old name and all the dark facts of his earlier life.

Now he was free. He had made up his mind. A new life for him, a new identity. Anything could be bought with money, even forged papers. And once Jean Valjean sold the bishop's silverware, he would have money, plenty of money. He would be truly free.

Then why didn't he *feel* free? On the contrary, with money at hand and a new life ahead of him, he felt more bound than ever before in his life, more bound than when he was on the rowing bench of the prison ship, more bound than when he was shackled on the chain gang. God had His hand on Jean Valjean, and His is the most binding grip of all. That grip never lets a man go.

Overwhelmed by emotion, Valjean raised his imploring hands up to heaven as the tears rolled down his face. Then he fell to his knees, and bowed his head.

God help me, Jean Valjean whispered silently, not realizing that he was praying.

## Chapter Four

### JAVERT

The man astride the black horse on this windy April afternoon was himself dressed in dark fabric from head to toe. Even in the spring sunshine, horse and rider presented a picture of darkness and shadow, a picture not softened by the grim expression on the man's face, or the tight set of his lips. He sat very straight in the saddle; his eyes, shaded by the brim of a stiff black cockaded hat pulled low on his forehead, were never distracted from the road ahead of him. He looked neither to right nor left.

Nevertheless, the man was acutely aware of every passing tree and newly flowering bush, every bird and stone within the long scope of his peripheral vision. Those piercing eyes never missed anything of any significance. However, he perceived them not as wonders of nature, but merely as details.

The man who was so intent on his destination was a policeman, Detective Inspector Javert, on the road to his new posting as prefect of police in the town of Montreuil, close to the sea. His intensity was nothing new. It was part and parcel of his personality, a rigidity of mind and nature that made the man not only inflexible but, in this time of widespread corruption, incorruptible as well. Javert's inflexibility made him an excellent detective, dogged and single-minded to the point of obsession. Like a trained bloodhound, once he'd caught the scent Javert could never be turned off the hunt. Nothing would prevent him from tracking his quarry until he'd trapped it. His record for the capture of criminals was superlative, and had led to his recent promotion to inspector, and now made him head of the metropolitan police of Montreuil-sur-mer.

What Javert lacked was the smallest iota of compassion, or any insight at all into the human soul. To him, everything was either black or white; there were no greys, and no excuses. Mitigating circumstances, pleas of desperation, were of no relevance to him, and he dismissed them without a second thought. Legal was legal, and illegal was illegal, and that was that. Those who commit illegal acts must be apprehended and punished. The tracking down and arrest of wrongdoers was not only Inspector Javert's duty, it was also his destiny. He clutched that destiny close to his very soul; it was his reassurance and his strength. It was his reason for staying alive.

As a result, Javert was alone in the world. He much preferred it that way. He had no family, no friends, and very few acquaintances outside the police sphere. Nobody knew his first name; nobody had ever called him by it. Actually, he had almost forgotten it himself. He was Javert, simply Javert. He did not remember his parents. Unnecessary and unwanted, as a child he had been abandoned at birth by his thief of a father and his unmarried prostitute mother and left to die. A helpless bundle, vulnerable in every way, the stubborn infant had lived instead. Javert grew up in an orphanage, and was released into the world at the age of twelve to make his own way in life. Intelligent and shrewd, he could have become a master criminal. Instead, he chose to work on the side of the law, defending what he thought of as absolute good against absolute evil.

As a child, Javert had never laughed, for there was nothing

in his young life to rejoice over. He never laughed now, even when his life was, by his own terms, a success.

Javert was ambitious, yet his ambitions didn't take an ordinary form. He wasn't interested in the politics of advancement. He had made steady progress in his profession by being the best at what he did, by bringing in the most criminals. Now in charge of a police force, he intended to continue tracking. Even though he was expected to occupy a fine office and sit behind a broad mahogany desk, he intended to stay active, remain in the field, the scourge of evil-doers.

If there was any real enjoyment in his life, it came only when he was on the trail of some malefactor, and closing in fast. For Javert, the thrill of the chase was capped only by catching up with his prey. His inevitable confrontation with the criminal, seeing the expression of terror and despair in the eyes of the wretched being – this was the fuel that fed Inspector Javert's innermost fires.

Coming from Paris, Montreuil would be a new sphere of activity for him. As yet he had no conception of what kind of town it was, or where the source of its wealth lay. But he would soon learn the vulnerabilities of Montreuil. One thing he knew: wherever there were men and women, there was crime, and it would be up to him as chief of police to ferret out crime and see the perpetrators brought to justice. And this he was determined to do. He was eager to get there and get started.

Once inside the city, Javert headed directly for the town hall in the centre of Montreuil. There he found the office of the prefect of police, where he was to present himself and his credentials. Outside the office were several gendarmes standing about idle, which made Javert narrow his eyes and curl his lip slightly in contempt. The moment he was officially in charge, these lazy loafers would be out catching malefactors instead of lounging around indoors. Behind a desk sat a plump young man in a more elaborate uniform, whom Javert at once perceived to be Captain Beauvais, his second-in-command, to whom he was expected to present himself and his documentation.

Javert remained at attention as Beauvais stood up slowly to greet him. He noticed that there was affability in the man's demeanour, but no sharpness or precision of movement, no snap. Something else that would have to change around here.

'Good afternoon, Captain,' he said crisply, extending his papers. 'I'm Javert, the new police inspector. Here are my orders from the Paris prefect.'

The cheerful Beauvais didn't bother to take the papers. He smiled a welcome. 'Yes, hello, Inspector Javert. I've been expecting you. I'm Captain Beauvais. How was your trip?'

'You didn't look at my orders,' Javert pointed out.

'Oh, I'm sure they're all right.' Beauvais gestured with one chubby hand as though to wave the papers away. 'Have you eaten? Would you like—'

'I'd like you to follow procedure,' insisted the other coldly.

Startled, Beauvais looked sharply at Javert. He saw a man with an expressionless face, but one whose hooded eyes gave away the intensity of his inner self. Easy-going though he was, Captain Beauvais was not unintelligent, and he had a keen sense of people. He could tell that Inspector Javert was a rigid man, one who did everything by the book. Beauvais caught the hint of an obsessive personality here. Normally, this wasn't a bad thing in a chief of detectives, but this man didn't look as though he could ever release his inner pressures. Javert might never explode, but he could very possibly implode, and collapse from within.

Accordingly, Beauvais accepted the official papers, and

looked them over with a care unusual for him. 'Everything's in order, Inspector,' he said. 'You are now in charge of the Montreuil police.'

Javert nodded in satisfaction. Although it had been something of a struggle, procedure had at last been followed. Refusing lunch – much to Captain Beauvais' regret – Inspector Javert preferred to start on his duties immediately. They began with a visit to his new theatre of operations. Beauvais took him on a walking tour of the city's heart, pointing out with some pride the great improvements that had in recent years been effected in Montreuil.

They passed a recently built boys' school, a sturdy stone structure with a large play-yard in which more than a hundred active boys were passing a noisy recess. Next door, construction was in progress on another sizable building, and a sign proclaimed that this was the site of the new girls' school, soon to be completed and in operation.

'Two new schools?' Despite himself, Javert was impressed.

'Yes.' Beauvais nodded, pleased and proud to be able to point out the fine facilities of his town. 'And there's going to be a park. Just as if we were a big city.' They turned the corner of the broad street. 'And here's the new wing to the hospital.'

A hospital, and with a new wing? Javert couldn't help the expression of surprise that came over his face. 'How is Montreuil paying for all these public works?' he asked.

'Not all of it is public,' Captain Beauvais replied. 'The mayor paid for them out of his own pocket. And he paid for an additional ten beds in the hospital.'

The mayor? Out of his own pocket? Most unusual, thought Javert.

The two men continued down what seemed to be a main

thoroughfare. On one side of the street was a large cleared open space, where many workers were toiling industriously, planting trees, laying gravel for walkways, removing mud and rocks into large barrels to be carried away in carts.

'Ah,' remarked Beauvais with gratification, 'here's our future park.'

Inspector Javert looked thoughtful. 'In Paris, things are miserable. Crime is rampant. Streets are filthy. Conditions here are much better.'

Beauvais nodded and smiled. 'Yes. Life in Montreuil has never been better,' he said with mingled pride and satisfaction.

'Because you have jobs? Is that why?'

Beauvais nodded again. 'Yes, that's part of it. In fact, shall I take you to our textile factory? That's our biggest business.'

'Very well.' Javert was curious to see this wonder which in addition to textiles had manufactured so much good for this small city. It must be a very profitable enterprise indeed. 'Who owns the factory?

'The mayor,' replied Beauvais. '*Monsieur le maire*. Originally, he was just one of the workers. He was known as Monsieur Madeleine. But when the factory went bankrupt five years ago – it's incredible to think of that now – he bought the whole works for less than five hundred francs.'

'How did he make it profitable?' asked Javert.

'He had the notion of dyeing the fabrics in large vats, using a production line of workers. That way, the colours are consistent. And he can produce so many they can be sold very inexpensively. Now he can't fill all the orders from England and Germany.'

The curiosity of a detective was burning now in Javert's breast. He had to see for himself this paragon of industry, ingenuity and philanthropy. Such a man of influence and power must be well worth meeting. As much as Javert despised those beneath him, he worshipped at the shrine of those above him. Authority was his god, and might never be questioned or challenged. Javert believed that his calling in life was to defend authority from the rebelliousness of the criminal. Sometimes he thought of himself as the divine watchdog, Argus of the Hundred Eyes, guarding society from that which threatened to tear at its fabric.

'On second thoughts, Captain, I should report to the mayor as soon as possible. Let's do that first.'

'Yes, sir,' agreed Beauvais. 'His house is near by.' He led the way off the main avenue and down a narrow side street.

'The mayor seems to be the force behind everything,' remarked Javert. 'He must be a man of genius.'

Captain Beauvais' chubby face looked suddenly hesitant. 'He *is* extraordinary. But I should warn you, he's also a little eccentric.'

'Eccentric? In what way?' Inspector Javert's curiosity was piqued even further by this description.

Beauvais nibbled at his rosy lower lip. 'Well . . . he's shy,' he answered slowly. 'Lives like a hermit. He didn't even want to be mayor. He tried to refuse the honour, but the town fathers insisted.'

Javert looked surprised. 'Not ambitious? And, even so, he's this successful?' Something didn't connect here; there was a discordant note that made him uncomfortable. Inspector Javert preferred that every fact fit neatly into its own pigeonhole.

'He's a mystery,' Beauvais admitted with a Gallic shrug. 'Some people think he's crazy. But I like him. I like him and I feel sorry for him.'

To Javert this was the most surprising fact of all. '*You*

feel sorry for the mayor?' He seemed genuinely taken aback, which was a rare experience for Javert.

'Because he's lonely.' Beauvais stopped and indicated the house they were standing in front of. 'Here we are.'

Javert stared in disbelief. He was looking at a tiny two-storey house, two or three rooms on each floor, the whole thing not much bigger than a cottage. It was impossible to reconcile this with what ought to be the dwelling of an influential mayor of a prosperous city. 'He lives . . . here?'

Captain Beauvais smiled. 'Strange, isn't it? Only a little better than a workman's house. But yes, it belongs to *Monsieur le maire.*'

He led Javert to the front door. 'Wait here. I'll tell him you've arrived, and then you can come in.'

Without ceremony, the captain entered a small side garden. A tall man of perhaps fifty years was sitting at a plain white-painted wooden table under a tree. Despite the coolness of the early spring afternoon, the man was dressed only in shirtsleeves, with no jacket to protect him from the vagrant breezes. But the linen shirt was a clean one, not darned or patched or shabby, and the man himself, with freshly shaven cheeks and chin, and neatly combed long hair, presented an image of modest respectability.

He was poring over a small volume; his lips moved as he read the sentences out loud to himself under his breath. As he heard footsteps approaching, the tall man quickly shut the book and covered it with some papers from the sheaf on the table.

'Good afternoon, *Monsieur le maire,*' began Beauvais. 'The new inspector has arrived. He wants to report.'

'That's all right. He doesn't have to.'

Captain Beauvais suppressed a smile. It was obvious that the mayor didn't know Javert. 'Oh, but *Monsieur le maire,* if you don't permit the inspector to report, I think he will burst into tears.'

'Ah, well then, we must not let that happen, eh, Beauvais?' The mayor stood and led the captain into the house, through the kitchen and into a small, plainly furnished sitting room. Beauvais went to fetch Javert.

As soon as the inspector entered the room, he saluted the mayor with an efficient snap of his right wrist. *'Monsieur le maire*, I am Inspector Javert. I have the honour of reporting to my post as your prefect of police.'

The moment the mayor's eyes fell on the inspector, a spell of dizziness threatened to overcome him, and he fought it back with all his strength. Javert! He knew that name and he knew that face. Captain Beauvais had previously referred only to 'the inspector'. With the man in front of him now, the mayor recognized Javert at once. He was a ghost from his past, an old enemy. The mayor saw in his mind's eye a younger Javert, dressed not as a prefect of police but in a guard's uniform, yet with the same cold, implacable face. But did Javert recognize him?

'Uh . . . I'm sorry . . .' stammered the mayor. 'You are . . . ?' He kept his face slightly averted, and his eyes cast down.

'Inspector Javert,' repeated the policeman a little nervously. Was anything wrong with his posting? Surely everything must be in order. 'You were expecting me? Paris should have informed you—'

'Do you have papers?' the mayor interrupted abruptly.

Javert almost smiled in relief, on solid ground now. 'Yes, *Monsieur le maire*. I apologize. I should have presented them immediately.' Reaching into his breast pocket, he produced his papers and offered them to the mayor.

But the other man didn't take the papers; he didn't even glance at them. 'Good. Thank you for coming.' To Beauvais, he said, 'Make sure he's settled comfortably,' and to Javert he only added, 'Good day.' Then he stood up and left the room swiftly, his pulses thudding heavily in his ears. The interview, such as it was, was over.

Javert stood perplexed. He'd never experienced anybody like this strange mayor before. Was he himself to blame for the man's brusqueness? 'Did I . . . did I make a mistake?' he asked Beauvais.

The captain hid his amusement. He thought that this must be a rare thing indeed – to see Javert embarrassed and at a loss for words. Very few men could have ever witnessed this.

'We had him over to supper once,' the amused Beauvais remarked. 'He said "hello" when he came in, "thank you" after dessert, and "good night" at the door. You got complete sentences. He must like you.'

Monsieur Madeleine hastened out of his sitting room to his small bedroom, shutting the door behind him. Throwing himself on his narrow bed, he gave himself over to the trembling that engulfed all his limbs. His breath rasped in his throat as the terrible memories came flooding back.

Javert! He'd recognized the police inspector at once. Javert! How well he knew that face – older now, perhaps, but essentially the same as when he last saw it years ago. Yes, he still possessed the same gimlet eyes, the identical stern brow, the same cruel set of the lips. The face of the hunter, the eyes of the obsessive. A wave of coldness made the tall man shiver. His teeth chattered, the coldness of Javert's implacable nature freezing his heart.

And so now the man had risen to become an inspector of police, and the prefect right here in Montreuil! How ironic was fate; how the gods must be laughing now!

The mayor felt once again the heavy weight of the shackles around his ankles. The chains seemed as real and as chafing as they had years before, when they *were* real. In his mind, he was once more sitting at the galley oars. He could feel the cutting sting of the lash; his shoulders ached from the whipping and the hard labour of the rowing bench.

Vividly he remembered the chain gang, the racking days and nights of work without rest. He could hear the curses and abuses of his captors beating at his ears. He felt again, as clearly as if no time at all had passed, the ugly injustices of his captivity. And, standing on the galley deck at Toulon, he once again saw the prison guard Javert.

For this man, this mayor, this philanthropic rich Monsieur Madeleine, was none other than Jean Valjean, fugitive, former criminal, violator of parole, stealer of silverware and mugger of a defenceless child. The unexpected sight of an old enemy, Javert, brought it all back in the flash of an eye. He felt trapped, a hunted animal staring down the barrel of a gun.

What should he do now?

## Chapter Five

### FANTINE

*J*avert! Unmistakably Javert! I'd know those icy eyes anywhere! Did he recognize me? Think! I must think!

As his heartbeat slowly returned to normal, Valjean was able to think more clearly. He didn't believe Javert had recognized him. The man had showed no sign of it, only a nervous deference to mayoral authority. Of course. Why should he recognize in the person of today's solid citizen the fugitive of half a dozen years ago?

Jean Valjean's physical appearance was very different from what it had been six years ago. These days he was beardless, always clean, he didn't shuffle when he walked, or look like the hunted creature he used to be. Valjean was no longer merely a near-human, to be counted less than a dog; he was a prosperous man, useful and respected.

Six long years had gone by since Bishop Myriel had ransomed Valjean's soul and given him to God. He had made excellent use of those years. With his new identity and the money he got for selling the bishop's heirloom silverware, he had established himself as an honest person. Working hard, 'Monsieur Madeleine' had been able to buy a failing business and expand it into a money-making operation employing many men and women. The working conditions in his factory were excellent; he was famous for treating his male and female workers fairly, with dignity and respect.

He paid them a living wage and saw to their physical and moral needs.

Oddly enough, when he disposed of the silver, Valjean never even considered selling the bishop's candlesticks. They were too precious to him as a visible symbol of that man's saintliness. Valjean had stolen a finger, and the bishop had given him his whole hand. The candlesticks were a constant reminder of his good fortune, his own conversion, and God's grace.

In those half-dozen years since he'd settled down here in Montreuil, Valjean had changed his life completely, and with his money and position had changed many other lives for the better. He had lived modestly, even frugally, while his factory earned him vast sums of money. He had saved up a great deal, but had given away much, much more than he'd saved, in various works of charity both public and private.

Shy and reclusive, still insecure in his new identity, Valjean lived alone, in his tiny house, denying himself every luxury, content with a roof and a loaf of bread. He never entertained and only rarely socialized with others, making an exception only when he felt it was unavoidable or that a refusal would cause another person pain.

Usually he drank cold water or simple cider, or, occasionally, the simplest and cheapest of the local wine. Valjean tasted meat only rarely, and ate mainly the fruit and vegetables he grew himself in his little garden. Without realizing it consciously, Valjean was following in the self-denying footsteps of the good bishop who had set him free from evil.

Intolerant of his own ignorance, he was even teaching himself to read and write, using a child's primer and a slate. The work proceeded slowly, because Valjean took nobody who might help him into his confidence. It was this school book he had hastily hidden from Captain Beauvais' sight earlier. Montreuil already accepted the fact that their mayor and chief benefactor was illiterate; in fact, they pointed to it almost with pride. They took pleasure in the fact that *Monsieur le maire* was so honest and hardworking a man who had come so far from his humble origins, but whose origins in ignorance he had not abandoned.

Jean Valjean didn't agree with them. He detested his ignorance. He recognized his inability to read or write as a point of shame, not pride, and he kept his attempts to school himself a secret from the world.

Valjean had never wanted power or craved authority over others. He had not sought to become mayor; the office was forced upon him. He had not been permitted to refuse. But in the last six years, in all his doings with men Jean Valjean strove to be fair and just and charitable. It seemed to him that he'd more than made up for the crimes of his earlier life by the good deeds of his later life, but then how could he be sure? He was no judge; only God the Father was fit to judge the value of a man's life.

Valjean tried with all his heart to be a good man – one belonging to God of his own free will – and to live up to the saintly bishop's faith in him. Even so, he understood that in the eyes of society he would always be regarded only as a fugitive, a criminal to be apprehended and brought back to prison for violation of parole, for the destruction of his legal documents, the criminal acquisition of illegal documents and the assumption of a false identity. Never mind that under his new identity he had devoted all his waking hours to charitable deeds. If he were ever caught and his true identity revealed, only a life sentence in the worst of conditions awaited him. No mitigation possible for the changed circumstances of a man's life. No mercy for the converted.

And now this new life and Jean Valjean himself were in grave danger. The sudden appearance of Inspector Javert came like fate knocking at his door, beckoning Valjean on to his destruction. He was under no illusions; to the rest of the world, all his years of being good faded into nothing compared with his sin of breaking his parole. There was no doubt. This man Javert appeared out of the shadows as the watchdog of the public good. Surely God must have His reasons for posting Javert to Montreuil.

Jean Valjean saw how it would be. The tiniest misstep on his part, the smallest clue, imperceptible to others, would soon stimulate Detective Inspector Javert to action. If Javert hadn't recognized him today, surely it must be only a matter of time before he would, before those gimlet eyes would pierce *Monsieur le maire*'s soul to find the wretched fugitive Jean Valjean crouching beneath. Because Javert, that most obsessive of policemen, guardian of the public good, was now right here in Montreuil, Valjean knew that he must be prepared to flee at a moment's notice.

He would have to lay plans for an immediate getaway.

The mayor's textile factory stood on a rise near the outskirts of Montreuil, near a river into which it could discharge the waste from its dye-vats. It stood in a large clearing from which all the trees had been cut down, so that maximum sunlight could pour through the factory windows. It was a long, narrow one-storey brick building, erected about forty years earlier and modernized by Valjean when he took the factory over.

Inside, the factory was divided in two, one half as a workshop for the male workers, the other half the female dyers' workshop. As Madame Blanquet, the factory forewoman for the female dyers, led the way, Javert and Beauvais climbed a short set of wooden steps, and entered a large office. The interior wall of the office was made up of a large, many-paned glass window that commanded a total view of the factory floor, showing all the activity. With great interest, Javert went over to the window and scanned the workshops.

He saw four large vats in each half of the factory, one for each colour, in which workers tramped the fabric down into the colour with their bare feet, similar to wine-makers trampling grapes. There were also steam-powered engines which manufactured and cut the fabric, and many wooden racks for drying the skeins of material. On either side of the factory, men and women, using long poles to manipulate the skeins, were shoving the heavy fabric into the dye-vats and pushing them under so that the fabric would take the colour evenly when it was trampled underfoot.

It took teams of workers, one at each corner, to manipulate a single large skein. A great deal of attention was paid to the edges and corners of the fabric, which tended to float up to the surface of the vat and not receive an equal amount of dye.

Steam rose from the hot liquid in the vats, curling up to the skylights in the roof. It was hot work, and hard work, but it was not impossibly difficult labour. In the earliest days of the Industrial Revolution, workers were accustomed to heavy jobs and long hours. At least, working here for *Monsieur le maire*, they were paid enough of a wage to cover rent and buy food to fill their children's bellies. Their labour was not exploited or treated with disrespect.

Javert watched curiously; he was most intrigued by the apparent equality of the sexes here. 'The men and women are doing the same work, aren't they?'

'Yes.' The forewoman nodded. 'Identical work. *Monsieur le maire* redesigned the factory to keep the sexes apart.' She didn't bother to keep the pride out of her voice. This was a model factory, and all acknowledged it to be so.

'I told you he was eccentric,' grinned Captain Beauvais.

Madame Blanquet sniffed indignantly. 'Not eccentric, Captain. He cares about honest working women and wants to protect their virtue.'

'Very proper,' Javert said stiffly. 'And very wise.' The inspector's opinion of the human race, particularly poor or working-class members of it, was not a high one. Potential criminals all. Just let them lose a job and they all went bad. As for men and women, Javert believed firmly that if they were not kept apart from each other, unspeakable animal acts and sexual abominations must surely follow. He stared through the window at the women's workshop, and one particular worker caught his eye.

He saw a very pretty young woman, who appeared to be no more than twenty-four or twenty-five years old. She was tall yet slight of build, and moved gracefully, her long yellow hair caught up under a protective kerchief. The girl was one of a team of four women pulling a heavy skein out of the large vat of blue dye, one woman at each corner of the fabric. She seemed upset and on the verge of crying. Why? Javert's eyes bored into her, the detective looking for that damning bit of information that would condemn the girl.

Suddenly the young woman looked up and caught Inspector Javert's eye. At once, a shiver passed through her, and her hand slipped. Her corner of the fabric dropped into the dye. As she reached for it, she bumped into Madame Victurien, the woman next to her, knocking the fabric out of the other woman's hand. The entire skein fell into the vat and was submerged.

'You did it again!' shouted Madame Victurien. She was a middle-aged woman, a widow, sour of face and of soul, unpleasant of manner. She particularly disliked the young and pretty Fantine, and seized upon every opportunity to make her life miserable.

'I . . . I'm sorry . . .' stammered Fantine.

'You've ruined another one! They're going to dock my pay now!'

Seeing the quarrel below, the forewoman left the office hurriedly and rushed to the factory floor, followed at a discreet distance by Javert. 'You two again?'

'It's not my fault!' yelled Victurien. 'She's incompetent! She knocks into me—'

'All right! All right!' With irritation, the forewoman put up a hand to stop the complaint. 'Fantine, I'm going to move your place.'

The girl nodded imperceptibly, but a feeling of relief flooded through her. She had been afraid she was going to lose her job, and that must *never* happen! That would be the worst thing in the world! She desperately needed every sou she could scrape together. As she gathered up her things hastily, Fantine didn't notice that a letter, addressed to her, fell out of her pocket and drifted on to the workbench next to Victurien. Neither did Victurien notice the letter.

'Goodbye and good riddance!' huffed Victurien.

Fantine gave a defiant little toss of the head. There was no love lost between herself and the sour Madame Victurien, but Fantine was afraid of the rough edge of the older woman's tongue. Now that she was leaving this intimidating woman behind, a few drops of courage began to run through her veins. 'It was an unforgettable experience working with you, madame. But I'll forget it anyway,' she said sarcastically, with another toss of her golden head.

'Enough!' barked Madame Blanquet. 'Let's go, Fantine.'

As she led the girl to another place in the women's workshop, Javert left. Nothing of interest here, nothing requiring his intervention or authority.

'What a tragedy!' Victurien addressed her fellow workers with elaborate sarcasm. 'We've lost our princess. We'll have to return to our drab lives. Well, we can't all get by on our looks—' At this moment, she broke off as she spotted the letter on the bench beside her. A letter to a dyer! And Fantine herself could neither read nor write! A rare thing indeed! Who knew what interesting or useful information such a letter might contain? Putting her hand over it to shield it from her fellow workers, Victurien surreptitiously slipped the letter into her own pocket, to be read later.

Promptly at ten to eight the following morning, Jean Valjean waited impatiently on the Pavement outside the Lafitte Bank. It seemed to him a great deal of time passed before the bank's shades were pulled up and the front door unlocked, but it was in fact only ten minutes. At eight on the dot, Valjean entered the building and was greeted with great deference by a clerk who ushered him immediately into the president's imposing, mahogany-panelled office.

Sitting under the brass-and-crystal chandeliers, Valjean and Monsieur Lafitte soon completed their transaction. But the banker was troubled. He was used to the fact that from time to time *Monsieur le maire*, Lafitte Bank's best and most prosperous client, took large sums of money out of his accounts. Those removals were usually quickly followed by the news that there was to be a new scheme to make Montreuil a better place, paid for by *Monsieur le maire*. A library, a school, the expansion of the hospital, hot lunches for the poor, all of them underwritten by Monsieur's bank withdrawals.

But this one seemed to Monsieur Lafitte to be different from the other transactions. For one thing, it was a considerably larger withdrawal, nearly three times the amount that the mayor usually took. It left the client with a much smaller balance than usual. Then, too, there was a haste to this particular transaction that made Monsieur Lafitte uneasy. *Monsieur le maire* wanted the money at once, and he brought with him a travelling bag to put it in. He was taking it away with him on the spot, and he was going away alone.

'I'd feel safer if you had an escort,' suggested the banker.

'Don't worry, I can handle myself,' Valjean answered grimly. Then he seemed to recollect himself; at least, his public persona. 'There's no time,' he added hastily. 'I have to leave right away.'

The banker brought the tips of his fingers together and cleared his throat. 'I hope the urgency does not imply distress,' he said with great delicacy. 'And I trust you are aware that this institution is at your service. Monsieur's credit is impeccable—'

'Thank you.' Valjean nodded gravely. 'But this is a . . . a . . . business opportunity. No crisis.'

Monsieur Lafitte the banker smiled a wintry smile. A business opportunity. Of course. He had great confidence in *Monsieur le maire*'s business sense. Whatever this new enterprise might be, soon even more gold coin would be rolling into the vaults of the Lafitte Bank.

From the bank, Valjean hastened to his factory. Placing the heavy satchel of money on his desk, he sent for his foreman and forewoman. 'I'm leaving for the day,' he told them. 'Urgent business. I'll return tomorrow.'

The foreman nodded, but the forewoman looked troubled. 'Before you go, I've received disturbing information about one of the girls.' She took out the letter that Fantine had dropped, and which Victurien had gleefully passed along to her. 'I haven't questioned her, but I have reason to suspect she has a child and she's not married.'

The news surprised him; somehow Valjean expected that all of his workers were above reproach. Morality had become very important to him since his conversion. He held his workers to a high standard of behaviour.

He didn't bother to glance at the letter held out to him by Madame Blanquet, who'd forgotten that *Monsieur le maire* could barely read. If he had taken it from her, if he'd slowly made out the words that had so tortured Fantine, he surely would have reacted with his customary compassion.

Or if there'd been time for Valjean to see the girl for himself, if he'd seen the desperation in her eyes, the sorrow in her soul, he would have recognized the purity of her nature, and extended a hand to help her, as he had done to so many others.

But Jean Valjean was in a hurry, and his thoughts were distracted, therefore he had no time for puzzling out letters one word at a time, or for reading the heart of a wretched young woman. Just as he reached the door, he turned.

'Is she a whore?' he asked brusquely.

It was the language of the streets, of the prisons, and a word that had not escaped Jean Valjean's lips in many years. His mind was elsewhere, and he wasn't even aware that he'd spoken it. For safety's sake, he usually guarded his tongue.

The forewoman bit her lip, embarrassed by the mayor's blunt language and about the position she found herself in. She couldn't afford to lose this job; *Monsieur le maire* was a generous employer, and hers was a respected place. 'I don't hire ...' She could not bring herself to repeat Valjean's word. 'I don't hire women who sell themselves.'

Jean Valjean chided himself. 'Of course you don't,' he said

kindly. 'I apologize. I don't want our girls to be exposed to
. . . to bad elements. Whatever you suggest . . .'

'I suggest dismissal,' Madame Blanquet said in a firm
tone.

Valjean nodded and opened the office door, the heavy
satchel in his other hand. His thoughts were now back on
his money bag and his plan. 'I trust your judgment,' was
all he said.

If only Jean Valjean could have seen into the future at that
moment! If only he could have seen what the consequences
of his answer would be! But he spoke never dreaming that
these four simple words would have the power to change
the course of so many lives, including his own, irretrievably
and for ever.

## Chapter Six

FANTINE AND COSETTE

**M**ollified, Madame Blanquet nodded. 'Thank you, *Monsieur le maire*,' she said quietly, and her mouth set into a grim line. The forewoman could not afford to allow anything to threaten her position or the trust that *Monsieur le maire* had in her. The girl would have to go, and immediately.

Returning to the factory floor, Madame Blanquet called Fantine off the line. She took her to one side and confronted her at once with the damning letter. The girl gasped and instinctively clapped one hand to her pocket, where she still believed the incriminating document was hidden. The pocket was empty.

The forewoman waved the letter under Fantine's nose like an angry red flag. The girl saw it with a sinking heart, and realized that she was cornered. She knew well what the letter contained. Even though she was unable to read, she always took every letter from a certain Madame Thenardier, postmarked Montfermeil, directly to the letter shop, where a professional reader, using a pointer to prove that he was reading every word, read the contents aloud to her for twenty sous. Then Fantine would dictate her answer at a cost of twenty additional sous plus postage.

In the letter being waved under Fantine's nose, this Madame Thenardier wrote asking for more money, because

Fantine's daughter Cosette was ill and needed medicine. Also, she wrote, the monthly boarding fees were going up again because little Cosette was getting so big she was eating much more food, and the Thenardiers could no longer continue to feed her at the old rates.

Then came the accusation – *Fantine, you gave birth to a child without a legal father, and then you gave it away!* Madame Blanquet's words drummed in Fantine's ears. The damning letter proved her charges beyond a doubt.

'No, madame, never!' Fantine wept. 'I would never abandon my own dear little girl! I have only boarded her with good people, caring people! I pay all of her expenses myself. Cosette is my daughter, and I love her. I could never bear to be parted from her for ever. Someday, she will come and live with me—'

Madame Victurien watched the confrontation from a distance, her face creased by an ugly smile of self-satisfaction. She was glad in her pinched little soul to see her enemy so humiliated and disgraced. The other women workers witnessed the scene as well, and they grinned like wolves to see 'Princess' Fantine brought so low. Their feelings were a mixture of ill-will and disgust.

It was no secret that most of the factory women were jealous of Fantine, of her youth and beauty, her slenderness and grace, her willowy height, her lovely long yellow hair, sound teeth and playful manners. They were by no means unhappy to see her lose her job. Most of all, they despised Fantine, not so much for bearing an illegitimate child, but for the fact that she'd been clumsy enough to be caught out in her sin. What a stupid girl! How foolish to carry the incriminating letter right into the factory! Thanks to Madame Victurien, who was able to read, all of the women workers now knew to the last syllable what Fantine's letter contained.

'Nevertheless, you are dismissed from here.' Madame Blanquet shook her head firmly. Her hands remained folded over the apron she wore. 'I want you to go this very minute.'

Fantine gasped in disbelief as she heard the unthinkable word. Dismissed! 'You're dismissing me for having a baby, and you ask why I boarded her?'

'You're not being dismissed for having a child. You're being dismissed for having a child out of wedlock and then pretending to be an honest woman,' replied the forewoman impatiently.

'But I have to earn money to feed her,' protested Fantine. 'How can I work *and* take care of her? I *have* to lie!' It was a cry from the very depths of her miserable heart.

The forewoman scowled. 'You make it sound as though your lie is my fault,' she told the girl indignantly.

Fantine's face crumpled in panic and tears began to spill from her eyes down over her cheeks. 'Oh God! I'm sorry, madame. I'm upset. I don't mean to argue. My Cosette is a sweet little girl . . . an innocent little girl. Don't punish her for my sin. I was stupid. I fell in love—'

'In love! That's always the excuse,' the other woman spat contemptuously. In the name of love, a woman thought she had permission to behave like a whore on the streets!

'Yes, you're right,' sobbed Fantine, fighting for her survival, in desperation now. 'I'm bad. I'm a bad person. But the Thenardiers are good people. They have two daughters of their own. My Cosette can play with them. She won't be so lonely. She's better off with them. Only I have to make money. Please! To pay for her medicine! Just a month,' she begged. 'Please . . . I'll be good . . . I'll work hard.' Fantine began to cry wildly – great, loud, gulping sobs which she was unable to control. Even the torment of more public humiliation could not keep those tears bottled in.

But Madame Blanquet would not budge an inch. She had a job to do, and she had to fulfil the trust placed in her by her employer. She felt that her own position in the factory was somehow compromised by the sins of this wretched young woman. And this she would never allow. '*Monsieur le maire* cares about his workers,' she said piously. 'He cannot have women of questionable morals influencing the girls. I'm sorry. But you must leave here at once.'

Jean Valjean had been trudging for hours, carrying the heavy money bag. While other men slept soundly indoors, he was travelling on foot and by night. Only his great strength, the muscles in his long legs and broad shoulders, kept him going. A less powerful man would have collapsed by the side of the road many kilometres ago. At last, he reached the marker he was looking for, the crossroads about eighteen miles north of Montreuil. He looked around intently, in every direction. Nobody. He stood very still, straining his ears in the darkness. Nothing. He was out here totally alone.

Reassured, Jean Valjean turned off the main road and made his way through the tall trees deeper into the forested area, disappearing into the morning ground mist.

Dawn was just beginning to break in the eastern sky. Even in the dim light and swirling mist, Valjean knew this place. He had been here six years ago. It was here, among these trees, that he had hidden out for a night and a day before deciding that Montreuil was far enough away from his past to give him a chance at a safe clean start. These woods had been lucky for him once before. He was counting on that luck again.

There! There was the special tree he was looking for, a tall, broad oak, centuries old. He remembered it well. It would be easy to locate and easy to recognize in future. But, just in case . . . Valjean set down the money bag and took his clasp knife out of his pocket. He carved a deep X on the tree trunk, down low near the upthrust roots, where it wouldn't be spotted unless one knew in advance where to look for it.

He opened the bag. On top of the stacks of money was a small shovel. Valjean took it out and began to dig in front of the tree. He worked feverishly, although his shoulders were aching with the effort. When the hole was deep enough, he placed the money bag inside and filled the hole in, trampling the soil down over it. Then he smoothed the surface with his hands until it was level, and brought small branches and leaves to lay over the spot until it was concealed. He stood up, walked a few steps away and turned, looking back at the hidden place. He walked in another direction and turned again. And yet again, always checking the spot where the hole had been dug, with a sharp, critical eye.

No, everything looked normal. You couldn't tell that a hole had been dug there or that the ground in front of the tree had ever been disturbed. His money was safe. Jean Valjean nodded his head, pleased. He trudged back to the crossroads and started on the long road back to Montreuil. He hoped to reach home before afternoon. Tomorrow he would return to his factory and it would be business as usual. Nobody would have missed him, and nobody would ever suspect that, under a tree miles away, a small fortune was hidden in the earth, only waiting for the day when Jean Valjean would be forced to leave Montreuil in haste and for good.

Fantine received fifty francs from the factory as her severance pay. It was a generous settlement, the same one that *Monsieur le maire* insisted on paying any worker he had to sack. She could have lived on it for several weeks, eating and drinking frugally, and paying the rent on her tiny room.

Instead, Fantine sent the entire sum to the Thenardiers to pay Cosette's latest boarding fees. She did this without question or a murmur of complaint.

Over the few years the little girl had been with the Thenardiers, Fantine's expenses had risen steadily. Every letter she received was a fresh demand for francs. More money for clothing, more for food. Fantine paid it without a murmur, happy in the thought that her precious child was being well fed and warmly clothed. She read with a hunger that might be called avidity the Thenardiers' accounts of Cosette's progress, of how tall she had grown, and how plump, of what a pleasant life she was leading.

Giving her daughter away had been the hardest thing Fantine had ever been forced to do. But what choice did she have? She had arrived in Paris at the age of fifteen, all alone, without a relative or friend in the big city. In fact Fantine had no relatives in the world, having been orphaned at thirteen. She came to Paris hoping to find decent employment as a house servant, one that would afford her a snug roof over her head and bread in her belly. Her wants and needs were very modest. Fantine had no true conception of just how beautiful she was or what that beauty might be worth in venal terms. She was barely out of childhood and had no experience of life or of the desires of men.

But someone else spotted her beauty and revelled in her childish naïveté. Felix Tholomyes, an idle and dissolute young student, the lazy son of wealthy parents, licked his lips at the sight of Fantine's round cheeks, plump bosom, narrow waist, shapely arms, golden hair, bright blue eyes and shining teeth. But Tholomyes was far from stupid. He knew that he had to proceed slowly, so as not to frighten his virginal little pigeon away. She was too delicious a prize to lose.

Felix wooed Fantine romantically – with nosegays of

flowers, meals in cafés, carriage rides, chocolates, glasses of wine and brandy, a lace scarf, a pair of pretty earrings. He overwhelmed her with his little gifts and his murmured words of undying love into her soft ears, while his fingers softly caressed her neck and the curves of her breast. This was the first man, apart from the loutish boys back in Montreuil, ever to pay Fantine any masculine attention. Is it any wonder that the girl fell completely in love and gave herself over to her passionate lover, body and spirit?

The first months of her affair with Tholomyes were an idyll of amour and romance. Fantine had never even imagined such happiness or so much pleasure. She abandoned herself to her lover and gave up all thought of employment and a useful life. They moved in together and Felix paid all their expenses from the generous allowance his parents made him. She and Tholomyes would sleep late, and have their breakfast at a café, usually with other students and their mistresses. Black coffee, heavily filtered, and buttered rolls with fruit *confiture*.

Their dinners were usually roasted fowl, grilled trout or sherried mushrooms with veal kidney, all of them served with fresh vegetables and fragrant white bread. Fantine put on five pounds from rich desserts alone, but Felix would kiss those extra pounds with lust, assuring her that she was more beautiful than ever.

All Paris was their playground – the parks, the River Seine, the restaurants and inns, the cabarets and street fairs. Not for this merry group were the museums or cathedrals. Their pursuits were only of pleasure. Felix, 'the student', never attended classes or sat for examinations. All he cared about was sensual pleasure and lively entertainment. His chief fear was of being bored.

By the time she was seventeen, Fantine had become pregnant, and her pleasures began to diminish as her belly grew. Tholomyes spent his evenings out in cafés, drinking wine with his friends while Fantine stayed behind alone, lying on their bed, sick to her stomach and aching in all her organs. Poor child! She still believed in her lover's devotion, and cherished the hope that the birth of their baby would bring them closer together, would perhaps even convince Felix to marry her!

Nothing could be further from the truth. When Cosette entered Fantine's world, Tholomyes left it. He moved out. As for marriage, men never married their mistresses. Why should they? They'd already had the enjoyment. What else did these fallen girls have to offer? Felix Tholomyes would marry only when his parents chose a suitable bourgeois wife with a large dowry for now and a decent inheritance for later.

For the first couple of years of the child's life, he continued to visit Fantine whenever desire for her overcame him, and on those occasions he would leave her several hundred francs. With careful scrimping, Fantine made the francs go as far as possible. This meant that she would go without new clothing or adequate food, while pretty Cosette was dressed in silk trimmed in hand-made lace, with satin ribbons in her baby-fine ringlets which were as golden as her mother's. She wore kidskin booties on her chubby little feet, and the finest, freshest food filled her little round stomach.

After Felix grew entirely tired of Fantine, his financial contributions to his daughter's welfare began to diminish to nothing. At last, too late, Fantine realized that he had never truly loved her as she'd loved him, and that his only love was himself. She knew at last that her dreams of marriage to him were only childish fantasies.

The plain, unhappy truth was that she was a young woman with an illegitimate child and no means of support. It was time for her to find work, but this was not easy in

Paris, especially for one burdened by a three-year-old to look after. Again and again she applied for employment. Again and again she was turned away.

After much painful thinking and many painful tears, Fantine decided to return to Montreuil, to go home. It was very difficult to write to Tholomyes, to inform him of her decision, and to beg him to help her with expenses this one last time. She needed money to leave Paris.

It took Felix Tholomyes almost three weeks to answer Fantine's tear-stained letter, but when he did, it was with a paltry one hundred francs, and a cold note advising Fantine that he did not intend to send her any more money ever, and to order her never to get in touch with him again. If she dared to attempt to contact him, he wrote, he would turn the matter over to the Paris prefect of police, who would charge her with prostitution.

And this was the sorry end of Fantine's hopes for enduring love and a normal family life!

The only thing left for her to do was to sell everything she had in order to raise money. All her furniture, even her clothes – the finery that Felix had lavished on her in happier times. Because she was so obviously desperate, the dealer took wicked advantage of her, paying only a hundred francs for goods worth many times more. He actually offered her fifty francs more if she would throw in little Cosette's beautiful clothing, but this Fantine absolutely refused to do. Her little daughter would always have the best while the breath of life was in Fantine.

With two hundred francs, Fantine was able to pay her debts before she left. It never occurred to her to skip out on what she owed. Fantine had an honest heart and was above-board in all her dealings. After the debts were paid, she was left with only a paltry eighty francs, barely enough to cover her and Cosette's expenses to Montreuil.

So, with a broken heart, and a toddler in her arms who was dressed like an angel, with only eighty francs in her purse and a suitcase filled with Cosette's fine clothing, Fantine set out on the road from Paris to Montreuil, intending to get home with as little expense as possible.

She paid a few sous to travel on the cheapest form of transportation next to walking, those shabby vehicles – *les petites voitures* – which travelled between Paris and the suburbs. When she reached Villemomble, the end of the line, she lifted Cosette into her arms and began to walk.

## Chapter Seven

### THE THENARDIERS

After an hour and a half of steady walking Fantine found herself in Montfermeil, a small town on the road to Montreuil. It was little more than a village, but it was a picturesque and charming place, with tidy front gardens and colourful window boxes decorating every house. The village was surrounded by farmers' fields and orchards, with fruit trees now in bloom.

As she trudged through the cobbled streets, Fantine came to a small stone inn, fronting the road. In front of the inn, two little girls – sisters – were sitting side by side in a swing, laughing happily, their slippered feet pumping the air as they swung high. The girls were neatly dressed, plump and healthy, with rosy cheeks and an air of superiority. They must be very much beloved by their parents, thought Fantine, to be so at ease with themselves and with life. There was such wholesomeness in the sight of them that Fantine had to stop just to admire the two happy little girls.

Their mother, who was sunning herself near by while keeping an eye on the road for potential customers, took note of the young woman's appreciation of her children. Like all mothers everywhere, she was gratified, and gave Fantine a bright, welcoming smile, beckoning her to come over.

These two little charmers in the swing were the young daughters of the Thenardiers, the couple who owned the inn.

Madame Thenardier herself, a tall, redheaded woman with coarse features and small, piercing eyes, was out enjoying the fine weather, sitting on the stone front steps. She looked at Fantine with curiosity, observing that the young woman's clothing was shabby and dusty from her journey. It might have been a pretty frock once, but that was a long time ago. In sharp contrast, the child in her arms, a lovely little thing with huge blue eyes and golden hair done in long ringlets tied up with ribbons, was dressed like a miniature empress in a flowing silk dress with a broad lace collar. Fine clothing like that must cost a small fortune.

Madame Thenardier was no fool, especially where money was concerned. Shrewdly, she sized up the situation. This girl obviously had no husband, only a child. Ah, but did she have any money? *I will soon find out.* Money was the Thenardiers' only deity, and they were extremely pious in their worship and pursuit of the holy franc. If this girl had any money, and was as friendless, alone and unprotected in the world as Madame Thenardier believed her to be, then this was a young woman worth talking to indeed!

Inviting Fantine to sit down beside her and rest her feet, the innkeeper questioned the naïve young woman with shrewdness, and soon had most of her story from her. Her imagination easily supplied the rest – the seduction, the abandonment, the fall from prosperity into poverty.

Meanwhile, the two young Thenardier daughters, Eponine and Alzelma, attracted by Cosette's beautiful baby face and exquisite clothing, left their swing in order to play with her, treating her like a precious little doll. When Fantine saw her darling so happily engaged with the other two little girls, tears filled her eyes. Thoughts at once wishful and regretful made a turmoil in her brain. If only they could settle down here, at this wonderful inn, with this wonderful family! If only she and

Cosette could partake of even a little domestic happiness such as this!

'Look!' remarked Madame Thenardier with instinctive cunning. 'Three sisters.' Her words went directly to Fantine's heart, as though an arrow shot from a bow.

At that moment an idea was born, an idea Fantine hastened to share with Madame Thenardier. It was necessary for Fantine to travel to Montreuil to find work, but what if she were to leave Cosette behind, to stay with these loving people and be a foster daughter to them? Would they welcome the child? On what terms might such an arrangement be made?

The older woman had already formed an idea not dissimilar to this, because she had sniffed out a fine profit to be made. She broke into a broad, warm smile. Yes, yes. What an excellent plan! They – the Thenardiers – could hardly wait to be of benefit to the mother and her sweet baby. They would look after the precious little one's welfare, Madame Thenardier assured Fantine, as though she were their own. And rest content that she and her husband would be punctilious in every regard. They would report on Cosette's progress to Fantine regularly, through the mail. As to the cost – well, they certainly had no desire for or expectation of profit. *No, no, let us not discuss money.* All it would cost Fantine was reimbursement for whatever funds they might be laying out on Cosette's behalf. It would be a privilege and a pleasure to raise a little girl as fine and beautiful as this one. Cosette would be no less than a beloved baby sister to their own two children. Eponine and Alzelma would play with her and take good care of her, too.

Madame Thenardier also promised that she would always keep Fantine's name alive in her daughter's heart, that she would tell Cosette how much Fantine loved her, how much she missed her and always prayed for her, and how one day she would return for her and they would be together always.

As for Fantine herself, it was decided that she would travel onward to Montreuil, find work, and mail money back to the Thenardiers every month, to cover little Cosette's expenses. Eventually she would send for her daughter to come and live with her. It was the perfect solution, soon arrived at, soon implemented.

Teary-eyed, Fantine handed over Cosette's bag of beautiful clothing, almost all of the eighty francs for the child's first year of lodging, and Cosette herself. Although she believed it was for the best, Fantine felt her heart breaking in her chest as she let her little daughter go to strangers. But what other solution presented itself? No, this seemed to be the perfect answer to the problem of Cosette's nurturing. These were good people, caring people. She could hardly ask for a better foster situation for her precious daughter.

If she had only perceived the truth about the character of Madame Thenardier, Fantine would have snatched up Cosette and carried her out of there on the run. She would have carried her in her arms all the way to Montreuil, and never let her out of her sight.

If she'd known what the Thenardiers were really like underneath their thin veneer of kindness and friendliness, what vile, rapacious monsters they were, and how bullying and cruel to everyone outside their immediate family – they really did love their two daughters, but nobody else – she would have gladly had all her fingernails pulled out with pincers before letting them get their hands on little Cosette.

But Fantine didn't know; she had no way of knowing. How could she possibly imagine that Madame's words, so honeyed and affectionate, masked intentions of the

utmost evil? Fantine herself did not lie, and so she never
suspected untruth from the lips of others. How could she
know that, after she continued on her journey, the first
act of the Thenardiers towards Cosette was to strip the
baby of her beautiful clothing, dress her in rags and sell
her laced-trimmed garments to an expensive children's
boutique in Paris?

So, happily ignorant of reality, with many kisses and many
tears, Fantine said farewell to the love of her life, turned
her back on her darling Cosette and walked on towards
Montreuil, her arms already aching from emptiness.

It was Fantine's intention to get work as quickly as
possible, send money for Cosette's support, and save up
as much as she could from her wages, with the sole aim
of bringing Cosette to Montreuil to live with her. They
would have a little house together and Fantine would
engage a kindly, grandmotherly nanny to look after the
child while her mother worked to earn them all a living.
What a beautiful dream!

To that end, Fantine intended to deprive herself of every
pleasure that cost anything, even a few sous, in order to live
in the cheapest way possible. She was already accustomed
to going without; a few more little sacrifices could hardly
hurt. Any self-denial would be worth the early return of
Cosette to her mother.

But things weren't working out quite as Fantine hoped.
She soon obtained employment at *Monsieur le maire*'s dye
factory, and was paid a living wage. She ate meagrely, and
lived in one small room. She kept her old clothing clean
and mended, so that she would not be forced to buy new
things. Yet she never managed to save, not even a few sous a
month. This was because the Thenardiers continually raised
their price for Cosette's support. Month after month brought
new demands. Every franc and sou she could scrape together

Fantine sent promptly to the inn at Montfermeil, passionately kissing the envelope as her personal greeting to her beloved Cosette. If only she could kiss her baby's sweet cheek!

Fantine's only consolation was that Cosette was doing so well. The little girl was thriving, happy, and being treated like a princess. She knew this because the Thenardiers told her so. Every letter they sent was much the same as the last one – Cosette was as healthy as a horse, and eating enough for two children. It was costing a horrendous amount, and the poor Thenardiers were at their wits' end for money, or so they would tell Fantine, and had to have more.

Their petitions were endless: little Cosette had outgrown her shoes; little Cosette had to have a new winter coat; little Cosette had a cough and needed some medicine. Money, send more money. It was only for Cosette's benefit. The Thenardiers were going broke maintaining Cosette in a fine style, or so they swore. *Mademoiselle Fantine can have no idea how expensive it is to bring up a child as pampered as Cosette.*

Fantine would close her eyes and remember what she had seen of Montfermeil – the pretty cobbled streets, the flower boxes in the windows, the fields and fruitful orchards. She would think of Cosette there, eating plums and cherries from the fruit trees, running through the field, her little white pantalettes peeping from underneath her muslin frock as she darted around in happy play. The thought of it was the only thing that kept Fantine going on with her wretched life.

So, somehow, Fantine managed to scrimp some more on her own pitiful living expenses, denying herself a candle at night, not eating more than two small meals a day, doing without a warm coat, keeping her own broken shoes for yet another year. She stuffed the holes in the artificial leather with bits of torn rag. And, always, she sent the kind-hearted

Thenardiers more money. How could she begrudge it? Didn't they have Cosette's best interests always in mind? In Fantine's aching heart, the dream of a normal life with her child was kept alive only by her faith in the strangers who were raising her daughter.

After she had been working at the dye factory for several years, Fantine's future with Cosette looked further away than ever. Whatever remnants of the dream remained depended on her remaining employed, so her dismissal from *Monsieur le maire*'s factory was catastrophic, a calamity so terrible it made her feel faint to think of it. What would she do now? She had nowhere to go and nobody to help her, nobody on whom she might depend.

Fantine blamed her current desperate situation on one person alone. Not on Felix Tholomyes, who lied to her, seduced her, threw her over and broke her heart, a man who had refused to support his own daughter. Not on herself, for having been weak enough to give in to his false words and his insincere promises. Not on Madame Blanquet, the woman in authority who had actually fired her. Not even on the sour Madame Victurien, who was dishonest enough to read a letter not intended for her, and vicious enough to give it to the forewoman and make its contents known to all.

No, the one and only person Fantine blamed for her present misfortune was the man whose insistence on high morals had led inevitably to her own dismissal. Fantine blamed *Monsieur le maire*. She felt for him a hatred so intense it shook her thin frame whenever she thought of him. The pious, wealthy, mealy-mouthed hypocrite who sat in judgment on those less fortunate than himself! May he rot in hell and be damned for ever! She cursed his name, Monsieur Madeleine. Fantine was not usually given to hatred and enmity, but this one man she wished dead a thousand times over.

Now her situation was critical. Fantine was down to one small meal a day, and that meal was almost always soup, to which she added more and more water as the days went on, as well as greens that she picked in the nearest open field. Dock and nettle, dandelion and weeds – these were the staples of Fantine's diet. Meanwhile, she scoured Montreuil for a job, willing to take any work for any wage, just to keep the francs flowing to the demanding Thenardiers. But everyone turned her away, because everyone in town seemed to be overly familiar with the details of Fantine's sin.

At last, with her back to the wall, the girl sent for the furniture dealer and sold every stick she owned in the world except her bed. She would have sold that too, and slept on the bare floor, but the dealer told her the bed was worthless, broken down and of no use. For the lot he gave her only fifty francs. Of course, he took merciless advantage of her. The furniture was worth at least a couple of hundred. But Fantine never knew how to strike a bargain favourable to herself; in every transaction she just closed her eyes to what few rights she had, and allowed herself to be trampled on, as usual.

'Nice doing business with you.' The furniture dealer leered at Fantine. He too, along with the rest of Montreuil, was in on her guilty secret, and his lustful imagination ran riot at his mental picture of this beautiful young girl, naked, writhing in sinful congress with some man.

It was Fantine's bad luck that her landlord, a scowling, squat, hairy brute named Chevrau, walked in on her just as the last of the furniture was being bundled down the stairs. His eyes fixed themselves at once on the fifty francs in her hand.

'What's going on?' he demanded suspiciously. 'You skipping out?'

The girl nibbled at her lower lip. 'I . . . I sold it for extra money,' she admitted in a near-whisper.

'You owe me a month's rent,' growled Chevrau.

'Not till next week.'

'Pay now, or you're out. I got people who want the room. Thirty francs. Come on, you've got fifty in your hand.' He held out one grubby mitt with its filthy nails and made a grab for the money.

Fantine clutched the francs more tightly, her face a mask of panic. 'I'll pay you fifteen. I'll give you the rest next week,' she pleaded.

'How? They fired you.'

Fantine's heart sank. 'Who told you I was fired?' she asked in a weak voice.

Chevrau leered. 'This is still a small town.'

'I have a job,' Fantine said hurriedly. 'I start next week. The new apothecary hired me—'

'Don't lie!' Chevrau interrupted harshly. 'Everybody knows your story. You've got a bastard kid. Nobody's going to give you work.'

But she knew that already. An overwhelming sensation of hopelessness washed over Fantine, nearly drowning her in sorrow. Her arms and legs felt weak, as though they couldn't support any weight. Her voice was barely above a whisper when she said, resignedly, 'I'll find work. I'll get you the rest. Please. Take half.' With a sinking heart, she handed him fifteen of her fifty precious francs. How was she to survive on the pitiful remainder? What could she send to the Thenardiers?

Chevrau reached for the money, and his gross, hairy fingers closed over it tightly, trapping Fantine's little hand as well. He leered at her again, ogling her soft bosom, which was rising and falling in panic, like the downy chest of a small trapped bird. 'Don't look so worried,' he told her in oily tones. 'Things aren't that bad.' His leer widened, and his eyes flickered over her body. 'You've still got a bed.'

At this suggestion, Fantine's eyes widened in horror, then shut tightly, to keep his brutish image out. Was it about to come to this? Would she have to buy the barest necessities of life with the sale of her self? She couldn't breathe; she was suffocating. All she could do was to shake her head – no, no, no. She went on shaking it long after Chevrau left. When at last she realized that she was alone, Fantine collapsed on the bed. In the nearly empty room, she sobbed piteously, her narrow figure racked with despair.

## Chapter Eight

### MIND, HEART, BODY AND SOUL

In the months that followed, autumn turned to a long, paralysingly cold winter. At last, winter reluctantly loosed its hold and gave up its place to spring. During this time Inspector Javert gave no hint at all of recognizing the fugitive Jean Valjean under the robes of the beloved *Monsieur le maire*, and Valjean began to breathe more easily. Yet he continued to take precautions. For one thing, he didn't go back to retrieve his money from the forest. It was safely hidden; let it stay there. He wasn't sure when he might come to need it, but whenever he did, it would still be in its dark hole under the tree, waiting for him.

Besides, he didn't need it now. More money was pouring in all the time from the dye factory profits. He had increased production, and his account at the Lafitte Bank was soon almost as large as before. Jean Valjean increased his public charities as well, building another new wing on to the hospital, for children this time. He had never forgotten the poor little chimney-sweep he'd robbed. The new wing had special facilities for the treatment of lung diseases in children. Chimney-sweeps were frequent patients there, made ill by the oily soot they were forced to breathe and swallow. In this new wing they were always given the finest medical care available, paid for by *Monsieur le maire*.

The other change Jean Valjean made in his life was to

invent a disguise for himself that would hide him more effectively from Javert.

Valjean was no longer quite so uncomfortable in the presence of the detective; they had become, if not friends, then certainly close acquaintances. After all, the mayor was the highest authority in Montreuil, and therefore he was Inspector Javert's superior. Javert reported to *Monsieur le maire* frequently. He loved to make reports, and his reports were always masterpieces of detail and expatiation.

Also, it was necessary for the prefect of police and the mayor to make frequent public appearances together, such as the day when *Monsieur le maire* cut the ribbon to open the public park that he had donated to Montreuil. After many months of labour, the park was finally finished, a pleasant, leafy place with many trees of different kinds, colourful flower-beds and blooming shrubs.

The park covered several acres. There were winding paths for strolling, many wrought-iron benches for sitting, and stone fountains ornamented by fat cherubs sculpted in marble. Around the perimeter of the park ran a broad straight path, wide enough for horses and carriages. There was even an open place in the centre of the park, a band shell surrounded by chairs for outdoor concerts, and a small puppet theatre to show delighted children the adventures of Pierrot and Pierrette, and funny Harlequin in his brightly patterned costumes.

The day the park was dedicated was a bright day in late spring. The sun shone brightly and all of Montreuil turned out for the occasion. The brass band, its buttons polished and its uniforms freshly pressed, played in unison, or as close to unison as it was able. Boys and girls, dressed in their Sunday clothes, waved small tricolour flags. Women wore new bonnets, with gay ribbons, and men had little bunches of spring flowers in the buttonholes of their coats.

Red, white and blue bunting decorated the bandstand and fluttered from the balconies overlooking the park.

It was *Monsieur le maire*'s function to declare the park open and to dedicate the central fountain, a marble sculpture of a graceful Grecian woman clad in carved draperies, who held a large water jug in her hands, from which water would flow when the fountain was activated. She represented the abundance of the water of life, and was widely supposed to bring good luck to Montreuil.

It was one of the highest moments in Jean Valjean's life when he pulled the heavy cloth cover off the statue, revealing the fountain for the first time to the townspeople. There were cheers and applause; the band broke into the 'Marseillaise', and the little children waved their flags enthusiastically. Valjean felt very proud.

After the dedication day, one of Jean Valjean's greatest pleasures in life was to stroll through this new and beautiful park, to sit on one of the benches and listen to birds singing in the tree branches above. He greatly enjoyed the sight of courting couples and the pleasure that old people took in the park's beauties and comforts. Most of all, Valjean loved to listen to the children laughing as they watched the puppets' antics in the puppet theatre. Children's laughter sent ineffable longings stirring through him. Marriage and children – he had missed these in his life, and it was too late now. He was too old. But he longed for a child, a little daughter perhaps, to call him 'Papa', and to show him a childish affection. His eyes would fill with tears at the thought.

After many months of their acquaintance, Valjean had learned something of Inspector Javert's nature, and, oddly, there was comfort in the knowledge. Everything the prefect of police did was by the book; the rules must be followed without deviation. There was no room for mercy, clemency or excuses in Inspector Javert's philosophy. Valjean now understood the policeman as a man who would never willingly challenge authority, who was eager to crush those below him, but who revered those above. It was this reverence for authority which informed Javert's nature, and made him so dogged in the pursuit of evil-doers.

Therefore it was necessary for Valjean to make a better show of his superiority and the social gulf between mayor and policeman, to create new layers of authority between Inspector Javert and *Monsieur le maire*, as protection for the fugitive Jean Valjean beneath. In other words, a disguise.

Where before the advent of Inspector Javert his dress had been simple and unostentatious, now Valjean bought new finery – mayoral robes and golden chains, handsome suits of the finest wool, even a large, full wig, suitable to his office. He now wore all his regalia whenever presiding at some public occasion, but his everyday dress also was nowadays more costly and impressive, better suited to a wealthy businessman and outstanding citizen. Valjean was correct, of course. Javert was dazzled by the trappings of authority, and *Monsieur le maire*'s new official splendour only increased Inspector Javert's respect for him and widened the distance between the two men.

The disguise was so generally well received, and the mayor was treated to so many complimentary phrases, that Valjean began to wear fine clothes and his new wig every day, even to his office in the factory.

Captain Beauvais noted and applauded the changes in the mayor's personal appearance, and put them down to Javert's good influence on him. Beauvais approved because he thought it was a fine thing for the mayor of Montreuil to *look* like the mayor of Montreuil. A tall, handsome, imposing mayor always created an excellent impression on important visitors.

With the new wig the disguise was now complete. Jean Valjean was barely recognizable as the modest 'Monsieur Madeleine' or the retiring *Monsieur le maire*. No two images could be further apart – the filthy, ragged criminal, as savage as an untrained animal, and the splendidly dressed and bewigged, beloved and philanthropic figure that Jean Valjean presented now. He even seemed to relax his reclusive shyness a little, although he still slept with one eye open, a relic of his old habits of survival.

Yet, underneath all his apparent security, there still lurked a potent germ of the former terror. Valjean knew that he had to maintain a perpetual vigilance. Everything could fall apart in one unguarded moment, in one act of carelessness. And then Javert, like a sleeping cat roused by a rat, would be awake to pounce.

Meanwhile, what of Fantine? How did she survive the winter? Not easily, as you may suppose. She couldn't find employment anywhere. At first, every now and again, she was able to earn a day's wages doing the filthiest chores – scrubbing out sordid lavatories and greasy restaurant kitchens for fifty sous. With this money she was able to eat, although only the most meagre of meals, little better than scraps. For coffee she made a bitter brew of acorns, those few she could pick up under the oak trees after the squirrels had completed their harvest. The cold weather cut through her delicate skin like a knife. Fantine could not afford to buy fuel, and made do by burning whatever she could glean without paying. Sometimes it was turf, sometimes only dried animal dung. Neither gave out much heat; it was barely better than nothing. For cooking she burned whatever twigs she could pick up in her travels, but these green branches burned badly, with a great deal of smoke.

Light, too, was forbidden to Fantine. In the brief days

of winter, when the nights were long and daylight left the sky at an early hour, Fantine was forced to sit in darkness, without oil for a lamp or tallow for a candle.

Food and drink, heat and light were thus accounted for. This left Fantine with two major problems – how to pay the rent on her room and where to find money for the Thenardiers.

In order to keep a roof over her head in winter it was inevitable that poor Fantine would have to give in to the lustful desires of the lascivious Chevrau. This she did only with the greatest reluctance, feeling nothing but loathing for him and for herself.

Even then, even with her naked beauty clutched in his sweating hairy arms, the landlord continued to berate her and demand money from her, telling her that what she was giving him was not worth the free rent she gained in exchange. The truth was that Chevrau had never in his life embraced such beauty and grace as Fantine's, such youth and firmness of flesh, but he was too brutish to be appreciative. He made her life a living hell with his frequent lecherous demands and his verbal and physical abuse. Possibly because he secretly despised his swinish self, he despised Fantine even more for yielding to him and letting him use her so shamefully.

But all that was nothing compared with the terror of not having the money for Cosette's support. Fantine agonized over it night and day; every time a letter came from Montfermeil she dreaded opening it, knowing that it would hold louder and louder demands for money from the Thenardiers. She had nothing to send, and it was only her continued faith in the Thenardiers' kindness that kept her from going insane with worry over her daughter. People as innately good as the innkeeper and his wife would certainly continue to care for Cosette, even without their monthly francs. After all, how many times had they sworn in the past that Fantine's little girl was every bit as dear to them as their own precious daughters?

Yet Fantine lived in fear that Cosette would cost the good people so much money that they'd be forced to turn her away. In reality, though, that would never happen. From the day when Fantine had handed her over, little Cosette had earned them a small fortune, and had cost the Thenardiers virtually nothing. The child had been afforded only the barest subsistence. She was fed mainly on scraps, those few bits left over from the Thenardiers' dinner table, even though they continually billed her mother at a rate for the finest gourmet fare.

As for her clothing, Cosette wore whatever was outgrown by the two Thenardier daughters, and she wore those garments to rags.

The money Fantine sent for clothes was actually spent on clothes – but for the Thenardier daughters, not for Cosette. From the hundreds and hundreds of francs that Fantine had sent them over the years, barely ten had actually been spent on Cosette. The Thenardiers dined well, dressed well, put money in the bank, while Cosette slept on a pile of straw covered with rags. Cosette ate a little better than the dog, but not so well as the cat. She suffered from chilblains in the winter and heat rash in the summer. She was frequently ill with a racking cough, but never once was the doctor called in to treat her, although Fantine sent extra money on demand many times for Cosette's 'doctor bills'.

So, although they kept hinting to Fantine that they might have to turn her child away because they could no longer afford to keep her, the Thenardiers would never actually willingly part with little Cosette, even after they had milked her mother dry. No, the child was too useful to them as an unpaid menial, an extra pair of hands to do those loathsome jobs that nobody else wanted. The Thenardier daughters kept their own hands as white as milk and as soft as cottage cheese, but Cosette's hands were raw and blistered, covered with scratches and burn marks. She worked from early dawn to after dark, doing manual labour; she toiled far beyond her strength, and she never complained. She didn't dare complain, because if she did, she would be beaten harshly and given no dinner.

Perhaps it would have been easier for Cosette to bear her miserable existence if Madame Thenardier had kept her promise to Fantine, to speak to the child of her mother's devotion, of the sacrifices Fantine was making on Cosette's behalf, and how she vowed that some day they would be together for ever. But Madame Thenardier had never kept any of her other promises, so why should this one not fall by the wayside as well?

All that Cosette knew of her own mother was that Fantine had not wanted her, and had given her away to the first people willing to take her, and now she was dead, and Cosette should be grateful night and day to the blessedly kind Thenardiers, who kept her at enormous expense to themselves, without hope of recompense. This pious lesson was repeated so often that little Cosette had it by heart.

Fantine had only two things in the world left to sell, so one day she brought all of her fading courage to bear and crept like a mouse into the wig-maker's shop. She wore a tattered shawl around her head, covering her hair. The proprietor waved his feather duster at her angrily, motioning her to the street, and Fantine shrank back at the scornful glare with which the wig-maker met her. Wordlessly, she removed the shawl, and took out the bone hairpins and combs that held her long hair up and away from her face.

Loosened, the golden rain fell into a thick cascade over Fantine's shoulders and down her back, a living thing of great beauty. The wig-maker's eyes opened wide, and he put out one hand to lift the locks and assess them. The weight was heavy, the texture like satin. Rarely had he seen a head of hair like this one. The wig-maker, enthralled, couldn't help caressing Fantine's lovely tresses. His heart swelled greedily; women's hair of this quality would easily bring in a hundred francs, perhaps even one hundred and fifty.

'Ten francs,' he offered brusquely. 'Take it or leave it.' He was bluffing; he'd have raised his offer to fifty francs if Fantine knew how to drive a bargain.

What could Fantine do? She felt humiliated by the entire process. Unable to argue, she accepted his offer. She might have lived a couple of weeks on ten francs, but instead she sent seven francs straight to the Thenardiers with the promise of more to come.

Seven francs wouldn't even begin to satisfy the Thenardiers. Cosette's lodging bill had risen to nine francs a month, and Fantine was already three months behind. Where would she get the rest? Fantine had only one thing more to sell.

The spirit seemed to go out of her when she sold her hair. Although she couldn't put it into words, Fantine's hair was a precious symbol of her lost youth and lost innocence. It was her greatest beauty; Felix Tholomyes had told her so many times. She herself, modest though she was, recognized its luxurious quality. Whenever she lost heart, just sitting quietly and brushing out the lengths of it had held a kind of peacefulness that always made her feel a little better. Now her long hair was gone, and with it went all that had remained of her youth.

Which left her with only one more decision. And why not make the leap? Wasn't she already prostituting herself to the vile Chevrau? And for no profit but a cheap, shabby room? Why not turn a real profit while she was about it? Even without her long flowing hair, a woman's crowning glory, Fantine knew she was still a pretty girl – young, fairly fresh. Men had always found her desirable; the time had come to make that desirability pay off. She might be totally inexperienced for life on the street, but life on the street appeared to be the only future open to her.

Such hypocrisy! How cruelly ironic that a young girl who has made one mistake in life should be so reviled by a pious and moralistic society, so utterly rejected and despised that, instead of being allowed to do honest work, to change her life for the better and rejoin the human race, she is instead forced into deeper and deeper degradation, into a downward spiral of ruin that can have but one miserable outcome.

So Fantine was forced to go out into the night, to approach strangers and offer herself for money. It was either that or kill herself. Fantine would have much preferred to die. Only the thought of Cosette kept her alive. For what would become of the child if her mother deserted her for ever? Fantine knew that somehow she had to earn money to support her daughter, and this was the only avenue open to her. The world already considered her a whore; why not prove them right? Having lost everything, what did she have left to lose?

She would soon find out. The humiliation and shame she felt in selling her hair or sleeping with the monster Chevrau would be absolutely nothing when compared with how she would react to selling her entire being to strangers.

## Chapter Nine

### FAUCHELEVENT

**T**he largest concentration of the population of prostitutes
in Montreuil was to be found in the dark side streets
and alleys near the army garrison where the military was
stationed. There were many young and lusty soldiers billeted
there, away from home for the first time, lonely, and with
money to spend.

At first, Fantine had some modest success in her new
profession. As a new face on the street, a young and pretty
one, men were attracted to her and were willing to pay to
possess her. For a few months, Fantine's firm body was
quite popular and she had no problem soliciting sexual
partners. She earned money and was able to pay some of
her outstanding debt to the Thenardiers. But her success
as a whore didn't continue for long.

Without the simplest street survival skills, Fantine soon
found herself at a disadvantage among the other whores
– she was neither competitive nor combative, and she was
not naturally lustful. She was, moreover, inhibited and oddly
modest. Each time she sold herself, each time she bared her
breasts, it was with shame and reluctance. Fantine could
not easily make up false seductive blandishments such as
the other streetwalkers employed to attract men. She could
scarcely utter the words men liked to hear – praise of their
powers as lovers, their strength and endurance, their good

looks, their generosity. She was unable to offer them delights beyond their imagination; those promises died on her lips. She couldn't even thank them for choosing her. All she wanted was to get the transaction over with and pocket the few francs she earned. Her clientèle, disappointed with her modest ways and her uncomfortable silences, soon forgot about her beauty. They began to seek out more demonstrative and sexually imaginative prostitutes to give them the uninhibited sexual pleasures they craved and were willing to pay for.

Also, Fantine found that the other whores resented her and were unwilling to share the street or their doorways with a newcomer, particularly such a pretty newcomer. If there was a camaraderie among them, it didn't extend to Fantine, unless it was to unite against the new girl. They harassed her mercilessly, abusing her verbally, kicking her and pushing her out of the sheltering doorways and into the night.

The prostitutes chased Fantine from corner to corner, clawing at her, tearing her clothing and scratching her face. Fantine was unable to fight back, and soon found that her personal territory was so restricted that she could not effectively compete. Her corner of the street was the darkest and most remote. Almost all the soldiers were picked off by the other whores before they even reached Fantine.

The life of a whore was much, much harder than Fantine in her naïveté had supposed. She had to be out walking in the alleyways in every kind of weather, whether it rained or snowed or was unendurably hot. She was expected to look and act enticing, when all she felt was revulsion. She had to endure the abuse and punishment heaped on her by the other whores.

She had to find a place to conduct her business that

would not be snatched away from her. Men sometimes cheated her, refusing to pay for favours received, or paying her less than half of what was agreed on, and defying her to do anything about it. Fantine wasn't brave enough or tough enough to carry a knife or razor with her, with which to defend herself against the cheat.

If any of the Montreuil pimps had taken Fantine under his wing, nobody else would have dared to take advantage of her. If they tried, they would face a savage beating – or much worse – by a brutal protector. But Fantine had no procurer; none would take her. She was too tame, too bland, not sexy enough, and not a good bet to survive the street and the life for very long. She cried too easily and didn't know how to fight back. She wasn't worth the expense of time or energy. Panders and prostitutes alike agreed – this little Fantine was a total waste of skin. She didn't have the heart, mind or soul of a whore.

Fantine herself wasn't eager to get a pimp. She had seen the other girls suffering beatings at the brutal hands of their 'protectors'; when the procurer was dissatisfied with the earnings of his whore he thought nothing of punching her black and blue. The whores were also horribly exploited. The procurers, brutal idlers, made sure their women worked hard and delivered up to seventy per cent of their earnings.

These men put gaudy clothing on their own backs, smoked fine cigars, ate and drank up the labour of their women. What could the whores do? The pimps afforded them the only protection they could expect, and many of the women were actually in love with them. They accepted the beatings as an inevitable – even necessary – part of their life.

In addition to all Fantine's other woes, there was also the matter of the police. In bygone years, the gendarmes were hardly a problem to the streetwalkers. They were easily bought off, some with money, others with sex. But now Inspector Javert patrolled the streets personally, taking the night shift like a common patrolman, and this was a man who was, unluckily for the whores, incorruptible.

No amount of money interested Javert, and as for sex – he looked on whores as nothing but common criminals, and with such contempt that their advances withered and died under his scorn. Javert could not be bought, threatened, tempted or persuaded to veer from the course of righteous pursuit. Naturally, the gendarmes under his command were forced to follow their leader, which effectively put an end to their favourable treatment of the whores. No more bribes, no more free sex meant no more looking the other way.

This was the life of a prostitute in Montreuil – to be beaten by her pimp, harassed by the other whores, cheated by the customers, continually under the threat of disease, and pursued by the police who needed very little incentive to make an arrest. This was the life to which Fantine was so ill suited, but it was the only life that had accepted her.

The presence of an army garrison in Montreuil was, in Javert's eyes, a honeypot, and the whores were the bloated flies buzzing around it to steal a bit of sweetness. He doubled the number of gendarmes assigned to the district. Almost every night of the week, he prowled through the streets himself, taking the ten o'clock shift to relieve Captain Beauvais. The sight of his rigid figure in its dark uniform sent a chill of horror into the bones of the prostitutes. They kept expecting arrests, and, when the arrests didn't follow, the chill deepened. What did Javert have up his cursed sleeve for them? Why was he waiting to pounce?

*Monsieur le maire*'s dye factory continued to prosper. Using the increased profits, Valjean kept expanding it until it was now the largest employer of men and women in Montreuil.

There was talk that their philanthropic mayor would soon
be receiving a medal, a Legion of Honour or a Chevalier
perhaps, from none other than King Louis XVIII. It would
be a reward for the mayor's many acts of charity and the
immeasurable good he had brought to the city. The citizens
of Montreuil blessed the day that 'Monsieur Madeleine' had
come to their town. The story of his rise from humble worker
to factory owner and successful entrepreneur was told over
and over from one mouth to another ear, and always with
fresh embellishments.

At the insistence of Inspector Javert, protection was set
up for the flow of cash out of the factory and into the bank.
*Monsieur le maire* attempted to refuse, but the police chief
stood firm. If it was not the law, it should be, he said. There
was not a city in France where the business owners did not
make use of the gendarmes to protect their income.

At last, Valjean reluctantly gave in. So, three times every
week, the forewoman and foreman from the factory brought
out the rich profits from the safe in *Monsieur le maire*'s
office and gave them to a bonded teller sent from the Lafitte
Bank. Under the watchful eye of Javert they allowed the
money to leave the factory for the bank, accompanied by
a couple of his armed policemen. There was no more fear
of robbery. This new way of doing things made everybody
feel personally safer, and the responsibility for the secure
bestowal of the funds was lifted from the employees'
shoulders.

'The mayor asked me to thank you for coming by and
standing guard when we receive payments,' the foreman
told Javert one afternoon, after the teller from the Lafitte Bank
had locked up two large strongboxes and carried them off
to the bank under the protection of Javert's gendarmes.

'Merely performing my duty,' Javert replied courteously.
'Large sums of money are a temptation.'

They were standing in the factory courtyard, not far removed from where a large dray was being loaded with heavy crates filled with dyed fabric on its way to market. The driver of the wagon, a sixty-year-old worker known only as Fauchelevent, was struggling with the horse, who was having difficulty going forward with so sizable a load. Fauchelevent tugged hard at the reins, trying to compel the horse to move on.

'Come on, you lazy beast!' he roared, taking his whip to the poor animal. The horse, harnessed to a cart that was overloaded, took a couple of staggering steps, then stopped, paying no attention to the driver's threats and curses. Its back legs buckled, causing the dray to tip. Fauchelevent lost his balance on the seat, suddenly pitched forward and fell off the wagon to the ground. He landed between the cart and the horse, and lay there, stunned.

The wagon's forward wheels crumbled into splinters, driving the front end of the vehicle towards the ground, pinning old Fauchelevent beneath it. There was barely room for him to crawl out. The old man moaned in pain, and pleaded for help.

All at once, the horse's back legs, which had already buckled with the weight of the unbalanced cart, snapped and shattered. With a loud scream, the poor animal dropped like a stone to the earth. The large wagon, now without any front-end support, dropped too. It fell on old Fauchelevent, covering his body completely, leaving only his head free. Now there was no way he could crawl out from under the dray. He was trapped, with the life slowly being squeezed out of him.

Suddenly, all was pandemonium. The crippled horse kept shrieking, uttering high-pitched neighs of agony. Fauchelevent too was weeping in pain and fear as he stared his death in the face. Workers were running everywhere, some trying to unload the dray to lighten it, while others tried to lift the wagon off Fauchelevent's injured body. It was an impossible task.

In his office, Valjean was dictating a letter to the Reverend Mother of the Petit-Picpus convent in Paris. The convent had always been a favourite charity of the Bishop of Digne. Valjean was offering, in loving memory of the sainted bishop, a generous contribution towards their work with the poor. Suddenly, the foreman burst in without knocking, sweat pouring down his face.

'Monsieur! There's been an accident!' The excitement in the man's voice, bordering on panic, brought Valjean to his feet at once.

Leaving his papers scattered on his desk, the mayor ran down to the courtyard, followed by the panting foreman and his office clerk. Before he reached the outer door, he could hear the frantic shrill screaming of the dying horse and the rasping pantings of the desperate Fauchelevent, whose chest was being crushed by the weight of the wagon. The old man was trying to draw breath into his lungs, but without success.

With one glance, Jean Valjean comprehended the situation and took immediate steps to bring it under control.

'Get crowbars!' he ordered. 'We need leverage!'

As a couple of workers scrambled to obey the mayor's orders, others slid boards under the wagon in an effort to pry it off the man. All at once, a shot rang out, and then another. The screaming horse fell silent. Coolly, Inspector Javert holstered his pistol, and his hooded eyes stared down the startled looks of the crowd.

'I was being merciful.' But there was no mercy in Javert's eyes, just as there was no mercy in his heart. It was only a horse; it was in the way. Now it was dead. Why should anyone care?

Now the crowbars arrived, and they pushed them under the wagon to lever the vehicle off Fauchelevent, who was in a bad way.

'Everyone together!' ordered Valjean. 'Now!'

With a terrible effort, they managed to raise the dray an inch or two above the ground, giving the old man a tiny breathing space. But the factory workers were unable to manoeuvre the crowbars in the tiny space, so they were forced to let the wagon drop once more on Fauchelevent.

'He's doomed,' remarked Javert coldly. He had taken no part in the attempted rescue, but stood observing it without emotion.

Jean Valjean wouldn't accept that. Something *had* to be done. The man's life must be saved. Without thinking, he tore off his costly jacket, which knocked the wig off his head. Concentrating only on the dray and the old man, Valjean dropped to the ground and crawled towards the back of the wagon, which still had wheels. There was a small space between the back wheels and the ground, and Valjean, on his belly, managed to crawl there and pushed himself into it. Face down, he too was now effectively trapped.

'Get ready to lift!' he shouted. Two men manned the crowbars. 'Now!'

While the workers began to ply the crowbars for leverage, and others pulled at the sides of the cart, Jean Valjean exerted a terrible effort. He pushed his body upward, against the floor of the wagon. His powerful shoulder muscles strained, and the blood surged into his neck and face. Using his great physical strength alone, like Samson, he began to raise the wagon from the earth.

Slowly, a half-inch at a time, the front end of the dray left the ground. Two factory workers rushed forward and pulled Fauchelevent clear. He was half unconscious, and in great pain. But he was alive.

*Monsieur le maire* was still trapped under the rear wheels. His own strength was exhausted; the effort to free Fauchelevent had been enormous. Around him, workers toiled to lift the dray high enough for their employer to free himself.

'Hurry, monsieur! We can't hold it!' cried the foreman.

He had only seconds to spare. Using his elbows and knees, Valjean wriggled forward until he was clear. He remained on the ground for a few seconds, panting. His shirt was torn, and great holes in his trousers bared his knees to view. He was filthy and covered in a film of sweat. His hair, without the benefit of the imposing wig, was plastered wildly to his cheeks. Then, slowly, his legs and thighs still trembling with the effort of strength he'd expended, Valjean stood up.

A great cheer went up; *Monsieur le maire* was alive! Their beloved patron was alive! He was a true hero! Using only his own strength and daring, he had rescued old Fauchelevent. Nobody else could have done it but their own *Monsieur le maire*!

But Inspector Javert wasn't cheering. He was staring at *Monsieur le maire*, and he wasn't seeing a hero. He wasn't seeing a factory owner, or a philanthropist, or even a good and pious human being. He was seeing a ghostly figure from out of his past. Javert's memory, which was as sharp as a dagger, held an indelible image, one that appeared to match what he was looking at now. He remembered a tall man, filthy, panting, covered in sweat. His keen internal eye was able to superimpose one image upon the other. A perfect match.

This man was older than the man in his memory, but Javert perceived only the similarities, not the differences. He pictured the younger man's muscles heaving with effort and fatigue, his body trembling as *Monsieur le maire*'s was doing now. But instead of standing in the courtyard of a prosperous factory, he was sitting in chains, straining over the oars of a prison galley. Javert was seeing a phantom from his past, a tall man of incredible strength and viciousness, a fugitive who had broken parole years ago and disappeared.

He was seeing Jean Valjean.

## Chapter Ten

### JAVERT'S NOTEBOOK

Inspector Javert wasn't the only one to be shocked by a vision from the past. Jean Valjean had recognized the policeman the very first moment he'd set eyes on him in Montreuil. Javert was one of the guards at Toulon, at the time when Valjean was on the galleys. For months, Valjean had been carrying on business as usual, keeping up his persona as *Monsieur le maire*, yet all the while dreading the day that would bring an encounter such as this.

When they faced each other across the bloody courtyard, Valjean covered in filth, with torn clothing and wild hair, he saw the shock of recognition on Javert's face, and knew that the police chief had made the connection. Yet Valjean thought he also saw some hesitation there. Could Javert believe his eyes? Was there evidence that the highly respected mayor of the city might in reality be nothing better than a common criminal and fugitive? Or was the strange resemblance in the two faces merely a trick of Javert's memory?

Valjean believed he might still have some time; perhaps he wouldn't be forced to flee at once. If he were to behave as usual, return to his business, present a calm exterior, maybe Javert's suspicions would be allayed. And even if he remained suspicious, Javert was not the sort to act quickly or rashly. He was an inflexible, methodical man who believed above anything in strict legal methods, step after step. He would gather proof before he struck out.

Valjean knew well that Javert was possessed of a dogged determination and that, once he formed a suspicion, he would follow up on it and nothing could distract him. He would take his time, build his case, be sure of his facts. But what could he prove? Valjean's papers were all in order, the finest forgeries money from the silverware could buy. He went over them in his mind, deciding that they looked genuine enough to pass even the strictest scrutiny. But had he left anything out? Had he closed all the loopholes? Yes, he told himself. Yes, he had been very thorough. His very survival depended on it.

*But I must be twice as vigilant as before*, he told himself. *Inspector Javert can make no move until he has proof. Don't give him proof or opportunity to dig up proof.*

Jean Valjean was correct in his surmises. A strong suspicion had been born in Javert's mind, but he needed corroborating evidence that the beloved *Monsieur le maire* was the despicable fugitive Valjean. Evidence was his first priority. So it became business as usual, both for Jean Valjean and Inspector Javert. At least for now.

As the months went by, Fantine grew more and more ragged. Her few clothes were so old and patched it was a miracle they hung together at all. But she dared not waste a franc on anything new. The Thenardiers had raised their rates again; they were now up to ten francs a month for Cosette's board.

Eventually, Fantine realized that not buying a new dress for herself was a totally false economy. The other whores bought finery, powders, rouges, long gloves, tortoiseshell combs for their hair, sparkly fake jewellery. Dressed up, perfumed and pomaded, the women equipped themselves to entice customers, so whatever francs they spent returned to them tenfold.

But Fantine couldn't see her way clear to improving her appearance at the cost of Cosette's welfare. So her cash investment in her profession was limited to some paint for her eyes and mouth and one new dress, a bright red frock made of artificial silk. It was the cheapest one she could find, and it wouldn't last long, since Fantine had to wear it every night. With her closely shorn head, and make-up plastered all over her pale face, she looked older, unhealthier, less attractive. When she sold off her hair, Fantine had given away a large part of her good looks.

As her beauty faded, Fantine's clientèle, too, became more wretched. She was far less tempting now than when she had first taken to the streets. No longer did the handsome, uniformed, generous soldiers seek her out. Now it was the dregs – beggars, cripples, farmhands, labourers in dusty overalls, all of them negotiating her price in sous instead of francs.

Eventually, as her good looks and her ability to earn money began to dwindle under the stress of her situation, Fantine herself began to harden, cheapen and coarsen. This was inevitable, if she were to survive. The very sweetness of her nature was turning to vinegar on the streets. Every day, her freshness eroded under the assault of men's sweating bodies. Every day her heart was a little more callused, her mind a little more debased, and her soul a little darker and further from God.

Soon she too would be carrying a weapon and stealing money from her customers, which was a regular practice of the other whores.

As a result of her wretched life, Fantine came to hate, fear and mistrust the human race, especially men, and of men, especially *Monsieur le maire*. Only the shining thought of her little Cosette kept her going one day after the other. The hope of someday reclaiming her child was all she had to cling to, and it possessed her utterly, to the point of obsession. Even as she submitted to rough hands and the unpleasant closeness of a strange male body, stinking of garlic and stale sweat, Fantine kept Cosette fixed so firmly in her mind that all other sensations were blocked out.

What did Cosette look like now? Was her hair still as curly and golden as it was when she was three years old, the last time Fantine saw her? Was she tall for her age? What did her voice sound like? Was she learning to read and write? Did she say her prayers to *le bon Dieu* every night?

Yet with time even Cosette's baby image began to fade from Fantine's memory. She no longer perfectly remembered her daughter's facial features, so she replaced her forgotten face with one of the angelic cherubs pictured in the stained-glass windows of the church. Yes, that was her Cosette – an angel! So many years had passed since she'd seen the child! She was almost six years old! Would Fantine recognize her if she saw her now? Would Cosette know her mother? The only thing left was a white-hot obsession to see her again, to reclaim her daughter as her own.

But every day drove that prospect even further away, and made Fantine's hopes grow ever more dim.

So did Fantine's days and nights pass, slowly and with agony of mind, body and spirit. Her life, once so full of promise, her good nature and affectionate heart, her healthy, youthful beauty – all were eroded daily by the misery of poverty and shame, of degradation by herself and abuse by others. At the age of twenty-four, Fantine looked at least ten years older. She was ill, coughing all the time and bringing up blood. In addition, she was so scrawny from scrimping on food that her skin was beginning to hang slackly on her bones. Soon, nothing at all would be left of the sweet young woman she once had been, and in her place would be the new Fantine – wretched, sick, despairing, ugly, debased, lost to the world, to herself and to heaven.

Fantine didn't know it, but the gendarmes were already keeping an eye on her. Not as a person – whores were not human beings to Javert – but as a statistic, a prostitute new to the red-light district. Javert was a great one for statistics. It was one of the ways he kept tabs on crime, by cataloguing it. His small black notebook never left his possession. In it he recorded every fact, every morsel of evidence, every thought that was or could possibly be connected to crime.

Captain Beauvais stood concealed in a doorway, his own notebook in hand, watching night business being transacted between the prostitutes and the soldiers under the streetlights. His surveillance was interrupted by a figure appearing suddenly at his side, out of the darkness.

'There are more than ever,' said Javert in a low tone.

Beauvais gave a start of surprise. 'Oh, Inspector, you startled me.' He touched the bill of his kepi with two fingers of his right hand. 'Yes, I've counted four new girls.'

Javert nodded sombrely. 'You see, Captain, when a town grows, crime grows with it.'

'Yes, sir. Shall I get the men and we'll make arrests?' It seemed to Beauvais that Javert was placing a special emphasis on surveilling prostitutes, as though they were even greater criminals than murderers, arsonists, thieves and perverts. The prefect of police appeared to hate whores with an intense passion, taking their presence in his jurisdiction as a personal affront.

'No.' Javert shook his head decisively. 'Did you check off the regulars?'

'Yes, and I've noted the new girls.' Beauvais handed his superior officer his notebook.

'Good work.' Javert stole a glance at his captain. 'I can hear the scepticism in your voice, Captain. But information is all we want for now.' The police notebooks, filling up fast, were all part of Javert's plan, a plan that would be revealed in due course.

'Yes, sir. Is it ten o'clock? I didn't hear it ring.'

'I'm early. I was restless,' Javert answered in a low tone. 'You heard about Fauchelevent and the cart?'

Beauvais nodded. 'I've heard about nothing else. It's all people are talking about in Montreuil.'

'An incredible feat,' said Javert thoughtfully. 'Has the mayor always been that strong?'

'He is a big man,' Beauvais replied, 'but I didn't know he was that strong.'

'Didn't it show when he was young?'

The captain shook his head. 'I didn't know him when he was young.'

'Oh, that's right,' Javert said carefully. 'He moved here. Where *is* he from?'

Beauvais thought for a moment, trying to bring to mind whatever he actually knew about *Monsieur le maire*. 'Well, he came here from Paris. But that's not where he was born. You know, I think—' Then he shook his head, his knowledge exhausted.

'Didn't you check his papers when he arrived?' persisted Javert.

Captain Beauvais' brow furrowed as he tried to recall. 'I suppose I did. Don't remember.'

A muscle jumped in Javert's jaw, signalling his anger and contempt. Captain Beauvais' casual attitude was damnably irritating! At once he stopped pumping the captain; he realized he wasn't going to get any more information from this inefficient imbecile, at least not tonight, and he didn't want to make the man suspicious. 'Perhaps you didn't,' he said dismissively. 'Why should you?' He peered out into the street. 'Ah. How about her?'

As he took out his notebook, Beauvais followed Javert's gaze. He saw Fantine in her garish red dress, her face masked in paint, stepping into an empty doorway to wait for the next customer. She moved slowly, her shoulders slumped in shame. Beauvais recognized her as much from her shorn head as by her face. 'Yes. She's new.'

*She's new, but she's a criminal type if ever I saw one*, thought Javert. He made a careful note in his book.

The infirmary was dark and quiet. Fauchelevent slept fitfully in his bed, under clean, starched sheets. He was dreaming again of the terrible accident. A figure appeared beside him, and laid a paper down on the nightstand. Fauchelevent stirred in pain, moaned, and woke up.

'Who is it?' he called out, alarmed. Then, in relief, 'Oh, it's you, *Monsieur le maire.*'

'Take it easy, old man, nothing to worry about. I'm buying your horse and cart,' whispered Valjean.

What horse and cart? The horse was dead, the dray little more than a collection of splintered boards. They had no value. Puzzled, Fauchelevent reached for the envelope and opened it. He gasped in surprise. Inside was a thousand-franc note, the only one the old man had ever seen.

'The doctor says your kneecap is broken and you won't be able to do your old job,' the mayor continued. 'I've written to the Petit-Picpus convent in Paris on your behalf. The sisters need a caretaker and a gardener.'

Tears leapt into the old man's eyes. He reached out and grasped Valjean's hand, pulling him closer to the bed, addressing him in a hoarse, cracked whisper.

'*Monsieur le maire*, I'm sorry. I'm so sorry.' The tears spurted out and rolled down his cheeks.

'Sorry? Sorry for what?'

'Monsieur, I used to . . . I was angry at you. Because when you came here, you were a worker like me, and you got rich, while I had troubles.'

Valjean smiled down at the old man, and his voice was gentle. 'We've all had troubles. And we all need help from time to time.'

But the old man kept shaking his head. 'I don't deserve your help. I've said terrible things about you.'

'Fauchelevent, no one deserves help,' said Valjean kindly. He placed an encouraging hand on the old man's shoulder and gave it a gentle squeeze. 'They just need it. What's important now is that we're friends. All right? Rest now. I'll let you know when I have an answer from the convent.'

Valjean moved away silently as the old man wept, his tears half shame and half gratitude. He heard the choked blessings that Fauchelevent was calling down on his name, and his heart was heavy with pity.

True to his word, as soon as the man was able to leave the hospital, hobbling on a wooden crutch, Valjean hired a carriage and horse and sent Fauchelevent down to Paris. He also dictated a letter to the mother superior of the Petit-Picpus convent, begging her to allow the old man to recover fully before beginning on his duties, and enclosing an extra hundred francs for Fauchelevent's care. *Monsieur le maire* had been so generous to the convent that his smallest request was instantly granted.

Soon, news arrived in Montreuil that Fauchelevent had almost completely recovered from the accident, and was already working half-days, and it was difficult to tell who was the more grateful to the mayor, the sisters for getting a good and honest workman or the caretaker himself for his new, secure place.

Fantine, dressed in the ragged clothing she wore during the day, carried the latest letter from Madame Thenardier to the letter shop. Outside, under the sign that read 'Letters Read and Written', she stopped, clutching her side as a long spasm of painful coughing racked her thin body. When the coughing fit passed at last, she drew the ragged shawl more tightly over her shoulders. Covered by a cold sweat, she felt the blood in her veins almost freezing.

She laid twenty sous on the reader's podium and handed over the letter. The reader took up his pointer and read out slowly:

> *Dear Madame:*
> *The ten francs a month we agreed on is no longer enough. Cosette grows bigger by the minute. She enjoyed her sixth birthday party and the new doll we bought her. We love her, so we won't charge for the presents, but she needs a new coat and shoes. We can't afford to pay for them. And she eats more than both our daughters put together. Beginning right away you must send twenty francs a month or you'll have to come and fetch her.*
>
> > *Sincerely,*
> > *Thenardier*

Twenty francs a month! Fantine's head began to swim, her eyesight darkened and she rocked back on her heels and came close to passing out. Twenty francs! Where would she find twenty francs a month? It might as well be twenty thousand! This would be the death of her!

The reader put down his pointer and took a clean sheet

of paper out, laying it on the desk. He raised his pen and looked at Fantine questioningly. 'Will there be a reply?' he asked.

But what could she possibly tell the Thenardiers? A savage cough took hold of her and Fantine's entire thin body shook with it. The taste of blood filled her mouth.

## Chapter Eleven

### THE CENSUS

Valjean was sitting at his desk in the dye factory office, slowly making out a letter of thanks from the mother superior of the Paris convent, thanking him for sending them Fauchelevent, when his clerk came knocking on the door.

'Inspector Javert is here to see you.'

The mayor looked up, startled and alarmed. This was the first time that the inspector had requested an audience since the day of Fauchelevent's accident, that awful day when the two of them had locked eyes and Valjean had seen the long-dreaded recognition in Javert's.

'Tell him to wait,' he said, flustered. Then he quickly put on his coat, buttoned it up to his lace collar, put on and adjusted his wig.

Javert was sitting in the outer office when the mayor opened the door. 'Come in, Inspector,' Valjean invited with a surface calm he didn't feel inside.

'I have exciting news, *Monsieur le maire*,' said Javert as he followed Valjean into his office. He held out a letter. 'Paris is interested in my plan.'

Valjean pretended not to notice the letter as he took his seat behind his desk. 'What plan is that, Inspector?' He waved the prefect of police to a chair.

'It's in the letter, sir,' and the inspector held the document out to the mayor.

'Why don't you tell me, Inspector? You said it's your plan.'

'I beg your pardon. I forgot. I apologize.' Javert put the letter into the breast pocket of his uniform.

'Apologize for what?' asked Valjean, looking sharply at the inspector.

'I forgot you don't read,' Javert said smoothly. 'Your clerk mentioned it. You must have neglected your education to make your fortune, I suppose.' His hooded eyes scrutinized the mayor's face very closely, looking for confirmation of his memory's image of that criminal of long ago, and finding it. The wig and the fancy clothing couldn't hide him now, thought Javert with ugly satisfaction.

This was so obvious a fishing expedition that Valjean didn't even bother to acknowledge it. He was, in fact, making steady although slow progress with his reading, but so far it was his own secret. 'What is Paris interested in, Inspector? I'm all ears,' he said mildly.

Javert's thin body suddenly seemed to take on substance, puff up. He sat rigidly at attention. 'Because of Montreuil's extraordinary growth during the past seven years, I've proposed we make a detailed census.'

A census! The mayor appeared to mull this over, but the very word filled him with alarm. 'Well, that would be interesting,' he replied calmly. 'But how is it a police matter?'

'Modern law enforcement demands modern methods,' Javert answered stiffly, 'and that means information. For example, how many people have moved here in the last decade? Where did they come from? What's their background? Is our criminal population home-grown or are they outsiders? Without information, we cannot know how to control the dangerous elements.'

Valjean felt a chill of dread. His first reaction, of alarm, was evidently more than justified. It was clear that Javert's plan, regardless of officious words like 'modern law enforcement' and 'dangerous elements', was little more than a widespread net intended to entrap anyone Javert suspected of anything. Including, he realized, Jean Valjean himself. No, *especially* Jean Valjean.

His long years as a convict had sharpened Valjean's survival instincts. He knew a trap when he smelled one. Nevertheless, he kept a calm exterior. 'You might be making a mistake, Inspector,' was all he said, and his voice was as bland as his words.

Javert glanced sharply at the mayor. 'A mistake? What mistake is that?'

'Sometimes people move to a new town to start with a clean slate. You may be doing more harm than good by prying into their private lives.'

This reasonable suggestion Javert rejected brusquely. 'An honest man has nothing to fear from the truth. And having a criminal background isn't a private matter. For example, Paris knows that my father was a thief and my mother a prostitute. If my mother or father were to move to Montreuil, I would want everyone to know who and what they are.'

*My God, he means it!* thought Valjean, appalled. 'Even if they had reformed themselves?' he asked pointedly. He was under no illusions now. He understood Javert's meaning to the last syllable – it was Jean Valjean and only Jean Valjean for whom the ferret Javert was setting his trap. Any other felon he managed to ensnare by this census subterfuge would be so much lagniappe.

'Reform is a discredited fantasy,' retorted the policeman. 'Modern science tells us that people are by nature law-breakers or law-abiders. A wolf can wear sheep's clothing, but he is still a wolf.'

The two men – the inflexible policeman and his enemy,

the wolf in sheep's clothing – locked eyes for a long moment. Then Valjean threw back his large head and burst into a genuine peal of laughter, startling Inspector Javert.

'I was just thinking, Inspector, that you've been unlucky.'

'Unlucky? I don't understand.'

'You've had the misfortune of being assigned to a pretty dull post,' explained Valjean, still smiling. 'You would be happier in Paris where everyone, either by nature or experience, is dishonest.'

It took Javert a moment to assimilate this pleasantry. He did not smile. There was not a scintilla of humour in the man. 'Indeed. Well, I'll see if I prefer Paris. They've asked me to report to the deputy prefect to explain my idea further. I'll be gone for four days.'

'We'll miss you. Good luck,' Valjean said drily.

Inspector Javert stood up. 'Thank you, and goodbye.'

Valjean opened the drawer of his desk. 'One moment.' He took out a thick packet tied with a ribbon and offered it to Javert. 'Here's a farewell gift.' He smiled gently at the gendarme.

Javert's eyes opened wider, and a smile of contempt touched the corners of his lips. *A bribe. The fugitive is handing me a bribe. How little he knows Javert!* 'You're offering me . . . a gift?'

*Monsieur le maire*'s smile held steady, and he looked directly into Javert's eyes. 'Yes, Inspector. My papers.' He untied the ribbon and handed the gendarme the contents of the packet, one by one.

'Baptism certificate . . . passport . . . working papers from the Marseilles docks . . .' Javert's heart began to sink and his disappointment grew as he studied the mayor's documents, which were so artfully forged that they appeared to be totally genuine. Even the seals must be authentic.

Valjean was enjoying this moment. 'I wanted to get your census off on the right foot. Pleasant journey, Inspector.'

It was a long ride to Paris, but Inspector Javert, mounted on his black horse, arrived outside the city walls with the same cool demeanour he had been displaying when he rode out of Montreuil. His back was straight in the saddle, his eyes hooded, his full lips pressed together. He regarded the men and women crowded around the wall, waiting to get into the city, with undisguised contempt. Without a word, he urged his mount around the waiting carts and wagons to the head of the line, where he was admitted at once, ahead of everyone waiting. Why should Inspector Javert wait? Was he not prefect of police for the city of Montreuil?

Paris was as filthy and crowded as he had thought it would be. The unpaved or cobbled streets ran with sewage and dirty water. Javert moved his horse cautiously through the dirt, careful not to splash mud or something unspeakably worse on his handsome uniform.

There were areas of Paris boasting elegant parks and wide paved boulevards, beautiful, ornate theatres and opera houses with fine crystal chandeliers and gilded balconies. There were large shops and small boutiques, overflowing with the latest men's and women's fashions, the most expensive perfumes, opulent jewels and furs.

But these luxuries were not intended for the poor people of Paris. Even after a bloody revolution and its even bloodier aftermath, the social structure of France had changed but little. The rich got richer, and the poor got children. Those who had saw no reason to share with those who had not.

This *arrondissement* of the city, a section housing only the poor, was a very long way from the broad avenues and boulevards. Here, instead of sturdy stone mansions with iron gates, were broken doorways and icy alleys crowded with the homeless sleeping on bits of board or old burlap, while their starving children ran the streets begging for a coin or a scrap of food.

At the sight of Javert, in his smooth coat and gleaming boots, the beggars tried to crowd around his horse, their scrawny hands held out imploringly.

'Give us something, monsieur, anything. A few sous. A bit of bread.'

But Javert rode coldly through the crowd. The misery of these poor people raised no emotion in his breast apart from disgust. His only outward reaction was to aim a kick at a little boy of about seven, who dared to lay a hand upon his horse. The savage lunge connected with the child, and sent him reeling across the cobbles.

Javert rode on. Several of the homeless, recognizing their enemy, picked up stones and threw them after his departing back, but they were so enfeebled by hunger that the stones fell far short of their target. The inspector did not even bother to look back. Nothing that this ragtag mob could do would have any effect on him.

A man with a mission, he rode to the *arrondissement* that contained the offices of the prefecture of Paris police. Reaching the imposing building, he dismounted, tied up his horse and went inside to enquire after the office of Georges Chabouillet, the deputy chief of all Paris police. Regardless of his 'deputy' title, the man greatly outranked Javert, who understood well that this was Paris, the capital of the civilized world, while Montreuil was merely Montreuil.

Nevertheless, Javert was greeted cordially by Chabouillet. 'Inspector Javert, the prefect was impressed by your proposal. I expect him to approve a budget for your census within the month.' In a vast, high-ceilinged office,

Deputy Chief Chabouillet sat across from Javert at a large mahogany desk covered in official papers.

Javert's face didn't change expression, but his eyes brightened. 'Thank you, sir. That's excellent news.'

Chabouillet scowled. 'So I suggest you drop this request for an investigation of the mayor.'

*No, impossible!* Javert half rose from his chair in protest. 'Sir, I was a guard for a year on the galleys in Toulon. I saw Jean Valjean perform exactly the same feat of strength as the mayor did with the cart. The rowing makes them strong—' Javert pointed to his upper back. 'Here. Since the connection was made in my mind, now I am no longer dazzled by the disguise of his wealth, I've grown more certain every day. Indeed, now that I recognize his face and voice so clearly, I'm amazed I didn't know him right away.'

'Well, Javert, I don't doubt—'

'Sir, I am prepared to denounce him!' The inspector's face kindled with passion, and his eyes burned.

Chabouillet drew back, astonished by Javert's sudden vehemence. 'Denounce him? Without proof?'

But Javert was relentless. 'If there is a trial, the evidence will be found,' he promised grimly.

'But he showed you papers and they were in order,' protested Chabouillet.

The inspector scowled deeply. 'I checked the baptism certificate. It's a copy,' he retorted. 'Eleven years ago, there was a fire at the parish. The original records were destroyed. All his documents are based on that copy.'

Deputy Chief Chabouillet kept shaking his head. This business was going much too fast for his liking. 'Your identification alone is not enough to subject the mayor of Montreuil to a trial. File a report and I'll recommend we investigate.'

Inspector Javert turned his burning eyes directly on the

deputy chief, as though he wanted to bore a hole in the other man's soul. 'Sir, Jean Valjean was a thief who showed no remorse at his trial. Claimed he had a right to steal. He attempted to escape four times. And he broke parole as soon as he was released.' Javert's voice began to tremble with the only emotion he allowed himself – fiery indignation in the face of wrongdoing. 'It makes a mockery of our institutions to have a corrupt and depraved man in charge of our industry and our government.'

But the deputy chief would not be moved by rhetoric. 'Javert, I said file a report,' he said sternly. 'I'll investigate at this end . . . discreetly. But do not denounce him without proof. Be patient. He's not going anywhere, is he?'

Inspector Javert opened his mouth to speak again, then thought better of it. He realized that nothing more he could say would change Chabouillet's mind. Rising from his chair, he made a short, stiff bow and left the room.

Once back on the street, Javert knew exactly what he had to do next. He mapped it out as he untied his horse and mounted up. Prisoners who were paroled and sent from Toulon to Pontarlier were required to follow a specified route, and to show their yellow passports to the police chiefs at certain stops along the way, so that authorities could monitor their whereabouts. The last city where Jean Valjean had shown those documents was Digne. Digne, then, was Javert's next destination.

Once there, it was not difficult for him to locate the gendarme who'd reported Valjean's presence in the town, turning every innkeeper and landlord against him. This was the very same gendarme who had arrested Valjean and dragged him back to the bishop with his knapsack filled with stolen silver.

The man had aged and grown fatter with the years, but he was still on the force. Javert found him sitting in a run-down tavern, half drunk, his uniform dishevelled, his undershirt showing torn and dirty under his open jacket. Disgusted, Javert sat down at the same table, and began to question the gendarme closely about Valjean.

'Yeah, I remember him,' the policeman grunted with a belch. 'Couldn't believe he got away with it. But the bishop was a fool. Famous for being a fool.'

'Yes, yes,' Javert said impatiently. 'But do you remember Jean Valjean well enough to identify him?'

Another belch, longer and deeper. 'Excuse me. Sure I can identify him. Where is he? Is he here?' The man looked around the tavern eagerly, as though expecting the thief Jean Valjean to emerge from the woodwork like a cuckoo from a carved German clock.

'No. Be patient. When the time is right I will take you to him. Meanwhile, say nothing to anybody. Do you understand?'

The officer grunted again, and nodded his head. His beady little eyes glistened. It would be a pleasure, confronting Jean Valjean once more and pointing the finger of accusation at him.

## Chapter Twelve

### JAVERT AND FANTINE

'No more credit for you, you whore, do you hear me?' Chevrau's greasy lips contorted in an angry scowl, and he raised his voice until it filled the narrow room and ricocheted off the grimy walls. 'From now on, you pay in cash . . . and in advance! If you don't have the money to pay what you owe me, get your lazy arse up off that bed and out into the street! I'm not in the business of giving away money, you hear me? If you can't pay, move out!'

Fantine could barely raise her head to answer. The room was so cold that she could see the rising vapour of her breath. The thin, patched blankets she kept wrapped around her didn't even begin to take the chill off. She'd been coughing almost without stop for weeks now, and was ill, pale and exhausted. Her lungs ached miserably, from the cold and from the consumptive disease that was eating her alive.

Outside, winter had returned with a roar to Montreuil; icy winds blew in from the sea, and the people had already begun going to bed early. As soon as the pale sun left the sky, they closed their shutters against the blast of Boreas, and huddled under plump feather-filled quilts in warm rooms where the hearth fires were not allowed to go out.

Fantine possessed none of these – not wooden shutters to keep out the winter winds, not quilts, not a warming fire. All she had was an icy room, a mountain of debts and a cough that drew blood from deep down inside her chest. All she had was her despair.

'So, what's your answer?' sneered Chevrau.

'I can't move.' Fantine shook her head wearily. 'I don't have money to pay in advance for a room.'

'Am I a charity?' demanded Chevrau roughly. 'You haven't paid me in four months.'

'I paid you,' she answered faintly. Actually, she *had* paid Chevrau a large portion of what he claimed she owed him, but she had no proof because he'd given her no receipts. She was at his mercy.

'I have bills, too,' Chevrau continued, aggrieved. 'And I can't spread *my* legs. Besides, it's not good business to rent to a whore. I'll lose tenants.' His little piggy eyes fastened on Fantine's thin neck, where a simple, inexpensive necklace lay close to her collarbone. 'What about that necklace? That's got to be worth something.'

'No, no, not this!' Fantine stuttered nervously. 'It's for my daughter. My daughter Cosette. I can't do that.'

'You'd better come up with something,' the landlord grumbled. 'I want ten francs or you're out!'

Fantine uttered a deep sigh, from her innermost soul. The morass of her life was so abysmal that no ray of light could make its way through. She was seriously ill, more gravely ill than she herself supposed. She was besieged for money on every hand – Chevrau, the Thenardiers, the cost of staying alive – but in frigid weather like the Montreuil winter how could she drag herself to the streets to earn a few sous? The cold cut through her to the marrow of her bones; she had nothing warm to wear, and her shoes were now more ragged hole than cheap leather. They were stuffed with rags, but still they let in the cold.

There was little business transacted in the streets on nights like this. It was too cold for the whores to be out in the doorways. Instead, they congregated in the warm taverns and restaurants, where they ate and drank and caroused with the soldiers and the other men out looking for a good time. Fantine was not welcome there; she was not of their sisterhood. She alone was consigned to the bitter cold streets, where every night of exposure to the weather made her illness worse and robbed her of her last vestiges of strength.

Desperately, she threw the blankets off and, assuming a grotesque pose intended to be enticing, offered herself to Chevrau.

'No,' he snarled, turning away in disgust. 'This time I want cash.'

Snow was falling thickly and silently. The streets and alleyways of Montreuil were already covered in a heavy blanket. The city was very quiet; who would willingly be out wandering in weather like this?

Duty was stronger than even the most severe snowstorm. Inspector Javert and Captain Beauvais were out in the snowfall, sheltering in a doorway that overlooked a slum street with its busy, lighted taverns. Beauvais was not there willingly; he longed for the creature comforts of his warm home and the steaming tureen his wife set on the table every night. But duty was duty; this he understood.

For Inspector Javert it was a different thing entirely. No matter how terrible the weather, Javert would never miss one night of duty, one inclement night of observation for his 'census', the gathering of information that appeared to be his latest obsession. What Beauvais didn't know was that, apart from this census, Javert's true passion was gathering every scrap of information he could glean about *Monsieur le maire*. This he did in secret, and he was assembling a thick dossier on the man he believed to be Jean Valjean. Soon he would be ready to make his move.

At the other end of the street, the two officers saw a tall, thin whore, shivering in a dirty red dress, walking slowly up and down in front of one of the cafés. Inside, a group of men was drinking and eating, some of them with their arms around prostitutes. These were soldiers and others with money to spend and time off in which to spend it, snow or no snow.

Observing Fantine, the only whore parading her wares out on the street, the two policemen could see everything that was going on. As the woman slowly marched back and forth in front of the café, hoping for an emerging customer, three men came through the door.

They were rich and foppish, well dressed, haughty, and obviously quite drunk. All three were wearing heavy, warm greatcoats with several capes, and tall silk hats. They were smoking cigars and they carried canes, but did not bother to use them, even on the slippery ground. The walking sticks, with their carved shanks and gold-tipped ferrules, were for ostentatious display only.

'Good evening, monsieur,' Fantine said timidly, as she approached the first of them. She raised one hand to lay it on his arm.

Taken aback at being so addressed, offended by her closeness, the fop grabbed the woman's arm before she could pollute him by her touch. He stared down at Fantine. He saw a haggard prostitute, her thin cheeks covered in heavy make-up which did nothing to disguise her unhealthy pallor. Bones were showing at her collar, and her fingers were as bony as a witch's.

'God, you're hideous,' he drawled, and he blew his cigar smoke into her beseeching face.

Fantine had made a mistake and she knew it. She had

crossed over the line separating class from class, and she no longer possessed the beauty that was the passport for such a crossing. She struggled to free her arm, but the fop's fingers only tightened on it cruelly. 'Well? How much?'

'A . . . a franc,' stammered the woman.

Another cloud of cigar smoke hit her in the face. 'You're joking.'

'Fifty sous?' Fantine's words were barely audible.

'Fifty sous? To screw a corpse?' The man laughed harshly, turning to his two companions. 'Look at her. She doesn't have a drop of blood in her veins.'

Stung by the sound of their derisive laughter, Fantine pulled her arm free. She turned, walking as quickly as she could to get away from this cruel man and his friends.

But he was not yet willing to let her go. Bending down, he scooped up a large handful of wet snow. 'Mademoiselle, how about a sou?' he called after her. 'I have a sou. I have a sou to spend on you.'

A sou! A small handful of pennies! This was beyond insult! This was too much! Fantine saw red. She whirled around as anger heated her frigid veins, coursing through her blood like liquid fire. She would tell the miserable bastard a thing or two.

But before she could get a word out, she felt herself seized by a hard, elegantly gloved hand and shoved roughly against the wall. 'But first . . .' hissed the fop, and he raised the hand he'd filled with snow and thrust it down the front of Fantine's dress, against her naked breasts. 'Let's give your tits some colour.'

The shock of the icy contact, so achingly cold against her helpless body, caused Fantine to cry out in pain. Captain Beauvais, ready to intervene, took a step forward out of the shadows, but Inspector Javert grabbed his arm and prevented him from taking another step.

The second fop shoved a fistful of snow into Fantine's open mouth. 'And have something to drink,' he sneered.

Twisting her head this way and that, while her tormentors kept her pressed against the wall, Fantine spat the snow out. She began to cough violently. Her persecutor let her go. Maddened by her humiliation, she lunged forward, clawing at his face. He staggered backward, lost his footing on the treacherous icy snow, and fell in a heap. Fantine threw herself on top of him, still clawing at him.

At once, the fop's friends pounced on Fantine and with some difficulty pulled her off. Driven to frenzy by her rage and humiliation, she turned her attack on them, punching and kicking. Laughing at her misery, poking at her with their fancy walking sticks, they easily fended her off.

The disturbance brought the café doors swinging open. The merrymakers poured out into the street to enjoy the spectacle of a skinny, consumptive prostitute in a mêlée with three drunken gentlemen. Roaring with laughter, they poked one another gleefully. This was unexpected but welcome entertainment!

Captain Beauvais' face mirrored his discomfort. This was a spectacle as unfair as a bear-baiting – three healthy men against one wretched young woman. 'Sir,' he said to Javert, 'this *is* a disturbance. May I intervene?'

'I'll do it,' Inspector Javert retorted brusquely. He emerged from the shadows and strode up the street, approaching the crowd. Beauvais followed him, keeping a respectful distance. As soon as the men and women from the café recognized him as the prefect of police, they melted back into the restaurant. Nobody in Montreuil with any sense wanted to fall foul of Inspector Javert.

The inspector pushed past the three fops and confronted Fantine, who was cowering and shivering in her soaked dress. 'It's not my fault!' she cried as soon as she saw Javert. 'They started—'

He didn't bother to utter a word. Instead, with his open hand, Javert slapped Fantine hard across the mouth. She dropped like a stone to the frigid ground. Captain Beauvais suppressed the gasp of horrified surprise that threatened to escape his lips.

'Go home! And be quick about it,' Javert snarled at the three drunken rich men, who scrambled to obey. Then, as Captain Beauvais stood there unable to move or speak, Inspector Javert laid his hands on Fantine. 'You are under arrest.'

Jean Valjean was in his bedroom, practising his writing, forming the letters again and again on a sheet of paper, when he heard tapping at his window. He looked up, startled, to see Captain Beauvais' face peering in at him through the falling flakes of snow. Rising, Valjean went to the window and opened it. The officer's face was troubled.

'Sir, you asked me to tell you if he went too far. Well, I've kept my mouth shut long enough. Tonight he went too far . . .'

It was warmer in the Montreuil police station than out in the streets. Still Fantine could not stop her shivering. She shivered because she was very ill. She shivered because her skimpy clothing was wet clear through, and she was soaked to the bone. But mostly she shivered out of fear. Fear of what was going to happen to her, especially fear of Inspector Javert.

Javert sat filling out forms at the desk, ignoring Fantine's deep coughs, her pathetic little whimpers and the chattering of her teeth. He didn't even look up when she brought a great gob of bright red blood up from her lungs and wiped her mouth on her sleeve. Whores suffered from all sorts of diseases; it was a punishment from God.

Javert finished writing out the indictment, folded it, sealed it and sent for the sergeant of police.

'Have her taken to the prison,' he ordered. To Fantine he said, 'You're getting six months.'

'Six months!' Fantine gasped, and put her thin hand over her wildly beating heart. 'What about Cosette? What will happen to her?'

'Who is Cosette?' demanded Javert.

'My daughter. If I don't send the Thenardiers money, they'll turn her out.'

'Is your daughter in Montreuil?'

'No, sir. She lives with the—'

'Then she's not my concern.' Javert cut her off without interest. He stood up from the desk and started for the door, but Fantine threw herself on the floor at his feet and began to beg.

'Inspector! Please! Listen to my side,' she implored in desperation. 'I know I hit the gentlemen. I know I was wrong, but do they have the right to put snow down my dress? Especially when it's the only one I have and I need it for work. I'm sorry. I didn't mean to argue. It won't happen again. Please, Inspector,' she sobbed, 'please be merciful.'

Inspector Javert didn't deign to look at her. He was deeply offended that a diseased whore should even dare to touch the cuffs of his trousers, let alone take up his valuable time with her nonsensical babble. He considered such as Fantine below even the most wretched citizen. In Javert's eyes she had no rights at all. Indeed, he didn't even recognize her right to go on living. For what reason? With what purpose? He nodded to the sergeant, who detached Fantine from his trouser leg, pulling her up roughly.

'All right,' Javert said roughly. 'I've listened to your side. You're still getting six months. Nothing can change that.'

'One moment, Inspector,' a voice near the door rang out. Javert turned in surprise. Unseen by him, Jean Valjean had entered the room.

'*Monsieur le maire?*' said the Inspector, puzzled.

Fantine, too, saw him, and scrambled to her feet. She was already half crazed. Now the sudden appearance of the mayor pushed her entirely over the edge. Unthinking, she ran towards him, planting herself right in his face. 'It's you! You fired me! You did this to me!' she accused the startled mayor. Then, before anybody could move to stop her, she spat full in Jean Valjean's face.

Immediately, the police sergeant grabbed the woman by the arm and hauled her away from the mayor, who stood quietly wiping the spittle from his face. He seemed unmoved by the incident. Then he turned to Javert.

'Let her go.'

'What?' What was the man up to? Javert could not believe what he was hearing.

'Let me explain, Inspector. I was crossing the square when you arrested her. I asked people what had happened and they told me it was entirely the fault of the men who attacked her. In fact, *they* should be under arrest. Now that you've heard this new evidence, I want you to release her.'

'I don't understand,' cried the confused Fantine. 'Is he really the mayor? He said I can go. He is the mayor, isn't he?'

The sergeant let go of her arm, and she began to sidle towards the door. 'Well, I'll be going, then. I won't . . . I won't be any more trouble.'

'Sergeant, have you gone blind?' snapped Javert. 'She's walking out. Who told you she could go?'

Once again the sergeant laid his hands roughly on Fantine, who uttered a low, despairing whimper.

'I did,' Valjean said coldly. 'I am the final judicial authority in Montreuil, and I say she's innocent.'

'She spat on you.' Javert was absolutely furious that his authority should be challenged in this way, but he kept himself firmly in check. As much as he detested the mayor, the inspector recognized his authority. The shock was that the man seemed to be exercising his authority on behalf of a common whore. A whore, moreover, who had just spat into his face.

'She was upset,' Valjean said calmly. 'I forgive her.'

'She insulted you. In front of my men, she defiled you.' Javert's words choked in his throat painfully; they were as sharp as nettles.

'That's my concern, Inspector.'

Javert's control began to slip. 'No, sir, you are wrong,' he declared passionately. 'You, *Monsieur le maire*, are the personification of order, morality, government – in fact, the whole of society. You don't have the right to forgive her for debasing all of us. You don't have the authority to destroy justice.'

'I have the authority, Inspector. Under articles nine and eleven of the Criminal Code I can order her release. Sergeant, she is free.'

Fantine looked warily from one man to the other, not knowing whom to believe, but well aware that her fate depended on the outcome of this struggle. She felt as though an angel and a devil were fighting for the possession of her soul, and in that she was not far from the truth.

'I cannot allow that, monsieur,' Javert said in a strangled voice. 'I was there. She attacked a man—'

'The decision is mine,' Valjean interrupted icily. 'She's free.'

Javert's gorge rose and he tasted a metallic tang in his mouth. This man was challenging his official authority. To be so ill regarded in front of his subordinate was not to be borne! 'She will not go free while I am in charge of this post,' Javert announced defiantly.

Valjean's calm exterior showed no change. 'In that case, Inspector, under article sixty-six, until tomorrow morning you are relieved of command.'

Javert recoiled as if he had been struck. '*Monsieur le maire!*' he gasped.

'You are dismissed, Inspector. Leave immediately.'

The mayor was implacable. There was no emotion in his voice, and that told Inspector Javert more than anything else that nothing would dissuade him.

'You're free,' the mayor told Fantine. The girl gasped emotionally. Then, completely overcome by her ordeal, she fainted in a heap at Jean Valjean's feet.

## Chapter Thirteen

### VALJEAN AND FANTINE

Carrying her in his arms, Jean Valjean brought the semiconscious Fantine to his own little house, and up the stairs into his bedroom. There he laid her gently on the bed, wrapped thick blankets around her and sent for the doctor to come with all possible haste.

Fantine seemed to be in a stupor, brought on by an excess of emotion, the stress of what she had endured on this awful night, and her fever, which was escalating. She alternated between crying out wildly and struggling with the blankets, and sinking back on to the pillows mute and exhausted. Before long the exhaustion won out and took complete hold of her. She could do nothing but tremble in all her limbs and mutter over and over, 'Cosette . . . Cosette . . . my little Cosette.'

Valjean watched over her with infinite pity and sadness, that such a young woman should have been so degraded and her life made so miserable. The words that Fantine had flung at him in the police station burned in his thoughts like fiery coals. He was to blame. Had he not dismissed her, this would not have happened to her. The guilt was his, all his. No one else was to blame.

And the worst part of it was that he remembered nothing of it, and didn't even recognize the young woman's face as that of a former employee. How could he have been so blind when he had prided himself on looking after the welfare of all his workers? Here was one worker whose welfare he had not only ignored but endangered, perhaps even destroyed. Surely, Valjean thought mournfully, the sin of pride must be the most unforgivable sin of all, leading inevitably to the others.

'I doubt she'll survive,' the doctor said gravely. 'She talks constantly of Cosette. Who is she?'

'Her daughter,' answered Valjean.

The doctor shook his head. 'She needs all her will to fight the infection in her lungs. Perhaps if she has the girl with her . . .' He looked enquiringly at *Monsieur le maire*.

'I understand,' Valjean nodded. 'Thank you, Doctor.'

'You'll need nurses. I can't arrange for them until the morning. The convent will send nursing sisters. What about tonight?'

'I'll take care of her tonight.'

'Try to keep her body warm and her head cool.'

He let the doctor out. Carrying a basin of warm water and a soft cloth, Valjean entered the bedroom. Fantine was in his bed, on clean sheets, under a warm blanket, more than half asleep. Her thin face was covered with a mix of smeared rouge, dirty snow and dried, caked blood. Yet, underneath the mask, he could discern the remnants of what once must have been remarkable beauty. He sat down on a chair near the bed and began to wipe the girl's face clean.

Fantine was drowsy from the pain-killing draught the doctor had given her, but at the touch of the washcloth on her face she opened her eyes. 'Why did the gossip bother you? You didn't have to fire me.'

'Your clothes are damp. I'll take them off, and get you into—'

'That's all right. There won't be a charge. You deserve a free one. But I don't understand—'

No, no, she had misunderstood completely why he had brought her here to his home. Embarrassed, Valjean hurried to get Fantine under the covers.

'—why 're you? being so kind after you were so mean.'

'I was preoccupied. I didn't know. If you'd come directly to me . . .' Valjean kept his face turned away to hide his guilty blushes; he found it difficult to look this young woman directly in the eyes.

Fantine strained towards him, trying to lift her head high enough to kiss him, but the mayor gently pushed her back down as he wiped her cheeks clean of the last traces of blood and dirt. 'You need rest.'

'You don't want a kiss?' Fantine said plaintively, in a near-whisper. She was in his debt and had no other currency to offer. How, then, was she to pay him back?

Valjean dropped the cloth into the water, rinsed it out and squeezed it in his giant hands, then placed it gently on her brow. He leaned close and spoke to her softly, yet intensely. 'I want you to rest. Don't worry. I'll bring your daughter here.'

Fantine opened her eyes, and they were filled with hope. 'You're going to the Thenardiers?'

Valjean shook his head. 'No, I can't. I'll send them money to bring Cosette here.'

'She can't live with me,' whispered Fantine unhappily, thinking of her cold, bare room and the lascivious landlord Chevrau. It was no place for an innocent child.

Valjean smiled down at her. 'She'll be happy with you,' he reassured her. 'She'll attend the school. You won't have any more worries. Cosette will be with you and, when you're better, I'll find work for you.'

But Fantine continued to shake her head. 'You don't understand,' she whispered unhappily. 'I'm a whore. And Cosette has no father.'

Valjean placed his muscular hand over her thin one. 'She has the Lord,' he told her softly. 'He is her father. And you are His creation. In His eyes you have never been anything but an innocent and beautiful woman. Now rest, child.'

The gentleness in his voice and words reassured her. Her eyes drifted shut and her head relaxed on the pillow. She fell into a deep sleep, and Jean Valjean sat on the chair by her bedside all night, watching over her as she slept and resolving that she would never want for anything again.

In the days that followed, Fantine showed a marked improvement. Under the tender nursing care of the sisters from the local convent, and nourished by tasty hot broths made of fresh-killed chickens, the hollows in her cheeks began to round out somewhat, giving her some look of health. But it was a deceptive appearance, since her diseased lungs were far gone, beyond a cure. She still suffered greatly from night sweats and sudden high fevers and, worst of all, frequent bouts of deep coughing that left her powerless to speak or even move.

Nonetheless, she was an altogether different person from the miserable whore who had spat in Jean Valjean's face and begged at Javert's feet. In her entire life Fantine had never known such kindness as she was experiencing now, at the hands of *Monsieur le maire*. His acts of generosity, unlike the gifts from her first lover Tholomyes, arose not out of the desire to possess her but out of the desire to possess heaven. The mayor was a true Christian, in that he imitated Christ. His joy in doing good was as infectious as the disease in Fantine's chest, and she caught some of that joy.

Soon she would be seeing Cosette. *Monsieur le maire* had promised it faithfully and was working towards it daily. Fantine trusted him completely. She would lie back in her bed, warm and fed, and dream of her little daughter with the golden curls. The mayor had advised her not to allow herself to think of the years she'd lost, but instead to keep her thoughts and hopes fixed firmly on the future. It was good advice, and Fantine did her best to follow it.

She pictured a future in which Cosette, wearing a starched school pinafore and carrying books in a strap over her shoulder, would come running into the kitchen of a bright little house in which her mother was waiting for her with a glass of fresh milk and some just-baked white bread. She pictured a small bed which Cosette would kneel beside to say her prayers to Jesus, and where she would kiss her mother goodnight.

Fantine imagined sewing pretty dresses for Cosette, braiding her hair and tying ribbons at the ends, hugging her watching her do her lessons on the oak table near the big stove, by the light of real wax candles. These were wonderful, fulfilling dreams, and in them Fantine always saw herself as healthy and strong, well able to raise a child by the fruits of her own labour.

But when the racking coughs seized her and the blood welled up from her lungs to her mouth, then her dreams dissolved into the reality of pain and Fantine had to force herself to stay alive until she could see Cosette. That became her only future – to lay eyes on her precious daughter one more time.

With a heavy heart, Jean Valjean observed the young woman's struggle to survive. According to the doctor her chances were far from good, but Valjean, too, was determined that Fantine should stay alive long enough to see her child again. He had pieced together her story, and he honoured her for her courage in the face of so much ill fortune and degradation. In an ideal society, one formulated on Christian principles, he thought, cruelty such as Fantine had endured would be outlawed. He bitterly regretted the unwitting share he had in bringing Fantine so low. It caused him many pangs of guilt, and made him more resolved than ever that Fantine's future – what there might be left of it – should be assured and happy.

No trouble or expense was too much for him to go through for Fantine. Without a word, he had given up his bedroom to her, forbidding anybody to tell her about it. He was sleeping in his little sitting room, his tall body stretched out on a couple of chairs. The discomfort didn't bother him; in fact, he welcomed it. It was a trifle compared to what Fantine had suffered.

As he had promised, the doctor had contacted the Montreuil convent, and the mother superior promptly sent nursing sisters over to take turns looking after the sick girl.

Three days after he had brought Fantine home, the mayor entered her bedroom with a letter in his hand. She was sitting up in bed, propped against pillows. She looked beautiful – her face showed that translucent purity and rosy glow not uncommon in tubercular patients, who ran frequent hectic fevers. Her cropped hair curled charmingly short around her small, well-shaped head, like a golden cap. When she saw Valjean, she broke into a radiant smile.

'Come in. Please come in.'

Jean Valjean nodded to the nun who was arranging a bed tray for Fantine, with a bowl of thick soup and a piece of fresh white bread. He smiled broadly at the patient. 'You look better every day,' he told her.

'Liar.' Fantine grinned. Then she spotted the letter Valjean was carrying. 'That's Thenardier's handwriting! Is something wrong?'

The mayor handed over the letter. 'Here, read it.'

But Fantine shook her head. 'I don't know how. You read it to me.'

Jean Valjean looked embarrassed. 'Well ... I'm still learning myself.'

'We're a fine pair.' Fantine smiled.

'My clerk read it to me. Thenardier writes he can't bring Cosette because you owe him money.'

'But I don't! I paid—'

'And I, too, sent him money,' the mayor put in. 'It's an obvious lie. He could have brought her and been paid in person.'

Fantine's cheeks glowed with patches of colour, more febrile than before. She pushed her tray aside and threw the covers off, attempting to get out of bed. 'I'll go get her—' she began breathlessly.

'Impossible.' Valjean put out a restraining hand to keep Fantine safely under the covers. 'The trip would kill you. And it isn't necessary. Thenardier thinks you've come into money. He's become a little greedy, that's all. I've posted three hundred francs, one hundred and fifty more than he asks. My clerk wrote to him that the extra was for bringing Cosette. She'll be here in four or five days.'

His words brought a measure of calm to the young woman. She sank back against her pillows, and her expression became dreamy. 'How wonderful,' she whispered, 'to see my Cosette.'

'You should eat, my dear,' the nun protested mildly.

'I'll let you have your lunch. You *should* eat,' echoed Valjean.

'No, don't go! I mean, what about you? Don't you eat?' Something in her voice, a loneliness that resembled his own, caught at Jean Valjean's heart. He nodded to the nun, and she picked up the lunch tray and handed it to him. He carried it out of the room.

While the sister brushed Fantine's hair and dressed her in a new frock, Jean Valjean made a simple luncheon for two, and set it out in his sitting room, using a tablecloth and linen napkins. If only it weren't winter! There would be flowers in his little garden. Stepping outside, he cut some evergreen branches and brought them inside. Their piny smell filled the small sitting room with the freshness of the outdoors.

When Fantine was ready, Valjean lifted her in his powerful arms and carried her down the stairs to lunch. She weighed nothing; it was like carrying a kitten. They sat across from each other, talking, while the mayor tried to slow the pace of his own eating to match that of Fantine, who merely nibbled slowly at her simple food, and had to be coaxed to swallow a mouthful.

But as they talked they drew together like friends, and soon they were laughing together. Valjean felt a surge of happiness such as he had never known in his life before. He thought he could ask nothing more of God than to let this moment last for ever. Let Fantine go on living, and let them sit across this table from each other for all eternity. That would be his idea of heaven. The love he felt for this helpless girl was pure and strong. He wanted nothing more than to make her smile and to be her champion and benefactor for ever.

It was this happy scene which Inspector Javert saw when he peered through the sitting-room window of *Monsieur le maire*'s house. The sight of Fantine, dressed in clean clothing and smiling happily, of Jean Valjean coaxing her to take another bite as though she were an infant, the sight of the obvious happiness on both their faces, burned through Javert's retinas with real pain.

The tableau he was witnessing was an abomination to the inspector – a wicked fugitive consorting with a prostitute under the guise of respectability. It was like a hard blow in his face. It defied everything that was moral and right.

Javert struggled to gain control of himself and his righteous anger. When he was more composed, he went around to the mayor's door and knocked, loudly and insistently.

'*Monsieur le maire?* It's Inspector Javert,' he called out, and knocked again.

After a moment or two he heard footsteps within, and the door was opened. 'Yes, Inspector?'

'Sorry to disturb you. I've received an urgent request to assist in an investigation in Arras. I'll be gone for two days.'

'They need you in Arras? What for?' Valjean wanted to know.

'To help find a missing person. I've put Captain Beauvais in command.'

'Thank you, Inspector.' The mayor nodded. 'Good—'

But Javert could contain himself and his indignation no longer. It burst out of him with the words 'She's a prostitute!' Pulling his infamous black notebook out of his uniform pocket, he tried to show it to Valjean. 'I can show you over fifty instances of her crimes!' he protested.

The mayor refused to look at the pages. 'Then why didn't you arrest her?' he asked grimly.

'Because whores are a social necessity. An ugly necessity. But controlled, they can be a benefit.'

Valjean had heard enough. The man's cold-hearted point of view was totally repellent to him. 'Safe journey, Inspector,' he said, and shut the door firmly in Javert's face.

## Chapter Fourteen

### ARRAS

Ten days after Jean Valjean had dispatched three hundred francs to the Thenardiers, a letter arrived from Montfermeil. Valjean took it to his factory office, where his clerk read it to him. He listened to the innkeeper's words with rising anger, tapping his fingers impatiently on his desk.

*Our little lark, our darling Cosette, is eager to be with her mother. But she has a cough, 'like my Mommy's', the sweet angel said. The physician advises she's not well enough to travel now. I'll bring her when she's stronger. Meanwhile, the medicine is expensive. And the doctor's bills are criminal. Fantine owes us another fifty francs—*

'All right, I've heard enough,' growled Valjean, enraged at the unmitigated gall of the man, denying a sick mother her child while attempting to suck more and more money out of the situation. The Thenardiers had already made themselves rich off Cosette, but they were still greedy for more.

'Do you want to dictate a reply?' asked the clerk.

'No.' Valjean shook his head in disgust. 'Instead, write this note for Fantine to sign. "Monsieur Thenardier: You will hand Cosette over to the bearer. Regards . . ." '

The clerk finished scribbling and handed over the note. Valjean stood up and moved to the door of his office, but before he could reach it the door was opened. Inspector Javert was standing in the doorway, and he was obviously agitated. His lips were working strangely, twisting around as his teeth chewed at them.

'Inspector?' Jean Valjean had never seen the man showing any emotion before this, but his face was troubled and paler even than usual.

Without preliminary greeting, which was in itself a departure from the inspector's customary formality, Javert announced, 'I need to see you immediately. Alone.'

Valjean didn't like the sound of this. An alarm bell went off inside him, but on the surface he displayed nothing but calmness. Meanwhile, Javert was pacing nervously up and down the office, saying nothing, still biting his lips.

The mayor waited a moment or two, but Javert remained silent. 'I'm in a hurry, Inspector,' said the mayor quietly.

It cost Javert an obvious effort to speak. 'Monsieur, a serious, a . . . grave violation of the public trust has been committed,' he declared solemnly.

If the alarm had not been sounding so loudly inside his head, Jean Valjean would have found Javert's pompous solemnity almost amusing. As it was, he found it frightening. What information had the man uncovered that affected him so strongly?

'Yes?' was all he said.

'An inferior has shown a complete lack of respect for the law. He must be exposed and punished.'

This was the moment Valjean had been dreading. The inevitable confrontation with the implacable uniformed bloodhound of morality. How far had Javert progressed towards exposing him? Would he have time to make his escape? 'Who is the offender?' Valjean asked through dry lips.

'I am,' said Javert. 'I've slandered you, *Monsieur le maire*. I'm here to ask that you demand my dismissal.'

Javert's words caught Valjean totally by surprise. What was he talking about? This must be some kind of lunacy! 'Inspector . . . I don't understand—'

But Javert was determined not to be interrupted until he had said everything. 'You may say that I can resign. But resignation is honourable, and I don't deserve it. I must be punished. You treated me unjustly, *Monsieur le maire*, over the . . . about the woman. This time you must treat me justly. You must dismiss me.'

The mayor didn't understand a word of what Javert was babbling about. 'For God's sake, Javert, what for?' he cried, at the end of his patience.

'I denounced you to the Paris prefect of police. I swore that you were a convict who had broken parole.'

Valjean's blood ran cold and he suppressed a shiver. Denounced? To the highest police authority in France? For a long time he'd felt Javert's hot breath on the back of his neck, knowing that the man was tracking him, following him into his private life, and possibly drawing closer to the truth every day. But he had no idea that things had progressed as far as this. What evidence had Javert unearthed? What witnesses? In what area had he made his mistakes? 'You said I was . . . what?'

'A convict. I had no proof. Only a memory. The memory of a man, Jean Valjean, whom I guarded twenty years ago on the galleys. I denounced you without a shred of evidence.'

'You denounced me,' repeated Valjean woodenly. His brain was racing, looking for a way out. Yet his old instincts made one part of his mind suspicious of all this.

One train of thought told him that the inspector's sudden bizarre declaration might even be a trap, set to catch him off guard and force him to come out with something that was better kept hidden.

'Yes. I was a fool. They told me I was wrong. They said you couldn't be Jean Valjean. And they were right. I've just returned from Arras where I saw the real Jean Valjean.'

'The . . . *real* Jean Valjean?' the mayor repeated dully. Once again he couldn't comprehend what Javert was saying. How could this be?

'Yes. Two weeks ago a man who called himself Champmathieu was arrested outside Arras for poaching apples. At the departmental prison, a convict took one look at Champmathieu and said, 'I know him. We were in prison in Toulon twenty years ago.'

'I didn't believe it,' Javert continued. 'I went to Arras to see for myself. Well, there's no question. Champmathieu *is* Valjean. I apologize, monsieur. I look at you now and it's obvious you're not a convict.'

'Now you don't think I'm a convict,' said Valjean carefully, part of his brain still fixed on the idea that this might be Javert's trap.

Inspector Javert shook his head vigorously. 'Of course I don't. I've seen Valjean with my own eyes. I must have been out of my mind to think a great man like you could be a criminal.'

'This man . . . he admits he's Valjean?' asked the mayor slowly.

Javert made a little sound of disgust. 'Of course not. He pretends to be a halfwit who can't understand the charges. What else can he do? Valjean has broken parole. That calls for life imprisonment.'

'Life imprisonment,' echoed Valjean dully.

'I left a deposition,' Javert continued. 'But they don't

need my testimony. Brevet, a trustee, made the original identification, and now two other convicts, Chenildieu and Cochepaille, have come forward. They knew Valjean even better than I. They will identify him at the trial.'

Chenildieu and Cochepaille! Jean Valjean remembered those names well. They had been his comrades on the galleys, if convicts might be said to have comrades. Now, for the first time, he began to suspect that this might not be a contrivance of Javert's after all. Perhaps it wasn't charade, but the real thing.

Yet it still troubled him. How could Chenildieu and Cochepaille identify as Jean Valjean anybody other than himself? Was the resemblance between Champmathieu and Valjean so remarkable that one might be mistaken for the other? Or, perhaps, had the other two convicts made some kind of deal with the authorities, maybe to reduce their own sentences in exchange for their trial testimony? Either way, they would in effect be sentencing a man who was not Jean Valjean to a lifetime of imprisonment.

'When is the trial?' asked Valjean.

'Tomorrow.'

'Tomorrow,' echoed Valjean thoughtfully. 'How long will the trial take?'

'No more than an afternoon. The evidence is overwhelming. I returned immediately so you could dismiss me and press charges for slander.' Javert was back on that again; the subject made Valjean very uncomfortable. Only he himself knew that the inspector had committed no slander.

The mayor had a great deal to think about. 'I need to consider . . . I was just on my way home. Walk with me, Javert.'

The two men left the factory together and walked side by side through the melting snow of the icy streets in the direction of *Monsieur le maire*'s modest home. For several minutes neither spoke, then Valjean broke the silence at last.

'Javert, you are a . . . stern man,' he said, searching for the kindest word. 'But you're honourable. Your offence is minor. I want you to remain prefect.'

'*Monsieur le maire*, that's impossible!' Javert cried out, genuinely shocked. How could the mayor, Montreuil's highest authority, dismiss a deep-dyed offence as 'minor'? It was almost insulting.

Valjean tried to calm the man down. 'You've exaggerated your offence.'

But Javert would not allow himself to be pacified. This affair had been weighing on his rigid conscience like a heavy stone. The events at Arras had come as a complete and unpleasant surprise to him. He'd had a taste of triumph; he was so close, he'd thought, to holding *Monsieur le maire* in the palm of his hand. He was getting ready to close his fingers in a death grip.

One sworn statement by a couple of convicts and Javert's hand was suddenly empty. Worse, he had proved to be wrong. Wrong! Almost worst of all, the Paris prefecture of police would learn of it, and the information would go on the inspector's record. At the very least. His spotless reputation for duty would be stained, a prospect he couldn't endure.

But the worst thing about the whole Arras fiasco was that Inspector Javert now knew himself to have transgressed against an innocent man. He had defied authority, only to have his defiance come back to slap him in the face. And it was that for which he demanded to be punished. This he would accept with all the arrogance of humility.

'I have not exaggerated, monsieur. I resented you. I chaffed at your authority and out of revenge I slandered you. If a subordinate of mine had done that, I would have broken him. You said just now I am stern. I am not stern. I am harsh. I have treated others who break the law harshly, and I was right. If I should now treat myself less harshly, that would mean all my past acts were unjustified. You must punish me, monsieur, or my life will have been meaningless.'

Valjean sighed deeply. It was very difficult for him to understand a man whose soul was so inflexible and so unforgiving. To the inspector, mercy was not allowable, and forgiveness the worst punishment of all. 'Then blame me, Javert,' he said, looking into the other man's eyes.

The inspector stopped and turned to the mayor, dark eyes meeting blue ones. 'Blame you, *Monsieur le maire?*'

Valjean nodded. 'I order you to forgive yourself. Blame me for that mercy. You will remain prefect. Those are my orders.' Even as he spoke, something inside him cried out strongly against his words. Something inside him longed to dismiss Javert and make him leave Montreuil for ever. To buy his own safety at the cost of the other man's honour.

But he could not. Jean Valjean knew that Inspector Javert was right; the man he called *Monsieur le maire was* a liar and a fugitive, a breaker of paroles, a destroyer of documents, a common criminal worthy of a lifetime of hard labour.

Javert was silent, his thoughts in turmoil. But the mayor had authority over him, and he did not dare to disobey. Reluctantly, he agreed to stay on. He lowered his head in assent.

If Javert's thoughts were tortured, how much more so were Jean Valjean's! Everything seemed to happen so suddenly. Thanks to events at Arras, suspicion had been diverted away from him, and he was once again *Monsieur le maire* to Javert and the rest of the world. Once the trial was over and this Champmathieu sent away in the identity of 'Jean Valjean', the real Valjean would be safe for ever. The books would be closed.

On the other hand, the wrong man would be sentenced to life imprisonment. A man whom Javert described as a halfwit who didn't even understand the charges against him! And the only hand that could be held out to save him was the hand that would condemn itself to the same fate.

But then again – let us suppose that this Champmathieu is about the same age as the real Jean Valjean. And suppose, moreover, that he was merely sentenced to ten or fifteen years for the original offence, poaching another man's apples off the trees. Wouldn't that really amount to the same life sentence? Could Champmathieu be expected to survive ten or fifteen years' hard labour? So what difference could it possibly make under which name he served out his time?

And wasn't a wealthy, religious man who provided employment to others and made generous philanthropic contributions a more worthy member of society than a half-witted drifter who stole apples? *I will double my good works*, vowed Valjean to himself. *I will spend every waking hour in charitable pursuits. I will be worthy of Champmathieu's sacrifice.* His unwilling, unwitting sacrifice.

*After all, all Montreuil counts on its* Monsieur le maire, he told himself. What about his factory and the many workers he employed, who depended on him for their living? What about Fantine and her little Cosette? He'd made promises in that direction, promises of support and protection. What would they do, all of them, if *Monsieur le maire* was languishing in prison for life?

Jean Valjean entered his house and went upstairs immediately to see Fantine. His mind, however, remained ill at ease.

Fantine was not well today. Feverish and coughing, she

was twisting this way and that on her pillows. Her anxiety for her daughter, whom she had expected to see a week ago, made her temperature rise. Her hair was tangled and wet with perspiration. The attending sister bathed her hands and cheeks with a cool cloth, but nothing could bring Fantine ease except the sight of Cosette.

She rallied a little when the mayor came in, and allowed him to help her into a sitting position. When he showed her the letter and declared his intention to go personally to fetch Cosette, she even smiled. Weakly, she signed her name to the authorization he'd brought her.

'Will you go get her today?'

'Yes. Tonight.' It was best to get out of town right away, thought Valjean.

Something in his voice or his face struck Fantine as different. He appeared terribly troubled, as though wrestling with some great problem. 'Is something wrong?' she asked breathlessly.

In answer, the mayor leaned over and dropped a kiss on the young woman's forehead. Her small hand, surprisingly strong, grabbed at his jacket, preventing him from moving away.

'Monsieur,' she said earnestly, her face very close to his so that she could see his eyes, 'I'm going to do my best. I'm going to get better for my girl. But if He chooses to take me, will you look after Cosette?' she begged. 'I know I don't have a right. So many people depend on you. I'm being selfish . . .'

Her breathless words, uttered with such an effort, moved him greatly. Valjean wrapped his strong arms around Fantine in a loving embrace. 'You and Cosette will always be safe with me. I swear it.'

Reassured, Fantine loosened her grip on his jacket and fell back on to the pillows. Cosette would be safe. She had the mayor's solemn vow for it and she had seen the truth of it in his face. As Valjean left the sickroom, Fantine closed her eyes wearily.

So Jean Valjean went to bed with his mind made up. In the morning he would go to Montfermeil, not Arras. His own security was more important than that of a dull-witted thief. He would stay away from Champmathieu's trial.

But he couldn't sleep; his thoughts were a constant torture. He tossed on the narrow chairs while his conscience tormented him. His head ached ferociously as he wrestled with his demons. He had planned for none of this. When Inspector Javert had first arrived in Montreuil, Jean Valjean had made a plan for escape, a simple plan. Get a lot of money, then cut and run. He'd prepared the money; it still lay buried in the little forest.

At that time, nobody else's fate was involved in the plan. Apart from his mayoral duties Valjean had no responsibilities. Now things were very different. Now a man stood accused of a crime he did not commit; his only crime was that he resembled the fugitive Jean Valjean.

Even Fantine and Cosette were not as pressing on Valjean's mind as Champmathieu. If he ran, he could legally hand his little house over to Fantine's ownership, and provide her with enough money to live on comfortably for ever. Even if she died of her illness – God forbid! – Cosette would be well provided for. But as for Champmathieu, money could not buy him out of his predicament. No, only Valjean's own surrender would take that burden off the poor man's shoulders. In the morning, he would go to Arras.

On the other hand, the retarded man was to be punished anyway, for the theft of apples, so why should two men suffer the same fate when only one had to bear the burden? Wasn't the misidentification of Champmathieu a gift from

God Himself, thought Valjean, and wouldn't it be sinful to refuse it? He would not go to Arras.

But wasn't it even more sinful to accept? Suppose it was Satan holding out the gift, not God? For years he'd tried to live a purely Christian life. Was it Christian to allow another to pay for his crimes? As far as his merits versus those of Champmathieu went, weren't all human souls, evil and good alike, fully equal in the sight of God? Only God, on that Day of Judgment, could assess their true worth. It was no more than vanity and sinful pride for Valjean to expect that on the dreaded day his own soul would shine more brightly than that of an apple thief.

And yet – the thought of being free for ever from fear, of never having to cut and run and become a fugitive again – how wonderfully tempting! How easily attained! All Valjean would have to do was keep his mouth shut and stay away from the trial at Arras.

What could be easier? Even before Javert had knocked on his door today, Jean Valjean had made his mind up to go to Montfermeil himself, get little Cosette back from the greedy Thenardiers, and bring her back to Fantine. He'd even had a letter of authorization drawn up for that purpose, hadn't he? Wouldn't that act in itself be the saving of two innocent lives? He had already formulated the plan of going the very next day, and Montfermeil was in the opposite direction to Arras.

So all he had to do was to say nothing and stick to his original plan. Whatever happened in the courtroom at Arras had nothing to do with *Monsieur le maire* of Montreuil. With his mind made up at last, the exhausted Jean Valjean fell into a restless sleep.

## Chapter Fifteen

### CHAMPMATHIEU ON TRIAL

Jean Valjean hired a carriage and driver to carry him north to Montfermeil. They set off at 4.30 in the morning, hours before the sun was up. It was a quiet trip; the roads were empty at this ungodly time of night. The clop-clop of the horse's shod hooves on the road was very soothing. It was the perfect opportunity for the mayor to get some sleep. But he couldn't sleep. His thoughts kept tangling around one another like the ancient classical statue of the Laocoon, in which men and serpents are locked in a death struggle. He tried to keep himself focused on two objectives – getting Cosette back from the Thenardiers and home to Fantine, and being safe at last from Javert and others like him who might follow.

But his thoughts kept turning back to Arras and the trial set for this morning. How could it be otherwise? For the first time in more than six years, security lay within Jean Valjean's grasp. Not the false security of forged documents and a money box hidden under a tree, but the real security of an unassailable reputation, of a stain lifted from him and transferred elsewhere. He'd made his decision, and he believed he'd made the correct one. So why did he keep thinking about the tribulations of one Champmathieu, a wretched, ragged apple poacher?

Lost in his thoughts, Valjean was unaware of the miles

passing below the carriage wheels. So he was startled to realize that the coach had already reached Digne, which was on their route to Montfermeil. He saw ahead of him the spires of the cathedral, and soon they were passing the bishop's small house, which had stood empty since the bishop's death some years ago. The new bishop turned his back on poverty, and held court in a mansion befitting his grand rank.

'Stop!' cried Valjean, rapping on the roof of the carriage. The mystified coachman obeyed. The mayor got down from the carriage and went to the gateway of the cottage. The iron gate was almost off its hinges, rusty with age and disuse. Valjean put one hand on it and, suddenly, as though the gate were a magical entrance into other worlds, as soon as his hand touched the rusting iron he was struck by a clear vision from the past.

All at once, it was not night around him but bright morning. He was years younger, standing in that little garden, looking down at the bishop. The old man, his injured head wrapped in a bandage, was stuffing heavy silver candlesticks into Valjean's knapsack. He was looking directly into Valjean's eyes. There was an expression of such purity and goodness on the bishop's face that it was painful for Valjean to witness it. The old man's gaze seemed to pierce through his chest until it reached his very soul.

And once again he heard those words, as clearly as though the bishop were speaking them in the here and now.

'Jean Valjean, my brother, you no longer belong to evil. With this silver, I've bought your soul. I've ransomed you from fear and hatred. And now ... I give you back to God.'

The vision vanished. In its place was a great emptiness, the emptiness of possibility. For the first time in many hours, Jean Valjean's thoughts were clear. He turned and made his way back to the carriage. 'Take me to Arras, please,' he said to the driver.

The driver's eyes opened wide in astonishment. 'Arras? But ... but ... then we've been going in the wrong direction.'

*Exactly*, thought Valjean. *For years I have been going in the wrong direction*. 'Yes, it was a mistake,' he said out loud. 'Turn us around.'

The driver flicked his whip and the horse made a slow semicircle, so that the coach now faced south. 'To Arras, then,' the coachman said, and Valjean nodded. A great weight seemed to have been lifted from his spirit.

'To Arras.'

By the time they reached the courtroom at Arras, it was mid-morning. Jean Valjean felt a sudden stab of hope. What if he were too late? What if Champmathieu had already been sentenced? He ordered his driver to wait for him, just in case.

A tall uniformed official was guarding the heavy doors.

'Is this the courtroom?' asked Valjean.

'It is that.'

'May I enter?' asked Valjean politely.

'Can't let you in.' The doorkeeper shook his head. 'It's full.'

'Full?' Valjean heard the words with mingled relief and dismay. 'There are no seats?' Maybe he wouldn't be called upon to stay after all. Perhaps they wouldn't want or need his confession. Justice might be well served even without his participation.

'Jammed,' the doorkeeper said with some satisfaction. 'We've got two great cases. Just finished with the woman Limosin. She murdered her baby. Unfortunately, they ruled out premeditation. All she got was life imprisonment. Now they're doing Valjean – a galley convict who broke parole. Take one look at him, you know he's evil.'

So he wasn't too late after all! 'He looks like a bad man?' asked Valjean, as a thin ray of hope dawned. Perhaps this was fate, God trying to tell him something. If he couldn't get into the courtroom and this Champmathieu was a really bad fellow . . . perhaps, after all, he wasn't needed here. He'd tried, hadn't he? Surely good intentions counted for something.

'Crazy and cruel eyes,' said the doorkeeper, who prided himself on his expert insights into good and evil, innocence and guilt, formed after many years of opening and closing a courtroom door. 'You can see he's capable of the most heinous crimes. He'll get hard labour for life. It's a shame,' he added. 'They should execute him.'

'So I can't get in?'

'No, not a chance.'

Well, he'd done the best he could. What else could anyone ask of him? God would have to be satisfied with his gesture. His carriage was waiting. Valjean had turned to leave when the doorkeeper's next words stopped him in his tracks.

'Unless . . . unless Monsieur is a public official,' said the man, eyeing Valjean's expensive coat and polished boots. 'There are two seats reserved for them right behind the judge. Best seats in the house.'

That clinched it. His destiny demanded a confrontation. Valjean sighed inwardly and turned back. 'I'm the mayor of Montreuil,' he announced in a hollow voice, and the door was opened wide with a flourish. The high reputation of *Monsieur le maire* of Montreuil had reached Arras.

The trial of Champmathieu was already under way when Jean Valjean took his seat behind the judge, who was wearing a sumptuous robe of office and a thickly curled wig. Despite his high position, the man was no more than five and thirty years old.

'This is an honour, *Monsieur le maire*,' the judge greeted him cordially.

'Thank you, *Monsieur le président*,' Valjean replied with equal cordiality, and his eyes raked over the courtroom. The doorkeeper was right. There was not an empty seat in the entire room. And upstairs, in the gallery, a crowd of ragtag spectators regarded the spectacle below with the glee of children at a circus. Over the judge's shoulder Valjean could see the prisoner.

Of Inspector Javert there was no sign. True to his word, he had stayed away from the trial. No doubt the humiliation of his 'error' was more than he could be expected to bear. Valjean almost smiled. Poor Javert! To be deprived by his own pride of his greatest triumph, to have lost the chance of seeing himself thoroughly vindicated! Most of all, to be absent when his old enemy confessed his crimes! Poor Javert indeed!

The accused was sitting in the dock. Champmathieu was a tall man, broad of shoulder and bearing a striking resemblance to the Jean Valjean of his convict days. He was wearing rags, and was filthy and unkempt. His hair was long, and his beard rough. But there was one striking difference between the two men. Whereas Jean Valjean, even at his lowest ebb as a convict, had been a man of ferocious intelligence, Champmathieu had the dull eye and slack mouth of the mentally challenged. He was of low intelligence and little comprehension.

'Continue with the examination,' said the judge. The prosecutor nodded. He was even younger than the judge, only about thirty, and his robe and wig were far more modest. But he had an air of what the ancient Romans called 'gravitas', a serious solemnity.

'You pretend to be simple,' the prosecutor addressed Champmathieu. 'So I give you a simple question to answer. Are you or are you not the convict Jean Valjean?'

The prisoner in the dock nodded vigorously. 'In the first place . . .' he began, then stopped, looking confused. 'What was the fist place?'

'Your Honour,' said the prosecutor, 'the accused refuses to answer. That proves his guilt.'

*That proves nothing*, thought Valjean, *except that the man has no understanding of what's going on here*.

The word 'guilt' seemed to penetrate the fog in Champmathieu's addled brain. He grew excited, and started to rise up from his seat, but the bailiffs pushed him down again. Specks of foam dotted the corners of his lips. 'You're wicked!' he cried. 'That's what I was going to say. Only . . . I forgot your name.'

At this the gallery roared with appreciative laughter. This was better than a play. And they already knew the ending. The poor buffoon below was to be found guilty and sent up for life. They shouted and jeered happily, exactly like ancient Romans watching a Christian being fed to a lion in the amphitheatre. Bread and circuses, that was what the mob was looking for in this courtroom. Bread and circuses, with the French judiciary as the Emperor Nero.

Champmathieu was first startled then gratified by the onlookers' mockery. His feeble mind accepted their laughter as a kind of tribute. He began to play to the gallery. 'I'm a person who . . . what's the word? I'm one of those who don't eat every day. I'm . . . I'm hungry! That's the word for it. When I saw this branch of apples, lying on the ground, I took a couple. I was hungry.'

As the men and women in the gallery laughed again, Valjean felt a strong pang of pity for the poor creature in the prisoner's dock. The people were right to mock, he thought, but not to mock the accused. No, this trial was itself a mockery. Couldn't these people – the judge and the prosecutor and the other lawyers – see that this miserable man was helpless? There was no way he should have been called to testify on his own behalf.

'You've already been found guilty of poaching,' the judge said sternly. 'This is about a different offence. Answer the prosecutor's questions.'

'He asked a question?' The prisoner sounded genuinely puzzled, whereupon the spectators roared with laughter once again.

'Are you or are you not Jean Valjean?' demanded the judge.

Champmathieu tried to think. 'You say I was born in Faverolles. That's very clever, telling me where I was born, because it's more than I know. My parents were tramps. If you ask me, Jean Valjean was lucky. Not everyone gets to be born in a house.'

The prosecutor turned to the judge, and made his appeal. '*Monsieur le président*, in view of the shrewdly calculated denials of the accused, who is trying to pass himself off as an idiot, I call the witness Brevet to the stand.'

'So ordered,' the judge agreed.

A man of about sixty, dressed in a grey prison smock, was brought in and led to the witness stand. This stand was facing the judge, hence it also faced Jean Valjean, who was seated directly behind him. Valjean knew this man from long ago, from his old life. He stared hard at Brevet, as if daring the man to recognize him. But Brevet barely glanced at him, and showed no signs of recognition.

'Brevet,' began the prosecutor gravely, 'I remind you that what you say may destroy a man's life. You must be absolutely certain of your testimony.'

'My memory's good,' Brevet announced cheerfully. 'Best thing I got.'

'The accused will rise.' One of the bailiffs helped Champmathieu get to his feet.

'Do you recognize this man?' the prosecutor demanded of the witness.

'Yes.' Brevet nodded. 'I was the first to recognize him. So I ought to get credit.'

'Never mind who was first,' snapped the prosecutor. 'Who is he?'

'That's Jean Valjean. We served nineteen years together in the galleys. He came to Toulon in 1796 and went out in 1815. He looks older, of course. Looks stupider too, but that's probably age.'

'*Monsieur le président*, I call the convict Chenildieu to the stand.'

'You can step down,' the judge ordered Brevet. 'The accused will remain standing.'

Chenildieu, a small man dressed in the red smock and green cap of the life prisoner, took Brevet's place on the witness stand.

'I repeat my warning,' the prosecutor said solemnly. 'A man's life can be destroyed by your answer. Do you recognize the accused?'

'I can't help but recognize him.' Chenildieu shrugged. 'We did five years on the same chain. What's the matter?' he challenged Champmathieu, laughing coarsely. 'No hello? Didn't you miss me?'

'Hello,' said Champmathieu sheepishly, and the courtroom rocked with laughter.

'Sit down,' the judge ordered Chenildieu. He'd heard evidence enough from this one.

'I call Cochepaille to the stand,' announced the prosecutor.

Cochepaille too was dressed in the uniform of a lifer.

He was tall and very hairy, almost ape-like, and wasn't a lot smarter than the poor fellow on trial. 'I warn you as well,' the prosecutor instructed, 'your answer can ruin a man. Do you recognize the accused?'

'Yeah. He's Jean Valjean. We called him John the Crowbar 'cause he's so strong. He's a good guy.'

Valjean could tolerate this scene no longer. A man innocent of this offence was being crushed by the heavy weight of mistaken evidence. He leaned forward in his seat and whispered to the judge. 'May I address the court, *Monsieur le président?*'

The judge raised one eyebrow, but the eminent and famous mayor of Montreuil was not someone to be denied. 'Yes, certainly, *Monsieur le maire,*' he replied courteously, although he was puzzled.

Jean Valjean got slowly to his feet. There was no going back now. 'Brevet, Chenildieu,' he called out in a deep, strong voice. 'Look at me. Don't you recognize me?' The prosecutor drew in a sharp breath, not knowing what might be coming next.

The baffled men and women in the courtroom gallery stirred and began to nudge one another, murmuring in surprise. Something was going on here, something different, something interesting, but they weren't quite sure what. Nevertheless, their curiosity and attention were excited, and their laughter trickled away into silence.

Jean Valjean left his chair and came down into the courtroom, close to the witnesses. 'I recognize you, Brevet. Remember the checked braces you used to wear? You were an informer at Toulon, and I see you're still a snitch.'

Brevet stared back, astonished. His memory twitched and revived a little as he brought to mind the face and form of the old Valjean, the one he knew back on the galleys. The tall man standing before him triggered that memory. Despite his fine clothing and his cleanliness, he looked and sounded very familiar. 'J . . . Jean?' he stammered.

'Yes. Hello, Brevet. And you, Chenildieu.' The audience murmur grew louder as the gallery began to comprehend something of the wonder it was witnessing here.

'Don't look at my fancy threads,' Valjean continued. 'Don't look at my scraped chin. Look in my eyes. You called yourself 'godless', right, Chenildieu? And you've got a scar on your right shoulder. I gave it to you the night you tried to kill me. Remember? When I pinned you on the stove.'

'It *is* you,' breathed Chenildieu, and a woman in the audience cried out, 'Oh my God!' The judge uttered a gasp of astonishment, and the prosecutor scowled as he watched his case against Champmathieu evaporating.

'Show the court your scar,' ordered Valjean. Without question, Chenildieu obeyed, pulling the smock away from his neck and revealing an old burn scar on his shoulder.

'And you, Cochepaille, in the bend of your left arm there's a date tattooed. It's the first of March 1815, the date of the Emperor Napoleon's landing at Cannes. Show them.'

Astonished, the convict rolled up his sleeve and there was the tattoo, almost lost in the fur of his hairy arm. Valjean turned to face the judge, who was staring down at him in amazement, the gavel held limp in his hand.

'I know them, *Monsieur le président*, and they know me,' he said firmly. 'I'm the man you want. I am Jean Valjean.'

*I am Jean Valjean.*

The announcement was met with stunned silence in the courtroom. It was broken by Cochepaille, who called out, 'Hey, he's right! It's John the Crowbar! How do you like that?'

Now the courtroom exploded in an excited buzz, every-body talking at once, while the judge rapped his gavel in vain, demanding silence. He still couldn't quite understand. How could so prominent a philanthropist, so great a magistrate as *Monsieur le maire* of Montreuil, present himself in this courtroom as a fugitive and felon? No, something was terribly wrong. This must be a kind of misguided self-sacrifice, some insane act designed to spare a worthless convict.

'*Monsieur le maire*,' the judge began, 'I know you to be a kind man, but this is—'

'Kind? A kind man?' Valjean interrupted, agonized. Nothing could stop him from confessing everything now, from spilling out into the courtroom all the secrets that had weighed on his conscience for so many years. 'Before I was arrested I was as ignorant as Cochepaille, but not kind. In the galleys, I was as mean and 'godless' and as devious as Brevet, but not kind. I'm still not kind. I've tried to become an honest man. I've tried to repay the world for my crimes, and I thought . . . I thought only yesterday I was about to . . . . about to find some happiness.' He stumbled over the words, remembering his affection for Fantine and his hopes for Cosette, then he recovered his composure.

'It's a terrible thing to say, but I wish I could keep my mouth shut and let this poor wretch suffer for me. Continue your investigation, *Monsieur le président*, and you will find more proof that I am Jean Valjean.

'I have things to attend to. When you're ready to arrest me, the court knows where I can be found.'

And, before anyone could move to stop him, Jean Valjean pushed his way through the stunned onlookers and out to his waiting carriage.

'Montreuil,' he said to the driver. 'And hurry.'

## Chapter Sixteen

### THE DEATH OF FANTINE

Jean Valjean arrived in Montreuil several hours later –
tired, dusty and in a great hurry. Before he reached
the city, he transferred from his conspicuous carriage to a
modest wagon, easily overlooked by any possible pursuers.
He'd bought it on the road, right from under the driver.

On reaching Montreuil, he drove the wooden wagon first
to his factory. By now it was almost sunrise. He ran up the
stairs and knocked on the door of the little apartment where
his clerk lived, on the second floor of the factory building.
The man opened the door in his nightshirt, his hair sticking
out in all directions, eyes still heavy with sleep.

'I need you in the office right away,' the mayor said
without ceremony, leading the half-awake, baffled clerk
to his office and seating him at his own desk.

Valjean knew that it was only a matter of a few hours or
even less before Javert would come searching for him. He
didn't have much time left, and there was much he had to do
to wind up his affairs. While he paced back and forth, dictating
his intentions to his clerk, the man sat stunned, unable at first
to comprehend the size and shape of his employer's plan.

Yet it was a simple plan, simply expressed, and it wasn't
long before the clerk realized that *Monsieur le maire* was
quite serious about what he wanted to do. This was no
mere rich man's whim. The clerk began to scribble rapidly,

covering many sheets of foolscap paper. At last the ledger entries were completed, and the appropriate papers were soon drawn up to Valjean's satisfaction. He signed them and set his seal to them.

That part of his plan completed, Valjean took the wagon home to his little house, where he washed hastily and changed into fresh clothing. He found the nursing sister, Sister Simplicity, in the kitchen, preparing a dose of medication for Fantine.

'Monsieur?' The nun turned, surprised to see him. 'You're back so soon?'

'I don't have the girl yet. I'll be leaving in an hour. How is she?' Valjean's voice dropped as he asked about Fantine; he knew that the news could not be good.

Sister Simplicity shook her wimpled head sadly. 'The cough's much worse. There's blood all the time now. She's . . . I think she's only hanging on to see her daughter.' The nun's eyes were sad; she had come to care for the pathetic young woman she was nursing.

'I need to see Fantine before I go. If you must wake her, do so.'

The sun was coming up as the uniformed rider spurred his horse up to the city hall. On a stone bench outside, Captain Beauvais sat taking a break, smoking his pipe. He watched lazily as the rider dismounted and tied up his horse. The man appeared to be in a towering hurry.

'Excuse me,' the rider said to the captain. 'I have an urgent message for Inspector Javert.'

'I'll take it up to him,' said Beauvais, holding his hand out, but the rider held on tightly to the paper. 'Can't. Delivery by hand.' He lowered his voice to a whisper. 'This is a special warrant from Arras.'

'All right, follow me,' Beauvais conceded. 'I hope it's good news. The inspector's in a foul mood.'

He led the way inside and up the stairs to Javert's office, little thinking that in a minute or two the inspector's mood would change totally.

Jean Valjean tiptoed into Fantine's room and sank into the chair next to her bed. Her eyes were closed. He watched her silently, while his mind went over the events at Arras. He was aware that he had very little time left; the authorities would be after him by now, looking to arrest him, with the bloodhound Javert baying in the lead.

The young woman slept restlessly, tossing with fever. Her cheeks were stained bright red, the rest of her skin so pale that light seemed to shine through it. Her tangled hair was wet with sweat and plastered in little curls to her forehead. Valjean thought he saw death unmistakably in her face. The sister was right; Fantine could not last long. As Valjean watched over her sadly, she opened her eyes.

'Monsieur, you're back—' She tried to rise, looking for her daughter, but Valjean shook his head. With gentle hands he settled her back among her pillows. Sister Simplicity bent over the head of the bed, ministering to her, wiping the bloody foam from her lips.

'No, no. Don't excite yourself,' he told her in a near-whisper. 'I don't have Cosette yet. Please don't worry. I'm leaving in a few minutes. I can get to the Thenardiers' and be back here tomorrow night.'

Fantine sighed. Tomorrow night. Only one more day and night until Cosette would be here. It was so hard to hang on. 'I'll be strong and wait.' She tried to smile through trembling lips.

'Fantine, I have to ask you—'

'I was dreaming just now,' she said softly. 'About you

and me and Cosette. We were at her confirmation. She looked so beautiful and so happy. But she didn't know me. And I cried—' The girl's face began to crumple as she remembered the lost feeling of her dream.

'Fantine, if something were to happen, if you couldn't care for Cosette—'

'I know I'm not going to live long, monsieur,' she answered simply. Reaching her hands to her throat, she unfastened her little necklace and laid it in Valjean's hands. 'Would you give this to my Cosette? I bought it for her. Could you give it to her? Please?'

Valjean's fingers closed around the necklace. 'Yes, I'll give it to her,' he promised.

'She can stay here with you, can't she?' begged Fantine. 'She'll grow up to be a fine respectable young woman. You'll raise her, won't you? Promise me, monsieur!' Tears formed in her eyes, matching the tears in Valjean's.

'Yes, I'll raise her. I promise,' he answered gravely.

'He lies so well, doesn't he?' Javert stood in the doorway, his clothing awry, his usually sombre face alight with elation and his voice trembling with triumph. He was flushed and panting, having run here on foot at top speed the moment he read the warrant from Arras. This was the most joyous moment in his long and joyless career. 'He's had a lot of practice,' he sneered. 'A lifetime of lies.'

At the sight of Inspector Javert, Fantine started in fright and screamed out loud. She grabbed at the mayor's coat. 'Monsieur, save me!'

'Don't worry,' Valjean said gently. 'He's not here for you.' He disengaged Fantine's grip. 'All right, Javert, I'm coming.'

'What does he want, *Monsieur le maire*?' Fantine cried shrilly. The sight of Javert terrified her so much that she began to tremble. Sister Simplicity tried to draw the blankets up over the girl's shivering body, but Fantine pushed her away. She couldn't take her eyes off Javert, like a small bird in the presence of a cobra.

'He isn't mayor any more,' yelled Javert, seizing Valjean by his collar and trying to pull the large man out of his chair.

Valjean stood up meekly. 'Inspector, please,' he whispered urgently. 'Let me talk to you in private.'

Javert's eyes sparkled with malice. 'What? Speak up! People don't mumble when they talk to me.'

'Monsieur? What's wrong?' begged Fantine, near hysteria. She didn't understand what was happening here. Why was the inspector bullying the mayor? It didn't make sense. Her head ached furiously trying to puzzle it out.

'I want to ask you a favour,' Valjean whispered, so that Fantine wouldn't hear.

'I told you to speak up,' Javert snarled.

Valjean began to speak very rapidly, as though racing against time. 'Give me two days,' he pleaded. 'To fetch her child. I'll pay. I'll pay anything you like. You can even come with me—'

'Are you joking?' laughed Javert harshly. 'Let you go for two days? Do you think I'm that stupid?' A bitter note erupted in his voice. 'Yes. You do. And why not? How you must have laughed—'

'Javert . . . I *beg* you . . .'

'—while you forgave me. Oh, generous, kind mayor.' Javert's lips twisted sarcastically. 'No! No, you can't fetch things for your whore!' he spat. 'You're going to the galleys. And this bitch is going to jail.'

Fantine couldn't breathe. She struggled to sit up in bed, wheezing, trying in vain to get some air into her lungs. '*Monsieur le maire*, what does he mean?' she cried.

Javert whirled on her in fury and hatred. 'Listen to me, slut! You'll never see your daughter again. You're going to prison. He can't save you this time. There's no *Monsieur le maire* any more. He's a criminal. He's from the galleys and that's where he's going.'

The nun tried to shield Fantine from Javert with her own body, spreading her full black skirts out to keep the girl from the sight of the policeman's mad-dog face. Javert shoved Valjean forward, towards the door.

Valjean lost his balance, stumbled and fell, his head banging the table that stood beside Fantine's bed. Fantine uttered a loud scream and collapsed back on to her pillows, her eyes rolling up in her head, her mouth opening slackly. She lay utterly still. The sister bent over her anxiously, searching the young woman's face for a sign of life.

Valjean held on to the table leg as though bracing himself to get up, but still he lay on the floor. He was thinking furiously about his next move, if he had one. All his prisoner's survival skills were starting to kick in.

'Get up!' yelled Javert, kicking him viciously.

All in one motion, Jean Valjean rose from the floor, clutching the table in his hand by its leg. He smashed the table against the wall. Water from the washing pan spilled over Fantine, the bed, the floor. Bottles of medicine rolled on to the floor, some of them breaking, spilling their contents. Now Valjean was fully erect and facing Inspector Javert. In his hand was the table leg, a thick bludgeon, a weapon. His ancient instincts, the instincts of a convict, had taken him over completely.

For a long moment, the two men stood glaring at each other. Valjean's face was wild and primitive, Javert's alight with an incandescent joy. The joy of the hunt. Now he had his quarry in full sight. *Monsieur le maire* of Montreuil was no more. In his place loomed the brutish Jean Valjean, fugitive, convict, evil-doer. This was the man Javert remembered from long ago, this evil savage with powerful hunched shoulders and glowering face.

It was Inspector Javert's deepest conviction that evil could never change. Instead, under the veneer of civilization the brute would always lurk, ready to come out snarling. Javert's view of the criminal was of something subhuman, and Jean Valjean, with his wild eyes and the wooden club in his hand, seemed to him the living validation of his theory.

'At last ... It's a pleasure to see you again, Valjean,' hissed Javert.

At this moment Sister Simplicity dropped to her knees by the bedside, crossed herself and began to pray. Valjean turned his head slightly. Out of the corner of his eye he could see Fantine lying limp, her eyes open, staring, bloody spittle on her lips. She wasn't breathing.

'Sister?' he cried, but the nun's head only dropped lower as she fingered her rosary and prayed for the immortal soul of the poor sinner, the miserable Fantine.

'You killed her!' Crushed by grief and despair, Valjean dropped the table leg.

'Show me your hands,' Javert ordered. Still stunned, Valjean obeyed without question. He held his hands out, and Javert pulled a set of handcuffs from his uniform pocket. The policeman moved towards his enemy and snapped one of the iron cuffs around Valjean's right wrist.

But before he could fasten the cuff, the powerful Valjean moved swiftly, pulling the policeman's right hand towards him and switching the handcuff from his own wrist to Javert's. He snapped the cuff shut and shoved Javert up against the wall, securing his other wrist and locking the handcuffs. The tables were now turned; the hunter had become the prey. Grabbing a fistful of the inspector's hair, Valjean yanked his head away from the wall.

'There's nowhere to hide, Valjean,' gasped Javert, defiant.

In answer, the tall man only growled and smashed Javert's

forehead against the wall. This was the bastard who had killed Fantine!

'You don't have papers!'

And again, Valjean smashed Javert's face into the wall, even harder this time. He wanted to see the man's head explode like a melon dropped on a stone pavement.

'I'll ... I'll find ... you ...' mumbled the inspector through a red haze of pain. Another crash of his forehead into the wall, and the inspector slumped to the ground, unconscious.

Breathing hard, Jean Valjean let go of Javert's hair and turned to the terrified nun, who shrank away in fear and confusion. By the furthest stretch of the imagination, there was no way that Sister Simplicity could equate this violent savage with the Christian man she knew, the kind and generous *Monsieur le maire*. She was afraid that this stranger would kill her and Inspector Javert.

But Valjean had no intention of harming anybody. His rage against Javert had passed, and he was now interested only in Fantine. He bent over the bed, searching her face to be sure that she was dead. With the gentlest touch imaginable, he closed her eyelids and bent to kiss her on the brow. Silently, he renewed his vow to her, that he would always care for and nurture Cosette. He would leave for Montfermeil now, and get the child away from her greedy keepers. Both of them would run and both would hide. He would take her with him wherever he went. He would keep his promise to Fantine, and give Cosette a good life, somehow.

Then Valjean withdrew a wad of bills from his pocket and pulled some of the money off. 'She repented, didn't she? She made peace with God?' he asked the nun.

'Yes, monsieur.'

Valjean thrust the money into her hands. 'Please, see that she's buried properly. And pray for her soul ...'

Sister Simplicity nodded and lifted a tear-stained face up to him. 'Yes, monsieur.'

Without another word, Valjean hurried from the room and down the stairs, heading for his wagon and escape. He had not a moment to waste. Grabbing a bag, he opened the street door, only to confront Captain Beauvais, who was standing outside. Valjean froze, and for a long moment the two men stared dumbly at each other.

'Are you a convict? Is that true?' Beauvais demanded.

'Yes.' Valjean could see no reason to lie. Not now. Not with Javert lying wounded and unconscious upstairs.

'Where's the inspector?' Beauvais wanted to know.

Valjean jerked his head to indicate the house. 'Inside.'

The police captain took his gun from its holster and pointed it at Jean Valjean. 'Did you kill him?'

Valjean shook his head.

'That's a pity,' smiled Beauvais. He turned his gun over, and handed it butt first to the tall man. Then he turned around, showing Valjean the back of his head. 'You'd better hit me hard enough to make a lump,' he said ruefully before he was knocked out.


'Where is he?' Javert demanded. His forehead was black and blue, and a large swelling was still forming over one eye. Behind him, Captain Beauvais was clutching a handkerchief to a painful lump on the back of his head. The two officers were followed by a sergeant and two gendarmes.

Valjean's clerk, his foreman and forewoman, sitting at their desks in the factory office, looked up startled as the police stormed in, with Javert at their head.

'He left a half-hour ago,' the clerk replied.

'On foot?' asked Javert impatiently.

'On a wagon.'

'Which way?' demanded Javert.

'The southern road,' the clerk said reluctantly. He hated to give his employer away, but he did not dare lie to the police. Inspector Javert intimidated him, just as he intimidated everyone he met. The clerk had no idea what *Monsieur le maire* might have done to bring the law down on himself, and he was certainly afraid to ask.

Inspector Javert snapped into action, barking out commands. 'Commandeer the mail-coach. Not you, Beauvais. You two. Go.' He turned to the clerk again. 'South? He went south? You're sure? Not to Paris?'

'Ask anybody.' The clerk shrugged. 'Everybody here saw him leave.'

'How much money did he take?'

The clerk shook his head. 'He didn't take any.'

But Javert did not believe him. 'Show me the books.' The clerk handed over the ledger, and Javert scanned it carefully. 'I don't understand. You say he transferred ownership of this factory?'

The clerk nodded. 'Yes. He's given the factory to all the employees. Here—' and he pointed out the appropriate ledger entries. 'Shares have been apportioned by seniority. He withdrew nothing for himself.'

In flight, Jean Valjean's first act was to retrieve his money from under the oak. He located the tree, checking the mark he'd carved in the trunk, and paced off the distance, then began to dig. Within minutes his spade had touched the metal of the box, and he hauled it up out of the ground. As he had expected, the money was still there, intact. Valjean smiled a bitter smile. Money was the least of his worries now. Working quickly, he filled up the bag he'd brought with him. There was more than enough in here to carry him many miles away. Paris was his destination. In Paris he thought he'd be safe.

# Chapter Seventeen

## THE CHASE

In the same hour that Jean Valjean was digging up his hidden money, Inspector Javert and two gendarmes, along with their sergeant, were climbing hurriedly into the commandeered two-horse mail carriage. The sergeant clambered into the driver's seat and took up the reins. Captain Beauvais, head bandaged, made an effort to get into the carriage with them, but Inspector Javert waved him off.

'You stay here, Beauvais. You probably have a concussion, and you should rest.' Beauvais obeyed without a murmur; his heart wasn't really into a chase after the man he had come to like and respect as *Monsieur le maire*.

As soon as everyone was on board, the sergeant yelled to the two horses, cracked the whip and they drove off swiftly, heading south. In the fever of pursuit, Inspector Javert jiggled impatiently on the seat next to his sergeant, as though by his movements he could make the carriage go faster.

Meanwhile, having retrieved his money, Jean Valjean was back in his wagon, driving north to make good his escape, as quickly as his horse would go. Which was not nearly fast enough, he knew. He expected that by now Javert and his men would be hot on his trail.

With any luck, the police would be starting off in the

wrong direction, because Valjean had deliberately turned south as he left the factory. It was his hope that his people would unwittingly give the police false clues without having to lie. Once out of sight of the factory, he'd backtracked his wagon north by another road until he reached the forest by the crossroads, intending to pick up his money and continue further north. His destination was Montfermeil and, beyond Montfermeil, Paris. A man and a little girl could lose themselves in Paris more easily than just about anywhere else in France, he thought. There were thousands of twists and turnings in the streets and alleys; many thousands of places to hide. With the money in the bag, he and Cosette could start a whole new life together.

But, even if Javert was in pursuit to the south, Valjean knew that, any time now, the inspector could order a change of direction. The police had a description of the wagon, and they knew what Jean Valjean looked like and was wearing. So, if no other traveller reported seeing him on the southern road, Javert would understand Valjean's tactic, and turn his forces to the north. He might already have dispatched a second force in the other direction. And, without a doubt, they would be driving a faster vehicle than Valjean's old wagon, probably with two horses to his single nag.

Jean Valjean was under no illusions about Inspector Javert. Even before his rise to prefect of police, Javert had long held a well-deserved reputation among convicts as a devil-inspired bloodhound. The man never let up; he was implacable. Once he had caught the scent, nothing but capture or death would put an end to the hunt. In pursuit of duty, Javert could not be turned aside. Jean Valjean's only hope was to throw Javert off the scent. Somehow he'd have to trick him; he couldn't hope to outrun him in this rig.

Valjean reined in suddenly, stopping short to avoid a disastrous collision with a peasant walking across the road behind a flock of geese. The horse reared up; it would have thrown Valjean from the driver's seat except for his firm hand on the reins. As he watched the peasant continuing to cross the road slowly, bent nearly double by age, his broad-brimmed hat shadowing his face, an idea began to form in Valjean's brain.

The mail carriage was too slow for Javert's liking. At this rate of travel they'd never catch up with the murderous Jean Valjean. He kept urging his sergeant to drive faster, faster. But the sergeant was having rouble with the horses. The road was far from perfect; it was pocked with holes and with winter damage. Pockets of muddy ice from a snowfall earlier in the week still dotted the road here and there, making for slick and dangerous driving. The horses were nervous, sensing the dangers of the surface. This was a road requiring prudence, not excessive speed.

But prudence was not in Inspector Javert's vocabulary in the pursuit of a fleeing criminal. 'Faster!' he kept shouting, punching his sergeant in the arm. 'Faster!'

'We're going too fast now, sir,' gasped the officer, trying hard to keep control of his steeds. Even as he spoke the words, the carriage veered, and the vehicle's right wheel dropped into a ditch. The coach shuddered and shook, nearly pitching the sergeant out on his head.

'Give me those reins!' yelled Javert, furious. 'Before you get us stuck in a ditch!' He pushed the sergeant out of the driver's seat and slid into it himself, grabbing the reins and snapping the horses hard with his whip. The animals neighed in fear and rolled their eyes, shaking their manes. But they obeyed the sting of the lash.

The police took off again at a more rapid clip, almost running down a peasant coming towards them on the road with his flock of geese, from the opposite direction. The birds squawked and spread their wings in confusion, dashing around crazily to get out of the mail-coach's way, while the peasant trudged on by, his old shoulders bowed, his expression unreadable under a broad-brimmed hat.

Inspector Javert had suffered a demoralizing blow when the Arras police had identified old Champmathieu as the fugitive Jean Valjean. His own accusations against *Monsieur le maire* of Montreuil had come back against him, staining his spotless record, and no doubt making him an object of scorn and derision at the police prefecture in Paris. To top it off, the incredible insult of Valjean's high-handedness in rejecting Javert's offer to resign, just as though he were an innocent man and not a damned criminal! Javert would never forgive him for that; he would pursue Valjean to the grave if it cost him his own life.

It was small consolation to Inspector Javert that Valjean now stood before the world revealed as that same fugitive Javert had known him to be. The blot on his record would be erased, and Paris would cease to laugh at him, but that was not enough for Javert, not nearly enough. The only thing that would bring Javert total satisfaction was to see Jean Valjean in chains. And the arrest would have to be brought about at Inspector Javert's own hands. Nothing short of that would be enough. He would ride a thousand miles and more, if need be, to capture his prey. Nothing else mattered so much to him. This was an affair that had gone well beyond duty. Valjean's criminal defiance was something Inspector Javert took personally.

Yes! Up ahead! Javert could just make it out now. He could see a wagon, travelling south. The man at the reins . . . was he? Could he be? Javert's eyes strained to see. Yes, it was Jean Valjean! Who else?

'Ha!' cried Javert triumphantly. 'There he is!' They had him now! And he gave the tired horses the whip again, compelling the poor beasts to run even faster.

The wagon up ahead wasn't travelling rapidly. This stretch of road was very bad, and Valjean's wagon moved slowly and carefully, swerving to the left to avoid deep mudholes on the right. The distance between the two vehicles was diminishing fast. Now Javert thought he could discern the fine cloth of Valjean's coat. Yes, he knew that coat and hat very well. Part of *Monsieur le maire*'s precious new finery. Well, fine clothes wouldn't help the fugitive now. Only a few more minutes, and the man would be within his grasp. Javert's heart began to pound with excitement, and the pulses beat quickly in his ears. His face was flushed with triumph and he felt a ferocious elation swelling inside him.

Faster, they needed to go faster! They were getting very close now. So close that very soon Javert would be able to reach out and grab Valjean with his own two hands.

'Sir, look out!' cried the sergeant suddenly, his voice filled with alarm. He pointed up ahead of the carriage, to where a large mud-sink covered almost the entire right side of the road. They were heading straight for it. Javert tugged hard at the reins, trying to pull the horses up and avoid the hazard, but it was too late.

The coach went out of control as the horses' hooves slid in the mudhole, and it shot off the road on to the rocky shoulder. The rear wheel hit a boulder, pitching the vehicle forward and knocking one of the horses down into the mud on its side. In a grinding screech of wood and metal the mail carriage came to a crashing halt.

The sergeant and the two gendarmes were thrown out on to the ground, and lay there groaning. Javert himself was trapped upside down in the driver's seat, helplessly watching Valjean's wagon still crawling down the road ahead. He was getting away! No! Impossible! While there was breath in his body, Javert would never let that happen.

Struggling free, he dragged himself out of the wreckage, stunned by the sudden onslaught of agony from his left side. On the road, his men were trying to move, wincing in pain, but Javert ignored them as he ignored his own injuries. He jumped on to the shoulder of the road and began running along it after the wagon. His head, chest and shoulder ached abominably; Javert was certain he'd cracked a few ribs, but that didn't stop him. He had to catch up with Valjean! He was not going to let him get away, not again! He would run him down himself, like a lion going after a gazelle.

It was getting very hard for him to breathe; painful stitches racked his side, but Javert kept running. The wagon ahead of him was tantalizingly close, but the inspector could see that the road beyond it was straight and clear of mud. In less than twenty yards the wagon would be able to increase its speed and Jean Valjean – the criminal, the fugitive – would be making good his escape.

Inspector Javert was not about to let his fugitive be snatched from his grasp. *He's mine!* he thought, probably the same thought the lion has before it pounces on the fleeing gazelle. It would take a Herculean effort for a man with cracked ribs to catch up with a horse and wagon, but Javert forced himself to make that effort. His knees pumped higher and higher as the breath rasped in his throat. His injured ribs were pressing on his lungs, making it hard to draw in oxygen. Blood from his injured forehead began to well out and sting his eyes, but still Inspector Javert kept going. His only objective was to reach Jean Valjean's wagon, put the fleeing criminal in handcuffs, and march him back to Montreuil to face a righteous justice.

The wagon was only a few feet away now, but it was beginning to pick up speed as the road improved. Javert leaped through the air and landed on the back of the vehicle. For a minute he lay there gasping, hanging on by the tips of his fingers. As the wagon moved faster and faster, Javert's position became more precarious. His clutching fingers were aching terribly.

He could feel his toes dragging on the ground and knew that he was slipping. He was in danger of being flung down to the road, perhaps at great speed. He managed to hold on, to draw himself on to his elbows, to bring his shoulders into the wagon. Inch by painful inch, he pulled himself up until he was lying in the bed of the wagon. He was exhausted and aching everywhere. If Jean Valjean intended to attack him, now would be the time to do it. All he had to do was stop the wagon and overwhelm the fallen inspector.

But Valjean paid him no attention. It was as though he were completely unaware that Inspector Javert was lying in his wagon. Breathing hard, Javert hauled himself up and slowly made his way to the driver's seat. At last. Pulling out his pistol, he pointed it at Valjean.

'You're . . . under . . . arrest . . .' he gasped.

The man turned. Javert took one look at his face and drew back in astonishment. This man was not Jean Valjean. He was a much older man dressed in Valjean's clothing. He was, in fact, the old peasant with the geese who had gladly traded his flock and his old coat and hat for a wagon and a fine new coat and hat, and who, as he had agreed with Valjean, had set off driving south.

Meanwhile, miles away up the road and going north, Jean Valjean, dressed in the old peasant's clothing, was walking very quickly. He had dropped the geese off at a farmhouse, trading them to a surprised but grateful farmer for a stone flask filled with cold well water, a bit of bread and a handful of dried apples for the journey. Within hours, he would be in Montfermeil, getting Cosette back from the Thenardiers. Nobody would suspect him, because nobody would expect that the fugitive Valjean would be proceeding on foot. Not even Javert.

As for Javert, he and his men returned the worse for wear as the mail carriage, its left wheel wobbling badly, limped back into Montreuil hours later. On the surface, Javert appeared silent and morose, but under his silence a great fury was seething, mingled with a deep humiliation. He'd been led on a wild-goose chase. The wily Jean Valjean had outfoxed him at his own game and made a fool of him. Inspector Javert couldn't stand the thought of it.

There must be an Achilles' heel to the brute. He had a weakness, if only Javert could find it. He had to find it. *Think. I must think.*

When the policemen were finally back in the Montreuil prefecture, they collapsed in Inspector Javert's office. The doctor was summoned and arrived ready to bind up their wounds. The sergeant had an injured leg and would be on a crutch for weeks, but the other two gendarmes had suffered only bumps and bruises.

Javert was the most seriously injured. He had cracked three ribs and dislocated his shoulder. With excruciating pain, the shoulder was popped back into place, and the doctor bound up Javert's bruised torso. There was very little more he could do except prescribe plenty of rest and inactivity, both of which suggestions he was aware Inspector Javert would flatly refuse to follow.

'You've weakened the joint,' he said sternly as he wrapped the gauze tightly. 'It can pop at any time, so be careful not to strain it.'

But Inspector Javert was not paying attention. His thoughts were focused on the subject of Jean Valjean's weaknesses; he ran over them in his mind again and again. Always the same answer came up. Compassion.

That wretched Valjean suffered from compassion. Look

at how he'd sent old Fauchelevent to a new job with some nuns. How he'd given away a prosperous factory to the workers. Javert remembered how Valjean had hovered over that tubercular whore, how he'd lavished costly medical attention on her when it was obvious to everybody who had eyes that the tart was dying. He'd even made her a deathbed promise to look after her little bastard . . .

'The girl!' Javert cried out suddenly. That was it! It had to be! He laughed aloud, a harsh, brutal sound. He knew that that damned, foolish compassion of his would trip Jean Valjean up at last! He had gone to fetch the prostitute's daughter. With his own ears Javert had heard him swear to do it. Now all he had to do was find the girl, and he would have Valjean at his mercy!

It didn't take a great deal of detective work for the police to locate Cosette. Under interrogation, the women at the dye factory were only too willing to give him the information that Fantine had received many letters, even though she couldn't read. She would take them, Javert was told, to the professional letter-writer to be read to her. The letters were always about her bastard child.

Faced with the police, the scribe acknowledged immediately that he knew Fantine, and that he'd addressed so many envelopes to Thenardier at Montfermeil that he had their name and address imprinted in his memory. One look at Inspector Javert's face convinced the man to disgorge it. After all, the whore was dead now and would never again be handing over her forty sous. She was bad business. On the other hand, it was good business to co-operate with the police.

The scribe's information was all that Javert was waiting for. He determined to go after Valjean at once, on horseback, taking with him only two gendarmes in attendance. It would be faster. He was bandaged and swollen; there were ten stitches in his head wound, but Javert paid no attention to any discomfort. The saddle was no place for a man in his condition. A lesser man would be lying in bed, soft pillows piled under his head, with a large draught of laudanum for the pain.

But Inspector Javert was not a lesser man. He was a law officer burning with a sense of duty and more – he considered himself to be the watchdog of morality; he would meet his responsibilities no matter how difficult they might be to carry out. A criminal must not be allowed to flout the law and humiliate the law enforcers.

The chase was only just beginning.

## Chapter Eighteen

### VALJEAN FINDS COSETTE

The years had not been kind to Madame Thenardier. Time had added fat to her corpulent form and subtracted the last remnants of beauty from her face. Time and disappointment with her lot in life had changed her temper from reasonably amiable to unreasonably vicious. Greed, suspicion and bad temper had dug deep vertical lines around her mouth and between her eyebrows, so that, even in those rare moments when she wasn't scowling, she still looked as though she was.

Her husband the innkeeper was equally fat and ugly; the main difference between Monsieur Thenardier and his wife was that he was lazy and she was not. He was content with inactivity, and much preferred to sit idly by the fire, drinking with his customers. Madame Thenardier, on the other hand, was a whirlwind of useless activity. She was forever bustling about, sticking her nose into everything, constantly giving orders, criticizing and scolding. And yet, with all her comings and goings, little was accomplished, and the inn remained dirty, dusty and disorganized.

The target of Madame Thenardier's continual bad temper was the child Cosette, whom they kept as their only servant. The old woman was ever on the alert to make certain that Cosette kept busy and didn't try to cheat her – either by being lazy or by stealing scraps of food to feed her eternal hunger. As though the child had any opportunity to be lazy. She worked a nineteen-hour day, well beyond her strength, ate almost nothing, and slept on a pile of dirty straw with rats and other vermin scuttling around her. She never went to school, never had leisure to play, and was never even taken to church on Sunday, because that would mean outfitting her in decent shoes and a frock.

As long as Cosette remained ignorant and could neither read nor write, as long as she was kept friendless and away from other people, she would not realize how wretched she was or how unjust her treatment was. Thus she would continue to be useful to the Thenardiers as an unpaid servant.

In contrast to Cosette, the Thenardier daughters, Eponine and Alzelma, were flourishing. Years of easy living, rich food, leisure and parental indulgence had made them as plump and sleek as two house cats who live in a farmhouse kitchen. They were not yet vicious like their parents, but they were totally spoiled. Because Cosette did all the work, the girls had no chores to do except to keep the satin ribbons in their hair neat.

This was a raw night, windy and cold. There was no moon, and the skies were very dark. The door to the inn opened and Madame Thenardier glanced up sharply. Cosette struggled through the doorway carrying a large wooden bucket, filled to the brim with water. She shivered as she tottered under the weight of the bucket. Her legs were bare, and her feet, which were black and swollen with toil and the bitter cold, were stuffed into crude wooden clogs.

'There you are, you little slut!' she growled. 'What took you so long?'

'It's heavy,' Cosette said quietly. The weight of bucket and water combined would have been an enormous load even for somebody twice her size.

'It's heavy?' cooed Madame Thenardier, pretending concern. 'Here, let me help you.'

'Thank you.' But as the girl drew near, the innkeeper's wife thrust out a fat foot and put it on top of the bucket, increasing its weight by so much that Cosette gasped in pain. Her arm, which was already aching, was so strained that her shoulder was in danger of dislocation. She was forced to drop the bucket on her bare foot and cried out in pain. At once, Madame Thenardier cuffed her hard on both ears.

'Don't let me hear you complain again, you little bitch,' the woman snarled. 'You don't earn a sou. The least you can do is fetch water!'

Tears stung Cosette's eyes and she scurried to get out of the way of the blows, running under a table and crouching there. It was the only shelter she knew.

'I feed your greedy little mouth and all I get are smart answers,' the woman scolded. 'Not thanks, not a single thanks. Now do your work or I'll twist that ugly nose off your face.'

The little girl scurried to fetch some knitting and crouched over it, needles working furiously as tears rolled down her face.

At that moment Jean Valjean appeared in the doorway, tired, cold and dusty from the road.

'What do you want?' demanded the innkeeper's wife gruffly. This one didn't look too promising in his ragged peasant's coat. If he had some idea of a handout, she'd soon put him right. Food didn't come free.

'A room, please.' Valjean's voice was polite, but his eyes raked over the dirty dining room and its denizens with some contempt. The inn's kitchen stank of stale pork grease and mouse droppings; it was a revolting place.

'Rooms cost twenty sous,' barked the woman.

Valjean took out a fat purse and extracted a coin from it. 'I'll pay in advance.'

At the sight of the money purse, Madame Thenardier's manner underwent a change. All at once she became obsequious, bowing and scraping. 'Very good, monsieur.'

From his comfortable seat by the fire, Thenardier excused himself to his drinking companions, roused his fat behind and came closer to the stranger. Placing one arm around his wife's ample waist, he cooed at her. 'My dear, my sweet, my precious, you've forgotten, haven't you?'

'I've forgotten, have I? I do that, don't I? I forget things. What did I forget?' Madame Thenardier looked to her husband for her cue.

'We've rented the regular room. We've only got the wedding chamber left. I'm sorry, monsieur, but it costs forty sous.'

Although he recognized that he was being taken, and that there probably was no 'wedding chamber' in the inn, Valjean paid another twenty sous without a murmur, and sat down at a table. Excited by the prospect of extracting more coins from that bulging purse, the innkeeper came to fuss over him. 'Do you want supper?'

'Bread and cheese,' Valjean said shortly. He was busy studying the three young girls in the room, to see which one might be Cosette. Two of them were plump and beribboned and were dressed in the latest fashions, while the third child, barefoot and wearing only rags, was so thin one could virtually see the bones showing through her skin. Her face was dirty and her hair uncombed; there were bruises all over her, including a large one on her right cheek under her eyes. She had an expression of such sadness on her face that Valjean felt a pang. Surely no child should look so unhappy. This girl looked as though she didn't know the meaning of the word 'play'.

'That's all?' Thenardier looked disappointed. Even by his calculations, he couldn't charge as much for cheese as he could for meat. 'There's rabbit stew,' he said hopefully.

Valjean shook his head, repelled even by the thought of a stew from the kitchen of this place. He pointed at Cosette. 'What's she doing?'

'Who? Oh, she's making stockings for my daughters.'

The child was knitting stockings for others, while her own legs were bare. This was injustice indeed.

'She's not your daughter?' No, of course not, Valjean told himself silently. She must be Cosette. The child had nothing of the Thenardiers' coarseness. He saw Fantine in the child's features almost immediately. In her boniness and paleness she resembled Fantine at the end of her life. It caused him pain to see it. And she had the same luminous beauty as her mother, with fine, small features, large, wide eyes and an impressive slender height.

'That creature? No. Why? Does she interest you?' Again, Thenardier began to calculate. A virgin, no matter how thin and pale and ugly, must be worth at least a little something to a man with a purse full of money.

'Perhaps.' Jean Valjean kept his tone non-committal. 'What's her name?'

'Cosette.'

*Yes, I knew it. I'm not surprised*, thought Valjean. It was all just as he'd suspected. For years they had been exploiting and mistreating Cosette, the focus of all Fantine's hopes and dreams. Cosette the beloved, for whom Fantine had sacrificed herself body and soul, as well as giving up everything she had ever owned. This was the baby girl whom she had entrusted to the Thenardiers, naïvely believing their false promises to nurture her and care for her. It was a blessing that Fantine was dead, and couldn't see the sorry state of her little girl.

Far from treating Cosette as a daughter of their own, the Thenardiers had been lying to Fantine all that time. They had used the girl as a servant . . . no, worse, as a slave. They had made a fortune out of her, embezzling the money Fantine had sent for her daughter's support and spending it on their own spoiled girls, leaving Cosette with nothing but the meanest, barest subsistence.

'What are they worth?' Valjean asked, keeping his tone neutral.

'The girl?'

'The stockings.'

'The stockings?' Thenardier thought fast. 'I don't know. Probably thirty sous.' They were actually worth less than three sous the pair.

Valjean took the coin from his purse. 'I'll buy them.'

Coming in just then from the kitchen with the bread and cheese on a cracked, chipped plate, Madame Thenardier overheard them and caught a glimpse of the money. 'You want to buy the stockings?'

'I'm paying for her time,' Valjean explained. 'I want her to play.'

'Of course, Monsieur understands that I meant thirty sous for each stocking.'

Taking out another coin, Valjean laid it on the table beside the first, and turned to Cosette. 'You're working for me now,' he told her gently. 'You should play . . . or rest. Whatever you like.'

The little girl was confused. Nobody had ever spoken in such a soft voice to her; nobody had ever told her she could actually have time for herself, to play. She was afraid that she would be punished if she accepted. She turned to Madame Thenardier, the ultimate authority. 'Madame, is it true? Am I allowed to play?'

'Didn't you hear?' the landlady snapped. 'Yes, you must play. Hurry up. Start playing!'

Cosette rummaged under her skirt and pulled out her 'doll'. It was nothing more than a crude straw figure with a rag wrapped around it, but it was the only plaything Cosette had, and she loved it. She began to croon to it quietly, arranging and rearranging its 'dress', like a mother with a baby. Valjean watched her, his heart aching with pity.

A horse's hooves were heard on the road outside, and Valjean moved uncomfortably in his seat. Could it be Javert here already? He sneaked a look out of the window as the horse galloped by. No, it wasn't the inspector. But Valjean knew that soon it would be. It was a reminder for him to conclude his business here and get back on the road.

Thenardier leaned across the table to Valjean, his bloated ugly face twisted in a gross expression of lechery. 'Perhaps Monsieur would like Cosette to play on his lap?' he suggested with a leer.

'No. I'm heading to Paris. Is there a night mail I can take?'

'It already left.' The innkeeper shrugged. 'Next coach to Paris arrives at dawn.'

Valjean frowned, worried. This was a blow indeed. By dawn, Javert might well have caught up with him. He didn't doubt for a minute that the inspector was hot on his trail, or that Javert's first stop would be the inn at Montfermeil. The only thing he wasn't sure of was how much time he might have left. He had to leave now, coach or no coach. He couldn't sit still in one place, just waiting to be arrested.

As soon as Madame Thenardier returned to her kitchen, the innkeeper sidled over closer to Valjean. 'Well? You like our Cosette?' he murmured half under his breath, so that nobody else would hear. It was a blatant insinuation which caused Valjean to wince.

'I want to take her with me,' he replied.

Ah, wonderful. Now they could talk business. 'Monsieur, I have to tell you the truth. I adore that child,' whispered Thenardier.

Jean Valjean's eyebrows went up in amazement as he glanced over at the object of this so-called adoration – ragged, bruised, dirty, cold, downtrodden and terrorized. 'You adore her?'

'Yes, it's true.' The old hypocrite nodded. 'I'm not rich and I've had to pay over four hundred francs for her medicines. But I'm a stupid man,' he continued with false humility. 'I have no sense, just a heart. A big heart.'

'She cost you four hundred francs?' Valjean reached for his purse.

'Five hundred,' Thenardier amended hastily.

'Five hundred. All right. I want to leave with her right away.' He counted out five hundred francs.

But Thenardier's eyes were locked on the purse, which still bulged with money. There was more cash to be had and, if he were clever enough, a lot more. It was time to pull out the ace in the hole. 'I'm sorry, monsieur, but her mother gave her to us to protect her. I can't let a stranger take her away.'

'How much?' demanded Valjean, who wasn't fooled for a moment. All these theatrics, all this strumming on the heartstrings, was being played out over money.

Thenardier laid a hand on his heart, a gesture indicating honesty and affection, neither of which the man possessed. 'Monsieur, it isn't a question of money. What right do you have to the girl?'

'You don't want money? Very well.' And Valjean scooped the five hundred francs back into his purse.

Thenardier felt a sharp pang as he saw the money disappear into the leather bag. But all was not lost. The innkeeper had an advantage over this man; he knew that the stranger wanted the child, and he knew further that he himself intended to sell her. It was merely a matter of price. Negotiations were only just beginning.

'Of course I don't want money,' Thenardier announced piously, pretending to be offended. 'Even if you were to offer me a thousand francs . . .' He glanced at Valjean to see how the other man reacted to this figure, but Valjean said nothing. The figure duly escalated. 'Even *twelve* hundred francs. I couldn't give her to you. It's true I owe fifteen hundred francs and my whole life would be solved if only I had fifteen hundred francs . . . but no! No, I can't think about money. It's a question of law. All that matters is who has the right to the child.'

Jean Valjean had been rather enjoying Thenardier's bravura performance, but it was time to bring the curtain down on it. The innkeeper had spoken the magic words 'who has a right to the child'.

'That's a relief,' said Valjean, and he took Fantine's authorization out of his coat. 'Here's a letter from Cosette's mother, authorizing me to take her,' he said, laying the paper down on the table between them but keeping one large fist clenched tightly on the corner of it, as a kind of warning that Thenardier would understand.

As he read the letter, and recognized the notarized signature and the official seal of the mayor of Montreuil, the realization of his appalling mistake hit Thenardier between the eyes, like a pole-axe slamming through the forehead of a cow meant for slaughter. In his mind's eye he could see the five hundred francs he'd rejected flying away as though the coins had real wings. He could kill himself!

Worse, when his wife found out he'd turned down an offer of five hundred francs she'd kill him herself. His little mind scurried this way and that, looking for an opening to that purse of gold, like a mouse on the scent of a cheese. But nothing useful occurred to him. The door was shut.

Jean Valjean stood up. To the squat little Thenardier the man appeared to be seven feet high, and he cringed before this colossus.

'Get her dressed. Warmly,' Valjean ordered, and Madame Thenardier hustled Cosette into another room. Within a few minutes she brought the girl out again. She was wearing a dress and hooded cloak that had been outgrown by the Thenardier daughters; because of her height, the garments were short on Cosette, too. Her legs were still bare, and on her feet were her old wooden clogs.

'Stockings,' snapped Valjean shortly. 'Woollen stockings. And stout boots. Good ones.' Gone was his mild manner; standing before the Thenardiers now was a frightening figure of stern authority.

Madame Thenardier opened her mouth to protest about the cost, but thought better of it and shut it again. She led Cosette away and brought her back wearing warm knitted stockings and a pair of Eponine's boots, not the best ones, of course, but strong and serviceable.

Jean Valjean looked Cosette up and down, and appeared to be satisfied. 'Come,' was all he said, and he held out his hand to the little girl.

Cosette hesitated, looking from Monsieur Thenardier to Jean Valjean and back again. In the innkeeper's eyes she saw nothing but cruelty and hatred; in the stranger's eyes was something the child did not recognize, never having seen it in her memory. Kindness. The only person who had ever given Cosette love or shown her kindness was her mother Fantine, and Cosette had forgotten her a long time ago. Wondering, the little girl came to Jean Valjean and put her little hand into his great one, and they left the inn together, going out into the frigid night.

At dawn, Inspector Javert rode up to the inn with two gendarmes. He'd been in the saddle for hours. His injured body was stiff from the journey; his ribs and shoulder ached, and his head throbbed under its bandage. Still, the only thing on his mind was the capture of Jean Valjean.

Brusquely, the inspector filled the Thenardiers in on the case, stressing how dangerous the fugitive was and how vital that he be recaptured before he fled out of reach.

'You've seen him?' he demanded of the Thenardiers.

The innkeeper nodded his head slowly. He was really disgusted with himself. He'd missed the boat. Not once, but twice. If he'd only suspected that the tall man was a fugitive on the run, he would have known how to empty that fat wallet in moments. Moreover, there might be a generous reward for the apprehension of the man, and he'd just let him walk out of there, free as you please. This must surely be Thenardier's unlucky day.

'Where is he?' Javert brought his face very close to Thenardier's. At this, Madame Thenardier burst into tears.

'He kidnapped our beloved Cosette!' she wailed. Her grief was real, although her tears were not shed for the loss of the child, only for the loss of the francs.

'They left for Paris on foot,' the innkeeper informed Javert glumly. 'They can't have gone more than two leagues.'

*Paris. I knew it would be Paris.*

Javert barked a sharp order, and the gendarmes mounted their horses again. Stifling a grunt of pain, he swung himself into the saddle. It was but two hours' ride to Paris. He had to reach the city before Jean Valjean so he could set up blockades. Because if Valjean managed to get into Paris, he could lose himself there for ever.

Paris, Javert knew, was a gigantic cauldron in which men and women of all stations and rank mixed together in an upper world and a netherworld. It would be all too easy for Jean Valjean to melt into that disgusting cauldron and disappear. But Valjean was travelling under one severe handicap. He had a child with him, which would make it a lot harder for him to move around or to conceal himself. Compassion would prove his downfall after all.

## Chapter Nineteen

PARIS

The two of them, the man and the little girl, had been making their way towards Paris for hours, throughout the night. They stayed off the road – it was too dangerous – and trudged on through the woods parallel to the highway. The skies were dark, with no moon showing, while myriad stars remained hidden behind scudding clouds. It was hard to make their way through the heavy growth of trees and bush. Valjean feared that, with no stars or moon to guide him, they might stray off the way and become lost.

At last, a reddening in the east told the man that day was breaking and that they were in fact still heading in the right direction. After the sun came up, the cold abated a little, but Jean Valjean knew that with daylight they ran a greater risk of being spotted by any gendarmes in pursuit.

The sound of horses' hooves on the Paris road sent him and the child running deeper into the woods to hide behind a tree. They watched nervously as three riders sped past them. Valjean recognized them. Two of the Montreuil gendarmes, with Javert at their head. They were riding in the direction of Paris. Valjean placed his hand over Cosette's mouth so that she couldn't cry out, and only removed it when the hoofbeats had died away in the distance.

The two of them slogged on, stumbling over tree roots and being scratched by branches,

'Do we still have to walk in the woods?' asked Cosette plaintively. She shivered with the cold, even in her woollen stockings and little cloak. Her feet ached, because she was unaccustomed to wearing boots, and these were too large for her feet. But she held very tightly to Jean Valjean's hand and clutched her rag of a doll in her other hand. It was her only possession.

'Yes, we do. Are you tired?' Valjean looked down at the child.

'No, monsieur, I'm all right.' The words were courageous, but they was far from true; Cosette was *very* tired.

'Don't call me "monsieur", Cosette,' Valjean said quietly. 'People will think we're strangers.'

'What do I call you, monsieur?' the little girl asked.

'You'd better call me "Father",' replied Valjean.

'But you're not my father, monsieur, are you?' Cosette's voice was so feeble that Valjean looked sharply at her, concerned. She was flagging badly, obviously exhausted. She had used up all her meagre reserves of energy slogging through the woods at night.

'Want to ride on my shoulders?' He hoisted her up easily – she weighed close to nothing – and settled her on his shoulders. Cosette looked around, delighted by her new perspective.

'I can reach the branches,' she announced exultantly.

Her pleasure was infectious. It made Valjean smile. 'You're the tallest lady in France,' he declared.

'I'm the Queen of France,' Cosette laughed.

'That's right, you're the queen, you're the Queen of France,' Valjean laughed back. And he moved on, more quickly now that Cosette didn't have to walk.

The Monceaux Barrier was always a busy entrance into the city of Paris, but the roadblock set up by the gendarmes made it busier yet, with long delays. The barrier was a wall, as tall as a building, blocking off this section of the city. It was breached only by an arched entrance with a wrought-iron gate. In front of the gate snaked a long line of carts and peasants, waiting to bring their produce, fowl and meats into the city for sale. Next to the gate was a heated guardhouse, where a pair of sloppily uniformed gendarmes usually hung out lazily, keeping warm and barely glancing at the papers of those seeking admission to Paris. It was a day and an age when no honest man travelled through France, not even from one town to another, without his official papers.

But today the indolence and inefficiency of the Paris gate guards was only a memory. Under the sharp eye of Inspector Javert, they presented a picture of military neatness and industry as they went over the passports word by word.

The farmers were complaining and milling about, while Inspector Javert's men checked their papers and inspected their carts, searching for the fugitive Jean Valjean. Javert had selected the Monceaux Barrier as the most likely entrance that Valjean would try to come in by, given the route that led from Montfermeil. Although he had circulated his description to every portal and gatehouse and bridge into the city, Javert stayed to man this post himself.

He had to stop Jean Valjean before the fugitive got safely into Paris and disappeared from sight. Once in Paris, he'd be very difficult to unearth.

'Have your papers out and ready to be inspected when it's your turn,' called out one gendarme.

A peasant fumbled in his smock to find his passport. 'Wake up! This is Paris. We don't waste time here!' barked another gendarme impatiently.

Jean Valjean crouched down and watched the action from a hundred yards away. He and Cosette had continued to travel all day together, reaching the city wall an hour before sunset, more than a day after leaving Montfermeil. Valjean had carried the girl in his arms or on his shoulders most of the way.

He might have known that Javert would have this entrance patrolled. No doubt every entrance into Paris was covered by the gendarmerie, looking for him. But curse Javert for choosing this entrance for himself!

On Valjean's shoulders, her little arms around his neck, Cosette was fast asleep, still holding tightly to her beloved rag doll. Tears were still drying on her cheeks. Well, Valjean obviously couldn't get through the Monceaux Barrier. He'd have to find some other way to enter the city.

That wouldn't be easy. On the other side of the barrier, the city side, there were streets of houses crowded together, at varying parallel distances from the wall. If a man were really agile, he might climb the wall; the stones were irregular, providing footholds here and there. The wall was not impossible to scale.

But coming down off the wall to the city's streets was another matter entirely: just below the wall's ledge, on the other side, there was a row of sharp iron pikes, facing outward towards the houses. The pikes made it impossible for anyone to climb or jump down on the city side of the wall. This system effectively discouraged any attempts to get into the city by leaping over the wall.

The only way left was this: from the ledge on the wall's summit, a man might jump across to the roof of one of the nearer houses, then clamber down, inside the city. It was a dangerous undertaking, because the nearest houses were feet away, and the gap between wall and rooftop called for a jumper with powerful legs and shoulders and no sense of fear. A false move and he would be impaled on the pikes.

Valjean pulled out a map of the Paris streets and began to study it. There must be a way in, and he intended to find it. Suddenly, his eye fell on a street name that was familiar to him. And it wasn't far from the barrier. If he could only reach the rue Petit-Picpus . . .

Up the street, a fiacre, pulled by a pair of matched bays, came to a halt. Javert ran over to it. Six gendarmes climbed down and saluted, but Inspector Javert was more interested in the officer getting out of the vehicle.

'No luck yet?' enquired Deputy Chief Chabouillet.

'He was on foot,' Javert replied. 'And the little girl would slow him up.'

'Well, Javert,' said the senior officer, 'you said he was Valjean and we ignored you. Rather than apologize, I want you to know I've asked the prefect to transfer you to Paris. To work as my deputy.'

A surge of exultation flooded through the inspector. He was on his up way now. This promotion would go a long way towards soothing his feelings. Javert had been chagrined beyond measure that he hadn't been present in the courtroom at Arras, when *Monsieur le maire* had stood up and confessed that he was Jean Valjean. That certainly would have been one of the highest points of his career. But now that he had been assigned to the prefecture of Paris, Valjean would not elude him again. Javert would make his recapture his highest official priority.

'Monsieur, I'm honoured. Thank you.'

'Meanwhile,' continued Chabouillet, indicating the six gendarmes lined up awaiting orders, 'these men are at your disposal to find Valjean. Although I don't suppose you'll need them. Valjean thinks he's lost you. He'll walk right up to the barrier bold as brass.'

*I suppose he's right*, thought Javert. And yet, there was something about the whole thing that troubled him. He couldn't quite picture the Jean Valjean he knew strolling up to a bunch of policemen and attempting to bluff his way into Paris. That would be idiocy in the extreme. And Jean Valjean was no idiot.

Meanwhile, about fifty feet from the barrier, Valjean and Cosette were creeping quietly along the base of the wall. Night had fallen, and the only illumination was from the gas streetlamps which had just been lit at every corner. Valjean had to squint hard to see what he was looking at. He was searching for a gap between the wall and the houses on the other side, small enough to allow him to jump across to one of the rooftops. The house would have to be very close to the wall.

But Cosette was lagging behind, slowing him down. 'Wait here,' he told her.

'Don't leave me!' Cosette cried shrilly.

Valjean dropped down beside her, raising one finger to his lips. 'You have to be quiet,' he whispered urgently. 'I'm only going to look. I'm not leaving you.'

But the child was not reassured. 'Why do we have to climb the wall?'

'Madame Thenardier is chasing us.'

Just the mention of that awful name had an instant effect. 'She . . . is?' Cosette quavered, terrified.

'Yes.' Valjean nodded gravely. 'We have to go secretly or Madame Thenardier will get us.'

Leaving Cosette huddled at the base, Valjean quickly climbed the wall and crouched down low on the top ledge, scanning the nearby houses as his eyes got used to the darkness. Getting past the iron pikes would be very difficult; they were sharp enough to impale a large man, and certainly an even greater danger to a little child.

Javert scowled impatiently as he waited by the barrier for Valjean to appear. This business of checking every vegetable cart and farmer's wagon was going much too slowly. In addition, his doubts were growing. And then, like a flash, he had a revelation.

'He won't! Of course he won't!' he cried out suddenly.

'Pardon me, Javert? He won't what?' asked Chabouillet.

But Javert was directing his attention to the six policemen assigned to him. 'I want three men in each direction to walk the wall,' he ordered. 'Look for a small enough gap to jump on to a roof. Go!'

'I don't understand,' said the deputy chief.

'He has no papers, sir,' Javert explained to his superior. 'He can't come through the barrier. Somehow, he knows the houses near by are close to the wall. He plans to jump.'

Deputy Chief Chabouillet looked sceptical. 'With a little girl?'

Javert nodded grimly. 'He'd rather die than face justice.' He was right; he was certain of it. Valjean would try to jump from the wall on to a rooftop. Javert knew Jean Valjean intimately, almost like a blood brother. He himself had been witness to the man's almost unlimited physical strength. He had raised a heavy cart almost single-handed off the old man Fauchelevent. Javert understood the man's thought processes as completely as if he lived inside Valjean's head and saw through Valjean's eyes.

'Follow along with me, Cosette,' Valjean called down softly. In a low crouch, he made his way along the top of the wall, and the child below tried to keep pace with him. He was looking for a house that was not too far away from the wall, and one whose roof was about level with its top.

Inspector Javert was looking for exactly the same thing. Having abandoned the gatehouse by the barrier, he was inside the wall now, on the city side, moving from street to street. He kept calculating by eye the distance between the houses and the wall. He rejected one possibility after another. Valjean might be foolhardy but he was also shrewd. He'd choose a rooftop very carefully.

At last, Javert found an older house, one that had stood inside the wall for more than a hundred years. It was a yard or two nearer than the others. A likely prospect for Valjean. Javert whistled over to a gendarme, and positioned him directly under the gap. 'Watch here,' he ordered.

Up on the wall, Jean Valjean was still looking. Below him, Inspector Javert was still trotting from street to street, trying to locate other houses that would fit the bill. He intended to post a man by each one of them.

Valjean made his choice at last. He was exhausted, almost at the limit of his physical resources, but the rooftop he'd selected was only four feet away from the wall. It was now or never. He dropped down to the waiting Cosette. 'Hands around my neck. Hold tight.'

With Cosette clinging to his back, he climbed the wall again. Taking the girl in his arms, he tried to straighten up for the jump, but the added weight of the child made him wobble. The terrified Cosette screamed out loudly.

At once, Valjean dropped into a crouch and shook the child violently. 'Shut up! You'll get us killed!' he whispered intensely. His face was purple with anger. His rage only made Cosette cry harder.

Valjean fought for self-mastery; he would not allow himself to revert to the Valjean of the galleys. Was he not a human being? And was this child not under his protection?

'It's all right. I'm sorry,' he whispered, his finger gently caressing Cosette's cheek and wiping a tear away. 'We can't make a noise because Madame Thenardier will hear us. All right? Now, stand on my shoulders. I'll hold your hands.'

Still sniffling, Cosette took an uncertain stance on Valjean's shoulders, holding his hands tightly. He shifted his hands to her waist and the little girl squealed in fright.

'I've got you,' he whispered urgently. 'I'll hold you. You have to jump. I'll count to three and give you a push. But you have to jump.'

Cosette stood on Valjean's shoulders, staring at the gap. The four feet or so seemed like a vast distance, a deep chasm. The night's murky darkness frightened her, too. She shook her head, unable to move.

'Cosette, I'll buy you a doll,' Valjean offered to tempt her. 'Now jump!'

Cosette shook her head harder. No. No, no, no. She was paralysed with fear.

'I'll buy you chocolates,' Valjean promised frantically. 'I'll buy you chocolates every day. But you have to jump.'

No. Impossible. The child was transfixed by her terror; she could not move. The only solution open to Valjean was that he must jump first, and attempt to retrieve her in some other way. He had no time to waste. Without hesitation, he put the girl down and launched himself into the air, over the gap. He landed safely on the rooftop opposite and turned to look for Cosette.

Underneath them, Inspector Javert had just reached the same house Valjean had chosen. To him, too, it seemed a likely prospect for a jump, and he whistled over another of the gendarmes.

Seeing Valjean land on the roof, the girl called out, 'Father!'

'Shhh,' warned Valjean, his finger pressed to his lips.

'But you told me to call you "Father",' Cosette cried artlessly.

'Shhhhh!' Dear God, make her shut up! He still had to get her off that ledge.

On the street below, Javert pricked up his ears. Had he

heard voices? He looked up, and the gendarme likewise looked up, but in the night gloom neither man saw anything. Still, they continued to walk very slowly along the base of the wall, their eyes peeled for any movement above them or around them.

Valjean had to work quickly, to get Cosette over to the roof before she panicked and fell off the wall. He dug his toes into the lip of the roof, stripped off his jacket and wrapped each hand in one of the sleeves. Raising his arms high, he stretched the fabric between them, so it billowed out like a sail. He hesitated, then threw himself forward, off the roof. For a long moment he was suspended in midair, neither on the roof nor on the wall, with the street far below him. Then his hands reached the pikes opposite.

As Cosette shrank back, horrified, Valjean's jacket sleeves caught on the sharp points of the pikes, and he was suspended across the gap, hanging there by his toes on the roof with his jacket caught on the pikes. In this perilous position, he suddenly heard movement below him and looked down.

Javert! Valjean saw Inspector Javert and the gendarme on the street below him, not fifty feet away. Their backs were to him, but for how long? He drew back in terror. Then he heard another sound, even more dire. The jacket was tearing. If it ripped away from the pike, he would certainly fall into the street, directly at Javert's feet. If he weren't killed or maimed, he'd be sent away for life. In either case, Cosette would be left alone, abandoned on top of a wall. What would become of the child?

He must not fall. Too much was at stake. Slowly, Valjean slipped his right hand out of the sleeve and reached for the bottom curve of the pike. He grabbed it and held on, then, slipping his other hand out of its sleeve, he grabbed another pike and held tight. He was now a human bridge, suspended between the wall and the rooftop.

'Walk over me,' he whispered urgently to Cosette. 'Hurry.'

Still terrified, the child clutched Valjean tightly. She moved very slowly, crawling over his head, then his neck, then his back . . .

Below them, Javert heard a strange sound and looked up. Above him, between the wall and the nearest house, he could see a strange shadow, a slowly moving grotesque image. Valjean's eyes met Javert's, and he froze in horror. It was all over!

But Javert turned away without recognition. In the night, the shadow he had seen had no human form, no human face, no eyes. But only a few seconds later the image from his retina settled in Javert's brain and sorted itself out. A man, a tall man – Jean Valjean? A man was suspended above him, and a child was crawling over him to get to the rooftop . . . It was he! They had found him.

'Valjean!' Javert shouted, and pulled his pistol from its holster.

Cosette was across now, safe on the roof.

'Don't move!' yelled Javert, taking aim. In answer, Valjean pushed off with his feet, clinging tightly to the pikes. The inspector fired, and missed. Now the gendarme, too, was aiming a weapon at Valjean.

With bullets whizzing around him, Valjean pulled himself up on the wall, squeezing between the pikes and cutting his left leg. He felt the blood spurting. Across the gap, Cosette watched him anxiously, her large eyes round with fear. Another gunshot; Valjean ducked. He couldn't stay here, pinned to the wall like a target. Any moment now one of the policemen's bullets would find him and kill him. He had to move right away, to take the risk.

Standing up, Jean Valjean launched himself into the air across the gap. With a thud, he landed on the roof next to Cosette. His wounded leg buckled under him. He stifled a moan of pain, not wishing to alarm the girl.

He took her small hand in his and clutched it tightly. From the street, Inspector Javert yelled out in anger and frustration and fired again. Once again the bullet missed. Jean Valjean and Cosette ran, side by side, into the night, over the rooftops of Paris, to safety.

## *Chapter Twenty*

### THE PETIT-PICPUS CONVENT

As soon as Inspector Javert raised the alarm, the other five gendarmes came running to his side, followed by Deputy Chief Chabouillet. Deployed by the inspector, men ran along the side streets parallel to the house where Javert had seen Valjean disappear. He must have come down from the roof somewhere near here. And with an injured leg and a child along, he couldn't be travelling very fast.

After a ten-minute search, the officers turned a corner and found themselves cornered in an empty cul-de-sac, at the end of which stood a high brick wall, perhaps eighteen feet tall and at least a foot and a half thick.

Frustrated by the dead end, Chabouillet and the gendarmes turned around, ready to try another route. But Inspector Javert did not follow; he stayed where he was, his eyes busily searching the wall and the area around and above it. Something about this situation nagged at him. It occurred to him that it was just such an apparently impossible escape as this high-wall route which would tempt Jean Valjean. He would picture the discouraged police turning away from the scent to look elsewhere, just as Chabouillet was doing right now. A difficult task, to get over a wall like this, but one worth the effort to a fugitive.

'What's on the other side of this wall?' demanded Javert.

'A convent,' answered Chabouillet. 'The convent of Petit-Picpus.'

Even as the deputy chief spoke those words, Jean Valjean, holding Cosette tightly in his arms, was climbing a tall elm tree which overhung the convent garden. Now he dropped from the lowest limb of the tree into the garden on the other side of the wall. He fell heavily on his wounded leg, but apart from a sharp stab of pain there was no further injury.

'Now may we rest?' Cosette asked plaintively. 'Madame Thenardier can't climb the wall.'

Out of breath, Valjean could only nod. Javert can't climb the wall either, he thought.

But Inspector Javert was far from ready to give up on the convent. He led Chabouillet and his policemen to the front gate, which was locked. It was his intention to search the convent and its grounds. A strong hunch told him that Jean Valjean was somewhere around.

Deputy Chief Chabouillet was not in agreement. The convent of Petit-Picpus was large and powerful; for many generations the daughters of some of the most influential men in Paris had been educated at its school. The sisters came from important families, and the mother superior herself was descended from one of the noblest bloodlines in France. It would not do to annoy or offend the mother superior with a search of her premises by uniformed men.

'Until we've searched everywhere else, we dare not ask,' he told Javert.

'But it's for their protection,' Javert protested. The more he was discouraged from searching here, the more convinced he became that Jean Valjean was hiding somewhere in the building or the grounds.

'Javert, this is a strict religious order. The nuns are not permitted to look at a man, much less speak to one.'

'But you said it's also a boarding school for girls. They must be protected—'

Chabouillet scowled. 'The girls are daughters of the aristocracy, whose parents will kiss your feet if you are correct, and have you guillotined if you're wrong.'

Javert almost groaned in frustration. 'Sir, I know he's in there,' he pleaded. 'Just allow me—'

'I'm not going to wake up a building full of nuns who are terrified of men and search their beds,' the deputy chief said firmly.

'I have another idea,' Javert offered stubbornly. 'What if I were to write the mother superior a note explaining the circumstances and the gravity of the situation, and asking for her co-operation in the search? Just a note, nothing more. What could be the harm?'

Chabouillet thought this over for a moment, weighing his anxieties against his faith in Inspector Javert's instincts as a policeman. But Javert was right; what harm could a note cause? Reluctantly, he gave his permission.

At the back of the convent garden was a small cottage, where the handyman lived. Old Fauchelevent was in his bed fast asleep when Jean Valjean crept into the cottage. The intrusive sounds of his entrance woke the old man up with a start.

Fauchelevent peered into the darkness, seeing a small figure, child-size. Beside her, a huge man was limping towards the bed. Fauchelevent smelled Valjean's sweat and the acrid smell of his blood. He froze, unable to move.

'What?' the old man cried out in terror. 'Who are you?'

Valjean clamped his hand over the old man's mouth, stifling his cries. He leaned close. 'Now *I'm* pinned under the cart, Fauchelevent,' he whispered into his ear.

The police party approached the locked front gate of the convent. The doorkeeper opened his peephole, looked through it and allowed Inspector Javert to hand in his note, which he carried across the grounds to the convent, leaving the police standing at the gate. When he came back, the doorkeeper allowed the officers to enter through the gateway and approach the convent door.

When the mother superior read Inspector Javert's note, she came to the front door. It was an ironbound door of thick wood and in the centre of it, at eye level, was a grille of iron bars, bars so thick that no face could be seen through it. Javert could hear the rustle of the nun's heavy skirts, but he could make out nothing through the grille. Then he heard the metallic clang of the grille sliding open, and the sound of a woman's voice, low-pitched and grave. The woman herself remained unseen behind the heavy metalwork.

'Your note has been read, Inspector. We understand and appreciate your worry. But a search of our grounds, our school or our convent is impossible.'

She spoke with finality, and Javert's heart sank, but he wasn't quite ready to give up yet. 'If you would collect all the nuns, all the sisters and the schoolgirls in the chapel, my men could search everywhere else, and you wouldn't be in danger,' he explained feverishly. 'I don't mean danger, because my men aren't dangerous—'

'We are not afraid of men, Inspector,' the voice said through the grille. 'We are here to adore Christ. We don't live in fear, we live in love.'

Javert brushed the reproof aside. 'Yes, yes, of course. But you may have – in fact, I'm convinced you *do* have – a dangerous criminal hidden among your lambs. I can't protect you from out here.'

'We thank you, Inspector, for your concern,' the mother superior replied coolly. 'But we will rely, as we always have, on the protection of God.'

The iron grille clanged shut, the convent's last word.

Javert's fists clenched in anger and frustration. Valjean was somewhere in there; he would take his oath on that. And yet, he was as far out of Javert's reach as though he were on the moon. He turned to leave, and behind him he could hear the peephole of the doorkeeper's gate closing too, shutting the world out of the convent.

The following morning, Cosette still slept deeply on Fauchelevent's bed, wrapped in a warm blanket. Valjean wearily sat by the side of the bed, watching her intently, as intently as he had watched by her dying mother's bedside. Fauchelevent came in quietly.

'I've told the mother superior that you're my brother, and you'll be the new gardener,' he said.

Jean Valjean was happy to hear Fauchelevent's words. This was the place he'd been looking for, the one he'd seen on his map of Paris. The Petit-Picpus convent was the convent that had been a favourite charity of the bishop's, the convent he himself had supported with generous donations from Montreuil. Here the sisters had accepted Fauchelevent as a member of their family, and in their charity had allowed him to rest and heal.

Valjean was glad to be here, of all places. He believed that it must be the hand of God which had brought him to the Petit-Picpus convent, that he was destined to receive sanctuary here for himself and his little girl. He felt he was being repaid for his kindness to Fauchelevent, in situating him here. He knew, however, that he must never reveal his true identity to the mother superior or the sisters; it would only endanger them, and put them in a moral quandary. Valjean had two identities – hunted fugitive and convent benefactor. The sisters should not be required to choose between the two. As Fauchelevent's brother the gardener, Jean Valjean would blend in quietly.

He nodded. 'Thank you, Fauchelevent,' he replied. 'Good.

And tomorrow, can you arrange for the girl to go to school here? I can pay for it.'

'Yes.' The old man nodded. 'If you can pay, that'll be all right.' He looked curiously at the sleeping child. 'Who is she?'

'She's an orphan,' Valjean said softly. He looked down at Cosette. 'She will be with me now,' he added, making his commitment to Fantine, and now to Cosette, stronger than ever. The child slept on.

'A pity,' said old Fauchelevent in a low tone.

'What?' whispered Valjean.

The two men were standing at the rear of the convent church, watching from behind a pillar the beautiful ceremony in which four novices were taking their vows. The young women were dressed as brides, all in white, with flowers and veils. As the sisters' choir voices swelled to the arched and vaulted ceiling of the church, the lovely girls were married to Christ, each receiving a simple gold wedding band as a sign of her lifetime commitment.

'I was thinking of next year, when it will be Cosette's turn,' Fauchelevent replied. 'A pity.'

Valjean instinctively looked at the high pews in which Cosette, now sixteen years old and beautiful, stood with her classmates, watching the ceremony.

'Is it a pity to be devoted to Christ?' he asked.

'A beautiful nun is a tragic waste.' Fauchelevent shrugged. 'Well, even though Cosette is stuck here, at least you can see the world.'

Valjean didn't answer. He was as much a prisoner here at the convent as Cosette would be as a nun within these walls. The world was lost to him. But he didn't miss it; he was content to spend the rest of his days at the convent.

'Or Paris, anyway,' continued Fauchelevent. 'Aren't you

curious? You haven't been outside in ... how many years?'

*Nearly ten*, Valjean answered silently. Aloud, he said, 'The world never changes, brother.'

'It *is* changing,' declared Fauchelevent. 'You should have a look for yourself. You'd be surprised.'

It was true; the politics of France were undergoing another radical change. There was unrest everywhere, workers' anger rising daily against rampant unemployment, the bourgeoisie and King Louis-Philippe. Paris was the centre of the unrest, as workers and students formed an alliance under flags of red. But political change held no interest for Jean Valjean. He could still sense, after a decade inside these walls, the brooding, threatening presence of Inspector Javert outside somewhere, waiting to pounce on him.

Yet Inspector Javert had very few thoughts of Jean Valjean these days. His enemies were now the revolutionaries, especially the ungrateful young students who preached sedition, rebelled against authority and incited the workers to strike, using fiery rhetoric and time-worn promises of equality. As though there could ever be equality!

Nowadays Javert haunted the alleyways and cheap cafés where the revolutionary students congregated. Silently, he collected his evidence, making lists of witnesses in his little black notebook, and gathering names from his paid informers. Soon he would be ready to make an official move against them.

Jean Valjean walked silently up to the doorkeeper's gate. He could see Cosette on tiptoe, peering out at life through the peephole, as though she were a spectator at a play. It was the favourite occupation of her few leisure hours, but she believed it was a secret activity. The nuns would be angry with her if they found out that she was spying on the outside world.

Valjean stood for a moment, looking fondly at her. Over the last ten years, he had come to love her more and more as his daughter, just as she adored him as her papa. The girl remembered little if anything of her life with the Thenardiers, which was exactly as Valjean wished.

'What are you looking at, Cosette?' he asked at last.

'Oh! It's you, Papa,' said the startled girl. 'Just watching the people go by.' She put her eye to the peephole again. 'Look at her!' she cried. 'What a silly dress. Want to see?'

'No.' He shook his head gravely. The world was of no interest to him, not any more.

Cosette stepped away from the peephole, her face troubled. 'Papa . . .' she began tentatively.

Valjean said nothing, but looked deeply into Cosette's eyes. Clearly, she wanted to tell him something of importance.

'I don't want to take my vows, Papa,' she declared at last, through trembling lips.

'We promised the mother superior,' Valjean reminded her quietly.

She lifted her distressed face to his. 'Mother Superior told me I must go to Christ with a pure heart. With no regret. If I took my vows now, I'd be lying to God. That's a terrible sin, isn't it?'

Without replying, Valjean regarded her lovely sixteen-year-old face, with its wide eyes and pure brow. He could no more imagine Cosette committing 'a terrible sin' than he could think of himself flying like a bird. But she was a normal young girl, with a normal young girl's curiosity about the outside world. Valjean knew that what he considered security, Cosette considered imprisonment. She'd been shut into the Petit-Picpus convent for ten years now, spending her days in a schoolroom and her nights in a dormitory, supervised by strict nuns every hour of the day. She had no first-hand knowledge of the wicked world outside. Was it any wonder that she was tempted by the glimpses she stole through the doorkeeper's peephole? Was it any wonder that she craved a taste of freedom?

How could he blame her? How could he possibly tell her what their true situation was? That he was a fugitive, a criminal, and she a prostitute's illegitimate daughter? That he wasn't her real father? By now he *was* Cosette's father; she had no other. Who could possibly love her more than he?

Here at Petit-Picpus they were safe, allowed to live in peace. They enjoyed protection, and the welcoming presence of God. Within these high stone walls the nuns had created a sanctuary, a private universe of goodness and charity a million miles away from the teeming streets.

And yet it was those very streets that Cosette wanted so much to see. 'I want to leave, please, Papa,' she begged, not for the first time. If he could only keep her a child for ever! It was the dearest wish of parents from the dawn of time.

'My child, we're safe here.' Valjean spoke through the pain he felt.

'Safe from what, Papa?'

*May you never know, my dearest daughter.* Valjean wrapped his arm around Cosette's slender shoulder and pulled her close to his chest. 'We have everything we need. I can work. I can be near you. We have a good life here.'

Cosette snuggled up to him, peering up at his beloved face. 'Please, Papa,' she begged.

He looked down into her clear, beseeching eyes and sighed deeply. He had dreaded this hour for years, but it had now arrived. How much longer could he keep his daughter shut away from the rest of humanity? It wasn't fair to Cosette. Soon she would be a woman, and she needed to see the outside world through a vantage point greater than a chink in a brick wall.

Cosette's curiosity to see life was the natural feeling of a sixteen-year-old girl who'd been sheltered for ten years. The brief glimpses of men and women going by the convent walls had only served to tantalize her.

For ten years, Jean Valjean had known true peace of mind. Here, in this holy place, he'd felt in touch with God. He had worked the soil with his hands, surely the most natural kind of work that man can do – to follow the seasons, to make things grow and bloom. To Valjean the sweetest sound he'd ever heard was the music of the convent bells, telling the hours of prayer – matins, compline, nones and the others. And the sweet singing of the sisters as they raised their voices in praise of Christ.

Jean Valjean's troubled mind had been eased by the peaceful sight of the nuns going about their business, without haste, with slow, measured tread, their eyes cast down demurely, their minds busy with prayer, the black skirts of their habits full and billowing, the soaring white wimples like God's clouds, the rosary beads clacking at their waists. And the holy days – the saints' days, All Hallows, and especially Easter and Christmas, when the earth is truly blessed by Christ – these had brought calm and happiness to his tortured mind.

Now he was ready to give all that up, for Cosette, that she might see the world she longed so much to become a part of.

Valjean had money, plenty of money. Even the ten years of Cosette's school tuition had not drained his resources. They had few expenses, living as they did free of charge within convent walls. He could set up a modest but comfortable life outside for himself and his child.

Valjean knew that by going out into the world he would be leaving the deepest sense of security he had ever known. But he also knew that his best days were behind him, while Cosette's life had yet to begin. Ten years ago he had taken responsibility for that life. He had to fulfil that responsibility, to give the girl everything she would need to get on in life. And that meant giving up safety for risk. Only Cosette must never know about that risk, or what her father had sacrificed for her.

'All right, my child,' he promised her gently, 'we'll go out. We'll see the world together.'

# Chapter Twenty-One

## MARIUS

**H**is unrelenting search for those committing crimes against the state kept bringing Inspector Javert back again and again to the Saint Antoine section of Paris, one of the major hotbeds of revolutionary fever in this spring of 1832. He had his paid police informants in all the poverty-stricken quarters of the city, shady individuals who lurked in the shadows and who, under the innocent disguise of poor students or workers, would infiltrate the burgeoning radical movements in order to spy on them and expose their members to arrest and prosecution. In Saint Antoine Javert's informer was a man named Robineaux.

The radical students would gather in the low-priced cafés and *boîtes* of this slum section. Here, surrounded by the have-nots and *les misérables* of the slums and alleyways, the young revolutionaries formed into committees and organizations intended to pool their strengths, reinforce their ideals and maximize their effectiveness. One of the most active of these organizations was called the ABC Society. In French, the pronunciation of ABC is *abaissé*, which means 'oppressed'. It was a grim joke, filled with bitter meaning. Within the society, the radical spirit was unquenchable.

The radicals' common goal was to bring about a revolution that would abolish the inhumane and unfair conditions by which the wealthy oppressed the poor, and restore to the common people of France their natural rights as human beings. So far, the organizations were weak, under-equipped and undermanned, but they were gaining in strength day by day, and the police had already begun to take them seriously.

Two years ago, the people of France had united to rebel against the Restoration and the Bourbon king Charles X. But in the long run the revolution of 1830 fizzled out, then failed. The monarchy was restored, and another Bourbon, Louis-Philippe, was now on the throne. This time, vowed the radicals, they would not fail.

Javert walked through an alley in the wretched heart of Saint Antoine, on the lookout for his paid informant Robineaux. He found the snitch, dressed like a student, leaning against an open doorway, staring across the avenue to where a young man with flaming dark eyes was making an impassioned speech to a crowd of people assembled to listen and to cheer him.

Javert stepped into the shadows, so that nobody within sight would observe the two of them speaking together and add two and two.

'See the man making a speech? He's the leader of the ABC Society,' said the informer out of the corner of his mouth, without turning his head. 'It's the largest and most dangerous of the student groups. They want the king out, they want suffrage without limitation—'

'I don't care what they want,' snapped Javert from the shadows. 'I want to know who they are.'

Less than five minutes later, a fiacre, a one-horse taxi, pulled up in front of a church in the same Saint Antoine district. In it were Jean Valjean and Cosette, both of them dressed in dark, modest but well-made clothing, the garments of respectable members of the bourgeoisie.

Now eighteen, Cosette was even more beautiful in face and figure than she was as a child. Without her being really aware of it, she had become a young woman in the full flower of her charms.

Jean Valjean picked up a leather case and opened the taxi door. 'I have to go over some papers with Father Bernard,' he said. 'It's about the free food programme. I won't take more than five minutes.'

'I'll wait here,' said Cosette serenely. 'It's so nice out.' She smiled at her papa from under her demure lace bonnet.

'All right, my child, but don't leave the fiacre.'

The girl shook her head, exasperated as usual by her papa's overprotectiveness. He watched over her like a tiger with one cub, rarely letting her out of his sight. They lived together in a large, comfortable house on the rue Plumet, attended by a devoted servant, almost never seeing anybody. To the outside world, they were Monsieur and Mademoiselle Fauchelevent, well to do but reclusive, charitable but not social.

As far as her freedom went, Cosette thought she might as well have stayed in the convent.

'Yes, Papa, I'll stay put,' she sighed. After he had left, she sat for a moment or two, tapping one foot in boredom. The sun was shining warmly, and only a few soft clouds drifted across the sky. Cosette had all the energy of an eighteen-year-old, and she wished to be out of doors, walking, enjoying the day, not sitting like a parcel in this stuffy taxi.

Suddenly, she heard the loud sound of many voices cheering. Cosette peered out of the carriage. She could hear crowd noises clearly, but they were coming from around the corner; she could see nothing. Then she heard a single man's voice. It was raised as though he were giving a speech, but she couldn't make out the words. Cosette got down from the fiacre. 'I'll be right back,' she told the driver. 'Just wait, please.'

Curiosity led her to the corner and around it. Across the street she could see a crowd of men and women and, in their midst, a tall, dark-haired young man was standing on a wooden box, addressing them. His voice was impassioned, and his eyes flashed with a revolutionary fervour.

'Everything in our country is a crime,' he was saying, his raised hands balled into fists. 'Speaking out is a crime. Being poor is a crime. Being poor is the worst crime of all. And if you commit these crimes, you are condemned for life. Our government has no mercy. No pity. No forgiveness.'

'And it has no work for us!' called out a man dressed in the coarse garments of a stonemason.

'That's right,' Marius called back. 'And there's no work. And because there's no work, our children are starving. They're starving but we can't feed them. We can't protect them from the fevers . . .'

Cosette walked along the outer fringes of the crowd, her attention fixed on the young man. She was fascinated by his beauty as well as by his powerful emotion. He possessed a kind of charisma that the girl had never before encountered.

He was tall and quite thin, with hollowed cheeks and full, sensitive lips. His thick hair was in need of cutting, trailing on to his threadbare collar and falling forward into his eyes. Those eyes were his most remarkable feature – very dark, with a piercing, solemn gaze. The young man's eyes went directly to Cosette's soul, as though only he in all this world could understand her.

His rebellious words were strange to her, but she knew his face well. It seemed to her that she had seen it every day of her life, in her mind's eye, even when she was too young to comprehend the meaning of a stranger's face in her innermost thoughts.

Across the street observing the demonstration, Inspector Javert was also interested in the young man and his rhetoric. 'What's his name?' he demanded.

'Marius. Marius Pontmercy,' the informer Robineaux answered.

'Address?' Javert wrote the name in his notebook in his meticulous handwriting.

'He rents a room above the Musain Café.'

'Concentrate on him,' Javert ordered crisply, and he melted back into the shadows. He had no idea that, not a hundred yards away, around a corner, his old enemy Jean Valjean had just entered a church on charitable business.

Cosette pushed her way into the crowd, approaching nearer to the speaker's makeshift platform with each step. She was unaware that she was even walking, let alone coming closer to Marius Pontmercy. She seemed helpless, caught up in some kind of spell cast by this man's face and voice. She began to listen to what he was saying, and the passion in his words began to touch her, too.

'. . . the fevers that come from living jammed together like animals,' Marius continued with great conviction. 'And we have no money to pay for their medicine. Why? Tell me. Why are we powerless to save the people we love? You know. All of you know. Tell me why!'

'The king lied!' a woman called out from the crowd.

'That's right!' Marius called back. 'The king betrayed us. We were promised the vote! Do we have it? Do we have the vote?'

'No!' the crowd roared with one voice.

Cosette moved closer; now she was in the front rank of listeners, directly in front of the speaker. Not only his compelling voice but his words too were reaching her now, and she was afraid to miss a syllable.

'Where is the Republic?' demanded Marius. 'Where is the Republic our fathers died for?'

'Where?' echoed the crowd.

'Here! It's here, my brothers.'

Marius Pontmercy's eyes scanned the crowd, and came to rest suddenly on the lovely, attentive face of a well-dressed young woman, surely the last type of person he expected to see here. The girl was watching him, and fascination was written all over her delicate features. The expression of purity and goodness in her huge eyes was so moving that it threw Marius for a moment. His speech faltered, then stopped. He made a mighty effort, and recovered.

'The Republic is here! Here, in our legs and our arms.' Now he spoke directly to the beautiful young woman. 'It lives here, in our heads. But most of all it lives in our hearts. In our hearts *we* are the Republic!'

The people, inspired by the fiery words of the young student, cheered him loudly. Marius, elated, smiled down at Cosette. She blushed and turned away. But inside she burned to know who the speaker was.

Marius Pontmercy had been born twenty-two years earlier into an upper-middle-class family of comfortable means. From the day of his birth his family had expectations of him. It was expected that he would get a decent education at the University of Paris and enter the same trade as his father and his grandfather before him. He was expected to marry a girl from a good family who would bring with her a substantial dowry, and the two of them would settle down and produce sons to carry on the Pontmercy name. It was also expected that he would never tarnish that name. But Marius Pontmercy would not fulfil any of his family's expectations.

At the university, he became radicalized. Once in Paris, he saw for the first time the staggering scale of the injustices and hypocrisy that gripped France in the early 1830s. Men who had a trade or a craft and were willing to work could find no work anywhere. Their wives and children went hungry, often starved. They lost their homes and were forced to sleep in cold streets and alleyways. Meanwhile, in the dining rooms of the rich, the tables buckled under the weight of costly delicacies, bloody roasts and exotic fruit out of season. Food was wasted at every meal, food that could have fed the poor but was thrown away instead.

Marius was taught in his history class about the revolution of 1789, but when he looked around him he couldn't find its precepts of 'Liberty, Equality, Brotherhood' followed anywhere. What had happened to those glorious ideals? Where was the Republic for which men and women had fought and died? Why were the cruel and privileged still in power? Why was a king back on the throne? What had happened to the vote that had been promised to all? Why were the other promises to the people not fulfilled?

It was up to him, he realized, to Marius Pontmercy and his contemporaries, to help the people grasp the power that was theirs by the right of nature and the 1789 revolution. It was for the students to become radicals, to link up with the workers and the disenfranchised – '*les misérables*' – and bring about revolution again. Only this time, they'd make it stick. This time, the blood of Frenchmen would not be shed in vain. Marius had no hesitation; he expected to and was willing to shed blood, including his own.

So Marius Pontmercy, at the age of twenty-one, had turned his back on his origins and become a man of the people. He embraced poverty and its discomforts with an almost saintly pleasure. He gave up without a backward glance the pleasures of the table, the taste of wine in the wine shops, fine new clothing, polished boots, a comfortable feather bed. He joined the student radicals. He went to live in the Saint Antoine district with the poorest of the poor. He ate very little, and most of that little was vegetable soup, coarse bread and porridge. He drank only water. When his clothing became ragged, he stitched it clumsily together, and went on wearing it.

Marius eked out a meagre living, barely a subsistence, by doing an occasional translation for a publisher, annotating manuscripts, and other minor literary jobs which paid him almost nothing. In the past twelve months he had devoted his hours not to the study of Latin, logic and rhetoric, but to organizing the people's unrest and channelling it into righteous wrath, to addressing the people and rousing their revolutionary ardour. He was one of the student organizers of the ABC Society.

As for women, Marius Pontmercy had no time for romance. He no more thought of them than he did of the rare roast beef served up at his father's table. The true love of his life was France, the France that would emerge from revolution as an ideal state. So, when he looked into Cosette's clear eyes, across the mobbed square, he had no defences against her. Those clear eyes went through his heart like an arrow shot from ambush. To Marius she appeared like an angel from a purer, more rarefied part of the heavens. She inspired him. She was France as he'd always dreamed she'd be.

Marius finished his speech and came down from the box, looking for the beautiful young woman who had captured his imagination. Men and women crowded around him, comrades and workers, eager to touch him and speak to him.

'Fine words, Citizen,' said the stonemason. 'But I think we'll need more than arms and legs, don't you?'

Marius smiled. 'We need arms, that's certain.' But his eyes kept raking over the crowd, looking for the girl. Yes, there she was, on the outskirts of the throng. She was going away. He just caught a glimpse of her dark gown as she turned a corner. He had to follow her, to speak to her!

Cosette had never found herself in such a large group before. As other people pushed against her, or elbowed her aside, she became disoriented and a little afraid. Suddenly, she was eager to get back to the fiacre and her father. She hastened to the nearest corner and around it.

It was not the way she'd come; this alley was strange to her. She hurried along the rough cobbles, aware of the filth and the poverty on all sides. The hem of her dress became soiled by the running sewer of the street. Beggars thrust their cracked and bleeding hands out to her, aggressively demanding money. Many of them were children, barefoot, dressed in rags and piteously starved. The pathetic children awoke in Cosette a long-buried memory of bitter unhappiness and terror. The memory wrapped itself around her, frightening her and impelling her to flee.

She broke into a run, her heart beating quickly. She didn't look behind her, didn't see young Marius Pontmercy following her at a distance. Out of breath, she turned another corner and there, at last, was the church, and the fiacre, and her papa, his face crumpled in anxiety and anger.

'Where've you been? I told you not to leave the cab!' Jean Valjean's voice was choked with fury and relief.

'Sorry,' Cosette answered. 'I just got out for some air.'

A figure appeared at the head of the street. 'Who's that?' demanded Valjean.

Cosette looked. It was the young man from the rally. 'I don't know,' she said nervously. 'He was making a speech in the street—'

'Come. We're going home.' Taking her arm, Valjean

ushered Cosette into the fiacre. As he followed her into the cab, he turned to throw Marius another glowering look. He didn't allow himself to relax until the fiacre was safely out of Saint Antoine.

Marius stood watching until the taxi disappeared from view, taking the unknown girl away from him. Then he turned and went back to the quarter. He headed for the Café Musain, where he was to meet up with his best friend Enjolras, a valorous man, another student leader of the ABC Society. He tried to turn his thoughts back to the vital business of revolution, but a pair of large, pure eyes and a wide brow under a lacy bonnet kept crowding into his mind, elbowing out other thoughts.

Once at home in the handsome stone townhouse in the rue Plumet, Cosette went up to her bedroom, where she removed her bonnet and pelisse and hung them away in her armoire. She moved slowly, as though in a dream, lost in her own imagination.

Stopping at her looking glass, she stared at her reflection, almost without seeing it. Dreamily, she removed the pins from her hair, letting the golden mass of it tumble around her shoulders and down her back. She ran her fingers through it, enjoying the sensuous caress of its silkiness on her fingertips. In the looking glass, she saw a young woman, but she saw a young man too – a handsome dark-eyed boy with an earnest expression, and it was as though she were looking at herself through his eyes. Did he find her beautiful, this man whose name she didn't even know?

Out in the upper hallway, Jean Valjean watched his Cosette through her partly open door. He realized that she was totally unaware of his presence, unaware of anything except her reflection in the glass. Yet Valjean knew from the rapturous look on Cosette's face that she was not alone in her thoughts. And he recognized with a spasm of pain that in only a matter of hours the young girl had somehow changed into a woman.

A few hours later, Marius and Enjolras, smuggling weapons under their jackets, returned to their concealed meeting room behind the Café Musain. They gave the secret knock – three raps, a pause, two raps, a pause, then a single rap. The door was opened by a comrade who was in reality Robineaux, Javert's secret informer. The group was not aware of his real identity, and they trusted him.

The other members of the ABC Society were present, waiting for the two. 'Any luck?' asked Courfeyrac, who was the son of rich parents but who was dedicated to revolution. Sitting around the table with Courfeyrac were Grantaire, the group's cynic, with his usual glass of absinthe half empty at his elbow; Feuilly, a self-educated working man; and the easy-going Boussuet. They were cleaning and repairing a few old pistols, trying to get them into working order.

Marius and Enjolras opened their bulky jackets. They had smuggled in some five pistols hidden between the two of them, against their bodies. The two students unloaded them on the table next to the other guns, and the group began inspecting them.

'Maybe we're moving too fast, Marius,' said Enjolras. He was the intellectual of the group, but his tendency to over-think any action made Marius Pontmercy impatient.

'Revolution should always be rushed,' retorted Marius stoutly. 'Progress doesn't have time to waste.'

Enjolras shook his head in disgust. 'This is pathetic. Two weeks and what do we have? Barely enough guns for ourselves.'

But Marius would not allow himself to become discouraged. 'Then we'll do what revolutionaries have always done. We'll tear up the streets and throw cobblestones.'

'Great.' Enjolras's voice held a weary sarcasm. 'But they won't attack with sticks.'

'The word is,' Courfeyrac put in, 'they've got troops and artillery two hours from Paris.'

Enjolras shook his head. 'It's too soon.'

The light of revolution brightened Marius's face. 'If we don't do something soon, nobody will have the strength to fight. Listen to me. We must organize. We need to co-ordinate the stonemasons, the carpenters. We have to be ready to strike at a moment's notice. Because when our chance comes, it won't last long.'

The others nodded agreement, and bent again to their work on the pistols. Outside, in the skies over the streets of Paris, clouds were beginning to form. Red clouds, as red as the flag of revolution, as red as blood.

## Chapter Twenty-Two

### GAVROCHE

'**M**onsieur Fauchelevent's' programme of free food for the poor and homeless was proving very popular. Each day, more and more hungry people came to line up in front of the food tents, and they lined up earlier in the day to be sure of getting a meal before the food ran out. Jean Valjean kept increasing his donations of food, again and again, until he was bringing more than twice as many provisions as when the programme started.

Although the soup kitchen was nominally administrated by the Catholic church in Saint Antoine, Jean Valjean covered all the expenses out of his own pocket. But money and food were not the only thing he provided.

Valjean did not believe in cold charity. It was his conviction that just handing over anonymous money was like turning your back on fellow human beings. One must extend the hand as well, look into the eyes of the needy and acknowledge them as brothers and sisters.

Therefore Valjean and Cosette were deeply involved in the food programme, going to Saint Antoine every day to serve out the hot meals personally. Valjean supplied fresh food daily – good bread, plenty of vegetables like turnips, potatoes, onions, greens, barley, carrots, also fruit, and even meat. He supplied large kettles to cook soups and stews in, and a collection of plain earthen plates and pewter tableware. Whenever he could, he also handed out free warm clothing, used perhaps, but freshly cleaned and still serviceable.

Every day, rain or shine, the free soup kitchen was set up in the grounds of the Saint Antoine church, across the street from a park. Tents on metal frames were erected over long tables loaded with hot, nourishing food for the poor. As soon as the morning Mass was over, the hungry men, women and children formed a long line, waiting patiently, sometimes for hours, for their turn to be served. Once they'd eaten, they were expected to return their plates and spoons for washing. There were no other obligations. Need and – in the case of the church – piety were the only qualifications that had to be met.

Cosette and Valjean came every day to cook and serve. Cosette would cover her dress with a fresh white apron, and her lovely golden hair was bound up in a lace cap. On her face was a sympathetic smile, but her heart was sore at the sight of all these people without food or hope. Yes, it was wonderful to give them a meal, but a hot meal was only one of their many pressing needs. As she served them, Cosette looked into the worn, anxious faces of the homeless, and she felt a stirring she had never felt before. Marius's words, spoken from his podium that first day, came back again and again to haunt her. Especially that fervent question, flung in the face of authority: Why? Why had France failed these people whose only real crime was poverty?

The church insisted that the free meals be restricted to those who had attended the early Mass. No church, no food. Valjean, as a religious Christian, could not fault the priests for rewarding the faithful, although a part of him did feel that there was something a bit too authoritative about the ruling. He wondered: shouldn't charity be unconditional, available to each and every human being? Wasn't that what Christ Himself taught? But he said nothing, not willing to offend the priests by impertinent questions.

Of course, there was always a handful of those clever people who had learned how to beat the system. They managed to get around the rulings, avoiding the early Mass, but they still lined up for the food, counting on their audacity to get them past the snoopy priests.

Gavroche was just such a one. He was an orphaned street urchin, homeless, dirty and ragged, yet cheerful and optimistic. His age was hard to determine. Ten years old? Eleven? Gavroche himself couldn't tell you the answer. He was so wise in the ways of the streets that he might be fifty. He was a survivor, and often had little human barnacles clinging to him in hopes of their own survival. Today he was accompanied by two little homeless boys, perhaps five and seven years of age. To them, Gavroche was a hero, fearless and intelligent. Which, in fact, he was.

When the line of the hungry had moved along enough to bring Gavroche and his barnacles to its head, the elder priest gave him a severe glare.

'You again? I looked. This time, I'm sure you weren't at Mass.'

'I *was*,' protested Gavroche, lying through his teeth. 'I crossed myself so hard I have bruises.' He glanced up slyly at the priest from under the bill of his cap, to see how his words were going down.

But the scowling priest had heard this once too often to be fooled again. This wretched morsel of street trash was definitely not one of the faithful. 'Go on,' he snapped. 'No food for you today. Get out of the line.'

Instantly, Gavroche took his protest to the highest authorities – to Valjean and Cosette. 'Mademoiselle!' he yelled, waving his arms. 'They won't let us in! Monsieur!'

Valjean turned his head at the commotion. He was in his shirtsleeves, dishing steaming soup out of a large kettle into pottery bowls. When he heard Gavroche bawling, and saw the lad waving at him, he smiled. Here was one of his best customers. 'Oh, he's all right,' he told the priest. 'Let him through. We made extra for him.'

Grudgingly, the priest gave way, and the three boys came up to Cosette, who was busy filling plates with bread and apples, which were piled high on wooden trenchers on the table in front of her.

'How are you, Gavroche?' Cosette asked with a smile. This gamin amused her and touched her.

'I'm in excellent health, thank you,' the urchin replied, exactly like a fancy gentleman. 'No one is as kind and as beautiful as you, mademoiselle.'

Laughing at his flirtatious air, Cosette shook her head. 'Gavroche, you're such a convincing liar, I fear for your immortal soul.'

The boys held their empty hands out, and Cosette filled them with soup bowls, bread and apples. She added extra bread, touched by the wide, trusting eyes of the homeless boys.

'Gavroche, who are your little friends?' put in Jean Valjean.

The boy's face became more serious. 'Not friends, monsieur. These are my babies. I found them wandering the streets yesterday.'

'Where are your real parents?' Valjean asked kindly.

'We don't know, sir,' the elder of the boys said. 'Our father took us to the park. He said he was going for food, and he'd be right back.'

'He never came,' added the younger boy, and burst into loud sobs at the recollection. At once, Gavroche grabbed the little boy's nose between his fingers and held on tightly to it, pinching his nostrils shut. Astonished, the crying child opened his mouth in order to breathe, which effectively stopped his blubbering.

'Listen to me,' the urchin said sternly. 'Stop complaining. I told you, I'm looking out for you now, and we're going to have fun. Don't I make a good father, monsieur?' and Gavroche cast a sidelong glance at Jean Valjean.

Valjean regarded the street urchin with respect, mingled with pity. He admired the boy's courage and his plucky, impudent outlook on life. Gavroche's skinny frame was clad only in a ragged pair of breeches and a thin shirt.

'You'd make a better father with a real coat, Gavroche. Wait a moment—' He went off to see if there was something available for the child to wear.

As soon as Valjean was out of earshot, Gavroche leaned over the table, close to Cosette, and whispered, 'My friend wants to know if you will take a walk in the park with him.' He jerked his head in the direction of a park bench across the street from the church. Her heart dancing in her breast, Cosette turned to look.

There was Marius, sitting on the bench, smiling at her. Cosette, who was unused to strong emotions, felt a sudden frisson of unfamiliar feeling, and she shivered in the warm air. Immediately, she cast a nervous glance at her papa, who was coming back, bringing a second-hand thick woollen jacket for Gavroche.

'I understand, mademoiselle,' said the streetwise boy with a wink. 'Perhaps your father will take you for a walk through the park?'

Cosette nodded silently. She was torn between wishing to talk to Marius and not wishing to upset her papa. She was sure that seeing the young man would make Valjean very angry. But, more than anything else, she wanted to meet Marius. So far they had not had the opportunity to exchange a single word. She didn't even know his name. But her virgin heart had been touched by his sensitive face, his compelling voice and the noble sentiments he expressed so well.

'Bring your friends back tomorrow, and I'll have jackets for them,' Valjean promised the boy.

'Thank you, monsieur,' laughed Gavroche, proudly putting his new garment on. 'I hope you find your reward in heaven. Or somewhere even more fun!'

Gavroche winked evilly at the priest and hustled his 'babies' across the street to the park bench where Marius was waiting for him impatiently.

'He's here again,' Marius said glumly, indicating Valjean in the distance.

'He never leaves her alone.' Gavroche shrugged.

'He's not a father, he's a jailer,' the young man muttered darkly. 'Hey, shove off! Here they come.'

The meal was over; everyone asking for food had been fed. A crew of women was washing up the bowls and pots and bringing them into the church for safe-keeping. It was time for Jean Valjean to take his Cosette home for their own midday meal. She took his arm and they crossed the street to the taxi stand, where fiacres were waiting for fares.

'May we go for a stroll through the park?' asked Cosette, through trembling lips.

'What about our lunch?'

'But today is so beautiful,' wheedled Cosette. 'I don't want to go straight home.'

The two of them were coming closer to the stone bench on which Marius was sitting. He stared openly at Cosette, but she concentrated all her attention on her papa, to throw him off the scent and to keep him from seeing Marius.

'I think there were more people this week,' she observed.

'Yes,' Valjean agreed. 'There are more every week.' It

troubled him greatly, this rising homelessness and hopeless poverty. Generous though it was, the free food programme wasn't even a drop in the bucket to the need he perceived growing out there in the real world. There were so many injustices to be set right.

Now they were very close to the bench where Marius was sitting, and Cosette could no longer help herself. She looked directly at him, into his ardent eyes, and her cheeks flushed a dark red. Seeing Cosette start, Valjean followed her eyes and recognized the young man who had been shadowing his daughter. Instantly, he placed himself between Cosette and the insolent boy.

'We have to go. Now!' he told her urgently.

Cosette was used to obeying her papa. Without a murmur, she walked towards the taxicab. Marius half rose in protest, then sank back down, tense with frustration.

None of them noticed that the police informer was watching all three of them carefully from a half-hidden doorway.

The fiacre drove off, but Cosette's mood had entirely changed. She sat as far away from Valjean as she could get, her face morose, just staring out of the window without seeing. Stricken by remorse, Jean Valjean tried to coax her out of her angry mood.

'I can't wait until we're home and Toussaint gives us our chocolate cake. What do you say, Cosette?'

But she wouldn't answer. Her heart burned with indignation. How dare he keep treating her like a little girl, trying to bribe her with chocolate cake! Did he think her a child? Didn't he know that she was a woman? She turned her angry face to him, and Jean Valjean read in it all her scorn. It frightened him; how long would he be able to hold on to the girl he thought of as his beloved only child? He knew that he was overprotecting her, trying to shield her from the harsh realities of the world, which had broken her mother and killed her. But everything he did he did for her benefit. He couldn't bear the thought of losing her.

'Strangers can be dangerous,' he warned her, but even Valjean recognized the feebleness in his argument. It was so much more complicated! Cosette didn't deign to answer. They rode on in silence.


'Well?' demanded Javert. He held his notebook in his hand, ready to jot down anything that might be of interest to the police.

'They have two kegs of gunpowder stored in the back room,' Robineaux the paid informer told him. 'But guns are another story. They've only got ten and one doesn't work.'

Javert noted the information down. 'Is there a plan?'

The snitch shrugged. 'No one can agree on how to make a move. They argue and argue about whether the people are ready, but the truth is they're scared.'

'What about . . .' Javert checked his notebook. '. . . this Marius? Anything on him?'

Robineaux grinned sourly. 'He's in love,' he said scornfully. 'But he has to go to the park to get a glimpse of his beloved while she does her charitable work. He still hasn't managed to exchange a word with her.'

Javert snapped his notebook shut. 'Well, these puppies seem harmless. We should move you to another group.' Taking out his purse, he placed a coin in his snitch's hand. Then, as an afterthought, something occurred to him. 'Why doesn't she talk to him?' he asked the informer.

'Who? Oh, the girl. Her father's always there.'

'Why is her father always there?' Nothing significant so far, but Inspector Javert collected information automatically, like a reflex. One never knew when two separate facts might be put together and make one useful fact.

'He pays for the free food.'

Something about the remark triggered Javert's curiosity further. 'What free food?'

'I told you,' the snitch insisted.

'No you didn't. Who gets the food?' the inspector wanted to know.

'The local poor. The church distributes it to parishioners who come to early Mass.'

'And the girl's father pays?' Inspector Javert was always suspicious of those who led a publicly charitable existence.

'Yes. She helps hand it out. I know you like me to be thorough, so I checked. He's behind the charity.'

Javert took his notebook out again. 'Who is the father?'

The informer shook his head. 'A gentleman. I didn't find out much. Only his name – Fauchelevent.' He saw Javert's brows knit together for a moment. 'You know him?'

Something about that name ... he'd heard it before somewhere. A snippet of memory from the past ... no, it was gone. 'I don't think so. Our revolutionary hasn't said a word to the father either?'

The informer grinned, a shark-like leer. 'No. He gives the girl these long dangerous looks. Very romantic.'

'Don't assume he's that big a fool,' Javert replied. 'Maybe he's really in love with the father's money.'

Now Robineaux misunderstood the inspector's meaning. He knew Marius Pontmercy to be a dedicated young radical, not a fortune-seeker. 'No. With all due respect, sir, I—'

'They need guns,' Javert interrupted. 'Guns cost money. And it's rich, soft-hearted people who fund revolutions. Stick with Marius. I'll see you next week.'

\*     \*     \*

The following day, Cosette and her papa returned as usual to the church at Saint Antoine to serve food to the hungry. Cosette said little and kept her eyes lowered demurely, but whenever Valjean wasn't looking she scanned the park benches eagerly, looking for the young man who was occupying so much of her thoughts lately.

At last! There he was, sitting on his usual stone bench, smiling over at her. As soon as Cosette saw her papa leaving the food tent, carrying an empty soup kettle into the church, she felt emboldened to smile back. Marius waved enthusiastically at her, gesturing for her to come over.

This was the moment she'd been waiting for. Cosette bid the priest a sedate goodbye, and walked across the street to the park. Under her modest frock, her heart was pounding in triple time, and the palms of her clenched hands were damp. She could see Marius's beautiful dark eyes fixed on her face, and the intensity of his gaze made small beads of sweat break out on her brow.

What should she say to him? Cosette was so overwhelmed by the thought of actually speaking to him that she could think of nothing. Words were failing her. But surely he would speak first! And what would he say to her? Another moment or two and she would know.

But that moment was not to be now. Suddenly the figure of Jean Valjean loomed in front of her. She had been so intent on Marius that she hadn't seen him coming back out of the church and striding quickly towards her. Before she reached the bench, Valjean had signalled a taxicab over.

'Get in,' he said curtly.

'But . . .' stammered a nervous Cosette. 'May we go for a walk? It's so sunny and mild.'

Jean Valjean shook his head. 'I'm tired. Take me home. You can read to me in the garden.'

Cosette nibbled at her lip. 'Why don't you go home and lie down, Papa? I'll walk in the park.'

'Alone?'

The girl lifted her chin. 'Well, I'm going to have to walk alone someday.'

'Someday. Not today.' There was no mistaking the finality in his words and his tone.

'I know!' Cosette said brightly. 'Why don't you sit in the fiacre and relax, while I take a walk?' Her nervousness was evident.

'Don't play games, Cosette!' snapped Valjean.

'I'm not playing games,' Cosette answered, lowering her lids. She hated deceiving Papa, but she hadn't yet met or said a single word to the young man she kept dreaming about. It was her only wish, to speak to him and to listen to him. Was it so wrong to want to reach out to another human being? Especially to so handsome a one with such mesmerizing eyes?

'Get in. I'm your father,' Valjean ordered. 'Are you disobeying me?' There was genuine anger in his voice.

Her papa had never spoken to her like that in her life! Without another word or a backward look, Cosette followed Valjean into the taxi.

Another opportunity lost! With a groan, Marius sank back down on the bench. Then he saw something to make him smile. Young Gavroche had hopped unseen on to the footboard above the rear axle of the fiacre, and was being carried along, as comfortable as you please. In this way he could follow the mysterious 'Fauchelevents' to their home, so he could report back to his pal Marius on where they lived, and where he could find his lady love. He grinned at Marius and gave him a friendly 'thumbs-up.'

Greatly relieved, Marius grinned back and stuck his own thumbs up in the air.

And, on the next corner, Robineaux the police snitch flagged a taxi down and said to the driver, 'Follow that fiacre.'

## Chapter Twenty-Three

### COSETTE AND MARIUS

Jean Valjean's house on the rue Plumet was an imposing two-storey villa of white stone, fronted by a thickly planted garden. The street around the house was prosperous and respectably middle-class, but the neighbourhood itself was not particularly ostentatious or fashionable. Valjean especially enjoyed his home's proximity to the nearby Luxembourg Gardens, where he and Cosette took their daily walks.

But the home's greatest virtue was its privacy. The house itself was sheltered from the street by a stone garden wall, with a locked gate. Growing here and there in the garden were some handsome, very old trees with broad, heavy branches, affording a great deal of shade and privacy.

Valjean didn't want to call attention to himself or Cosette, so they lived well but not luxuriously, with only a single female servant to look after them and cook simple but ample food for their table.

Valjean had invested his money wisely, and although he had a generous income, he made certain they lived within it. His greatest expenditure was the generous amount he allotted to charity every month. He and Cosette also visited the aged, infirm and ill, gave freely to anybody in need, and went frequently to Mass. In every way, Jean Valjean attempted to provide a normal, useful and happy life for the young woman he thought of as his daughter

He had never revealed to Cosette any of the secrets of his life or hers. To Cosette, he was 'Papa'; she had never known another father. Their name, Cosette believed, was Fauchelevent, for so she'd been told. Her old uncle, Papa's brother, had worked for the sisters at Petit-Picpus until his death two years ago. Cosette seemed content not asking questions. She appeared to have only the dimmest recollection of her unhappy former life with the Thenardiers, and she didn't remember her mother at all. On the few occasions when she had asked him questions about her, all Valjean had ever told her was that her mother was dead. She seemed satisfied to know nothing more.

Jean Valjean hadn't yet given Cosette the simple little necklace that her mother had entrusted to him on her deathbed. He treasured it as his only real link with Fantine, whom he had loved as he'd never loved a woman before. He knew that someday he would have to part with it; he had promised Fantine he would. But giving Cosette the necklace would mean opening the door to the past. He would have to tell Cosette some of the circumstances of her mother's life, and he put that day off. That was how he'd dealt with Cosette for a dozen years – by putting off the day of reckoning, by keeping her sheltered from the ugly secrets that enshrouded them both.

Cosette was aware that 'Papa' was not in fact her real father. She had some faint and unpleasant recollections – a cruel woman, incredibly hard work, never getting enough to eat, a tall man who had come to rescue her, a long chase through a scary forest and, at last, a safe arrival at the Petit-Picpus convent and the beginning of a different life.

Yet Cosette didn't have any idea that she and her papa were fugitives from justice, or that he was a criminal. He was such a good man, so charitable, so full of feeling for suffering humanity, how could she ever imagine that he had once been a violent and unsavoury man who hated the world and everyone in it? She knew that for all their wealth they lived rather reclusively, with no friends, but she didn't know why. Papa didn't volunteer information, and Cosette knew better than to ask.

Besides, her life was calm and pleasant. Her papa was kindness itself, and the best company imaginable. She enjoyed spending her evenings alone with him in the sitting room. Sometimes she read aloud to him, while he listened with enjoyment. At other times, Cosette would play on the spinet and sing, which Jean Valjean considered the greatest pleasure of his life. For a long time the girl had the only companion she needed, and everything she wanted. Until now.

Now she yearned for something more, something vastly different from what she was accustomed to. Cosette could not even put a name to her yearnings, except that they were intimately connected to burning black eyes and a sensitive mouth. And now, for the first time, her papa had set himself against her, refusing to give an inch. Her wordless yearnings he dismissed as disobedience.

For the first time in her life, Cosette was questioning every aspect of her life here in the rue Plumet. Who was she, really? Who was Papa? Were they family? What was their true relationship to each other? What was her future to be? This morning Cosette had informed Papa that someday she would have to walk alone, and his only answer had been 'Someday. Not today.' Was this to be his answer to everything? 'Someday. Not today.' She couldn't bear it. She *wouldn't* bear it.

The girl had never been difficult, had never misbehaved. Recognizing the debt of gratitude she owed to the man who supported and protected her, Cosette had always been dutiful and obedient. It came easily to her; by nature she was a pleasant, kind and affectionate person. She possessed a large, warm heart and a deep well of sympathy for others.

But now a rebellious spirit was stirring in Cosette's heart. Why should she not be in some control of her own life? How long would Papa be authorized to make all her decisions for her? That might have been all right when she was six years old, or when she was ten or even fourteen. But she was a woman now, eighteen years old. She believed that she was mature enough to decide for herself, and to choose her own path in this life. Papa's unexpected opposition confused her and made her very angry.

Cosette was still angry when she stepped out of the fiacre. Valjean said nothing when he followed her into the house. Neither of them noticed Gavroche dropping silently from the rear axle of their fiacre. Nor did anyone notice the second fiacre coming to a halt at the far corner, or see the police informer peering out at them from inside.

By dinner-time, Cosette's open anger against her papa had somewhat diminished, but the questions stirred up by it had not. All day long she had remained in her room, thinking and brooding, going over the same questions in her mind again and again. She still felt sullen and depressed, and it was with reluctance that she came down to the candlelit dining room and faced Jean Valjean across a long mahogany table.

Their only servant, a sixty-five-year-old woman named Toussaint who suffered from severe stuttering, served them a simple dinner of thick soup and black bread. She replaced the ladle in the heavy tureen. 'W . . . w . . . will that be all?'

'Yes, thank you, Toussaint.' Valjean was always gracious and patient with the old woman's handicap. He dug in with relish, spooning up the tasty soup and biting into chunks of the bread. But Cosette merely stirred the soup around with her spoon, without transferring any of it to her mouth.

'You're not, you know,' she said suddenly.

Valjean looked up in surprise. 'I'm not what?'

'You're not my father.' Frowning, Cosette looked across the table at him. When he didn't reply, she continued. 'You never said you were. That is, until you became so angry and behaved so strangely today. That was the first time you said it. The very first time.'

Valjean struggled to keep his equanimity. 'You're right,' he said calmly, and took another mouthful of the soup.

'Well . . .' challenged Cosette. '*Are* you my father?' She waited for a reply.

Inside, Valjean's feelings were in turmoil. Her question was one he'd been dreading so much, even more than being discovered and arrested by Javert. How much should he reveal? What was it safe to tell her, and what would shake Cosette's secure world to its foundation? He drew a deep breath.

'Cosette,' he began slowly, 'I promised your mother I would take care of you. I know you think I worry too much, but strangers can be dangerous—'

'All right! All right!' Cosette interrupted, with a sudden shout.

'Cosette! What's the matter?' Valjean was taken aback; she had never behaved like this before.

The girl's face was angrier than Valjean had ever seen it. 'I don't want to hear that speech again,' she burst out. 'I know . . . there's something shameful. It must be me.'

'No, my child—'

'Or you. You're the shameful secret,' accused Cosette. 'Or maybe both of us. It doesn't matter. I can't talk to people, I can't go out—'

'Stop this, Cosette,' Valjean cried. 'It won't help—'

But Cosette was unable to stop. Her resentful feelings had been pent up for so long, and now accusations just came pouring forth. 'I think you're lying. I know the secret. The secret is that you want me here with you all the time. Night and day. You're lonely, and you want me to be alone for ever, so I'll be stuck with you.' Standing up, she flung her napkin on the table and ran from the room.

Cosette's angry, hurtful words struck Jean Valjean deeply. He couldn't dismiss them, hasty and ill considered as they were. He understood the turmoil of emotions she was feeling, and he recognized how much the girl wanted a measure of freedom. He knew that he had been oppressive, and he was sorry for it. Cosette, too, was a prisoner here.

Jean Valjean had kept her a prisoner, pampering her and cushioning her so that she wouldn't chafe against the bars around her. But he couldn't bear the thought of opening the door to her cage. Little birds aren't safe when they fly free. The sky is too big.

Getting up from the table, he followed Cosette out into the garden. She was sitting on a marble bench, weeping. For a long minute Valjean stood watching her, love and remorse gnawing at him.

'Cosette?' he said quietly.

The girl struggled to regain her self-control. Her sobs began to subside. 'Cosette?' Valjean said again.

'What?' she sniffled. But she kept her back turned to him.

'You're right. I'm not a father. I don't . . . I just want to protect you. The world isn't a safe place. Believe me. You're the only person I have. This is the only way I know how to do it. I'm sorry.'

Cosette heard a genuine sorrow in his voice and words, and his apology touched her deeply. She had always thought

Les Misérables

of her papa as such a large man, so strong, and so impervious
to pain. Now she saw him for the first time as vulnerable.
He had comforted her so often, and now it was her turn to
comfort him. She reached out for his hand. 'It's all right,'
she said softly.

'I want to be a good father, Cosette,' he whispered.

Cosette turned to him, and in the clear moonlight Valjean
could see tears glistening on her cheeks. 'You are. You're
a good father to me,' she told him sincerely.

Valjean smiled; Cosette's acknowledgment was a soothing
ointment on the wounds of his soul. 'Come, have your
supper,' he said gently.

'I'll be right in,' promised Cosette. 'In a minute.'

'All right,' agreed Valjean. 'Toussaint will save it.' He went
back into the house.

Cosette remained sitting on the marble bench. It was
getting colder, but she didn't feel chilly. She stayed lost in
herself, struggling with her new emotions, which threatened
to overwhelm and engulf her.

Suddenly, she heard a strange sound. She opened her
eyes and listened. Yes, there it was again. It seemed to
be coming from the locked gate at the further end of the
garden. She looked and saw a shadowy form by the gate,
and heard a voice whisper, 'Pssst!' And a small, square,
pale shape was pushed through the bars.

Cosette looked around. Her father had disappeared into
the house and she was totally alone in the garden. She moved
swiftly to the gate. There he was, the dark-eyed young man
she longed for, and he was pushing an envelope through
the barred gate towards her. She took it.

'What's your name?' whispered Cosette.

'Marius. And yours?'

'Cosette.' She opened the envelope. There were many,
many pages inside, all covered in a flowing script.

'C . . . C . . . Cosette?' It was Toussaint calling from inside the house. 'I can w . . . warm up your s . . . s . . . soup.'

'I'd better go,' Marius said hastily. 'I'll be waiting here tomorrow night.'

'I'm coming, Toussaint,' Cosette called back. She hid the letter in her gown. 'See you tomorrow,' she whispered to Marius. Then, almost dizzy with excitement, she turned away and headed back to the house, leaving an excited young man to dream of clear, dark eyes under a wide, pure brow and a lace-trimmed bonnet.

Even though she sat meekly down at the dining table, two spoonfuls of soup were all that Cosette could choke down. Her mind was on Marius – Marius! What a wonderful name – and on the thick letter hidden in her skirts. All she really wanted was to go upstairs to her room and be alone, with only a lamp and the letter. She longed to read every word of what he had to say to her.

'I'm going to bed,' she announced.

Valjean put his coffee cup down. 'But you haven't eaten,' he protested mildly. He was still worried about her.

Cosette came around to Valjean's side of the table and kissed her papa on his forehead. 'I'm not hungry. Thank you, Papa. Goodnight.'

And she left him to run upstairs to her precious letter. Jean Valjean sat for a long time over a cold cup of coffee. His heart was heavy with anxiety.

Marius Pontmercy was so fired up by meeting Cosette Fauchelevent and speaking to her, however briefly, that he had to take action, any action as long as it was immediate.

Never had Marius been so optimistic. He was in love with the most beautiful, most charming, most intelligent girl in the world, and he wanted nothing more than to bring about a world worthy of her.

Marius had declared himself in pages and pages of prose, and therefore the coming revolution now seemed to him only a few days away. How could it be otherwise, with the blood flowing so hotly in his veins? Tonight, he hoped and prayed, he would know how Cosette had received his words, and what she thought of him and his hopes for their future life together. He had an added incentive now – to make the world better not only for all Frenchmen but for Cosette especially. Would she stand by his side as a soldier-daughter of the revolution?

He was filled with energy. Fired up, he called a special meeting of the ABC Society at the Café Musain.

The upcoming state funeral of General Lamarque, a popular hero of the Hundred Days War, was anticipated with boiling indignation by the radicals. The man had struggled on behalf of the people and, now that he was dead, the authorities and the monarchy were planning to co-opt the occasion and turn his funeral into a bourgeois propaganda parade. It was around the funeral that the radical demonstrations were being planned. Groups like Marius's in Saint Antoine were working towards an uprising on the day of the obsequies. All over Paris, revolutionary fire was burning and spreading.

The ABC group was finally beginning to coalesce, as the students formed tight bonds with the workers. The workers had formed separate cells, like unions or guilds, one for each of the professions. By allowing the workers into their ranks, the ABC Society had forged special ties with the miners, the stonemasons and the carpenters, bringing them into the group. Enjolras and Marius had sent messages to the leaders of the three worker factions, promising immediate action if the workers would agree to fight with them.

Marius impatiently paced the meeting room at the back of the café, stalking back and forth while Enjolras sat quietly at the table, waiting for the others to join them. Enjolras still had some doubts about the timing of the planned uprising, but Marius had gone a long way towards convincing him that the time was right, and the time was now. His impatience was wearing down his friend Enjolras's caution. With them was one other comrade, the man who was Inspector Javert's secret informer – Robineaux. He was always with them; he said very little, but his eyes were everywhere.

It seemed hours before the agreed-upon secret signal sounded, coded knocks on the door. It marked the arrival of the workers at last.

They took their seats without greeting, and sat in silence for a moment, looking at one another, each man searching the others' faces as though the future was written there. Finally one of them spoke.

'All right. We're in,' the stonemason said grimly.

'Good.' Enjolras nodded.

'Now let's make a plan,' said Marius, and they bent over the table, studying a map of the streets of Paris.

The following evening, Jean Valjean came into the sitting room, dressed in his greatcoat and tall hat. He was surprised to find Cosette sitting near the fire, a book in her hand. 'Aren't we going for our walk?' Their quiet evening strolls together were very important to Valjean.

Cosette looked up from the pages. 'Not tonight, Papa, I want to finish my book.' Nothing under heaven would get her away from the house tonight, not when Marius had promised to return to her garden.

'We skipped it last night,' said Valjean anxiously. 'And you've been in all day. You need some exercise.'

Cosette shook her head and pretended to suppress a yawn. 'I'm too tired.'

Valjean looked keenly at her, noting how pale her

cheeks were, how nervous her expression. 'You'll be all right?'

Cosette smiled at him. 'Of course. I have my book. And Toussaint is here.'

Reluctantly, Valjean nodded his agreement. 'Goodnight, my child,' he said, and left to take his walk by himself. He had no inkling that, almost outside his window, events were beginning to flow together that would change not only his life and Cosette's but the course of French history. Or that he would be caught up in these events.

At last the front door shut behind Papa. Cosette was afraid he'd never leave, that he would decide to stay at home with her instead. Feverishly, she threw her book to one side. The only thing she could think about was Marius, Marius and his wonderful long letter. In its many pages, he had declared his love for her again and again, with ardour and sincerity and a matchless eloquence.

Cosette had shut herself away in her bedroom all day, and read the letter again and again, until its every word was burned into her memory. Never, she believed, had anyone received so moving a protestation of love and revolution, so mixed together in one communication! His passions ignited hers; as soon as her papa had left the house, impatience to see Marius again drove Cosette from her seat by the fire and out into the garden. He'd promised to come back again tonight. Maybe he was waiting for her even now! Soon he might even be declaring his love in person!

With a fire that set her limbs trembling, and a fluttering in her heart that she had never felt before, the girl Cosette hurried to meet her lover. She knew that this was the end of her innocence, that her love would take away her girlhood and make her a woman, and she ran eagerly to embrace her Marius and her destiny.

## Chapter Twenty-Four

### JAVERT'S NOTE

**O**utside the house on the rue Plumet, Marius was already watching in the shadows, waiting for Jean Valjean to walk down the street and turn a corner. When the coast was clear, he approached the Fauchelevent's garden gate. Within moments Cosette appeared, walking quickly. Without a word, she unlocked the gate and gestured silently for Marius to come inside and follow her.

Cosette led Marius to a tall oak tree with a massive trunk that stood near the garden wall. It was in full leaf, and the tree's thick, wide-spreading branches formed a shelter so private that it was like being in a world of their own. The two young people stepped into that shelter, and found themselves alone with each other, the rest of the world shut out. Cosette drew Marius's letter from her skirt and held it close to her breast, staring into his handsome face.

Ah, the letter! She had read it! She had kept it! Marius stood transfixed, anxious, his heart in his eyes. Above them, the canopy of oak leaves rustled in the cool evening breeze of late May. And then, miracle of miracles, Cosette leaned close to him and kissed his lips.

It was Cosette's first kiss of love, given out of the fullness of her virgin heart. It was shy and sweet, like a butterfly brushing a nectar-filled blossom with its delicate wings. But Cosette's precious kiss ran like a river of fire from Marius's lips through his veins until it reached his heart.

'I love you too,' she whispered, her first words to her lover.

With a soft moan of desire, Marius gathered Cosette up in his arms, and pressed her close to him. They kissed again, longer and deeper, losing themselves in each other's embrace.

At last they drew apart, each looking longingly into the other's eyes. No lovers before them, nor those who came after them, could possibly want each other more than Cosette and Marius did under their private oak-leaf canopy. 'Tell me everything,' Marius breathed.

'Everything? About what?'

'About you.'

'There's nothing,' Cosette replied honestly. 'Nothing to tell. I'm a very simple girl. I live a very simple life. I grew up in a convent, with lots of other girls, of course. My father lived there, too. My father's a very good man. I grew up in his love ... if you know what I mean. His love was my home.'

She hesitated, a little embarrassed about what she would tell him next. 'And then ... then I met you. And you, what about you?' She smiled shyly at him. 'You're a genius, aren't you?'

The boy threw his head back and laughed heartily. 'A genius? I'm a poor student. No smarter, no stupider than most.' But he was pleased nonetheless at her choice of words. A genius! What young man could object to being called a genius by a very pretty girl?

'Your speech was beautiful,' Cosette said softly. 'I didn't breathe while you talked. I was afraid I'd miss a word.'

'Well, when I saw you,' Marius answered lovingly, 'I forgot what I was talking about.'

Once more they gazed into each other's eyes, sharing looks of love and passion. Once more they kissed, and then again . . .

Jean Valjean left the Luxembourg Gardens and walked slowly down the back streets of his *arrondissement*, lost in thought. Cosette's words weighed heavily on his heart. He realized that her accusations were impetuous and overdramatic, yet he recognized the justice of her complaints. She was growing up; eighteen was an age at which young girls became women and were married. As much as he wanted to stop time and keep Cosette a girl for ever, there was no way that he could. That was in God's power alone, not his. He realized that their old life together – their shared piety and good works, books, music, quiet evenings at home, a young girl depending on her papa – was no longer enough of a life for Cosette.

Perhaps it *was* time for him seriously to consider loosening his tight hold on her. He couldn't protect her for ever. As precious as his own freedom was to him, hers must be of equal value to Cosette. He had lied, cheated, forged and stolen to gain his freedom; who knew what Cosette might do to gain hers?

Valjean arrived at the River Seine without realizing he had come so far. A stone wall, chest high, separated him from the river, and he strolled slowly alongside it for a while. Then he stopped and leaned on the wall, staring down into the dark river as it flowed silently past him, as though the water held the answers and the Seine itself could help him to solve his knotty problem. But the river told him nothing. The answer must lie within himself.

When Jean Valjean came home, he went directly upstairs to his bedroom. Opening a closet, he took down a box with a rope tied around it, and placed it on the bed. He stood regarding it for a minute or two, then he loosened the rope and opened the box. Inside was a worn and dirty child's dress, the dress Cosette had worn the night Valjean had taken her away from the Thenardiers. He lifted it out very carefully and laid it on the bed.

The dress was torn and full of holes, where Cosette had snagged it on sharp branches in their flight. Although it was crumbling away, this little frock was precious to Valjean, a reminder of where they'd come from, and what the two of them had endured to get here. The only other object in the box was a necklace, the little necklace that Fantine had entrusted Valjean with on her deathbed, begging him to give it to her daughter as a gift from herself.

Ever so gently, Jean Valjean lifted the necklace from the box and held the fragile thing in his huge hands. This cheap little necklace represented the truth about Cosette's former life. He turned it over and over, remembering poor, wretched Fantine and how he had cared for her, and thinking of Cosette, and of how much he was afraid to lose her. Tears came into his eyes as he struggled to make up his mind.

As soon as the fiacre turned into the rue Plumet and stopped at the corner, Robineaux dashed up to it. Chief Inspector Javert was waiting inside the taxi, his notebook out to record his informer's weekly report on the visits of Marius Pontmercy to the Fauchelevents. Javert was reluctant to let go of the notion that somehow this Monsieur Fauchelevent was funding the radicals, and obtaining weapons for them, and that Marius Pontmercy was the gunrunner and liaison between the money and radical groups like the ABC Society.

But Robineaux had little to add to the inspector's notes. In the past two weeks, Marius and Cosette had been meeting secretly by night, every night, in the garden at the rue Plumet. They had no idea that they were under

Robineaux's surveillance. And a deadly dull surveillance it had been, according to the police spy.

'This week the same as last? Every night?' Javert wanted to know.

'Inspector, they're in love,' the informer snorted. Then he sneezed loudly. 'It's perfectly nauseating. She leaves the gate unlocked and they stay in the garden till dawn. They even stay out there when it rains—' The man broke off to sneeze again, and once again. 'I haven't caught a gun supplier, Inspector, I've caught pneumonia.'

'And the father knows nothing?' Javert asked.

'This too, it seems to me, is not a surprise. Isn't the father always the last to know? I admit the whole experience has disillusioned me,' Robineaux whined. He blew his nose loudly into a dirty handkerchief. 'I certainly don't plan on having children. Especially not a daughter.'

The informer broke off to sneeze again, three long, hearty, wet sneezes that left him with a runny nose. 'Can I be reassigned? Perhaps I could infiltrate some nice anarchists, with a warm roof over their head?'

'Yes, yes, I'll handle this,' Javert agreed impatiently. 'You're relieved. Take two days off and report to me. You'll be reassigned.'

'Thank you,' Robineaux said gratefully. He hesitated, then ventured to ask, 'Just out of curiosity, sir, what are you going to do?'

'From what you've said,' Javert answered, 'Monsieur Fauchelevent is respectable and well-off.'

'Yes.' Robineaux nodded agreement.

'A little soft-hearted, perhaps, but a churchgoer, loving father, and so on . . .'

'Yes, absolutely. The whole neighbourhood speaks well of him.'

Javert allowed himself the luxury of a little smile. 'Then

I think he deserves to know his daughter has been seduced by a dangerous radical.'

These were harsh words from a harsh man, but Javert had not changed his opinion of the human race since he was a young policeman let loose on a world of criminals and evil-doers. He had witnessed many acts of kindness and charity in the years since then, but none of them had served to soften his mind to his fellow beings, or given him any insight into the human condition.

Chief Inspector Javert could never understand a man like Jean Valjean, for example, who had changed so completely from criminal to philanthropist, from an enemy of the human race to a benefactor.

Years of work as a gardener in the Petit-Picpus convent had given Valjean a genuine love of growing things. To work in the earth was one of his chief pleasures; he loved plunging his hands into the rich soil. He loved handling the immature plants as though they were his children, and most of all he loved seeing a plant come to fruit or to flower. On every fine day when he had some leisure, Valjean was to be found dressed in his old garden clothing which he had brought with him from the convent. He'd spend hours on his knees with a trowel or spade, bringing new life to his garden in the rue Plumet.

On this sun-drenched day in early June, his servant Toussaint walked slowly out of the house to find Valjean kneeling in the flower-bed, planting a new crop of annuals. He was grouping them carefully by colour.

'Ah, Toussaint,' he called out cheerfully at the sight of the old woman. 'Take a break from cooking and sit in the garden. What a glorious day!'

But Toussaint shook her head. She was here on an important errand. 'There's som . . . som . . . someone here . . . to see you,' she stuttered.

Valjean sat back on his heels, trowel in hand. He stripped off his work gloves and began to brush soil off his breeches. 'Who is it?'

'In . . . In . . . Inspec . . . Inspec . . .' Toussaint was having a problem just getting the words out.

Valjean stood up and started towards the house to greet his guest. 'Doesn't matter. I'll—'

'. . . tor Javert,' Toussaint finished at last. 'From the police.'

Valjean stopped, transfixed. He could hardly catch his breath. Javert! Here? This was so unexpected he barely knew what to do first. All he knew was that he felt impelled to run, to escape now.

Inside the house, Inspector Javert paced the sitting room, waiting for the master of the house to make his appearance. It was a large, well-furnished room, with comfortable divans, prettily inlaid tables, pleasant oil paintings in heavy gilded frames, and a spinet piano. The room was accented by a wide marble mantel over a fireplace in which a log fire burned cheerfully despite the mildness of the day. On the mantel stood a pair of heavy silver candlesticks.

They looked somehow familiar to Javert, those candlesticks. He strolled over to inspect them more closely. He had a feeling he might have seen them somewhere before, years ago. He tried to remember where, or under what circumstances, but he couldn't quite put his finger on it. His memory, so sharp ten years ago, was not quite as sharp today, probably because the growing political dissension in Paris was occupying so much of his mind these days.

Meanwhile, where was Monsieur Fauchelevent? How long was a high-level police chief inspector to be kept waiting? The stuttering old woman had gone out to the front of the house. The garden? Javert moved to follow her, but before he reached the sitting-room door the servant

Toussaint reappeared, coming in from the garden. Beyond her, Javert caught a glimpse of a figure disappearing hastily around the back of the house.

'Cou . . . cou . . . could . . . you wait . . . a . . . a . . . ?' stammered the servant.

'I'll wait,' interrupted Javert impatiently. 'Who was that?'

'That w . . . wa . . . was—'

'Yes?'

'A g . . . gardener.'

Javert accepted the explanation without further question. He'd observed that the running figure had been dressed in old working clothes.

As soon as he heard the policeman's name, Jean Valjean assumed that Javert had come to arrest him. How had the authorities found him out? What had given him away? But never mind that now. This was not the time for speculation.

With Inspector Javert in the house, Valjean had to make his mind up very quickly as to what to do. He had no time to waste. But he couldn't just take immediate flight, leaving Cosette behind without a word of explanation. Besides, he had given Fantine his word that he'd always look after her. He could never flee without taking her along with him; they would flee together, when the trail was cold. It would take him several days to arrange for sufficient money, to reserve transportation, to decide on a destination.

To run away by himself would be the work of a moment, but to run with Cosette required intelligent advance planning.

No, the best plan of all was to *pretend* to run, to set Javert off on a wild-goose chase, looking for him anywhere but here in the rue Plumet. For this he needed the immediate help of Cosette.

How much was it safe for him to reveal to her? Valjean

decided to inform her only that he had to leave, was unexpectedly called away, must go very soon. On the other hand, he would have to hide here, in this house, until it was time to leave. Most important of all, the police inspector waiting downstairs must not suspect that 'Monsieur Fauchelevent' was still in this house.

Valjean hurried to Cosette's room, and surprised her just as she was locking away a letter from Marius in the top drawer of her dressing table. She turned to her papa, flustered and guilty, but saw at once that he had something else on his mind. In a few words he informed her that there was some trouble, and told her she had to cover for him with a lie to the officer downstairs.

Cosette didn't understand. She had never seen her papa like this – rattled, almost panicked. And she could hardly comprehend what he was telling her, that she had to go down and give false information to a police inspector.

'But why?' she demanded, totally confused. 'Why say you're away—?'

'Cosette, there's no time to explain,' Valjean answered urgently. 'Tell him I won't be back for a weeek. If he asks questions about your past, say you have a headache and excuse yourself. All right? No details.'

'You're frightened,' Cosette marvelled. Valjean's fear had communicated itself to her.

'Yes. No. Please . . . just go. Try not to be nervous. He'll sense it. Be calm and composed.'

But calmness and composure were not easy for an eighteen-year-old girl who had no idea what she was really getting into. Cosette went down to the sitting room with fluttering pulses, to find a tall, thin man dressed all in black waiting for her. He stood up as she entered the room. With a bow, he introduced himself as Chief Inspector Javert, and his deep black eyes seemed to bore holes in her, making Cosette even more nervous.

Both of them sat down, facing each other across a small table. Through dry lips, Cosette began to stammer out the story that her papa had given her. Javert sat without speaking, but he appeared to be listening.

'. . . so you see, my father instructed Toussaint to say he's out when he's on one of his trips, so that no one will know we're just two helpless women here by themselves. Isn't it ridiculous that she worried about it with you, a police inspector?'

'When will he return?' Javert asked. He had barely listened to most of what the girl had told him, dismissing her as little better than a slut. But he had grasped that Monsieur Fauchelevent was presently not in Paris.

'Oh . . . a week. Hard to say,' Cosette replied nervously.

Taking his notebook out of his pocket, Javert began to write. 'I'm going to leave him a note. Do you have an envelope?'

'Right here.' Cosette fumbled in a drawer, and pulled out an envelope. Javert finished writing, folded the paper and put the note inside the envelope. He sealed it, and turned it over to address it.

'Fauchelevent,' he mused. 'I knew a Fauchelevent. Where did your people come from?'

Cosette froze. 'Uh . . . here . . . Paris.'

'Paris? Probably no relation.' He handed over the sealed envelope. 'This is for your father's eyes alone. And I'd appreciate it if you gave him the letter yourself.' A little irony he relished inwardly, although outwardly his icy demeanour did not change.

Cosette accepted the note with trembling fingers. Javert noticed her nervousness, but put it down to guilt on her part. This was a girl who was engaged in an illicit amour behind a loving parent's back. No wonder she looked nervous. Formally, he bowed and took his leave.

Cosette made her way slowly up the stairs to her bedroom, where Jean Valjean was waiting for her. Mutely, he questioned her with a look, and Cosette nodded, telling him that Javert had accepted the lie and was gone. She handed over the note, and Valjean turned away to open and read it.

Cosette shivered. 'What a horrible man! How do you know him? He has no feeling in his eyes.'

Suddenly, Valjean wheeled around, his face almost purple with rage, and shoved the note in Cosette's face. 'What does this mean?' he demanded furiously. ' "Your daughter has been seduced by a dangerous radical named Marius Pontmercy. She betrays you every night by meeting him in your garden." '

Cosette shrank back in horror. 'I . . . I don't know,' she muttered in a strangled voice.

Jean Valjean's hand shot out, slapping Cosette hard on the cheek, sending her rocking backwards. The girl gasped with shock more than pain. In all the years with Papa, he had never once struck her.

'Don't lie to me!' Valjean brought his face close to Cosette's. His eyes were dark with fury. 'Have you given yourself to this . . . this person?'

Anger flooded through the girl. 'Why should I tell you?' she cried defiantly.

Her defiance brought Valjean's hand up once more. He brandished it as a physical threat. 'Is it true? Every night? You see him every night?'

Cosette's head went back and her chin stuck out as she returned her papa's gaze. 'Well, go ahead. Hit me. Is that why I should tell you? Because you'll hit me?'

The sight of his hand imprinted on her flaming cheek, the

flashing of her courageous eyes, brought Jean Valjean back to his senses. He lowered his hand, and when he spoke it was much more quietly, yet with equal intensity. 'Tell me the truth, Cosette.'

Now it was Cosette's turn to be indignant. 'How dare you ask for the truth when you tell me only lies? Why does a policeman frighten you out of your wits? Who is he? *Who are you?*'

Valjean saw it all now. It wasn't he who had been under surveillance by the police. Javert had no idea of the true identity of Monsieur Fauchelevent. It was this Marius Pontmercy, the damned radical who had stolen Cosette from him, and who had unwittingly led the police and Inspector Javert straight to the rue Plumet. In setting his trap for Marius Pontmercy, Javert had also ensnared Jean Valjean.

'You don't understand,' he sighed. 'You've ruined me. You've ruined us.'

'You're right!' Cosette cried. 'I *don't* understand. How can I? You won't tell me the truth. What is it? Who are you?'

But Valjean could only shake his head. He couldn't bring himself to speak the words, not yet.

'All right,' said Cosette, more calmly now. 'I'm not going to lie to you. Yes, it's true. I love Marius. I'm not ashamed. I only have a corner of the garden to be with him in, but that corner is mine! It's my life. Is that what's going to ruin us? My life?'

Jean Valjean slumped on to Cosette's bed, his eyes empty, his lips trembling. 'Yes,' he said in a doomed voice, 'your life is the end of me.'

Baffled, Cosette held her hands out to her papa wordlessly. If only she could understand! Everything was changing so fast. What was happening to them, and why?

Valjean dropped his head into his hands. 'I can't hide from myself,' he said in a low voice. 'But I don't want to see the truth through your eyes.'

Whatever became of them now, Valjean knew that his life and Cosette's would never again be the same. The safety, the security in which they'd been living, was shattered for ever.

## Chapter Twenty-Five

### LAMARQUE'S FUNERAL

On the evening of 4 June 1832, the ABC Society met as usual in the back room of the Café Musain in Saint Antoine. But it was not their usual sort of meeting. Feelings were running very high, and a great sense of expectation infused the meeting with fever-pitch excitement.

Tomorrow, 5 June, was the date set for the state funeral of General Lamarque, and the city of Paris was a tinderbox only waiting for a spark to ignite an explosion. All over the city, radical groups such as the ABC Society were getting together to plan their strategy for the next day. Each group of radicals was to act independently of the others, yet with a concerted effort that would give the impression of a large army of the common man. If they had to use weapons, they would, and without hesitation. Nobody in Marius's little group knew how the following day would turn out. Would any of them die in the battle against the right wing? All of them? None? No matter what the outcome, the ABC Society was whole-heartedly committed to fight.

The common people of France were very angry that the Crown and the ruling classes, protected by the military, were attempting to steal their popular hero Lamarque from them, and wanted to bury him as one of their own. Lamarque had always stood firmly on the left, a strong supporter of liberty and humane rights for everyone alike.

A great soldier, one of Napoleon's marshals, a supporter of the beloved Emperor Bonaparte, a defender of the Republic, General Lamarque was never a puppet of the Bourbons. The working classes mourned his death bitterly, their bitterness increased by the insultingly pompous ostentation of his scheduled funeral. What right did the ruling classes have to bury Lamarque at all? He belonged to the masses.

Expecting trouble, the National Guard had marched twenty thousand armed soldiers, including heavy artillery, into the city. Ten thousand of these troops were assigned to escort the funeral cortège from Lamarque's house along the route down the Faubourg Saint-Antoine to the Louvre Palace, where the coffin containing the hero was to lie in state until the burial. The balance of the troops, heavily armed and ready to fight, were to be deployed around the city, concentrating on the trouble spots where revolutionary fever ran at its highest pitch.

The people also expected trouble, and they armed themselves with whatever came to hand. Those men who owned guns or could get hold of them carried them hidden under their coats or working-men's smocks. Others sharpened kitchen knives, shovels, tools and other implements into crude weapons. If it was a fight the Guard wanted, the working people of Paris would give it to them!

Feverishly, in the days and nights before the funeral, men and women all over the city set themselves the task of making bullets, melting down objects into molten lead for shot, casting metal casings and filling them with powder, sealing them with wax. Ammunition was scarce and precious, but the streets were filled with cobblestones, which could be pried up and flung with deadly accuracy from the barricades. Effective weapons, and free for the taking.

Barricades were going up all around the city, dotting the working-class sections that lined the funeral route. The revolutionaries used everything they could find – wooden carts, tree branches, vegetable stalls from the marketplaces, scrap lumber, all piled high to form crude protective barriers between themselves and the armed militia.

When the meeting of the ABC Society was over, the membership filed out through the back door of the Café Musain into the alleyway behind. There was a feeling of great excitement and anticipation among them – tomorrow was going to be a big day, the greatest in their lives! Tomorrow they would show the fat-cat right-wing factions the payback for stealing a hero from the people!

Marius broke away from the group and waved his friends a farewell. Tonight of all nights he had to see his darling Cosette, to share with her the feverish joy of the eve of revolution.

'Marius, not tonight!' Enjolras protested, as he saw him about to break away from the others. 'We need you to plan tomorrow's action.'

'Tomorrow's action? Tomorrow, my friend, we are not having an action. We are having a revolution,' Marius cried buoyantly.

'We can't tolerate this insult,' Courfeyrac chimed in. 'We can't allow the king to bury Lamarque as his hero.'

'Lamarque belongs to the people,' agreed Enjolras.

'I promise,' said Marius, 'I'll be back in an hour. Alert all the group leaders to meet here.'

But Enjolras reached out and caught hold of his jacket. 'Marius! Everything is ready. Everyone is eager. But we need you to take the lead.'

'Tell them it's on,' Marius responded, extricating himself from his friend's hold. 'Pass the word. Tomorrow our suffering will end.'

'This time we have to mean it!' Enjolras said vehemently.

'I mean it! Do you?' cried Marius.

'Yes!' they all cried.

'Long live the Republic!' Marius cheered.

'Long live the Republic!' the others echoed.

'We'll plan our tactics when I get back. When those bastards try to bury Lamarque, we'll bury them instead.' With this promise, Marius pulled away from the group, but little Gavroche, appearing suddenly out of nowhere, stopped him, blocking his path.

'Marius, have you seen my kids?' the child asked. His small face wore an expression of concern.

'Not now—' Marius pushed past Gavroche, eager to be on his way to Cosette, but the boy followed him, on a run. 'Have you seen my boys?' he repeated, catching up with Marius.

'No. Did you lose them?'

Gavroche pulled a pistol out of the waistband of his trousers and showed it to Marius. 'I had to go shopping.' He grinned proudly.

Between May and June of 1832, the French military and police authorities began to get some idea of just how widespread the political unrest was, and how close it was to igniting into real revolution. They began to take seriously those workers and students they'd been dismissing as mere nuisances. The French National Guard was mobilized and put on alert, and its troops awaited orders to march.

The scheduled 5 June state funeral of General Lamarque, who, although he had died of advanced age and natural causes, was now thought of as a mythical martyred hero of the left, became the obvious focus of radical anger. The city of Paris was burning with anger; perhaps tomorrow it would be burning with real fire. The Guard received its orders; of the fifty-four thousand active members, twenty-four thousand troops were brought into Paris itself. The balance were stationed in the nearby suburbs, ready to engage or to march.

On 4 June, in the central market district of Les Halles, twenty-seven barricades were erected, to shelter fighting men with guns. Other barricades were springing up everywhere along the funeral route. The city crouched down, tense, afraid, waiting, like a farm animal when thunderclouds appear on the horizon and the smell of lightning is in the air. There seemed to be nothing anybody could or would do to avoid the inevitable fighting.

At National Guard headquarters, the two highest-level officers of the prefecture of police, Chief Chabouillet and Chief Inspector Javert, were briefing the Guard general and half a dozen of his military commanders. With their superior knowledge of the Paris streets and alleyways, and their network of paid informers, the police had a tactical grasp of what they expected would happen tomorrow.

'There are twenty-four thousand troops in the city,' said the general. 'They can be reinforced by another thirty thousand in two days. The question, Prefect, is where do your informers think they'll make their first move?'

Javert's brows came together in deep concentration. He moved his forefinger over a large map of Paris to illustrate his information. 'Lamarque's funeral will pass through Faubourg Saint-Antoine. The stonemasons and carpenters have been on strike all week, so they're armed to the teeth and they'll start it there. Les Halles will be the stronghold. They'll go for the Arsenal on the Right Bank.'

'Excellent. Thank you,' replied the general. 'This gives us a clear picture. Well, we won't fight them for every inch.' He turned to his commanders. 'Cavalry, in the Place Louis Quinze I want four mounted squadrons. Municipal Guard – you take the Latin Quarter. Dragoons? Here.' The general rapped the map sharply to show where he wanted every regiment deployed. 'Twelfth Light Infantry – I want you between the Bastille and the Grève. We'll protect the Louvre with artillery. We won't try to suppress. We'll surround them.'

'And then they're doomed,' Javert said, half to himself. He felt a dark thrill at the thought. Those damned law-breaking radicals would meet a stern justice tomorrow, on their precious barricades.

Javert returned to police headquarters to make his own plans and to meet with his informer.

'Inspector, where do you want me tomorrow? Should I go back to the Café Musain?' asked Robineaux.

'Not right away,' Javert replied. 'Mingle with the crowd at the Antoine and see where it takes you.'

'All right—' But before Robineaux could take off, Javert stopped him.

'Fauchelevent, the soft-hearted gentleman. Did you find out anything about his background?'

'Certainly,' the informer answered. 'He's from Montreuil. Born and raised. Fauchelevent and his daughter Cosette lived there until ten years ago.'

'Cosette?' Unconsciously, Inspector Javert raised his voice in sudden excitement. Montreuil and Cosette – a connection was being made. He took hold of Robineaux by both arms, grasping him firmly. 'You didn't say her name was Cosette!'

'You didn't ask,' shrugged Robineaux. 'Inspector, I'm happy to talk to you. It isn't necessary to actually hold me in place.'

But Javert was in no mood for jest. His eyes drilled into Robineaux's skinny face. 'Describe him. Think carefully. Be precise. And describe him to me.'

Robineaux began to tell him everything he had learned

of the man called Fauchelevent, together with a detailed physical description of a tall, powerfully built fellow. Javert listened intently, saying nothing. But an unholy glee began to fill his dark heart. All at once, the oncoming revolution lost its importance. It paled next to the chance of capturing Jean Valjean after all these years.

Inspector Javert's old obsession with the fugitive had not died; it had merely lain dormant. Until now, when it emerged to bloom again.

Marius broke into a run when the house on the rue Plumet came into view. As usual, he came up to the garden gate and eagerly gazed at the house, waiting for his beloved Cosette to appear. But tonight there was no light on, no soft glow from the oil lamps perceived through the curtained windows. When he put his hand on the gate it yielded to him and swung wide open, to his great surprise.

What the devil—? Marius ran into the garden and came up close to the house. He peered in at the tall downstairs windows. Dark, all dark. The house appeared to be empty. He couldn't believe it. How could this be?

'Cosette?' he called, although he already felt a sinking in his gut. 'Cosette!'

His only answer was silence. The large house brooded, empty, dark, voiceless, a hostile creature lying in wait. Confused, upset, Marius backed away, bumping into the garden wall and slumping down, his back against the stones. Despair overcame him. Where was Cosette? How could he find her? He looked over at their tree, their beloved oak, which had sheltered their lovemaking like a conjugal roof over their head.

Suddenly, Marius thought he could make out something on the trunk of the tree. He came closer and peered at it. Yes, there in the bark, the letters obscure as though scratched in

very hurriedly, was carved an address: *18 rue de l'Ouest*.
Bless her! She had not forgotten him.

As he listened to Robineaux's description of 'Monsieur
Fauchelevent', Javert closed his eyes, a useful trick of
his that blocked out extraneous sensations and allowed
him to concentrate his mental powers. He visualized the
man being described – very tall, good-looking, large hands,
powerful shoulders. He knew this man. Then, unbidden, a
pair of silver candlesticks flashed upon his memory. Where
had he seen them? When?

And suddenly everything fell into place. Fauchelevent.
Cosette. Montreuil. Silver candlesticks. In his mind's eye,
Javert saw a small room in a small house, very different from
the house on the rue Plumet. Sitting on the mantelpiece, two
silver candlesticks, their value out of place in this modest
environment. Yes, the silver had belonged to Jean Valjean
in Montreuil! At the same time, Javert had a sharp mental
image of a heavy cart being lifted off a groaning old man
by one pair of massive shoulders, one person's strength. He
remembered it all. The old man's name was Fauchelevent!
And the child the dying whore Fantine kept whining about.
Cosette!

It all added up to one person! Jean Valjean! This 'Monsieur
Fauchelevent' must be none other than Jean Valjean, the
fugitive. Javert felt his heart swell, his pulses race. This was
better than anything he could have imagined. Drawing a
police net over a little fish, Marius Pontmercy, he had netted
a whale!

Swiftly, Chief Inspector Javert issued orders, and four of
his best and most trusted gendarmes accompanied him to
rue Plumet, where they met up with Robineaux. Even as they
approached the Fauchelevent house, Javert had the sudden
feeling that it was too late. The house would be empty, and

the bird flown. That 'gardener' he'd seen running off – a tall man. And that cock-and-bull story the girl had fed him – he'd swallowed it. Javert felt a momentary stab of anger at Cosette, at Valjean and at himself for not bothering to question her.

Carefully, the gendarmes searched the entire house, upstairs and down. They could find no clues to the Fauchelevent family's disappearance.

'No one and nothing,' Robineaux reported glumly, as he came out into the garden where an icily silent Javert was waiting. 'Clean as a whistle. He moves fast.'

'Yes, he does.' Javert nodded. 'But there's a way to find him.' He had used surveillance on the house of 'Monsieur Fauchelevent' to keep track of Marius Pontmercy; now he would use Marius as bait for hunting down Jean Valjean.

Wherever the girl had gone, the fool of a boy would be sure to follow her. In fact, Marius Pontmercy had already sought out Cosette in her new quarters in the rue de l'Ouest. She had been sitting for hours at the window of her bedroom, peering through the shutters, on the watch for him. When she saw Marius approaching the house, she opened the shutter, overjoyed.

As soon as he saw her, he waved exuberantly. Cosette put a finger to her lips for silence, and pointed to the nearby alleyway. Then she slipped noiselessly down the stairs and went out to meet him.

This meeting Jean Valjean had strictly forbidden. Cosette was not to see or speak to anybody, especially not Marius Pontmercy. Valjean perceived Marius as a threat to him in more ways than one. He had made plans for his escape with Cosette, and they had to lie very low until he could put the plan into effect.

Marius was deeply upset and angry when he heard what little information Cosette was able to impart. All she could tell him, in a voice filled with misery, was that her father was leaving France, and she was leaving with him.

'Why? For God's sake, why?' he demanded.

Cosette turned away, in torment. 'He has to leave and I have to go with him,' she said in a low tone. 'What difference does the reason make?'

'It makes a big difference,' protested Marius. 'Cosette, what's wrong?'

'His life is at stake,' she said helplessly.

'His life? How?' demanded Marius. She wasn't making sense.

'It doesn't matter how or why,' said Cosette, who didn't really know the reasons herself. She turned her face up to Marius's, and he could see sincerity mingling with deep unhappiness. 'I was an orphan. He saved me. He gave me everything I have. I must do whatever he asks. That's all there is to it.'

Marius angrily turned his face away. 'You don't trust me,' he said resentfully.

'No.'

'And obviously you don't love me.'

'No,' answered Cosette with a smile. Then she kissed him, winding her slender arms around his neck. Marius accepted her wheedling caresses with ill grace. He was still offended by what he perceived as Cosette's lack of candour. He felt she didn't trust him enough to confide in him.

'I adore you, Marius,' the girl declared. 'How can you say I don't? It's not my secret to give away. It's his. Listen – I know what we can do. We'll talk to him. He'll understand. He'll agree you can come with us to England.'

'England?' cried Marius, dumbfounded. 'Cosette, are you crazy? You know I can't. Tomorrow we're going to fight! We're going to restore the Republic! I can't run away!'

The situation seemed to be hopeless, a solution impossible. Cosette wasn't able to stay in Paris; Marius wouldn't leave Paris. What were they going to do? What would become of them? Cosette's face crumpled. 'Oh, Marius,' she moaned.

Marius's fists clenched and his jaw muscles trembled in anger. He hated this man who was taking his darling Cosette away from him. Monsieur Fauchelevent was an arbitrary tyrant! 'Why? Why to England? And why now?'

'Do you love me?' asked Cosette, fighting back her tears.

'Yes, goddamn it!' shouted Marius through gritted teeth. 'I love you! Do you love me?'

Now it was Cosette's turn to be angry. Why wouldn't Marius make the smallest effort to understand or sympathize? 'I told you. I adore you.'

'Then how can you leave me?' It was almost a wail, a cry from deep within him. Cosette lost her battle for self-control, and dissolved in tears.

'Oh God! Can't you understand?' she sobbed. 'He needs me now. He took care of me, and now he needs me!'

Cosette's weeping struck Marius hard. He couldn't bear to see his beloved so unhappy. He realized that his own anger had increased her misery, and he drew in a deep breath. 'When do you leave?' he asked quietly.

'He's not sure,' Cosette said thickly, through her tears. 'Tomorrow no one can leave Paris because of General Lamarque's funeral. He said we might leave the next day.'

Marius nodded dully. 'I'll be here tomorrow night. If I'm alive tomorrow.' It was a cruel, childish thing to say, and he knew it, but he couldn't help himself. He wanted from Cosette some of the sympathy she was reserving for her father.

'Please don't talk like that!' she begged, and her tears began to flow again.

Her heart was breaking in her breast; she was torn between the two men who loved and needed her. Both of them had valid claims on her, but she could only fulfil those claims for one. What if something terrible happened to Papa and she wasn't at his side to help? What if Marius was hurt or killed in the fighting, and she had turned her back on him? She couldn't bear either crushing thought.

Marius relented. He put his arms around her comfortingly. 'Of course I'll be here,' he murmured into her dark hair, kissing the tips of her ears. 'Don't worry. And you promise you'll meet me here tomorrow?'

Instead of words, Cosette gave her lover his reply by turning her face up to his and kissing him passionately on the mouth. For a few minutes, pressed close together, the two young people lost themselves in the present, and were able to forget for a little while their pain and their fears for tomorrow.

## Chapter Twenty-Six

### TO THE BARRICADES

The morning of 5 June 1832 brought rain mixed with sunshine, and a flurry of wild rumours mixed with very few facts. There were crowds strung out all along the route of the funeral cortège, and as the morning wore on, more and more people arrived, until the crowds turned to mobs. Thousands of students and workers came out, burning with revolutionary spirit. Shopkeepers locked their doors and put their shutters up, fearing destruction and looting if the mob became unruly. The centre of the city, around the Faubourg Saint-Antoine, was thick with the population of working-class Paris. Many had come to protest against the funeral; some had come for the spectacle of a grand state burial and a military display. Some had come to see the revolution begin and to take part in it; this last group was the most vocal of all.

But they all had one thing in common. They were waiting for the appearance of the sombre funeral cortège and General Lamarque's body. They were waiting to play a part in history.

Among the factors the spectators were most interested in was the deployment of the government forces. Radical scouts brought back reports that at the Halle aux Vins, the wine market, a squadron of dragoons was on the alert. The court of the Louvre was filled with artillery. In the

Latin Quarter and at Le Jardin des Plantes troops were spread out on every street. Other battalions were stationed all along the route. But by the time the information was passed from mouth to mouth, the number of the French troops had exploded from the factual twenty thousand to an army worthy of Napoleon and Wellington combined.

Rumours flew around every corner; a favourite was that the military were planning to use the funeral as a pretext for a massacre of the people. They would open fire whenever they chose, without regard to women or children. Another prevalent rumour was that the radicals were planning to hijack Lamarque's body and bury it secretly, in the dead of night. They would divert the body from the Louvre Palace and bring it to the Panthéon for the funeral service instead. How they were going to purloin the body from under the noses of ten thousand armed soldiers nobody could say, yet that particular rumour gained in strength with each telling and retelling.

Cosette stood with her papa at the half-shuttered window of the sitting room on rue de l'Ouest, watching the flow of men and women outside their hideout as they streamed towards the Faubourg Saint-Antoine. She had never seen so many furious, shouting people before. They all looked so intent, so purposeful, that it filled her with an uncomfortable awe.

'It's scary, Papa. Why are they so angry about this?'

Valjean turned from the window to look down at Cosette. 'Lamarque was a hero who fought for the Republic,' he explained.

'Then why is the king giving him a state funeral?' the girl wanted to know.

'He's trying to claim Lamarque as his own hero. It's a lie. It's the final insult. That's why they're angry.' He turned for a final look at the teeming streets below, then slowly closed the window shutters, safely shutting them in.

Two battalions of the National Guard escorted the flower-laden catafalque as it made its solemn way through the streets and boulevards of Paris. They carried muskets with the barrels reversed; the drums were muffled, and the horses' hooves were bound in black cloth so that they made only a ghostly clop-clop on the pavements and cobbled streets. The hearse itself was drawn by the flower of the regiments, handsome young men of a similar height, their uniforms immaculate, their boots and buttons polished to a blinding shine. They were accompanied by a full honour guard of sabre-carrying officers.

Directly behind the hearse marched the officers of the Invalides, carrying branches of laurel, the traditional crown awarded by Apollo to the heroes of classical antiquity. After them came troops of cavalry, preceded by mounted trumpeters, followed by thousands of soldiers marching in step.

Walking solemnly in front of the hearse, a cordon of priests bearing tall crosses was flanked by altar boys in their white lace surplices. The funeral recalled the triumphs of imperial Rome, and was designed to have the same effect on the populace as the old triumphs once had, by underscoring the monumental power of the ruling classes and reminding the lower classes of just who was in charge.

Behind the soldiers marched the official civilian groups in a flurry of tricolour flags – representatives from the universities and the hospitals, from the libraries and the theatre and opera companies and artisan guilds and other established organizations.

The common people thronged the sides of the boulevards, and crowded together on the balconies and at the windows along the route. The younger, more agile of the spectators shinnied up the tree trunks and perched in the branches, or stood on the roofs near by, all to catch a glimpse of the procession. Many of the people waved the red, white and blue tricolour flag of France, but many more carried defiant banners of brilliant scarlet, the blood red of revolution. Against the grey of the lowering skies, or in the occasional flashes of brilliant sunshine, the flags made a brave display.

As the cortège made its solemn procession through the streets, shouts from the crowd accompanied it.

'Long live the Republic!'

'Lamarque for the people!'

Paris held its collective breath. Something was going to happen, something historic; it was only a question of where and when it would erupt.

Those questions were answered at the Esplanade of the Pont d'Austerlitz. It was there the procession halted, snaking out for more than a mile behind the priests and the catafalque. It was a scheduled stop, to allow the great soldier and statesman Lafayette to make his personal farewells to General Lamarque. It was to be a solemn, historic moment.

But, before it could take place, a solitary young rider, dressed all in black and carrying a red banner, rode up to the cortège at a gallop and went directly to the hearse. He circled the catafalque, waving his red flag, then faced the crowd, holding his banner high as a signal of defiance.

'Lamarque to the Panthéon!' yelled the people. They raised clenched fists as a sign of their solidarity.

The dragoons did not fire; they had no orders to fire; the mob was very menacing and the soldiers very young. Suddenly, a group of young men, members of the ABC Society with Marius Pontmercy as their leader, darted forward towards the catafalque and picked up the harness.

They hitched themselves to the hearse and began to draw it forward. The dragoons scattered.

'To the Panthéon!' cried Marius.

'To the Panthéon!' roared the spectators.

But now the cavalry, more seasoned veterans, received orders to attack. The mounted soldiers began to gallop towards the young men pulling the hearse. As they charged, the troopers pulled their sabres out and brandished them. The crowd yelled in mingled fear and defiance. Some men threw stones; others ran away. The cavalry began to slash at the spectators, while the dragoons re-formed into a disciplined rank and aimed their muskets. Shots were fired. A few men fell. The killing had begun.

The crowd dissolved into a group of angry civilians and defiant radicals. 'To arms! To the barricades!' shouted the insurgents, showing the clenched fist.

It was the signal all Paris was waiting for.

Enjolras and Marius broke free from the hearse and raced back to Saint Antoine. There, together with Grantaire, Courfeyrac, Feuilly and the other members of the ABC Society, aided by some twenty others, they joyfully began setting up their own barricade outside the Café Musain. Grantaire and Feuilly pulled iron bars from the café's windows, while Enjolras and a few friends pulled up the cobbles from the streets, to be flung as missiles. Gavroche and Bahorel flipped over a cart with three barrels of lime; two women dragged a mattress over to add to the pile.

The barricade began to take shape. Courfeyrac and Marius ran up to an omnibus, which was coming down the street. They forced the passengers out and unhitched the horses. Then they rolled the omnibus over to the barricade and, with the efforts of many – pushing, heaving, straining – they tipped it over. It toppled on to the breastwork, giving the final layer of protection between the radicals and the soldiers.

'The Republic!' yelled Marius.

'The Republic!' echoed the others happily. Behind the solid fortress they'd built they felt invulnerable. Let's see the damned soldiers get past this!

Chief Inspector Javert, wearing the clothes of an ordinary working man, entered the office of his superior, Chief Prefect Chabouillet. The office was a beehive of confusion today; gendarmes and clerks kept rushing in and out with orders and dispatches. Paris was about to erupt into flames. It was the police's job to keep on top of it, working side by side with the military.

'Javert, your information was as good as gold,' Chabouillet began without ceremony, 'but the idiots in the Municipal Guard ignored your advice about the Arsenal and they've—' He broke off as he noticed for the first time what his second-in-command was wearing. 'Javert, why are you dressed like that?'

'I'm going undercover,' Javert answered grimly. 'I have the scent, sir, the scent of someone who's . . . very dangerous. I don't want to leave the job to an underling. It will be an important arrest, sir, the most important of my career.' His eyes were agleam with anticipation.

Chabouillet caught some of Javert's excitement. 'Indeed! Who is it?'

'I'd rather not say until I've got him,' Javert answered evasively. He was well aware that his prefect chief would react badly to hearing that he was going after an ancient enemy when all of Paris was about to explode.

The prefect looked gravely at his chief inspector. 'Be careful, Javert. We don't control the streets. Not yet.'

A wintry smile crossed Javert's icy features. '*I* control them, sir.'

Across the city, in the house in the rue de l'Ouest, Cosette stood at her window, anxiously looking out for Marius. It was getting late, and there was no sign of him. Her own street was deadly quiet; all the shutters on the houses and shops were closed, and the families were either holed up inside or had already fled the city. Nobody was out in the neighbourhood.

All over Paris, the streets were empty except for the soldiers and the radicals on the barricades, and long lines of refugee men and women, loaded with their possessions, running away from the fighting. In the direction of Les Halles, a column of smoke spiralled into the sky, almost obscuring the sunset. Cosette could hear, now and then, bursts of gunfire.

Where was Marius? Was he alive? Or, God forbid, was he lying dead or wounded and crying out for Cosette in his pain? Not knowing what was happening in the heart of the city was killing the girl by inches. She didn't turn away from the window when her father came into her bedroom with an empty valise and awkwardly began to pack up her dresses. He had just returned from a reconnaissance of their escape route.

'As soon as it's dark we'll go through the barrier. Hundreds are fleeing,' he told her. 'The gendarmes don't care who leaves. They're worried about the people coming in. So it's a perfect opportunity for us to slip out of Paris.' He looked sharply at Cosette, but she didn't move from her station at the window. She looked like an alabaster statue she was so white and still.

Valjean glanced down at the muddle he was making in his attempts to pack up her dresses. 'I'm not very good – could you help?' Cosette paid no attention. Valjean could see how upset she was. He stopped his packing.

'How . . . how bad is the fighting?' asked Cosette.

'I didn't go anywhere near it. I went the other way.'

She turned from the window to face her papa. 'But what are they saying?' she persisted.

Valjean shook his head. 'No one really knows what's happening,' he said gravely. 'The streets are full of experts. And they all say something different. No matter what the truth is, a lot of people will die tonight.'

*People will die tonight.* Cosette said nothing, but tears began to roll silently down her cheeks. His heart aching for her obvious misery, Jean Valjean approached her. He intended to embrace her, but Cosette turned her face away, looking out of the window again. Valjean stood next to her, feeling helpless, his arms dangling at his sides.

'Is . . . is it too dangerous for us to wait here until morning?' Cosette asked.

Valjean comprehended at once. She didn't want to leave now, without knowing what had become of her lover. 'He's on the barricades?'

Cosette nodded, biting her lip. 'I promised I'd wait. Even if he can't come, I have to wait—' She broke down suddenly in a torrent of tears. Valjean took her in his arms, patting her heaving shoulders. Her entire slender body was shaking and shivering with unbearable emotion.

'It hurts this much?' he asked softly.

'I'm sorry, I'm sorry,' sobbed Cosette. 'I know you don't understand. I've known him for only a few weeks, that's what you're thinking. He's little more than a stranger. I'm only a silly girl.' She raised her tear-stained face to look earnestly at her papa. 'But that's not what I feel. I feel he *is* me and that tonight *I'm* dying out there.'

In agony himself, Jean Valjean rocked his broken-hearted Cosette lovingly back and forth in his arms. 'I understand,' he told her tenderly. 'I do.'

In the years with Cosette, Valjean had known the only real happiness of his life. No father could love a daughter more than he had loved his Cosette. Now he had lost her, no matter what happened. Marius dead or Marius alive, Cosette belonged to him. She was lost to Valjean, never again to be his little girl. So he understood her feelings of loss only too well.

And yet, as the two of them hugged each other for comfort, there was a glimmer of hope in each of them. In Valjean, that Marius would not come before he could take Cosette away from here and make their escape good. In Cosette, the thought that Marius was alive and well, and would soon be with her.

Back in Saint Antoine, Marius had no time to think now of Cosette, but only of France, of justice and equality, and the battle to come. The barricade erected, about thirty men manned it, among them Marius, Enjolras and others of the ABC Society. They prepared themselves, hearts high, for the attacking soldiers. Buoyed up by their idealism, they felt no fear.

A few men and women turned their attention to providing themselves and their few guns with ammunition. Cartridges were in wretchedly short supply. A huge cauldron was set up in the Café Musain for melting down lead. Some of them poured off the molten metal into the bullet moulds, while others measured gunpowder from a keg into the cooled cartridges. Among the people working in the makeshift armoury was a dark man with gimlet eyes, wearing ordinary worker's clothing. It was Javert, undercover as a revolutionary.

Night was falling. Marius lit a torch and carried it to the top of the barricade. He planted it near their flag. The men, young and old, peered over the top, down the street, waiting for the soldiers to come; the street itself had become no-man's-land. They were poised on the brink of a different future, and they knew it. Not one of them had ever looked death in the eye before, let alone seen bloody, dying men with mutilated limbs and torn entrails. Therefore the young men were exhilarated, feeling that nothing could harm them. Those on the side of the angels must inevitably prevail.

Those among them who were older and had seen more of life had fewer romantic notions. They were perhaps a bit less fervent in their belief that *Dulce et decorum est pro patria mori*. Those were words of the poet Horace: 'It is sweet and proper to die for the sake of one's country'. The older men could more easily envision their own deaths.

Suddenly, from a distance, they heard a high reedy voice, a boy's voice, singing a parody of the Age of Enlightenment:

> *They're ugly at Nanterre,*
> *It's the fault of Voltaire.*
> *And stupid at Palaiseau*
> *All because of Rousseau.*

It was young Gavroche, dashing down the street towards them, ducking in and out of doorways so that he would not present a target. He scrambled halfway up the barricade, tossed a musket over the top, and followed it.

'Give me my musket,' he demanded of Enjolras.

'How did you get it?'

Gavroche tapped a small finger to the side of his nose. 'National Guardsmen shouldn't take naps. I need a bullet.'

Marius shook his head. 'We only have thirty cartridges. They're making more now.'

'I get one, right?'

'Gavroche, you're a boy,' Marius protested.

'And you're a student,' the child retorted impudently.

'Besides, you've told us nothing,' Enjolras reminded him.

Gavroche passed his information along. It hadn't been so hard to come by. Nobody ever notices a child; a little boy is able to go where adults cannot, find out things, carry information back, steal a musket. A child who can use his eyes and ears intelligently may be of great value to a revolution. 'They're bringing a cannon.'

'A cannon?' Enjolras gasped, incredulous.

'A little cannon. With grapeshot.' Gavroche looked around the barricade with complacence. 'It won't get through our mighty masterpiece. Now can I have a bullet?'

'How many are there?' Marius asked.

Gavroche wrinkled his small nose. 'Too many. I'm getting my bullet. They'll be here any minute. What do you expect me to do? Spit at them?'

Hopping down from the breastwork and dashing into the café, he ran to the back room where the ammunition makers were hard at work. There he demanded and received one of the newly made bullets.

Grantaire was sitting at a table with a man Gavroche had not seen before, a cold-faced man with gimlet eyes. 'Did my babies show up?' asked the boy.

'No. How can they show up now? The streets are all closed off.'

Gavroche winked knowingly. 'Oh, you go through the back alley, climb a fence or two and there's a clear route away from the fighting.'

'Here they come!' Enjolras shouted on the barricade, and everyone in the Café Musain scrambled out, to see uniformed troops moving into the far end of no-man's-land. They were setting up a cannon, wheeling it into position, loading it with shot and priming it with gunpowder.

Gavroche scrambled back on to the barricade, but Javert

remained near the café, his eyes fixed only on Marius Pontmercy. This Marius was his ticket to Jean Valjean.

'They're loading!' Enjolras yelled. 'Everybody back!'

Suddenly, a loud boom split the air as the cannon discharged. A load of grape slammed into the mattress and the omnibus, like a rain of hail. When the smoke cleared, the insurgents looked around, and did a mental head count. Everybody present and accounted for. Nobody was hurt.

'Nothing!' Grantaire crowed. 'It did nothing!'

Another boom sounded from the cannon, and another rain of grapeshot hit the barricade. Once more, the pellets had no effect, and the radicals broke into a cheer. They were still cheering, pleased with themselves, when the sound of steady drumming came to their ears from the near distance. The drums grew louder.

'They're coming,' breathed Feuilly, as a formation of National Guard troops rounded the corner and marched towards them. Their muskets had sharp bayonets attached.

The revolutionaries stopped their cheering and stared at the troopers, who were coming nearer and nearer. Perhaps for the first time, the young radicals realized that they were about to fight a real war.

## Chapter Twenty-Seven

### THE CAPTURE OF JAVERT

'Save your bullets!' shouted Marius. 'Don't shoot until you can smell them! Take your positions, men. Make every shot count! For the revolution!'

Now the soldiers were less than twenty feet away, marching towards the radicals without missing a step. They were so close that the rebels could make out their facial features under the brims of their kepis. Shouldering their muskets, the troopers took aim and fired.

Half a dozen of the rebels toppled on to the barricade, wounded or killed. But the others on the breastwork returned fire bravely, and the front row of troopers dropped to earth as though they were toy soldiers a child had knocked over.

Suddenly, an eerie silence fell. Both groups – soldiers and revolutionaries – stared at the bodies on the ground and on the barricade. An awful reality dawned on them, that men could kill one another, that dying for an ideal might be only death, not romance. For most of them, very young men on both sides, it was their first hard lesson of war.

But the battle was fated to resume. An old man on the barricade threw his empty musket down. He was out of bullets, but not out of courage. Grabbing the flag planted on top, he pulled it out and waved it, the banner fluttering in the evening breeze, his white hair waving around his head like a banner of his own.

'Long live the Republic!' he shouted.

A volley of shots rang out. The old man tottered and fell, mortally wounded, his body virtually torn apart by bullets. His death was a signal for the troopers to charge the barricade. They stepped over their dead and began to climb, their bayonets fixed for hand-to-hand combat.

The first skirmish in the battle for Saint Antoine was in full cry.

The rebels were almost out of ammunition; those who had one or two bullets left had no time to reload. At the first onslaught, one of the troopers ran Courfeyrac through with his bayonet. The young man died, his entrails punctured, blood gushing from his mouth. Little Gavroche raised his musket and aimed it at a very large trooper heading straight for him. He pulled the trigger and nothing happened; the stolen gun, too old to be accurate, misfired. The trooper raised his bayonet to stab him through the heart; the boy was inches away from death, staring transfixed at the wickedly sharp point of the bayonet as it came closer to his thin chest.

Suddenly, the large trooper staggered. A huge hole blossomed in his forehead. The man's eyes glazed over and he fell backward, dead. Gavroche looked around for his saviour, and saw Marius grinning at him. The grateful lad grinned back, giving Marius the thumbs-up.

Now the troopers were swarming all over the barricade, overwhelming the men and driving them down. Marius jumped to the ground and ran to the Café Musain. He picked up a keg of gunpowder and carried it back to the breastwork, dodging a trooper who tried to bayonet him. The keg was heavy and made climbing very awkward, but he managed to scramble to the top. He grabbed the torch and held it over the keg. Unquenchable fire burned in his eyes.

'I'll blow the barricade!' he yelled. 'Clear out, or I'll blow up everyone!'

The troopers froze; they realized that Marius was deadly serious. They didn't dare shoot at him; if he were hit, he'd surely drop the torch and the gunpowder would explode. If the Guard soldiers didn't abandon the barricade right away, they'd end up in bits their own mothers wouldn't recognize. One of the troopers jumped off the barricade and ran away.

'Hold your positions, men!' the Guard lieutenant ordered. But his order was in vain. None of his men was eager to be shipped home in pieces.

Marius Pontmercy lowered the torch until it was perilously close to the keg of gunpowder. When they saw that, the troopers broke in disarray, scrambling down from the breastwork, trampling over one another in their haste to retreat. In a moment Marius found himself alone on the barricade, watching the backs of the guardsmen as they retreated in double time across no-man's-land.

Marius made his way to the old man's body and lifted it up in his arms. As he carried it from the barricade, other rebels joined him, taking up their fallen comrades. Carrying the old man's body into the Café Musain, Marius laid it on a long table. The dead bodies of his fellow rebels were laid out beside him. For a lengthy moment, the living looked sombrely at the faces of the dead – their friends, their fellow warriors.

When Marius looked upon the dead face of his old comrade Courfeyrac, eyes staring, jaw open, and saw the gaping wound in his belly, tears filled his eyes, and some of the fire went out of him. But not for long. Within moments, his friend's death made him angrier than ever, and more determined that the revolution would prevail. Mourning could be put off until the battle was won.

'We'd better make some more bullets,' Grantaire said, and the others voiced agreement. There might a lull in this battle, but none of the radicals believed for a moment that the troopers wouldn't return in greater strength the next time.

'We have a little time,' Enjolras observed. 'They won't be back for a while now.' He saw a grim-faced Marius moving towards the alley door of the back room. 'Marius? You're leaving? Now?'

The young man turned, his expression turning a little guilty. 'An hour. I'll be gone only an hour.' Opening the alley door, he headed for a break in the fence.

As the alley door opened, they caught a glimpse of the two little homeless boys Gavroche had been looking for high and low. They were huddled together in the street, completely traumatized by the gunfire. 'There you are! Come to Papa, boys!' cried Gavroche in relief. He opened his arms and the children ran to him, hugging him joyfully. Although the difference in their ages was slight, the children regarded Gavroche as their only Father.

'Let's go, brothers. Let's rebuild the barricade!' Enjolras cried.

They ran to the breastwork to make repairs. In all the bustle, they didn't see Javert slipping past Gavroche and the children and entering the alley to follow Marius.

In the house on rue de l'Ouest, Cosette had not left her post at the window. Toussaint begged her to come and eat, but she refused. Even when the old servant brought her a tempting meal on a tray, she wouldn't quit the window long enough to eat a morsel of it.

When every passing moment didn't bring Marius back to her, Cosette began to lose heart. She could see fires glowing red in the night sky; all of central Paris seemed to be aflame. Where, in all that conflagration, was Marius? Alive? Dead? Not knowing was pouring cold water on the remnants of her hope, almost quenching it. But not quite. Within her inner core was the powerful belief that Marius would return to her. Their love was too strong to be broken, even by guns; nothing could keep them apart.

All at once, a pebble came flying through the air and hit the windowpane. Cosette jumped, startled. Was it possible? Hastening to open the window, she called urgently into the darkness. 'Marius?'

A hand waved back from a doorway in an alley opposite the house.

'Marius!' Cosette's hand flew to her throat in delighted surprise. 'I knew you would come!' She ran from her room to the front door. 'I knew you were still alive! I knew! No matter how far away you were, if they stopped your heart, mine would break!' She flung her arms wide, ready to embrace her lover.

But before she could get out of the front door, a large, powerful hand snaked out suddenly and covered her mouth. Cosette found herself twisted around, her arms held from behind. She was trapped, a captive, unable to move.

'Didn't you mean those words for me, Cosette?' Chief Inspector Javert hissed into her ear. 'Don't you love the law? It loves you. It protects you. The law protects you from criminals like . . .' The policeman pushed Cosette roughly through the doorway. '. . . this scum!'

Cosette screamed. There was Marius, lying on the ground, his hands bound behind him, his mouth gagged. It was Javert who had deceived her with the wave of a hand.

Javert came up behind her and tightened his hold, pinioning her cruelly. 'Where is he? Where is your papa?'

The girl only shook her head mutely.

'Poor Cosette.' Javert grinned. 'Didn't he tell you he was

a common thief? Didn't he tell you who you are? Didn't he tell you you're a bastard child?'

Cosette gasped, and her eyes widened.

'Didn't he tell you your mother was a whore?' Chief Inspector Javert was relishing this moment. He had waited for it for a very long time, more than ten years.

'So you tell me, *where is Valjean?*'

'Let go of her!' It was a roar of the purest fury, such as a tiger might utter when its cub is threatened. Jean Valjean appeared suddenly, right behind Javert, a pistol cocked at the policeman's head.

Javert loosened his hold on Cosette. She rushed to Marius and knelt beside him, taking off his gag and untying the ropes around his wrists.

'I found you,' Javert said with grim satisfaction. He seemed to be indifferent to the pistol aimed at his head.

'Congratulations,' Valjean replied ironically. To Marius, he said, 'Give me the rope.'

He handed Marius the gun, and took the rope from him. 'Who is he? An informer?' asked Marius.

'A policeman.'

'I'm the law, Valjean,' Javert said coldly. He didn't flinch when Valjean bound his hands tightly. Glaring at Marius, he added, 'I'm Chief Inspector Javert and you are a traitor.'

Marius shoved the pistol barrel up to Javert's temple. 'Shut up. I'm taking you to face the people's justice.'

In answer, Javert laughed scornfully. His meaning was plain; 'people's justice' would be meaningless when all the ABC Society at the barricades were dead, which would be in only a matter of hours.

Marius didn't mistake Javert's meaning. 'If we die, you die with us.' He pushed Javert ahead of him into the alley. He was taking him back to Saint Antoine as a prisoner of the revolution.

*Les Misérables*

'Marius!' cried Cosette, devastated. He couldn't be leaving her! Not so soon!

At the sound of her voice, the boy turned. 'Goodbye, Cosette.' His eyes met hers, and they exchanged a long, painful glance, filled with longing and meaning. 'I love you.'

'I love you,' she whispered back, and then Marius and Javert were gone.

Cosette slumped against the door frame of the house, stunned. She couldn't believe he was gone, possibly gone for ever. Even if he lived through the fighting, how would he ever find her again? Soon they would depart. Even now, Toussaint and Valjean were piling a cart high with their possessions. In just hours the three of them would be on a ship bound for England. Without Marius. She stared dully at the fires in the sky, knowing that somewhere inside them her love was risking his life every minute. Any one of the troopers' bullets might find his heart. No, it was too much! She couldn't think, she could only feel.

Jean Valjean came slowly over to Cosette. It weighed on him now that he'd let Marius leave so easily with Javert. His daughter's suffering was breaking his heart. 'We're ready.'

Cosette turned her face to him. All Valjean saw was her eyes, large, staring, despairing. 'He came to say goodbye,' was the only thing she could say.

Valjean made up his mind. He turned to Toussaint, giving her instructions. 'Take her to our old house.' Toussaint nodded and picked up the reins. Valjean folded Cosette into his arms and embraced her lovingly, kissing her on her forehead. 'It'll be all right. I promise you,' he whispered. Then he lifted her up and placed her on the cart. He struck the horse on its flank, and the cart started up.

Cosette looked startled. Wasn't Papa coming with them? Suddenly, she understood. He was going to Saint Antoine, to bring Marius back to her. They would meet in the rue Plumet. Papa was putting himself in mortal danger for her sake.

The girl turned around on the cart, reaching out for the man she thought of as her father. But he was gone, running towards the barricades and the fires of battle.

When he reached Saint Antoine, Jean Valjean found the rebels active, although the Guardsmen were in a fall-back position at the end of the street, across no-man's-land. The barricade was being rebuilt, stronger than before, with added materials found in the streets and alleys around the Café Musain. In the café itself, Valjean saw the dead laid out on the tables, and the wounded being tended by their comrades.

Chief Inspector Javert was in the café as well, gagged and tied hand and foot to a beam. Seated at a table was Grantaire, half drunk, and sitting with him was little Gavroche. When the child saw him, he broke into a beaming smile.

'Monsieur!' he cried. 'Good to see you!'

'Hello, Gavroche,' acknowledged Valjean. He gazed at Javert, unable to take his eyes off him. The lad noted the policeman and Monsieur locking stares, and began to explain.

'Chief Inspector Javert. Can you believe it? When we can spare a bullet, we're going to shoot him. In fact, that reminds me . . .' And the boy took off at a run.

Valjean left the Café Musain and returned to the barricade. He saw Marius at the top, directing the placement of some more protective material. When the young man saw him, he ran down to the street. 'What are you doing here?' He frowned. 'Where is Cosette?'

'Waiting for you in the garden where you fell in love,' answered Valjean. 'Go to her.'

'I can't. Not now. You know I can't.' The boy's face was tormented, yet resolute.

'I'll fight in your place,' Valjean volunteered. 'Go to her. She's your future.'

Marius shook his dark head. 'If we can't win here, then none of us has a future.'

'You have love,' Valjean answered quietly. 'That's the only future God gives us.'

Suddenly, there was the crack of a single bullet. And they heard Enjolras crying out, 'Gavroche! Get back here!'

Valjean and Marius climbed up the barricade, crouched down next to Gavroche's homeless boys and peered down the street. They saw little Gavroche kneeling beside a dead Guardsman, close to the enemy position. He was emptying the soldier's ammunition pouch of bullets into a small basket. Around him, on the roofs, there were at least three snipers firing at him. A second bullet whizzed, but struck the body of the dead trooper.

Gavroche chuckled. 'Can't kill him twice.' He moved to a second dead trooper, and began to rob him of bullets. More snipers took aim at the child. As he threw the bullets into his basket, Gavroche began to sing.

> *'I'm no lawyer, I declare,*
> *It's the fault of Voltaire.'*

There was a sudden volley of shots, coming from all directions. It was getting warm out there. Time to go home. Gavroche took up his basket and headed for the barricade in a crouching zigzag run, while bullets sped by him.

> *'I'm nothing but a sparrow*
> *All because of Rousseau.'*

He was close to the breastwork now, and had almost reached the safety of the barricade and his comrades-in-arms.

On the roof of the Café Musain, only a few yards away, Robineaux the informer aimed his musket carefully.

> *'There's joy in the air,*
> *Thanks to Voltaire,*
> *But misery below,*
> *Thanks to Rousseau.'*

Robineaux pulled the trigger. Gavroche straightened up, arched backward, and fell dead in front of the barricade. His basket, filled with the precious ammunition, fell from his dead hand, the bullets scattering across the street, useless now.

'Daddy!' cried the elder of the homeless boys, and the two children, sobbing loudly, embraced.

The others fell silent, shocked to their souls. Gavroche, cocky, impudent, merry, large-hearted, courageous, belonged to all of them. Everyone was fond of him. His death was the greatest blow the ABC Society had suffered so far.

Enjolras looked around. He had heard the shot that killed Gavroche, and knew it came from a different direction to where the troopers' snipers were. He glanced up at the roof of the Café Musain, and saw Robineaux ducking down out of sight. Robineaux, a traitor to the cause, a child murderer! Enjolras ran into the café and raced up the stairs.

Marius leaped down from the barricade and made his way carefully towards the body of Gavroche, to retrieve it. On the roof, Robineaux raised his musket again and took aim at Marius, but out of the corner of his eye he sensed something moving behind him. He turned, to discover a pistol cocked right between his eyes, and Enjolras grinning angrily at him.

Marius reached the body of Gavroche and lifted the boy in his arms. He weighed so little; Gavroche was always hungry.

For a moment he held the body high, like a defiant red flag, then he heard the sound of a shot, above him. He turned, to see the dead body of Robineaux falling from the roof.

Marius carried Gavroche past the twenty men left on the barricade, so that each of his comrades could see the dead boy, and be moved. Then he brought the body into the Café Musain, and laid it solemnly next to his fallen friends. Around him were the wounded, and the dying. Witnessing this was the bound and gagged yet scornful Javert, who showed no emotion at the sight of the dead child. Valjean quietly followed after Marius.

Enjolras joined them, and explained to Marius, loud enough for Javert to hear, that Robineaux was a police informer, a traitor, and now a corpse. Let the bastard Javert know that the ABC Society had flushed out and eliminated one of his own. The other insurgents, deeply angered by the death of Gavroche, gathered around the post where Javert was tied. They wanted a blood vengeance. An eye for an eye. One of them put a pistol to Javert's forehead.

'Proud of your work?' the rebel growled.

'You're next,' snarled another rebel. Javert didn't blink or show fear. Was it bravado? Only partly. In fact he was not afraid; there was no fear of death in Chief Inspector Javert. Death was equal to life; he saw no difference. Since he had never enjoyed life, he was not reluctant to leave it. As long as he'd done his duty.

Marius spoke to Valjean in an undertone. 'I'm staying.'

Valjean nodded; he understood. The child Gavroche had been his friend, too. Many times had the amused 'Monsieur Fauchelevent' handed over bowls of hot soup to the mischievous boy who cleverly avoided the necessary morning Mass, and who accepted the bowl with a wink. Valjean had seen how lovingly Gavroche had cared for the homeless little children he encountered in his daily adventures. He'd fed them, stolen warm clothes for them, put a sheltering, if humble, roof over their heads. Mass or no Mass, little Gavroche was what a true Christian ought to be. He should never have died so young.

And now came the sound of drumbeats, and the marching of feet. 'They're coming again,' shouted Enjolras. 'To the barricades!'

As the radicals ran out of the café, Valjean put a restraining hand on Marius's arm. He pointed to Javert, who still had a rebel pistol aimed between his eyes. 'One favour. Let me kill him.'

Marius thought for only a moment. Then he remembered Valjean's deep love for Cosette, and Javert's extreme cruelty to the girl. He took the pistol away from his comrade and offered it to Valjean with a polite bow. 'Be my guest.'

Now Chief Inspector Javert was to die, and at the hands of Jean Valjean. A bitter irony.

## Chapter Twenty-Eight

### THE SEWERS OF PARIS

Jean Valjean cut Chief Inspector Javert free from the post, leaving his hands and feet still bound and his mouth gagged. He led the hobbled policeman to the back door of the café and out into the alley. It was a nondescript place; the ground was very rough here, because the ABC Society had dug up many of its cobblestones to be used as missiles. The alley was full of holes, some of them large enough for a man to fall through. The fence was broken, leaving a narrow space between the buildings, through which a slender man might squeeze.

Valjean propped Javert against the fence and put the pistol in his pocket. He cut off his enemy's gag. Now he held only a knife in his hand.

'A knife?' asked Javert scornfully, eyeing the weapon. 'You're right. Suits you better.'

Valjean held the sharp knife close to Javert's throat. 'Why, Javert?' he demanded angrily. 'Why couldn't you leave me alone? I'm nothing! I'm nobody!'

'Yes, it's true,' Javert admitted. 'You're old news. You wouldn't have made an impressive arrest. I don't understand it,' he added in a low tone. 'I don't understand how you've managed to beat me.'

'I'm not trying to beat you, Javert! I want to live in peace.' But Valjean knew that Javert would never understand. Living in peace was beyond the man's comprehension. So was the concept of forgiveness and mercy.

A volley of gunfire reached their ears. The fighting at the barricades had started up again.

Javert smiled coldly at his enemy. 'Hurry up and do it. Your friends need you.'

In reply, Jean Valjean bent down and cut the ropes that were binding Javert's feet. Then he turned the inspector around and freed his hands from his bonds.

'What are you doing?' demanded the policeman.

'That way. Through the fence. You'll be safe.'

'You plan to shoot me in the back?' Javert asked suspiciously.

'I'm letting you go,' Valjean said simply. A sudden cheer came up from the nearby breastwork. He listened, and a smile spread over his face. 'They held again,' he said to Javert. 'You'd better hurry. They won't be merciful.'

For the first time, Javert appeared moved. No, he was much more puzzled than moved. This wasn't right. Matters did not develop like this. This was not criminal behaviour, and Jean Valjean was a criminal. 'I'd rather you didn't,' he said to Valjean. 'You should kill me.'

'What?' Valjean looked at him, incredulous, but Javert was perfectly serious.

'That's . . . that's what makes sense.' The agitated police officer found it a struggle to explain. 'I won't stop. Understand? I won't let you go. You should end this. Go on. Take out your gun. Take it out and shoot me.'

Valjean took the pistol out of his pocket and cocked the hammer back. Then he pointed it at the sky and pulled the trigger. There was a loud explosion. Hearing it, the rebels would assume only that Valjean had carried out Javert's execution.

'You're dead, Javert,' said Valjean, and went back to the

café through the alley door. He was ready to join in the fighting. This revolution had become his, too.

For a moment, Chief Inspector Javert stared after him, then he turned and pushed his way through the hole in the fence, disappearing from sight.

The fighting continued all night long, but in sporadic bursts. Each side inflicted casualties, but it was hard to see what was gained by either. The barricade still stood, even though as the night wore on more and more of its patriots were either killed or dying, or lying wounded in the Café Musain, moaning, shrieking, waiting for death to release them.

Did the rebels think they could win against uniformed troops, well trained, well fed, and armed with enough ammunition to fire again and again? Did the Guardsmen think that they could really defeat a closely knit band of brothers whose ideals would carry them to the grave, if need be? They could kill them, of course – the troops outnumbered the rebels ten to one – but they could never destroy their spirit.

As the besieged insurgents fought through the night, it became more than evident to them that defeat was inevitable; they were outgunned and outnumbered; bullets were as scarce as rubies, and even their piles of cobblestone missiles were dwindling fast.

Yet the rebels seemed to ignore the probability of death. They were imbued with love – love for their country, love for their comrades, love for their families, whom they would never see again. They felt somehow immortal; they would die as heroes and live for ever as heroes in the hearts of working-class Frenchmen.

The government troops attacked again and again during the long night. The rebels managed to fend off the enemy, because the barricade, virtually impregnable, still stood, and because the young revolutionaries fought with heroic vigour. But each fresh attack left behind more dead and wounded at the barricade. The numbers of the insurgents, small to begin with, were lessened with every onslaught.

When dawn arrived at last on the morning of 6 June 1832, it found the battle for Saint Antoine at a stalemate. The troopers had left their dead in the street, unwilling to risk their lives to get them back. But they had retrieved most of the wounded. No-man's-land was littered with the stiffening bodies of soldiers.

On the barricade, the few remaining rebels – Marius Pontmercy and Jean Valjean among them – were exhausted and stunned, beyond fear, beyond hope. Yet they were not disheartened, even though they expected to die today, perhaps even in the next hour. Each man intended to make his death count. The ideals for which they fought had become the centre of their lives, and were more important to them than mere continued human existence.

A rumble of heavy wheels came to their ears, and the revolutionaries peered through the early light. Twin caissons, each of them carrying a piece of heavy artillery, were being rolled into position, with a full army regiment behind them, backing them up. The rebels knew they were looking death in the face. This must surely be the end.

As he saw the cannon being loaded, Marius barked an order. 'Get down! Now! Get off!'

The first cannon fired, its missile striking the barricade dead centre. Men's bodies flew everywhere. Marius and Valjean made it to the bottom, but a second blast tore the centre wide open; the impact threw Valjean to the ground. A heavy rubble of cobblestones and iron bars collapsed on top of Marius, knocking him unconscious.

Clouds of smoke arose from the explosions, covering Marius and Valjean, and hiding them from the view of the enemy. With his huge, powerful hands, Valjean began to pull the rubble off Marius, desperate to find him alive. Yes, he was unconscious, but still breathing. Marius's leg was injured and bloody. Valjean hoisted him up on his shoulders and carried him under the cover of the smoke into the Café Musain.

The barricade had suffered a breakthrough. Covered by smoke, the government troops poured through the breach, surrounding the few remaining rebels, among them Grantaire and Enjolras.

Chief Inspector Javert, now back in uniform and accompanied by three gendarmes, followed the troopers. He watched coldly as the last remnants of the ABC Society were lined up against a wall.

'Long live the Republic!' Enjolras cried out just before the firing squad's bullets tore into his body, and he fell, taking his dreams of the 1832 insurrection with him.

'Can you walk?' Valjean asked Marius in a low tone. 'We have to get out of here. The soldiers will be here in a moment.' Marius was too groggy to respond, but when Valjean lowered him to the ground, and his injured leg touched the solid earth, he moaned loudly in anguish.

Marius couldn't walk; that much was clear. He would have to be carried. Valjean hoisted him up again and brought the young man, draped over his back, out through the back door and into the alley. Where should he take him? They'd never make it through the hole in the fence and, even if they did, the soldiers would catch them easily. He tried to find another way out, turning this way and that.

Then his eyes fell on the kerbing of the alley. Someone had pulled away a large number of cobbles there to use on the barricade. Completely exposed was the large rectangular grating covering the opening that led into the sewer system.

Javert followed the soldiers into the café, his eyes raking the dead and wounded, looking for Valjean. He wasn't there. Without hesitation, the inspector led his men through the back door and into the alley. Valjean must have come out this way.

But once in the alley, Javert hesitated. He had underestimated Jean Valjean before, and he wouldn't make that same mistake again.

'Must have gone this way,' said one of the gendarmes, peering through the hole in the fence.

But Javert wasn't so sure. Valjean knew that Javert was familiar with this way out; why would he take it? No, there must be some other escape route, one less obvious to the police.

'You two,' he said to the other gendarmes, 'check ahead and report back if they've caught him.' The two vanished through the hole in the fence. Javert looked around, then up. He remembered Valjean getting into the city ten years ago, over the rooftops. Would he try the same trick again, to get out?

'Let's check the roof.'

As he turned to go back to the café, Javert's foot knocked against a cobblestone. The stone, dislodged, rolled to the kerb and came to rest on top of the sewer grating. The grating immediately collapsed, and the stone plunged into the depths of the sewer with a loud splash.

The grate had been removed and then lightly replaced. Instinctively, Chief Inspector Javert knew that this was the escape route that Jean Valjean had chosen.

In many parts of Paris, the ten-centuries-old sewer system was ancient and, in 1832, it was in desperate need of repair. Later ages saw it expanded tenfold and modernized, and the filth contained, but when Jean Valjean dragged Marius Pontmercy down into its depths it was a running river, many miles long, of garbage and sewage. From every section of Paris branches of the sewer carried human waste and other unspeakably rotting stuff to the main sewer routes, and discharged them there at a series of intersections. It was a gigantic, sewage-filled maze. For that reason Valjean supposed that Javert would never suspect that he was using it as an escape route.

The stench of the sewer was quite literally unbelievable. It was as though hell yawned open and spewed forth the smell of damnation. Even the brick-and-stone walls sweated a filthy stink. Breathing was a problem for Valjean, and carrying the helpess, still-unconscious Marius Pontmercy on his shoulders was an even larger problem. He made his way inch by inch along the narrow ledge above the river of raw sewage below.

At the next sewer intersection, where branches met and spilled more night-soil into the main sewer line, Valjean straightened up and peered through the grating overhead. He could see the Guard and the army troops milling around above. There was no way to leave the sewer from this intersection. They'd have to go on.

Behind him, Marius groaned. He was coming to. Valjean slipped the young man off his shoulders and leaned him against the wall behind the ledge. The sound of scrabbling feet made him start with a cry. But it was only a couple of rats scurrying by on the ledge, at home in their environment.

Marius, feeling the jolt of Valjean's body and hearing his cry, roused himself fully. The first thing that hit him was the disgusting smell. 'Where . . . ? What . . . ? Are we . . . ?'

'Quiet!' Valjean ordered. 'Yes, we are. You're exactly where you think you are.' He saw, suddenly, a light behind him, bouncing off the walls. Someone was following them.

At the intersection, two dark passageways led away from

the centre. 'Which way? Do you know?' Valjean asked Marius, but the boy had no idea.

A voice called suddenly out of the darkness behind him. 'Valjean! It's over! Surrender!' Valjean recognized the voice of Chief Inspector Javert.

They had no time to lose; they had to choose an escape route. Valjean stuck his foot into one of the passageways and felt around in the sludge. Then he did the same thing in the other passage. 'That's uphill,' he told Marius. 'The other's down.'

'Downhill's the Seine,' answered Marius. The tunnel leading to the Seine river carried the largest burden of waste. Also, there was no ledge above the river of detritus. They would have to travel through raw sewage.

Valjean nodded, hoisted Marius up on his back again and headed into the downhill tunnel.

'Not downhill!' Marius protested. 'We'll drown in the shit!'

'Well,' answered Valjean, 'the shit may kill us, but it's the way home.' He headed into the pitch darkness, Marius clinging to his back.

Not far behind him, Javert slogged through the sewer, together with one hapless gendarme. Both men carried lanterns to light their way. They arrived at the intersection and saw the two passageways that had confronted Valjean. The gendarme pointed hopefully to the uphill tunnel, the tunnel with the ledge. 'This way?'

Javert shook his head and stepped off the ledge into the tunnel to the Seine. 'Unfortunately,' he said sardonically, 'he's smarter than that.'

Deeper and deeper into the darkness, Jean Valjean carried Marius. The filthy sludge from the tunnel floor rose to his thighs, making it much harder to move forward. Every step was an agony of labour.

'You can't carry me all the way,' Marius protested. 'Put
me down.'

'You can't walk,' Valjean said roughly. His words came
out pantingly; it was getting harder for him to catch
his breath.

Suddenly, with a terrible groaning sound and a sharp
crack of breaking wood, the aged and rotting tunnel floor
split under Valjean's feet, dropping them both into a pool
of sewage up to Valjean's neck.

'The floor, it's caving in!' he gasped.

'Let me go. I'm too heavy,' Marius protested again, but
Valjean paid him no attention.

'The sides are holding. I'm spreading out. I'm going to
wedge my feet. Keep your head up.'

Valjean hoisted Marius higher, took a deep breath and,
before Marius could protest further, sank down into the
sludge. The filthy sewage rose up over his mouth and
nose, to his eyes. Then, creeping along, his feet wedged
to the sides of the tunnel, and holding in his breath with
all his strength, he made his way deeper and deeper into
the darkness. After more than a minute, he bobbed up,
gasping for air, and took another breath. Then he sank
down again.

'Valjean!' called Javert from somewhere behind him.
'There's nowhere to go!'

The two policemen had reached the place where the
floor had cracked. Their lanterns revealed that the sludge
flowed much deeper here, and was much more difficult to
get through.

But the light from the police lanterns pierced the blackness
of the tunnel where Valjean was struggling, and showed him
that there was a narrow run-off tunnel, not much wider than
a large drainpipe, four or five feet to his right, at eye level.
He jerked up, gasped hard for air, and moved towards it.

'Follow him!' Javert ordered.

'Pardon me, sir?' asked the appalled gendarme with a sinking heart.

'Do what he's doing. Wedge your feet on the sides. Hurry! That's an order!'

Fighting his nausea, the gendarme lowered himself into the deep sewage and began to creep forward slowly. Meanwhile, Valjean had manoeuvred over to the run-off tunnel and placed Marius in position to enter it by climbing off his back. This was a slow process, taking almost all of Marius's remaining strength. Valjean was concerned that Javert and his men would be on him before Marius was safe. But at last, Marius was able to haul himself into the small tunnel and collapse.

As soon as he saw the young man safely inside the tunnel, Valjean began to do an odd thing. Holding tightly to the edge of the run-off tunnel, he bounded up and down, rising from the sewage and dropping down into it again.

*Jump up, take a deep breath, come down again into the sewage with all your might. Again. And again.*

Too late, Javert understood what Valjean was attempting to do. He was jumping up and down on the rotting floor of the sewer, bringing all his weight to bear on the ancient wood. The floor groaned beneath him. Inside the sewer, the gendarme's body trembled, feeling the floor give way.

Suddenly, the floor cracked and collapsed. For a moment it looked as though the young gendarme would be swept away to drown in sewage. But Javert caught his hand and pulled him to safety. The two were cut off, unable to go forward.

As for Jean Valjean, he threw himself into the run-off tunnel after Marius Pontmercy, and disappeared from sight.

Groaning, Marius crawled forward through the tunnel on his belly. It was a tight fit, and a hard passage. But at least they were out of the river of sewage. Behind him crawled Valjean. For a man of his size, especially one with extremely broad shoulders, this small tunnel was an even tighter fit. He was completely exhausted; the physical toll taken on him by the rigours of the sewers and the weight of Marius on his back had aged him years in less than an hour. Also, his legs and feet were swollen, bruised and sore. Making his way through the tunnel with his feet wedged to the sides, jumping up and down on rotting boards, carrying the weight of another person as he slogged through the sewage – all had added up to making Jean Valjean lame.

'Can you see anything?' he gasped.

'No,' Marius said over his shoulder. 'It could be a dead end.' He moaned, and stopped crawling. 'I . . . I . . . don't feel well . . .'

'Do you want me to push you?' Valjean asked.

But there was no answer. Marius had passed out, blocking the passage. Valjean took hold of the young man's thighs and began to push his body ahead. It was very slow going – push Marius a few inches, crawl up himself, push Marius again, crawl up again. It was excruciatingly hard work, and Valjean panted and gasped to bring air into his lungs. He had no idea where this tunnel went, or whether it went anywhere at all. Maybe they were trapped here. Maybe they would die here. Marius would die of his wound, and Valjean of starvation and exhaustion. It was so dark; he could see nothing.

All Jean Valjean knew was that he wasn't going back.

At long last, the journey came to an end. The run-off tunnel reached the main tunnel, the sewer came to an end at the Seine, and a large entrance led to the outside world. Unbelievably, they'd made it.

Valjean pushed Marius the last few feet, and followed him up. He could smell air ahead, and smell too the River Seine, the most welcome aroma in the world, he thought. He gave Marius one last push, and the boy suddenly disappeared. Valjean heard a thud. He followed. Crawling out of the tunnel, he suddenly found himself in open air, without any footing. He tumbled hard.

He found himself on the ground near Marius, who was still unconscious. Or was he dead? They were at street level, and there was a gate leading to the thoroughfare beyond, and to the River Seine.

Dizzy from his ordeal, Valjean wobbled to his feet and went to bend over Marius, to see if the boy was still breathing.

'Is he alive?' asked Chief Inspector Javert, who was standing near the gate, his gun drawn and aimed at Valjean's heart.

## Chapter Twenty-Nine

### THE END OF THE ROAD

'**H**e's alive, but he's pretty badly hurt,' Valjean replied without surprise. Somehow he'd always known, deep inside him, that this moment must inevitably come, when the pursuit would be over at last and he would face his pursuer, his implacable nemesis. Jean Valjean had come to the end of the road.

Chief Inspector Javert was standing just outside the street gate. Behind him, Valjean could hear the rushing sound of the River Seine as it ran swiftly by. Javert was leaning against a police fiacre, but his drawn gun revealed that he was in no way relaxed. With the inspector was a soggy and unhappy gendarme, obviously the man who'd had the miserable assignment of chasing Valjean through the sewers of Paris. At a gesture from the inspector, the gendarme helped Valjean to carry Marius to the fiacre and set him down inside.

'He needs a doctor,' Valjean said. Since Javert didn't move or reply, Valjean limped on his bruised legs over to the police inspector, who raised the barrel of his pistol to cover him.

'To make him healthy for the firing squad?' Javert's voice held a sneer.

'In a few days there'll be an amnesty,' Valjean pointed out. Javert nodded; it was the usual custom, otherwise half the men in Paris would have to be executed after every minor insurrection. 'It's me you want,' Valjean added pointedly.

Javert nodded again; that much was certainly true. This was the moment he'd been living for. For sixteen years, Inspector Javert had been galled by the fact that in the case of Jean Valjean he had not fulfilled his duty. The law-breaker was still at large, and the case was not closed. Now the chase was over. Javert had come to the end of the road.

'Arrest me and let him go,' Valjean said quietly.

A sardonic smile appeared on Javert's face, and his eyes glinted. 'To Cosette's loving arms?' he asked mockingly, but Valjean nodded 'yes' in all seriousness. 'That's all you care about?' Another nod from Valjean.

'And you've caught me. That's what you wanted.' It was an unspoken bargain. Let Marius go, and Valjean wouldn't struggle or try to escape again. It would all come to an end, here, now.

Javert thought for a moment, then motioned the gendarme over. 'Let him take the boy where he wants,' he ordered. 'Then bring him back here to me.'

When the fiacre pulled up at the gate of the house on the rue Plumet, old Toussaint came running out, her face a mask of worry. Fussing and stammering, she followed her master and the gendarme up the stairs to one of the bedrooms, where the men laid Marius out on the bed.

There he was, his face waxy, his dark hair spread out on the pillow. There he was, Marcius Pontmercy, the last and only remaining member of the ABC Society, the last and only survivor of the rebels' battle for the barricade of Saint Antoine. Where was his revolution now? It had lasted less than two days. Many men had died for the sake of *les misérables* of France. What would history say of them? Would future ages remember these men and boys, and

be grateful for their sacrifice? Would they be part of the
inspiration for a new, more successful rebellion?

Cosette came running in at once. When she saw Marius,
all bloody, filthy, his face very pale, his chest hardly moving,
she uttered a little cry, and knelt down at the side of the bed,
frantic. 'Is he dead? He looks dead!'

'He'll live,' Valjean reassured her. 'Toussaint, find a doctor.
Here's money. Promise him more. Promise any amount he
wants.' He turned his attention to Cosette. 'Don't lose your
head now,' he told her. 'You have to nurse him until she
gets back with the doctor.'

Cosette bent close to Marius, her ear on his chest.
'He's breathing. And his heart is strong,' she said, greatly
relieved.

Valjean looked long and earnestly at the girl. 'You know
what to do, Cosette? I told you everything. You'll take care
of him and you'll live a happy life.' He reached deep into
his pocket and handed something to her. 'Here, I promised
to give you this.'

Cosette took the object into her hands with wonderment.
It was a sweet, simple little necklace. She looked at Valjean,
her face a question mark.

'It was your mother's,' he told her gently. 'I loved her.
She was a good woman, Cosette.' His face softened at the
memory of beloved Fantine; suddenly, he looked much
younger and less careworn.

Cosette looked up from the necklace in her hands to see
her papa backing away to the door where the gendarme
was waiting. Suddenly, she understood everything. Papa had
brought Marius back to her with his blessing on their union;
he had given her her mother's last gift; now she would be
protected and safe. All this Jean Valjean had done, and only
for her. She realized that he was going back to give himself
up to the police. With a despairing cry, she ran to him.

'No, Papa!'

But Valjean was already at the door where the gendarme was waiting. 'We made an arrangement,' he told her quietly. 'I have to go. Promise me you'll be happy.'

'Not like this, Papa, not like this,' Cosette wept, throwing herself into his arms. Her heart was breaking. She had gained one love, but had lost another, and both were equally precious to her.

Jean Valjean enfolded his beloved daughter in his embrace and kissed her forehead. 'It's good this way, my dear. I stole something. I did. I stole happiness with you. I don't mind paying. Go to him . . .' He pushed Cosette away gently, towards the bed where Marius was lying wounded. 'He's your life now.' And, before she could turn back to him, he was gone.

Chief Inspector Javert was sitting on a low wall alongside the river's edge, just where Valjean had left him. He was scribbling in his notebook, his eternal notebook, companion of all his waking hours. Near by, the Seine rushed on by, its waters churning. The river currents were particularly strong here, fed by many tributaries from the sewers. When the fiacre pulled up, carrying the police officer and Jean Valjean, Javert carefully tore two pages from the book.

'Here,' and the inspector handed the pages over to the gendarme, 'this is an important memo to the prefect. A list of improvements for the force. Make sure he gets these pages before breakfast.'

'Should I return, sir?'

Javert pulled his pistol from its holster and pointed it at Valjean. 'No. Take the fiacre. I'll walk him to the Archives post.'

When the officer had driven off, Javert pulled out a pair of handcuffs. 'Your hands?' Wordlessly Valjean presented them.

*Les Misérables*

'I'm glad I had time to myself,' continued Javert. 'I needed to think about what you deserve. You're a difficult problem.' He locked the iron cuffs around Valjean's wrists, then shifted the connecting chain to his left hand while holding the pistol, trained on Valjean, in his right. Now Valjean was completely his prisoner, handcuffed and helpless.

Using the chain, Inspector Javert pulled Valjean over to the low wall at the river's edge. He climbed up on the wall, and tugged at Valjean's cuffs. Alarmed, Valjean resisted, setting his feet more firmly on the ground.

'Get up,' Javert ordered icily.

'Aren't you taking me in?' Valjean asked warily. He sensed what was about to happen. Javert intended to push him into the cold waters of the roiling river. With his hands cuffed, Jean Valjean would have no chance of survival. He would drown, and his case would be closed, with no further investigation. Or maybe Javert would shoot him first, and then dispose of his body in the Seine. Either way, Jean Valjean would simply disappear, and his fate would never be known. It would be as if he'd never existed at all.

'You're my prisoner!' Javert snapped. 'Do what I tell you.' His voice rose and cracked. 'You never . . . you don't understand . . . you don't understand the importance of the law.' Then, recollecting himself, he again assumed his customary detached demeanour. 'I've given you an order. Obey it.'

There was nothing Valjean could do. He was Javert's prisoner, his hands bound. His swollen legs aching, he climbed on to the low wall. Below him, he could see and hear the river rushing by.

'Why didn't you kill me?' demanded Javert. The question had been tormenting him ever since Valjean had released him in the alley behind the Café Musain.

'I don't have the right to kill you,' Valjean answered quietly.

311

'But you hate me.'

'I don't hate you.'

Incredible. Impossible. Not to hate? 'You must,' Javert protested.

'I don't,' Valjean answered calmly. 'I don't feel anything.' He was being honest. Over the years he'd been angry with Javert, resented him, but he had never hated him. To hate one must judge, and only God could judge a man's heart.

'Well, you've made me feel something . . . I don't like it.' Dully, Javert stared down into the rushing waters, then back at Jean Valjean. 'You don't want to go back to the galleys, do you?'

This was it, thought Valjean. Here was his choice; Javert was offering him the galleys or the river. Wordlessly, he shook his head. No, death was preferable to the galleys. He resigned himself to dying, hoping for heaven.

As he stared into the river, Valjean remembered the face of Fantine, whom he had loved and lost. Perhaps they would meet again. He thought of his heart's darling Cosette, and was glad that he'd been the instrument by which she'd been reunited with her Marius. They were young; they'd forget him; they'd be happy. There would be marriage, perhaps children.

'Then for once we agree,' Javert said coldly. 'I'm going to spare you the galleys, Valjean.' Yanking on the chain, he pulled him close. 'It's a pity the rules don't allow me to be merciful. I've gone so long without breaking a single rule . . .'

Suddenly, in a single, practised movement, Javert jerked the handcuffs off Valjean's wrists.

'You're free,' he said, and he pushed Valjean hard, so that he lost his balance and fell safely into the street. Valjean turned in astonishment to see Javert lock the handcuffs on to his own wrists and turn to face the rushing Seine.

For the first time, Javert allowed emotion to show on his face. It was bitterness, mingled with bewilderment. The policeman had pursued his enemy for sixteen years. He had always believed that he knew Jean Valjean inside and out, that he understood the way the man's mind worked, and that, *au fond*, Valjean was the self-same criminal whom he'd known on the galleys. But Valjean had proven him wrong. He was not the man Javert thought he was. He had changed, changed profoundly. How could that be? Change was not in Chief Inspector Javert's lexicon. His character had been set in childhood, more than forty-five years before. He had been in love with duty all his life, but in the end duty had rejected him for more interesting lovers.

So, in the end, Jean Valjean had beaten Inspector Javert. There was nothing left for him to do except this: Javert threw himself off the wall into the river, without an outcry or even a murmur. The waters began to close over him even while they carried him away, but Javert didn't struggle.

A shocked Jean Valjean rushed to the water's edge, in time to see the last of Javert as he disappeared in the strong current. He stood watching for a long time, but there was no further sign of Chief Inspector Javert. It was as if he'd never existed.

Jean Valjean turned away at last. His legs were very painful and his aching feet were swollen. It was a long walk to the rue Plumet, to his home, to Cosette and her Marius, his daughter and his son, but Valjean didn't even think of that. Happiness flooded his heart and he limped along without thinking of pain. The long, weary ordeal was over. He was free.

Like Valjean, France was battered and sore. In these last two days both had seen profound changes. But France would recover; Paris would rebuild. The next revolution would be stronger, more effective. Meanwhile, there was, for the survivors, freedom.